# ORCHARD
*a novel*

# Jack H. Bailey

## Also by Jack H. Bailey

*The Number Two Man*
*The Icarus Complex*

*Orchard* is a work of fiction.
Where real-life historical or public figures appear,
the situations, incidents and dialogues
concerning those persons
are entirely fictional.

Copyright © 2016 Wanda M. Bailey

ISBN: 978-0-9968356-0-2
LCCN: 2015921064

Published in the United States by The Four B's.

Cover and book design: Big Fig Design
Layout: Karen Borchgrevink
www.jackhbailey.com

For Scrappy

# INTRODUCTION

This much is true. It's 1899. Harry Orchard is a member of the fire-breathing Western Federation of Miners. While other members labor underground to harvest the riches of the earth, Orchard is paid to kill men who are a problem for the union. He's an interesting killer, well-liked by his peers and by the ladies.

After years of cat-and-mouse pursuit by legendary Pinkerton Charles Siringo, when he's arrested in 1906 for the murder of Idaho's former governor, Frank Steunenberg, he's killed nineteen men in Idaho and Colorado. Even today, in the silver mining towns of northern Idaho, his name is spoken in whispers by those familiar with his deeds.

# CHAPTER ONE

Harry Orchard lay back in the worn mohair seat, his brown derby tipped forward on his brow. Short-fingered square hands laced together on his vest concealed a heavy gold watch chain with its genuine Colorado nugget fob. In the poor illumination of the coach's coal oil lamps, he gave the impression of one asleep, but his senses were keenly attuned to the diverse sounds and odors surrounding him.

A damaged wheel on this or on the following car pounded rhythmically on the track, to the accompaniment of shrieking flanges as the train negotiated the sharp-curved downhill grade. On the upgrade earlier, he could hear the cinders hitting the top of the coach every time the engineer opened the throttle too wide and blew out the flue.

He could smell the toilet water on the nattily dressed gent seated across the aisle. The cloying fragrance, however, was hardly enough to overcome the smell of shit wafting from the patched pants of the boy in the facing seat, who lay restlessly against his mother's bony shoulder. They had gotten on at Mullan, just west of the ragged, mile-high Montana-Idaho border. Sleep had quickly overtaken the sickly looking woman, interrupted from time to time by her strangled coughing. Whoever was waiting for her should have already spoken to an undertaker or bought a pick and shovel.

Seated beside him, next to the steamy window, was a young woman who was there when he'd boarded at Butte. His several attempts to start a conversation with her had died aborning. She had smiled politely, but her brief responses to his comments didn't encourage him to press on.

He'd had a run of bad luck with the sweet-smelling gent across the aisle, who had also boarded at Butte. By the time the train stopped for supper in Missoula, the man, who had introduced himself as Leon Allison, had won a dollar from him, matching for two-bit pieces.

Orchard was curious about his occupation. With his fancy clothes, rakish hat, and as handsome as he was, he could have been a thespian. However, his muscular, work-worn hands seemed to hint at a hardier profession. However, this wasn't something one asked on such short acquaintance, so he'd have to live with his curiosity.

Above the train's constant mechanical clatter, rose the occasional raucous laughter of the four roughly dressed men seated several rows away, smoking stogies and passing a bottle from one bearded mouth to another. Strikebreakers, bound for the Coeur d'Alene, Orchard surmised, needing the whiskey to stiffen their spines for the dangerous game they'd chosen to play.

The region's newspapers had been full of the atrocities being committed in the Rocky Mountain mining camps by both sides in the ongoing struggle between mine operators and union miners. Greed versus need, Orchard thought; need epitomized by the dying woman in the facing seat. She was probably the wife of some poor stiff who was mucking out stopes ten hours a day for three dollars or less.

Through half-closed eyes, Orchard glanced sidelong at the young woman next to him. Not a great beauty, but not unattractive either. She had a plump fullness of face and figure which might delay the premature onset of old age which inflicted itself on the women of the mining camps, be they whores or homemakers. A widow perhaps, he speculated. His eyes drifted to her ungloved hands, lying ring-free and capable-looking in her lap.

A loud clanking of couplings announced that the engineer was braking for a curve. The smelly little boy, who had fallen asleep, opened his eyes to stare dully at the steamed-over window.

"Are we stopping, Momma?"

The boy's mother either didn't hear him or chose not to answer. The question seemed to startle the young woman. She gave Orchard an almost furtive glance when her eyes popped open and she caught him looking at her. She leaned toward the window to wipe at it with the palm of her hand.

"I don't think so," she told the boy, as she tried to see into the dark void outside.

Orchard liked the tone of her voice, which, along with the ample treasures rising beneath her melton jacket, made speaking to her imperative. He tried to think of something he could use for another entrée without sounding stupid. As the train slowed, the clatter of the flat wheel became more pronounced.

"Sounds like we've got us a flat wheel that doesn't want to get there."

He tipped back his derby and smiled at her, wondering if she'd even know what the hell he was talking about.

"Like me," she said, giving him a sad little smile. "My brother's wife is sick. He asked me to come to Wardner to help out."

"Wardner? Is your brother a miner?" Orchard asked.

"No, thank God." Her tone was adamant. "I live in Colorado and remember the last big trouble there, all too well."

Then, the conversation seemed to embarrass her. She turned away to try to see out the window again.

"Where in Colorado?" Orchard persisted, wanting to keep this fragile relationship alive.

"Goldfield, near Cripple Creek. It was terrible there for months."

She stared at her folded hands.

"So what does your brother do?" Orchard grinned at her. "Doctor? Lawyer? Indian Chief?"

"Edward's a watchman at...at one of the mills," she explained softly, with a nervous little laugh. Her eyes darted around the car, coming to rest for a moment on the man across the aisle, who seemed to be listening to them.

If Edward was guarding the Bunker Hill mill, that makes him a scab, Orchard thought, as he continued to smile at her. Almost every mine in the Coeur d'Alene, recognized the union and paid union wages. However Bunker Hill, the largest in the district, refused to recognize the union and paid its workers fifty cents a day less than the others.

The breaking point had been reached a month before when twenty union men were fired for no other reason than their union affiliation. Bunker Hill had declared that union men weren't welcome on its work force and was believed to be rooting out more. Now there were union pickets at the gates and Bunker Hill was importing non-union men from as far away as the New Mexico Territory.

Tensions had risen throughout the Coeur d'Alene, with some of the mining towns cowering in the face of bold acts of sabotage and not so bold acts of mayhem which had sent union and non-union men, alike, to hospital and graveyard.

"My uncle's a policeman where we live," the little boy piped up, suddenly coming to life. "He has a big gun to shoot people."

The boy's mother opened her eyes to look at them. When she spoke, her voice sounded like it was having trouble penetrating the phlegm in her throat. Listening to her made Orchard wince.

"Lawrence, this gentleman ain't interested in guns."

The boy giggled and said, "He wouldn't know a rifle from a rat trap, Momma. That's what Pa says about...about..." He screwed up his thin face trying to recall what the epithet was that his father probably applied to anyone who wore a suit and tie.

Orchard nodded his assent to the smelly little wretch's momma.

"The boy's right, ma'am. Guns have no place in my business."

He exchanged an amused glance with the man across the aisle, sat back and folded his arms. His right hand rested on the hard bulge of his brand new .38 caliber Iver Johnson Patent Ejector revolver, reposing in his shoulder holster. Six loads of protection for three dollars and sixty cents. A bargain, indeed.

"What is your business?" the young woman asked. Her tone indicated that she wasn't really interested; merely making conversation. At least, she was polite enough to do so. She could hardly have any other motivation on such short acquaintance.

Orchard took a business card out of his vest pocket and handed it to her.

"Peerless Crane And Cable. Our business is putting things up in the air." He had to suppress a chuckle at the irony of his response.

"You're a salesman, then?"

"Yup." He extended his hand. "Tom Hogan. Pleased to meet you."

She took his hand awkwardly, a flush spreading from her throat to her cheeks. "Glad to know you..." she glanced at his card, "Mr. Hogan. I'm Miss Shanks."

"Your travels take you to Colorado, friend?" The man across the aisle injected himself into the conversation.

Orchard shook his head dismissively. "No. Never been there. Our Denver office covers that territory."

"Strong union state," the man said.

"I wouldn't know," Orchard said, wondering what he was up to. "You a miner?"

"Was. Now I'm Secretary of the Wardner Miner's Union."

Miss Shanks leaned forward to stare at him. "Does the Wardner Union use blasting gelatin and murder to get what it wants, Mr...."

He touched his hat brim respectfully. "Leon Allison. You have the wrong opinion of us, miss."

The drunken men in the forward seats turned to look and listen, slack-jawed and red-eyed.

"I was engaged to a union man," Miss Shanks said. "He told me things."

"Was?" Orchard interjected hopefully.

"He was killed in an accident at the Gold King mine."

The recollection seemed to pass over her like a dark cloud.

Allison and Orchard both mumbled condolences.

"I'm surprised a pretty woman like you hasn't found someone else," Orchard blurted, trying to sound gallant.

The words came out louder than he had intended because he was trying to work himself back into the conversation before her apparent antipathy toward union men could be exacerbated by Allison. Unfortunately, those words attracted the attention of the drunken men.

A loud guffaw rose from the group. They turned to ogle him.

"Did you hear that fancy talking little shit?" an older man asked in a booming Irish voice. He turned to glare at Orchard. He was particularly ugly, his face pitted with smallpox scars under a shock of unruly gray hair.

"The drummer just wants to get her petticoat over her head, Alford," one of the younger men snorted, collapsing against the seat in a fit of hysterical laughter.

Orchard could feel himself getting angry. Next to him, Miss Shanks kept her eyes downcast. Across the aisle, Allison seemed to be enjoying the moment. Stinky little Lawrence would twist his head around to look at the men and then stare first at his momma and then at Orchard, apparently expecting him to discipline the four drunken men.

As though sensing his frustration and anger, Miss Shanks said, "Pay no attention to those men, Mr. Hogan." She sighed reflectively. "It seems like there's something about mining men that makes them take to drink more than others."

Lawrence's mother rolled her eyes and nodded her head in agreement. "They's all alike."

Was she including all men, Orchard wondered? Did her husband get himself boozed up before coming home to punch this sickly woman around? If so, the boy would probably be blabbing it in a minute.

Orchard tensed when the one called Alford heaved himself out of his seat and reeled down the aisle toward them.

"Sic 'em, Kildare! Go get 'em, boy!" rose the cheers of his drunken entourage.

Orchard glanced around the car, finding himself the center of attention and disliking it with a vengeance. He could ill afford a confrontation here. If he and this drunken loudmouth were standing behind a saloon somewhere, Orchard would have taken whatever action was necessary before he'd have allowed himself to be manhandled by someone twice his size. After all, that's what pistols were for.

The Irishman, Kildare, scowled at them with bloodshot eyes. His sinewy right hand, from which the first joint of the index finger was missing, gripped the back of the sick woman's seat to steady himself. His open shirt framed a thick mass of gray hair in which nestled a large medal of Saint Christopher.

"The reason we turn to whiskey, woman," he told Miss Shanks in his hoarse brogue, "is that we work our butts to nubs and still can't afford no fancy duds like the drummer here."

He paused to look at Allison.

"Or Fancy Dan, over there."

Surprisingly, it was Allison who introduced himself into the fray. He rose to stand in the aisle, almost nose-to-nose with Kildare. He was taller than he had appeared while seated. He smiled when he spoke.

"If you don't sit down and leave these folks alone," Allison said, in an easy conversational tone one might use with an unruly child, "I'll have to ask the conductor to put you off the train."

The expression which passed over Kildare's face was that of a man witnessing a miracle.

"Put me off the train!" He turned to look at his leering cohorts for approval. "Ain't no man rough enough to put me off this train."

Orchard remained coiled, right hand near the butt of his revolver. The two women stared at their feet, stiff with apprehension. The boy gaped in open-mouthed awe at Allison.

Once, Miss Shanks glanced at him. He tensed himself to rise so he could ally himself with Allison but decided to wait for more cards to be dealt.

"Then sit down," Allison said in a voice which had assumed a hard, commanding edge. "Sit down, or I'll invite you to step between the cars and I'll put you off myself."

After a moment of surprised contemplation, Kildare bellowed, "Lead the way, bucko. We'll see who leaves the train."

Allison exchanged an expressionless glance with Orchard, gave a slight shrug, and turned toward the door at the rear of the car.

"Are they gonna fight, Momma?" the boy wanted to know.

His mother glanced about nervously and put her hand over his mouth.

Kildare's three companions were so taken aback by the suddenness of the challenge and its acceptance that they were silent for a moment before snickering and nudging each other, confident of victory for their champion.

Orchard twisted in his seat to watch. Allison was either a madman or his coat concealed arms of steel.

When Allison opened the door, the car was filled with the raucous cacophony of the train's running gear. As he passed from view and the doorway was filled with Kildare's broad shoulders, Orchard saw the hand which slid into a pocket and his eyes caught the glint of a clasp knife's blade.

Lawrence's mother shrieked when Orchard stepped down hard on her foot as he scrambled into the aisle. He drew his Iver Johnson as he ran. Jerking open the rear door, he plunged into the narrow, swaying space between the coaches, arriving just as Kildare made a swipe at Allison with his blade. Allison ducked, but his handsome hat was knocked into the trees which lined the right of way.

Orchard jammed his pistol barrel against the seams in the Irishman's weathered neck.

"Toss the knife, Paddy," Orchard ordered, "or I'll blow your head clean off."

Kildare stiffened. His hand dropped and the knife flashed once as it bounced among the ties in the roadbed.

Orchard stared across the narrow space at Allison, who was regarding him with a mixture of surprise and disdain, his face illuminated by the light entering from the open door.

"You want me to shoot this son-of-a-bitch?" Orchard asked him. "He cost you a nice hat."

Allison shook his head. "No, you cost me a nice hat. If you'd pulled that pop-gun inside, we wouldn't be standing out here in the cold."

"You wouldn't shoot a man over a damned hat, would you?" Kildare asked in a subdued voice.

"I'd shoot you over a pair of dirty drawers," Orchard said, jabbing him again with the revolver. "What name do you want painted on your headboard?"

"My gawd! Alford Kildare."

"Where are you from, Kildare?" Allison asked.

"Bannack, Montana, most lately."

"You got a union card?"

"Not on me."

Allison looked at Orchard.

"I don't ride with scabs."

Orchard moved so he wouldn't hit Allison if the bullet went all the way through. He was distracted by a commotion inside the coach behind them. The partially open door was flung wide, revealing Kildare's drunken companions. They stood there, reeling with the motion of the train, more curious than hostile.

Allison reached beneath his coat and drew a heavy pistol.

"This is a private party, gents," Allison drawled. "Dust."

He covered the three unwaveringly.

They turned in their tracks, stumbling over each other. Orchard was watching them leave when Allison clubbed Kildare on the side of the head with the barrel of his heavy pistol. There was a hollow thud and Kildare fell headlong over the low chain barrier, miraculously bouncing clear of the unforgiving wheels.

Orchard peered over the chain where light from the car's windows was enough to reveal that the Irishman was still intact.

"Whew. Almost went under the wheels. Why'd you do that?"

"I thought you were going to shoot him."

"You afraid your fancy shirt'd get splattered?"

"Maybe. Let's go back inside. I've got a bottle in my valise. I'll buy you a drink while we discuss my new hat."

Orchard laughed.

"Don't get your hopes up, but I could use a drink."

They stepped into the thick coal oil scented air of the coach. Allison laid a hand on Orchard's arm.

"Were you going to kill him without giving him any edge?"

"No edge at all. Were you gonna let him carve you up before you pulled that cannon of yours?"

"I guess we'll never find out," Allison said, leading them to their seats.

"Is everything all right?" an anxious Miss Shanks asked, looking past them to see what had happened to Kildare.

Orchard nodded reassuringly, noting that the three drunken men had moved on to another car. He glanced across the aisle at Allison calmly opening his valise. What was his game? Somehow, he wasn't what he seemed. In any case, pulling the Smith on the drunks revealed him as someone to be reckoned with. These were times when a man who pulled a weapon had better be prepared to use it. Allison had given that impression.

If he'd known he was armed, Orchard thought, he could have remained in his seat, getting to know the comely Miss Shanks, while Allison was giving Kildare his edge between the cars.

"Where's the other man?" the boy asked, finally realizing that Kildare wasn't going to reappear.

"He wanted to stretch his legs," Orchard told the boy. "He decided to walk into town."

Allison passed two ounces of whiskey in a silver cup across the aisle to Orchard.

"Hobble," he muttered, smiling at Orchard. "He decided to hobble into town."

They had two more drinks of what proved to be some fairly decent whiskey. It was decent enough to allow Orchard to relax, without putting down his guard completely.

Allison leaned across the aisle to share the last of his liquid bounty.

"You're pretty fierce, Hogan. I wouldn't have expected you to be carrying iron," Allison said, shoving the empty bottle under his seat.

"I travel some dark streets," Orchard said, wondering why a union paper pusher would be packing a big Smith, the model made famous by Jesse James.

"I don't expect labor trouble is good for your business," Allison said. "Companies need to conserve their cash when they've got pickets at the gate and few men working underground."

Orchard nodded in agreement. He didn't wish to be drawn into a deep discussion of his work or he might be called upon to produce a catalog for Allison to peruse.

"Do you make calls in Burke?" Allison asked.

"I was there a couple of weeks ago," Orchard lied. "Don't like staying in that town. It's hell, with one street. Saloons on one side, whorehouses on the other."

Allison chuckled.

"That's Burke all right. I used to work in Burke Canyon at the Frisco."

Orchard wondered if Allison had been there in '92, when striking union workers had blown up the Frisco mill and killed several scabs in a fierce gun battle.

It was half past nine when the train clanked into Wallace, the Shoshone County seat and commercial trading hub for the Coeur d'Alene mining district. A few people left the car, hardly attracting Orchard's attention. The whiskey had made him drowsy and he would have drifted off if Miss Shanks hadn't asked him to help her open the window.

11

"I'm sorry to bother you," she apologized when he opened his eyes, "but it's awfully close in here."

With the train motionless, the air in the coach had become oppressively heavy. After a brief struggle, Orchard was able to raise the window, admitting cool, fresh, mountain air. It had started to drizzle. Small rivulets flowed from the station roof to splash noisily in puddles formed between the station platform and the tracks.

The sickly woman pulled her coat tighter to fend off the night air, which seemed to aggravate her coughing. Orchard and Miss Shanks watched the few people who crossed the platform only to disappear into the darkness, their departure marked only by fragments of conversation.

"It's lonely out there," she murmured as the voices faded away.

Orchard's reply was drowned out by two short blasts of the train's whistle, signaling the resumption of the journey to Kellogg. The noisy take-up of couplings was accompanied by the furious chuffing of the engine, when its drivers slipped on the wet track.

The train lurched away from the Wallace station, passing several illuminated buildings and scattered houses before it was swallowed up by the darkness of the pine-clad Bitterroot Mountains.

Orchard and Miss Shanks pitted their combined strengths against the window before it slammed down with an explosive sound. Laughing, they sank back into their seats. The combination of cool air and exertion had brought color to her cheeks, which was very becoming.

Orchard turned away to find Allison studying him intently. Their eyes met for an instant of mutual, almost telepathic communication before both looked away.

"Where are you staying, Hogan?" Allison asked when he'd finished stowing his cups in his valise.

"At the Galena House," Orchard told him, wishing immediately that he hadn't been so forthcoming. Allison's presence had triggered a warning bell whose muted notes were making him edgy.

Allison's raised eyebrows indicated either surprise or disapproval.

"A man of means. I heard rooms were a dollar and breakfast, four bits."

Orchard smiled, aware of Miss Shanks's awed appraisal.

"My company insists on first-class accommodations for its road men," Orchard said. "Where do you hang your hat?" He chuckled suddenly. "When you have one."

Allison ignored the slight abrasion.

"Mrs. Kessie's boarding house is the best I can do. I'm just a poor union man."

"Pa says union men are..." the boy blurted, before he was silenced by his mother's thin hand over his mouth.

"I take it your husband isn't in the union," Allison said lazily, seeming to enjoy the woman's startled reaction.

She bit her lip and shook her head, tears appearing suddenly. She coughed several times into her handkerchief, finally taking in enough air to speak.

"He has to work," she muttered. "We got nothing. We can't live if he don't have a paycheck. He has to work."

Her voice became almost inaudible. She turned away from them to stare out the steamy window. The little boy looked frightened. He moved closer to her.

Orchard gave Allison a hard look and shook his head as a warning. Scabs and strikebreakers made it possible for the mine owners to ride roughshod over the union, but he felt some compassion for the women and children caught in the middle of the often violent maelstrom. In this poor woman's case, her unfortunate choice must have been food on the table or opium-laced syrup for her cough. Food had apparently won.

Allison rolled his eyes and shrugged by way of apology, but gave voice to none. The boy pretended to ignore them, playing finger games with dirty hands.

"If you're staying in Wardner," Allison said suddenly, "you must have business there."

Orchard nodded agreement. Wardner, a mile or so up a steep canyon from Kellogg, was the first town to spring up in the wake of the great silver strike of '89. It could now boast of being the home of the giant Bunker Hill mill and concentrator, the largest in the Coeur d'Alene.

Wallace, to the east, was udder and teats for the string of rich mines on Canyon Creek and the rough-and-tumble towns of Gem, Frisco and Burke.

"Yes, I have some business with the Bunker Hill people," Orchard replied truthfully. "When I have business up Canyon Creek, I stay in Wallace."

"No need to explain," Allison said airily. "Not being a businessman myself, I was just curious."

The groaning of brake shoes warned them that the train was preparing to stop again. The car's forward door opened to admit a paunchy, harried-looking conductor who came down the aisle on a trot. Allison extended his arm to bar his path.

"Not another hot box, I hope."

Several axle journals had overheated between Missoula and Mullan, forcing them to stop so the brakeman could saturate the cotton waste in the journal box with oil.

The conductor tried to evade Allison's outstretched arm. He sounded harried when he said, "We're letting some men off at the Bunker Hill spur. Won't take but a few minutes. Kellogg station's just a mile down."

This last sentence he tossed over his shoulder as he hurriedly exited the car.

"What the hell's going on?" Orchard asked of no one in particular.

By the time he'd managed to raise the stubborn window again, the train was stopped. Rain was falling briskly now, adding to the eerie scene before him. The Bunker Hill spur ran alongside a fence of rough boards, perhaps ten feet high. Men in glistening slickers and gum boots lined the track. They carried rifles and lanterns.

As the men from the train began to appear, laden with bedrolls and baggage, they were herded through a gate by armed men in yellow slickers, toward a string of boxcars pulled by a small locomotive. Orchard didn't count them, but estimated that they numbered upwards of fifty. He thought he saw Alford Kildare's three cronies, but couldn't be sure in the poor light. He could make

14

out the sign above the gate, however: Bunker Hill Mining And Concentrating Company–Men Wanted–Strike Conditions.

From the head of the train came the sound of breaking glass. Someone yelled, "Rotten scabs! Bloodsuckers!"

Allison came to stare over Orchard's shoulder.

"Strikebreakers."

"A lot of rifles," Orchard said.

"Company police and special deputies," Allison said, returning to his seat. "Bunker Hill's planning to operate in spite of the strike. That takes a lot of imported manpower and plenty of rifles." Allison shook his head disgustedly. "They'll live to regret it."

That they will, Orchard thought, sobered by the sight of so many armed men. He couldn't help wondering if this assignment might be terminated by a rifle bullet. On the other hand, if the risks were high, the rewards were higher. One had to consider the compensating factors.

"My God," Miss Shanks muttered. "It's like Colorado all over again."

The train was moving again, rolling past the gate where the last of the debarking passengers were climbing into the boxcars. Orchard slammed down the window. The bastards!

There was little conversation between them until the train pulled into the Kellogg depot. Orchard helped the sick woman retrieve a newspaper-wrapped package from beneath her seat, helped her to her feet and assisted her into the aisle, glad to see the last of her and the smelly child as she dragged herself away.

He offered to carry Miss Shanks's cardboard suitcase but she declined, seemingly eager to get off the train. When they stepped down onto the depot platform, Orchard was immediately aware of the presence of more armed men, some with badges, standing in a group, closely observing the debarking passengers. One, a large, exceedingly ugly man, wearing a gum raincoat and carrying a double-barreled shotgun, studied everyone with almost pathological intensity. He looked vaguely familiar to Orchard.

"Let's find a hack," Allison said. "We can split it."

15

"And we can offer this lady a ride," Orchard said, smiling at Miss Shanks. She glanced at Allison and shook her head.

"No thank you. Goodnight, Mr. Hogan."

With that she stepped off the platform and vanished into the night.

Orchard watched her go, indulging in a momentary fantasy, at the same time, wondering if he'd ever see her again.

"I don't think that lady likes you, Allison."

"I think you'd like to get her petticoat over her head, Hogan," Allison drawled.

"Can't say it hasn't crossed my mind," Orchard said, eager to get off the platform.

He and Allison hadn't moved ten feet when they were accosted by the sheriff and the plug-ugly with the shotgun. The sheriff, with his drooping moustache, sheepskin-lined corduroy coat and three-dollar Stetson hat was an imposing figure.

"Allison, isn't it?"

The sheriff planted himself directly in front of them.

Allison seemed very relaxed when he said, "That's right, Sheriff."

The sheriff unbuttoned his coat to get at his handkerchief, revealing a Colt Peacemaker in a heavy leather holster. He blew his nose noisily.

Orchard took a closer look at the other man, red-faced, perpetually scowling. Gregory. Lyle Gregory. A union-baiting, bully boy from Denver who'd been a strikebreaker during the trouble in Telluride three years before. Orchard hoped the bastard didn't remember him.

"Who's your friend, Allison?" Gregory growled, jerking his head toward Orchard. "More union trash?"

"Easy, Gregory," the sheriff warned, stowing his handkerchief and looking at Orchard. "What's your business, friend?"

Orchard snapped out a business card and handed it to him. "Machinery sales."

The sheriff studied the card. "You been here before, then?"

"Many times," Orchard replied easily. "We haven't met because I stay out of trouble."

Gregory thrust his face closer. "I seen you in Colorado."

The son-of-a-bitch thought he remembered him. Maybe he wouldn't recall the details. Orchard had worn a stylish moustache at that time, which might muddle Gregory's recollection.

It had started with an exchange of insults in a Telluride saloon called the San Miguel. Gregory and one of his men wanted the billiard table where Orchard was playing. When the other man intentionally jostled him, spoiling a money shot, Orchard had terminated the dispute with a right fist, which had dropped the man like a steer in a slaughter house.

"I seen you up to no good in Telluride," Gregory repeated, stepping closer.

Orchard folded his arms, letting the fingers of his right hand slide beneath his lapel.

"I'm afraid you're mistaken, brother. You have me confused with some other handsome gent."

The sheriff pocketed the business card.

"The company you keep," he said, giving Allison a disdainful glance, "raises suspicions."

"Not much choice on a crowded train."

"I suppose not," the sheriff said, turning away.

"I still say I seen you in Telluride," Gregory said, joining the sheriff with obvious reluctance.

"Who was that mug?" Orchard asked Allison as they crossed the platform.

"Gregory? One of Bunker Hill's head breakers," Allison said. "He thinks he knows you."

"He's real fond of you union boys, isn't he?"

Allison's response was interrupted by the appearance of a heavy wagon, pulled by two frightened horses. The teamster driving it stopped next to the platform. Two burly Special Deputies dragged a small, manacled man out of the wagon box and hustled him, hatless and coatless, toward the train.

"What's that all about?" Orchard wondered aloud.

"Deporting another union man," Allison said. "Probably caught him trying to steal a shovel."

Despite his small size, the deportee put up a violent struggle, twisting, turning and kicking at the bigger men. At one point, they stopped dragging him and punched his face bloody, which only seemed to make him more berserk.

A wild-eyed young woman in a dirty dress and torn shawl came running across the platform toward the deputies. She carried a baby in her arms and was trailed by two wailing toddlers.

"Won't nobody do nuthin'?" she screamed to the world at large. "They're shippin' my man off."

Her appearance seemed to invigorate the prisoner who twisted and turned, trying to shake their grip on him.

"What are we gonna do?" The woman turned to those still on the platform. "These kids ain't et since yesterday. I got nuthin' to give them. Nuthin'!"

"Whack the son-of-a-bitch, Cyrus" one of the struggling deputies bellowed.

The deputy called Cyrus pulled a large blackjack out of his back pocket and hit the unruly deportee on the side of the head. The man's struggles ceased abruptly. He went limp in the deputy's arms.

"Goddamn you!" the young woman screamed. "You bastards!"

She rushed at them, hair flying. Cyrus tried to grab her but she fended him off with one arm, holding the screaming baby in the other.

Cyrus raised the blackjack. "Back off woman, or I'll brain the kid."

He swung at the baby but connected with the women's protecting shoulder. She wilted from the pain, almost falling down as she staggered backwards. Cyrus threatened to hit her again, waving the blackjack menacingly.

The other deputy, with the help of the conductor, stuffed the unconscious deportee onto the train.

Orchard set down his traveling bag.

"Watch my bag, Allison."

The deputy and the young woman circled each other. The two toddlers hugged each other, crying hysterically. Orchard crossed the platform and jerked the blackjack out of Cyrus's upraised hand. He was surprised by how heavy it was when he swung it hard and felt it connect with the bridge of the deputy's nose. The man went to his knees, eyes rolling around in his head. His blood gushed onto the platform, some of it spattering the screaming toddlers.

The sheriff and Gregory charged toward Orchard.

"Whoa, there," the sheriff ordered. "Drop that sap!"

Orchard tossed the blackjack under the train, keeping his eyes on the other deputy who was kneeling beside his downed partner.

The young woman sank down on the platform. The sobbing children attached themselves to her, grinding their eyes with dirty little fists. She extended a calloused hand to Orchard.

"Could you help us, mister?"

Allison approached, carrying their bags.

"This union man'll help you," Orchard said, turning to Allison. "Give this lady a dollar, Allison. Didn't you hear her? These kids ain't et."

A pained Allison dropped a silver dollar into the woman's hand and shrugged off her thanks.

There was an instant where time seemed to stand still. The sheriff and Gregory eyed Orchard warily while the injured man, blood pouring from a nose now twice its normal size, was helped to his feet.

In the background, the train began to roll out of the station, blowing steam and smoke.

"Get him out of here," the sheriff ordered, before turning his attention back to Orchard. "I'm gonna let this go, Hogan. He had no call to hit the woman, but if you ever interfere in law business again, you're goin' to jail."

"I wouldn't like that," Orchard said easily. "I've never been in jail."

And that was the God's truth. His history of deeds and misdeeds had never placed him under arrest or even questioned by the police in half a dozen towns. It was a distinction of which he was rather proud, considering that many in similar occupations had been arrested and, in several instances, lynched.

The old man driving the depot hack wanted fifty cents to take them to Wardner. The narrow road up the steep winding canyon was illuminated by flickering electric lights. Along the way, houses clung like ticks to the hillsides.

Allison had been silent until the lights of Wardner were visible. Suddenly, he looked directly at Orchard.

"You didn't care about that woman, Hogan. You just wanted an excuse to bash that deputy."

Yes, he had wanted to bash the deputy and Allison was right, it had nothing to do with the man's abuse of the woman. Striking the deputy and watching him spurt blood had relieved some of the uneasiness that had been building since he was confronted by Lyle Gregory. He should have settled his hash in Colorado, once and for all.

"Maybe. Man, there was a lot of lead shot in that sap."

"It did reroute the bastard's nose," Allison said with a chuckle.

"Didn't it, though?" Orchard replied, his attention suddenly diverted by the sight of Miss Shanks trudging up the road ahead of them.

"Pull up, Grampa," Orchard ordered when they came abreast. He jumped down to bar the way.

"If you'll tell me your first name, you can ride with us," Orchard said, reaching for her case.

"It's Bella, but I can't," she said, glancing nervously at Allison. "Ed could lose his job if I was seen in the same rig as a union man."

"So your brother's a scab," Allison said. It was more casual observation than condemnation.

Bella bristled. "He is not! He's a watchman at the Bunker Hill concentrator."

Orchard made a sweeping gesture which encompassed the canyon and the almost deserted, poorly lighted road.

"Come on, Bella. The best eyes in Idaho couldn't tell Allison here, from Governor Steunenberg in this light."

Orchard took her case from her and handed it up to Allison, before helping her into the hack. Allison moved up to sit beside the old man, to make room for her on the second seat.

"Where does Mr. Shanks live?" Orchard asked when they were moving again. He could tell that she was uncomfortable and hoped to stimulate some casual conversation to ease the tension.

"In one of the dump houses, whatever they are," Bella said. "I'm not sure where they are, either."

"I expect we can find out," Orchard assured her.

Allison looked at him and smiled benignly.

Orchard returned the smile, thinking, the smug devil knows what I'm up to and seems to be enjoying my attempts to establish a bond with this woman. Well, to hell with him. He'll soon be gone and I'll have her to myself.

Allison directed the old man to stop in front of Mrs. Kessie's boarding house, a two-story building of unpainted rough boards. He gave the driver two bits, grabbed his valise and jumped down.

"A good evening to you, ma'am," he said, nodding to Bella.

She merely nodded her acknowledgement.

"Stay out of trouble, Hogan," Allison said, cutting in front of the work-worn horse's drooping head.

Orchard gave him a friendly wave.

"I know you'll be there for me if I can't avoid it."

"Don't count on it," Allison said, turning to step up on Mrs. Kessie's porch.

Orchard watched Allison disappear into the boarding house. There were enough contradictions about the man to make him wary. He dressed in gentlemen's getup and yet he insisted on portraying himself as a poor, downtrodden union man. Caution, Harry, he told himself.

As they moved on, the canyon became wider. They passed the Galena House and several saloons, among them Fatty Kincaid's, louder and gaudier than the rest. At the end of the street, much of the canyon had been filled with mine tailings, creating an uneven sea of finely crushed rock.

The old man pointed to several lights on a distant hillside, across the tailing dump.

"Them's the dump houses," he told them, laying down the reins to fill his pipe. "The Shanks house is the one on the end."

"Thank you," Bella said, preparing to disembark.

"He'll take us over there," Orchard said. "It's too far to walk."

"I don't go no further," the old man said. "Tailing pile's too hard on the horse."

"I'll give you another four bits," Orchard said, searching his pockets.

"You owe me two bits," the old man said, squinting at Orchard through tobacco smoke as he lighted his pipe.

Bella was already climbing down. Orchard handed the man a quarter and got out of the rig. He was disappointed that he couldn't have finished their trek with a ride to Ed Shanks's door, but it was apparent that the old man couldn't be bought.

"Wait for me," Orchard told him. "I'm staying at the Galena House."

"We passed the Galena House," the old man said, beginning to sound a little petulant. "You shoulda got out then."

Orchard pulled open his coat so the old man could see that he was armed.

"I'll bet this horse could make his way home with a dead man driving," Orchard growled. "Wait for me, unless you want the horse to find out. I'm leaving my bag with you."

Bella had already started across the tailing pile, forcing him to hurry to catch up and take her case from her. It was immediately obvious that the uneven footing, in the dark, would have been too much for the horse. He hoped he wasn't scuffing his own good shoes.

"What were you talking about?" Bella wanted to know, picking her way carefully through the debris.

"I just wanted him to wait for me," Orchard said, glancing over his shoulder to be sure his order had been obeyed.

The girl who opened the door for them was as thin as a stick. In the light of the lamp she was carrying, she looked dirty and unkempt. From inside the house came the sound of coughing, not unlike the strangling gasps of the woman on the train.

"Bella? God, I'm so glad you're here," the girl said. "I'm Amy Neville. Been helpin' out."

"That's good of you, Amy," Bella said. "How is she?"

"Doctor says she's dyin'," Amy said, seeming to see Orchard for the first time. She poked at her hair self-consciously.

"This is Mr. Hogan," Bella said. "He gave me a ride up the hill."

Orchard acknowledged Amy with a curt nod and spoke to Bella as though the girl didn't exist.

"I don't know how long I'm going to be here, Bella, but I'd like to see you again. May I call on you?"

"Mr. Hogan, we just happened to meet on the train."

She gave Amy an embarrassed little smile.

"Isn't fate wonderful?"

Amy was staring now, mouth open.

"I've never really thought about that," Bella said, "but I don't know anything about you."

"You'll never get a better chance to find out," Orchard said. "I'll drop by in a day or two."

"You're very persistent."

Her tone sounded encouraging.

"In my business, I have to be. Goodnight ladies."

As he walked away, Amy whispered, "Handsome, ain't he? Not very tall, though."

"Tall enough, I think," Bella said and followed Amy into the house.

Orchard signed the Galena House register Thomas Hogan and pushed it back to the night clerk, an elderly man with an unfriendly manner.

"What room's Frank Bromley in?" he asked him, lighting a cigar with the automatic cigar lighter which stood on the counter. "I'd like you to put me across the hall, but don't tell him I'm here. I want to surprise him."

He gave the clerk a sly, conspiratorial smile, which elicited no response.

"Mr. Bromley's in room twelve," the man said. "I could put you thirteen."

Orchard shook his head.

"No, not thirteen."

"Fifteen? It ain't directly across the hall, though."

He studied Orchard with small eyes, as though waiting for him to reject the second choice.

"That'll be fine," Orchard said, picking up his bag and taking the simple key he slid across the counter.

Because the rooms were small, room fifteen wasn't that far from Frank Bromley. The room itself was spartan and uninviting with its iron bed and cheap window curtains.

Orchard took off his hat and coat, hanging them on the hook on the back of the door. He tossed his heavy canvas bag on the bed and undid the straps. He found a quart of whiskey, carefully wrapped and protected in two pairs of long underwear. The single glass tumbler on the washstand was cloudy and chipped, but Orchard filled it half full, took a deep drink and set it on the dresser.

From beneath his clean shirts, Orchard pulled out his Winchester take-down twelve-gauge pump gun, assembled it, made sure it was fully loaded and tucked it under the edge of the mattress. He then proceeded to put shirts, socks and underwear into a dresser drawer, checking first for the presence of lice or silverfish.

In the bottom of the bag was a small wooden box, its lid tied on with twine. Orchard set it on the bed next to his bag, untied the twine and opened the box to check his inventory. Two apothecary bottles, their stoppers secured with tape, six sticks of 2XX dynamite, a small roll of fuse, a bottle of sulfuric acid and a small tin box of blasting caps. On the top of the tin, a warning, in bold letters: DO NOT STORE WITH DYNAMITE.

When he'd pushed the bag under the bed, Orchard refilled the tumbler and sat down in the wooden rocking chair by the window to wait. He didn't know when they'd come for him, but among his few virtues, patience was uttermost.

# CHAPTER TWO

Kellogg's Bitterroot Hotel was a three-story edifice whose guests claimed it swayed when the winter winds came roaring down the canyon from Wardner. It did, however, boast several large rooms adequate for meetings and socials. Thus, it had been selected as the site for the negotiations between the Western Federation of Miners and the Bunker Hill Management.

Bill Haywood, the union's secretary-treasurer, chewing on an unlit cigar, was an imposing figure. Though his right eye was opaque, the result of a drilling accident years before, he shunned an eye patch, which he said would make him look like a pirate. To many western mine owners, pirate was an apt description. He rocked his big frame back in his chair until he was leaning against the flowered wallpaper. Hooking his heels in the chair rungs, he only half-listened as Charles Moyer, the union president, reiterated for the third time in as many days, the union's demands.

Haywood had lost interest. It might not be apparent to Moyer or John MacNamara, the president of the Wardner union, but they were shoveling shit against the tide. Frank Bromley and his people weren't going to be influenced by either veiled threats or cajoling. They needed to be hit hard by something that would command their immediate attention.

"We're not here to ask for the eight-hour day, gentlemen," Moyer declared. "We demand it."

He paused to take a sip of water from the glass in front of him. "We fought for the eight-hour day in Colorado, and I'm happy to tell you that it's now on the statute books of that state."

Frank Bromley, the managing director of The Bunker Hill Mining and Concentrating Company, adjusted his pince-nez to stare at Moyer over the tops of the lenses.

"This isn't Colorado, Mr. Moyer." He sounded tired. His voice had lost some of its earlier resonance. "The ten-hour day is the standard in the Coeur d'Alene and I see no reason to change it."

Moyer took another sip of water and ran his hand over his mouth and moustache. "I reckon that's because you're not down there, ten hours a day, six days a week, Mr. Bromley."

John MacNamara leaned on his elbows, pushing his big-shouldered body across the table to face Bromley.

"If you won't give on the hours, then by God, you got to give on the wages," he bellowed. "You can't have it both ways."

Haywood liked the handsome miner but gave him poor marks as a negotiator. His temper was the seething lava of an Irish volcano, ready to erupt at the slightest provocation.

"We pay what we can afford to pay, MacNamara."

As he spoke, Justin Whitehead, the Bunker Hill superintendent, glanced sidelong at Bromley, seeking approval. It was evident that he was somewhat in awe of Bromley, if not a bit insecure in the knowledge that Bromley might have considered the meeting too important to be left in his hands alone. Somehow, his elaborately styled gray hair and well-tailored suit set him apart from the rest of the group, including the conservatively dressed Bromley. A peacock among pigeons.

"I might remind you," Whitehead continued, "that ours is a dry mine. Men don't have the expense of gum clothing."

"Shouldn't have that, no how," MacNamara said. "No matter what, two dollars fifty above ground and three dollars below ain't a decent wage for men and their families."

Color was rising in MacNamara's face.

"The Bunker Hill has always considered the needs of family men," Whitehead responded in his sing-song condescending tone. "And the single men as well," he added, throwing a challenging look at the silent Haywood. "We provide houses for families and company-operated boarding houses for the unmarried men, at nominal rents, I might add."

Moyer drew himself erect. He pointed a finger at Whitehead. "Women and children are living in the mud under leaking tents, Mr. Whitehead, because you, yourself, signed the order for eviction from the company houses."

Walker Timmons, the young, rosy-cheeked lawyer who had accompanied Bromley from San Francisco, raised a plump hand.

"Let's get the issue of eviction in proper perspective, gentlemen. The houses were provided for Bunker Hill employees, not for men or the families of men, who picket our gates and threaten our workers with bodily harm."

"Your scabs, you mean!"

MacNamara was beginning to perspire, stains visible at his armpits.

Haywood rocked forward, the legs of his chair striking the linoleum floor with such force that the water in their glasses rippled.

"Gentlemen, it's after ten. With Mr. Moyer's permission, I'd like to propose we adjourn these proceedings until Monday to give you time to consider our proposals. May I conclude with a couple of pertinent comments?"

Haywood's booming voice seemed to intimidate everyone in the room. Even the unassailable Bromley listened.

"We've had no meeting of the minds here, either on hours or wages. The question of a company-sponsored medical facility didn't even seem to deserve

27

an answer." Haywood looked at each man with his good left eye. "I tell you, my friends, we're on the brink of crisis in the Coeur d'Alene."

"What do you mean by that, Haywood?" Bromley's tone was sharper than it had been all evening.

"I mean that the Western Federation can't be responsible for the acts of desperate men, Mr. Bromley, and the district's overflowing with them," Haywood said. "I'm not talking about rock-throwing and fist fights. I'm talking about all-out war."

He paused to take a kitchen match from his vest pocket and drag it across the polished table top until it ignited in a sulfurous flash. While he rekindled his cigar, he studied the Bunker Hill men through the smoke. There was no way to reach these men, sitting there in their expensive clothes. They had no concept of the miserable living conditions and the sickness which prevailed among the very people who toiled in the dank tunnels to provide them with their wealth. Well, he was going to get their attention.

"I don't think any of us wants a repetition of the troubles of 1892. Beatings, shootings and finally, the total destruction of the Frisco mill."

Haywood's eyes wandered to Moyer, who stared impassively at the table top. The union president had belonged to the powerful Burke union in those days. Though it was never proven, he was suspected of releasing the ore car loaded with giant powder which had leveled the Frisco from ball mill to settling tanks. To this day, the wreckage littered the mountainside as a reminder of the union's power.

"If you're threatening us," Bromley observed dryly, "let me assure you that I'll have no qualms about asking Governor Steunenberg to declare a state of martial law in the district at the first hint of trouble."

Haywood exchanged an amused glance with Moyer. "Maybe we're not speaking the same language, Mr. Bromley. This is the first hint of trouble. While you've been living in splendid isolation in San Francisco, out of earshot of the screams of men broken in the machinery, crushed in collapsing stopes or blown to bits in premature explosions, a revolution has been brewing here." Haywood paused to get his breath. "You hang tough on the hours and the wages and you sow the seeds of your own destruction."

Bromley rose abruptly. "I didn't come all this way to be browbeaten by the union. Gather up your things, Timmons."

The lawyer stuffed papers in his case and rose quickly, as did Whitehead, who was constrained to make a final comment. "If you're threatening destruction of the Bunker Hill mill, Mr. Haywood, I'd have second thoughts. It's well guarded."

MacNamara banged a big fist on the table. "By imported hooligans hiding behind fences built with scab labor."

"So we won't have anarchy like they had in Telluride," Whitehead responded smugly.

"Telluride," Haywood growled. "Where union men were arrested and beaten for walking picket lines. Even the town constable was a paid tool of the mine owners."

"Until he was murdered," Whitehead shot back.

At the door, Bromley paused to raise his hands in a signal for silence. "Enough of this senseless bickering, gentlemen. If the union has any constructive proposals, I can be reached at the Galena House until Monday, when I return to San Francisco."

"Good riddance," Haywood muttered when they were gone.

Moyer retrieved the opened but untouched bottle of Duncan and Duncan from the sideboard and poured each of them a generous drink. He downed his quickly and poured another for himself before shoving the bottle toward Haywood.

"That bastard Bromley is a hard nut," Moyer said. "I don't think he'll ever cave in."

"If he don't," MacNamara exclaimed, his face reddening, "the union agreements with the mines in Burke Canyon are just so many goddamned pieces of worthless paper. They'll go back to ten hours for the same pay. Just you watch!"

Moyer waited for Haywood to finish his second whiskey before asking, "You have any thoughts, Bill? We've got to find the vein pretty quick or quit drilling."

Haywood gave him a tight-lipped smile. Poor Moyer had been eternally optimistic from the first hours of the talks, and now that those talks were clearly in the shithouse, he didn't know what to do.

"I was pretty sure that Bromley wouldn't budge," Haywood said. "That's why I sent for Harry Orchard."

Moyer was startled. "You think dynamite's the answer? You heard what Bromley said about martial law. I don't want to put the boys through that." He shook his head emphatically. "No, I don't think we need Harry Orchard and his tricks yet."

Haywood shrugged big shoulders. "You give the orders, but you're dead wrong. The smell of powder's the only thing that might bring Bromley around. And you don't need to worry about Steunenberg. He's in office because labor put him there. The man carries a printer's union card, for God's sake."

Moyer leaned back to rub tired eyes. "Once in office, politicians tend to forget who put them there. They're more likely to remember who makes them comfortable."

Haywood shook his head.

"Not Steunenberg. He hasn't got enough in his pants to call the army down on us. Let me discuss a few things with Orchard, then you and I can talk about it some more before we go any further."

"All right, Bill," Moyer said, "but not one match is struck without my approval."

Haywood rose and stretched, his large fists almost touching the ceiling. "Well, then, I'm off to Fatty Kincaid's to watch the prize fight." There was a sparkle of mischief in his good eye when he added, "When the fight's over, we'll meet Harry at Kate's where we can be comfortable. Coming gents?"

Moyer shook his head but MacNamara scrambled eagerly out of his chair.

# CHAPTER THREE

Fatty Kincaid weighed three hundred and seventeen pounds, but moved with surprising agility in his self-appointed role as referee, in the first semi-professional prize fight ever staged in the Coeur d'Alene mining district.

The idea had come to him months before when he witnessed "Driller" Jack Smythe's one-punch knockout of a bullying hoist engineer from the Morning mine.

The event had occurred at a time when Fatty was, as usual, dreaming of ways to enhance his income. He'd sponsored everything from drilling contests to tobacco juice spitting competitions at his saloon, offering modest prizes. His motive, of course, was the hope of selling more beer and whiskey at the bar. He even offered a haven and opportunity to several whores who had been banished from reputable bawdy houses in the district.

They plied their trade on rickety bedsteads in the two upstairs rooms adjacent to his office. Fatty collected a percentage of their take, along with an occasional sampling of their wares; this on the desk in his office, since neither bed was up to the task of supporting him and the lady of his choice.

He had spoken to Smythe after his quick victory and the driller admitted, somewhat modestly, that he had once fought for the light heavyweight championship of British Columbia before he left the Sandon diggings to find work in Idaho. When the trouble between the miners' union and the Bunker Hill culminated in the strike against all the mines not honoring the eight-hour day pact, Fatty had approached the unemployed Smythe, obtaining his enthusiastic agreement to fight anyone the saloon owner chose to put against him, for a fee of fifteen dollars.

"Irish" Paddy Delaney, with his scar tissue brows and flattened nose had been arrested and jailed in Butte the week before for breaking up a whorehouse, assaulting the madam, two of the women and the brace of deputies sent to quell the disturbance. Fatty had seen Delaney defend his Pacific Coast title in Portland a year before, so he was sufficiently inspired to go to Butte to pay the boxer's fine after reading about his plight in the Spokane newspaper.

Now, as he struggled to separate the two sweating and bloody warriors, he reveled in the knowledge that he'd made a wise decision. Spectators stood two and three deep along the twenty-five-foot bar, keeping two barkeeps working at full speed. At least thirty more were packed into the area at the back of the saloon, where the two billiard tables had been pushed against the wall to make room for an arena.

Everyone entering either the guarded front or back doors paid twenty-five cents admission. Once inside the place, most could be counted on to spend at least another fifty cents at the bar. Additionally, Fatty had bet over forty dollars on his man, confident that Delaney's boxing skills were superior to Smythe's.

Fatty's cigar was out, clenched in the corner of his small mouth. His pink and white striped shirt was stuck to the mounds of fat around his middle, above the straining waistband of his pants, as he danced nimbly backward to the accompaniment of bare fists smacking unprotected flesh.

Since Portland, it was apparent that Delaney's training must have consisted mainly of bouts with cheap whiskey and loose women in saloons and cribs from Oregon to Montana. He had lost the toned muscles and flat belly of his prime; the roll above his tights an inviting and frequent target for Smythe's vicious body attacks. He had, however, retained enough of his past skill to prevent Smythe, an eager but awkward gladiator, from knocking him out.

There was no ring as such, only a seething mass of partisan spectators. They surged forward and back like the tide, cheering each blow Smythe landed and hooting derisively when Delaney lashed out with a successful hook or jab.

Another clinch gave Fatty the opportunity to roll his eyes toward the clock above the mirror of the back bar. Across the face was printed, DON'T SWEAR. The hands read quarter past ten. The fight, now in its sixteenth round, had been going on for over an hour. Fatty tried to calculate his gross thus far, but couldn't concentrate on the figures. If Smythe could stay up for another nine or ten rounds...

The faro dealer-turned-timekeeper, whacked a cuspidor with a large spoon, signaling the end of round sixteen. There was a welcome surge toward the bar for refreshments, a sight which gladdened Fatty's heart.

The fighters collapsed in the university chairs, appropriated from the poker tables. Smythe was immediately surrounded by his solicitous cronies from the Wardner union who fanned and encouraged him. One gave him a deep drink from a foaming schooner of beer.

Fatty, sweating more profusely than either boxer, knelt beside Delaney who was being tended by the half-drunk Indian swamper, Joe Gray Wolf.

"He's a tough monkey, that one," Delaney panted, his smashed lips framing bloody teeth. On his right temple, a knot the size of a hen's egg was rising and his pale skin was splotchy with livid welts where Smythe's blows had landed.

"Can you take him?" Fatty asked, at the same time wondering if he should put some money on Smythe as insurance.

Delaney spit bloody water in a proffered bucket and nodded. "He's strong, but clumsy. I'll take him out when the time comes."

"Yes," Fatty said. "When the time comes. Not just yet. A few more rounds."

"If me belly'll take a few more rounds."

Fatty went to stand in front of Smythe. The driller's angular face was relatively unmarked, the mat of hair on his torso concealing any evidence of Delaney's attacks. He was gasping for air, however, and his eyes seemed dull and lifeless."

Fatty leaned close. "You all right, Smythe?"

"A bit winded, Fatty, but man enough to lay your goddamn Irishman away."

"Good luck, then," Fatty said, going to a neutral position to wait for the sound of the improvised gong. He was pleased to see that more men were entering the saloon, among them, Charlie Siringo, known in the district as Leon Allison. He was surprised to note that the usually natty Siringo was wearing a dirty fedora with a frayed band. With him was a rangy, red-bearded miner from the Burke union, Klondike Davis. Davis was a troublemaker who had been jailed several times on suspicion of pro-union violence against non-union men.

Fatty and Siringo exchanged a wave across the smoke-filled room just as the timekeeper banged the cuspidor for round seventeen.

At the end of round eighteen, wherein Delaney had almost knocked Smythe to the floor with a hard punch to the side of the driller's head, one of the doormen advised Fatty that two men had refused to pay twenty-five cents to enter and were asking for a better price. In recognition of the fight's probable duration, and in the interest of fairness, Fatty reduced the admission charge to a dime.

This brought in the two men, who paid the doorman and went directly to the bar. Both wore the yellow slickers which Bunker Hill furnished to its imported special police. Their presence was greeted by a few hostile glances, but there was too much interest in the boxing match for trouble to do more than ferment.

Bill Cheyne, the smaller of the two, glanced furtively around the room, looking uncomfortable. His companion, Ed Shanks, a tall, scowling fellow, threw two dimes on the bar and ordered beer. Baldy Meekham, one of the barkeeps, eyed him coldly.

"This ain't a very safe place for non-union men, Shanks," Baldy told him. "If it was up to me, I wouldn't serve you."

Shanks leaned across the bar to growl, "Well, it ain't up to you, Baldy. Draw two and keep your jaw latched."

"This wasn't a good idea, Ed," Cheyne mumbled.

Baldy set down two schooners and picked up the dimes.

Shanks grabbed up the beers and handed one to Cheyne.

"Horseshit, Billy. We got as much right here as union men. Drink up. Nobody's gonna fuck with me, no how."

In the middle of the nineteenth round, after Smythe had struck Delaney with a jarring right to the head, the former Pacific Coast champion launched a fierce counter attack, driving the driller across the room until he had his back against the bar. The drinkers gave them room, allowing Delaney to press his attack. A powerful left hook to the face sent Smythe reeling backward toward the front door.

At that moment, Haywood and MacNamara stepped inside. Haywood, his stylish brown derby tilted above his blind eye, took in the spectacle with a look of great amusement. He was just in time to stop Smythe's staggering retreat with his arms and body. Haywood steadied the puffing driller before propelling him toward Delaney with a powerful shove. In the wild exchange which followed, Delaney dropped to one knee.

"Start counting, Fatty!" someone screamed. "He's beat."

The hooting and cheering seemed to shake the building.

Haywood, caught up in the excitement, roared, "Count the bloody bastard out!"

But it wasn't over. At the count of six, Delaney sprang to his feet, rushed the surprised Smythe and knocked him down with a mighty left hook to the jaw.

Smythe struggled to his hands and knees, shaking his head in a desperate attempt to clear it. Fatty restrained an eager Delaney, who was ready to deliver the coup de gras the moment Smythe raised his head. He was denied his chance at victory when the gong ended the round.

Haywood and MacNamara joined Siringo and Davis at the bar. After an exchange of greetings, Haywood threw down a silver dollar for a bottle of "the good stuff" and four glasses.

After the first round of drinks, Haywood asked Siringo, "How'd you do in Butte, Leon?"

"Found work for thirty men," Siringo said. "The Butte union's gonna raise the train fare."

"Good," Haywood said. "Some of the families are down to one meal a day, they tell me."

"How are the talks going with Bunker Hill?" Siringo asked as Haywood refilled their glasses.

Haywood's smile disappeared.

"We're getting nowhere. For my money, it's time to stop talking and start tearing things up."

Klondike Davis growled happily, "I'm ready for that!" His mood changed suddenly. "I think we got some Bunker Hill scabs in here."

He scowled at Cheyne and Shanks, who were hunched over the bar and apparently hadn't heard him.

"Not now, Klondike," Siringo said, putting a restraining hand on Davis's muscular arm.

Davis was adamant. "I don't drink with no scabs."

This time Shanks heard him, but Cheyne seemed to pretend he hadn't.

"I think that red-bearded son-of-a-bitch called us scabs, Billy," Shanks said in a loud voice.

Davis shook his fist at him. "That's what you are!"

"I'm a tally clerk and Ed's a watchman," Cheyne squeaked, trying to defuse the situation. "We ain't scabs!"

"You don't have to explain anything to this loudmouth," Shanks said.

He set his beer glass on the bar and spread his feet apart in fighting stance.

Haywood, MacNamara and Siringo watched the exchange escalate, at the same time giving considerable attention to the boxing match.

Davis stepped away from the bar to confront Shanks. "You work for Bunker Hill. That makes you a rotten scab, no matter what you do."

"We got families to support," Cheyne ventured.

"So do most of the union men," Siringo told him, "but they go hungry before we work for slave wages."

It was at this point that Davis swung at Shanks, hitting him a glancing blow on the shoulder. Siringo jumped between them and caught a grazing blow to the mouth thrown by Shanks, that split his lip. Instinctively, he reached inside his coat, but didn't draw his pistol.

Haywood put big arms around Davis and pulled him back to the bar.

"Only one fight at a time, gents," he bellowed.

He poured another drink and offered the bottle to Shanks in a peace making gesture. Shanks declined with an angry shake of his head.

The boxing match was now in round twenty with the two exhausted boxers clinging to each other and throwing ineffectual punches.

Shanks finished his beer and turned to watch the staggering boxers. He avoided eye contact with the union men.

"This fight's about done," he told Cheyne. "I'm gonna take a piss and we'll get out of here. My sister's due in tonight."

Shanks pushed his way roughly through the crowd, shoving aside those who were in his way. When the back door had closed behind him, Davis eased himself away from the bar to follow. He skirted the waltzing boxers and pushed through the impatient spectators, pausing for a whispered word or two, along the way. He lifted a billiard cue out of the wall rack and slipped out the back door. Three men followed.

Fatty looked at the two bloody and spent fighters collapsed in their chairs at the end of the round and wished the fight were over. His feet hurt and his shirt and trousers were as wet as if he'd walked through a rain storm. He had expected Delaney to dispatch the driller before now, his confidence dictating several more wagers including a twenty-dollar bet with Bill Haywood.

Behind the saloon, next to the outhouse, Ed Shanks was buttoning up his overalls when he heard the sound of the gong, signaling the beginning of round twenty-one. The shouts and catcalls of the spectators penetrated the thin pine boards of the saloon, drowning out his scream when he was struck in the left kidney by the hard swung billiard cue in the hands of Klondike Davis.

Irish Paddy Delaney seemed to sense that the opportunity to win the bout was fast eluding him. In desperation, he dropped his guard to launch a two-fisted attack on the panting Smythe. A ferocious right to the body followed by a solid left to the head staggered Smythe but failed to take him off his feet. Smythe's supporters yelled encouragement as they guzzled their beer.

Shanks sank to his knees. A heavy boot caught him on the face, knocking him sideways into the mud.

Smythe fought back now, also sensing the end. He missed with a hook to the head but landed hard lefts and rights to Delaney's body. The former champion grimaced with pain as he backed away, trying to protect his midsection.

Another boot caught Shanks in the groin. He drew up his legs in agony so intense he could make no sound. Davis swung the billiard cue again. It glanced off the bridge of Ed Shanks's nose to smash lips and teeth below.

Driller Smythe seemed to gain strength from Delaney's obvious discomfort. He pursued him across the room toward the bar, where the crowd melted away as they approached, both swinging wildly. A looping right fist to Delaney's jaw sent the professional to his knees. He tried to rise but Smythe struck him again on the left temple. Delaney's eyes glazed, he dropped his hands and pitched forward into the tobacco stained sawdust on the floor.

Klondike Davis tossed the bloody billiard cue into the weeds behind the outhouse and followed his three companions into the saloon. Behind him, in the puddle of his own piss, Ed Shanks lay still, making no sound.

When it was obvious that Paddy Delaney was down for the count, Haywood slapped MacNamara on the back, causing him to choke on a mouthful of whiskey.

"Fatty owes me twenty dollars," Haywood chortled. "I'll collect and we'll head over to Kate's."

Klondike Davis, a schooner of beer in each hand, pushed up to Siringo. Spots of blood dotted his shirt.

"A whale of a fight, Leon." He turned his back so Cheyne, who was watching them, couldn't hear. "We just beat the shit out of Shanks."

Siringo turned to MacNamara who was becoming red-eyed and unsteady on his feet. "Get Haywood the hell out of here, Mac."

"He's getting his money from Fatty. What's the rush?"

MacNamara reached uncertainly for the bottle on the bar but Siringo moved it out of reach. "There's been some trouble out in back. Get going."

MacNamara nodded dully and pushed his way into an appreciative crowd surrounding Driller Jack Smythe, Fatty Kincaid and Bill Haywood. Haywood was making capital out of the business of collecting his twenty dollars from the pained saloon owner.

"Our association always seems to cost me money, Bill," Fatty grumbled as he extracted a limp bill from his sodden pocketbook.

Just as MacNamara reached Haywood's side, there was a shout from the rear of the saloon.

"Git a lantern, somebody. They's a dead man layin' out by the shithouse!"

In response to MacNamara's mumbled warning, Haywood tipped his derby to a distracted Fatty and headed directly for the front door.

On his way to the back door, Fatty paused to glare at Delaney, still glassy-eyed, stretched out on a billiard table. Joe Gray Wolf wiped clumsily at his swollen face with a dirty, bloodstained towel.

"You cost me a lot of money, you barroom bum. I've got a mind not to pay you," Fatty growled.

Siringo skirted the stampede of the curious to corner Fatty. "Pay him, Fatty. He fought his heart out for you."

He pulled Fatty away from the table. "You heard anything?"

"Haywood's fed up with the negotiations. That I know."

Fatty moved his bulk toward the back door. "I better see what's going on outside."

39

"Any word of someone coming in from the outside to do the union's dirty work?"

Fatty mopped his red face with a bandana handkerchief and shook his head. "Not that I've heard, but with Haywood, anything's possible. You heard anything?"

"Nothing worth repeating."

An elderly man entered through the back door and confronted Fatty. "Somebody better get the sheriff."

# CHAPTER FOUR

Johnnie Neville, thin and ferret-like, in his shabby suit coat and over-alls, pulled the buggy up to the second largest house in Wardner. The largest belonged to Justin Whitehead, the Bunker Hill superintendent. He hopped down to tie the horse to a cast-iron black boy in painted livery.

"This here's Kate's place, Mr. Orchard."

Orchard didn't answer, taken by the elaborate scrollwork and stained glass windows. Light shown from every room in contrast to other homes on the street, hunkering darkly against the mountainside, as though put to shame by their neighbor's splendor.

"Big house. How many girls?"

"Five or six," Johnnie said. "That's not counting Kate. She don't work much no more."

"She's come a long way from Colorado," Orchard said, starting up the steep stairs to the front porch.

Johnnie hurried to catch up. "You know her, Mr. Orchard?" He might have used the same tone to inquire about Orchard's acquaintance with the Pope.

"Only by reputation, sonny. Ring the bell."

The muted notes of a piano filtering through the polished oak door were drowned out by the jangling bell when Johnnie twisted the handle. The door was opened almost immediately by a hefty and exceedingly plain young woman whose dress and somber manner seemed to say that she was hired help for all but the horizontal chores.

"I brung Mr. Orchard, here, Willi. Go tell Kate," Johnnie ordered.

Willi ignored the order and gave Orchard sort of a curtsy.

"Ya," she said, in a heavy German accent, "they vaiting upstairs. You go up, Mr. Orchard."

Willi stepped between them when Orchard mounted the staircase. "You, Yohnnie, in the parlor mit the girls."

At the end of the upstairs hall, a large woman in a green brocade dress was framed in a doorway. The light behind her danced on her abundant lacquered red hair. Her appraisal was accompanied by a slow smile.

"You don't look too damn dangerous, Mr. Orchard, but Big Bill says you're a holy terror." Her voice had an interesting, husky quality. "I'm Kate McCafferty."

"Well, Kate, you don't look like the best fuck this side of the divide neither," Orchard said, not to be outdone by this whore, or any other, despite her good looks.

"Any time you've got three dollars to spend, you can find out," she responded, still smiling.

"Three dollars? A day's wages. My, my, you must be good. They still call you Big Ass Kate?"

"Only behind my back, honey," Kate said. "Come in."

Kate stepped aside to reveal Haywood and MacNamara sitting side by side on a velvet settee, whiskey glasses in hand. MacNamara seemed to be having trouble keeping his eyes open.

Haywood smiled warmly at Orchard but didn't rise, or offer his hand. MacNamara nodded sleepily and closed his eyes.

"Hello, Harry. You're looking well for a man in your profession."

42

Orchard dropped into a Morris chair, put his derby on his knee, and accepted the glass of whiskey Kate poured for him. He watched her as she bent to fill Haywood's glass. She was indeed a handsome woman, despite a rear end of rather ample proportions. Though she'd made much of her fortune in the Coeur d'Alene, he'd heard about her in Colorado. The men who had bought her favors when she was one of Fannie Tatum's girls in two-mile-high Leadville spoke of Big Ass Kate with a kind of reverence.

"Who brought you here?" Haywood stared at Orchard over the rim of his glass.

"Young weasel named Neville," Orchard told him. "I left him in der parlor mit the girls."

"Don't poke fun at Willi," Kate warned. "I need one girl in the house who's more interested in staying on her feet than on her back."

Haywood downed his whiskey to become abruptly businesslike. "Bunker Hill's wiped its ass on my shirt, Harry. We've run out of color in the talks. I've decided it's time to tear things up."

Orchard glanced at Kate, who was lighting a cigarette. He raised a hand to stop Haywood from saying anything else.

"Let's have this talk in private, Bill."

Haywood was startled.

"Harry, we can talk in front of Kate. I'd trust her with my life."

"I trust no one with mine," Orchard said.

"You trust me, don't you, Harry?" Haywood sounded hurt.

"Only as long as you don't get your ass in a crack, Bill," Orchard replied. He found a cigar in an inside pocket, took it out and wetted it.

"Let's get down to business," Haywood said with a note of annoyance in his voice.

"In private, Bill, if you don't mind."

He grinned at Kate who was watching him with a curious expression. She gave him a little bow.

"I don't have to have a tunnel cave in on me to know when I'm not welcome."

She swept from the room and closed the door behind her.

Haywood shook his head unhappily.

"That was rude, Harry."

Orchard ignored the rebuke.

"What do you want me to do for you, Bill?"

Haywood leaned back on the settee, big hands clasped over crossed knees.

"Not for me, Harry. For the union. We're going to destroy the Bunker Hill mill and concentrator."

He stared hard at Orchard to measure his reaction.

"How much?"

Haywood's face darkened.

"How much what? How much money or how much dynamite?"

Orchard turned his tumbler, watching the lamplight reflecting in the convolutions of the cut glass.

"I know how much dynamite I'd need," he said quietly. "A load of buckshot in Frank Bromley'd be easier. I'm across the hall from him at the hotel."

Haywood sat up straight. His angry voice made the dozing MacNamara open his eyes.

"No! It's 1899. I want the world to remember the Western Federation in 1999."

"We blow the mill, the district's gonna be up to its ass in soldiers," Orchard said. "Remember Colorado."

Haywood was trying to light his cigar, finally getting it going. He squinted at Orchard through a cloud of smoke.

"Not a chance! Governor Steunenberg's got union sympathies."

"We'd have to move boxes of gelatin past guards with rifles. It sounds like suicide to me, Bill."

"The price is right, Harry."

"I'll need diagrams of the mill and at least a hundred boxes of dynamite."

Haywood relaxed.

"The powder houses on Canyon Creek aren't guarded. The Burke union boys can get you what you need."

He punched MacNamara in the ribs, causing him to open his eyes and sit up straight.

"McNarmara can get you the diagrams," Haywood continued. "There isn't much time, though."

"Why not? The mill's not going any place."

"I want it blown on Sunday when nobody's working."

"I'd make a bigger impression with a full shift in place. Slip in there the night before…"

Haywood shook his head adamantly.

"I'm not interested in killing people on this job. I want to do it while Bromley's here."

Orchard got up and put on his derby.

"It seems a shame to waste that much dynamite on just wood and steel."

Haywood looked closely at him. "You're not joking, are you?"

"I never joke about business, Bill," Orchard said. "I'll need a couple of hundred dollars now and you can put another two in my account when you get back to Denver."

"Done," Haywood said. "That's fair."

Orchard paused, hand on the china doorknob. "Can I trust all the union boys?"

"They're the least of your worries."

"How about Leon Allison? I was on the train with him tonight."

MacNamara nodded wisely and said, "Allison? Hunnerd percent," before closing his eyes again.

Orchard opened the door. "I'd watch him just the same."

Haywood got up and followed him into the hallway. "You're too suspicious, Harry."

At that moment a bespectacled middle-aged man came out of one of the rooms straightening his clothes. He gave a sheepish smile and hurried down the stairs.

When he was gone, Orchard said, "Suspicious, alive and out of jail. Keep an eye on Allison, you won't be sorry."

Haywood placed a hand on his shoulder.

"I feel better with you here, Harry."

Suddenly, the sounds of a violent commotion exploded from one of the rooms. A door was flung open and a young woman with a mane of blonde hair, clad in a flowered chemise, sailed into the hall and landed on her face.

Klondike Davis, barefoot, in his long underwear, stumbled out of the room. He picked up the girl by the hair. She spat in his face. Klondike slapped her and jerked her around by the hair.

Kate came charging up the stairs.

"Klondike! Stop it!"

Davis let the sobbing girl slump to the floor.

"The bitch was goin' through my pants while I was taking a piss."

Kate's expression changed.

"Damn it! I've warned her."

Kate grabbed the girl by the hair and pulled her to her feet. The girl seemed more afraid of Kate than she was of Davis.

"Pack up and get out, Pearl," Kate ordered, shoving her in the direction of the room.

Davis's face broke into a huge grin when he saw Orchard. He came to him in a rush and gave him a bear hug.

"Harry, you wild son-of-a-bitch," he bellowed. "Haven't seen you since that business in Telluride."

Various articles of Davis's clothing began to pile up in the hall as the girl fired them through the door. Davis released Orchard and put on his shirt. His hat and boots hit the floor with a thud, ending the barrage.

"That's right," Orchard said, "and you haven't changed your duds, either. You've still got blood on your shirt."

Haywood, in the sitting room doorway, was amused by the reunion.

"Harry, you might want to talk to Klondike about that other piece of business."

Orchard nodded agreement but had reservations about Klondike Davis, a wild, violent man whose emotions overruled his judgment. In Telluride he'd shot the aged constable for no reason other than that the old man wore a badge and had the nerve to ask them where they were going.

"I intend to," Orchard said, looking at Kate, "but first, I have a proposition to discuss with Kate."

Orchard offered her his arm and they went down the stairs together.

# CHAPTER FIVE

Shortly after leaving Fatty Kincaid's saloon, Siringo left Main Street and followed the railroad tracks. The rain had stopped, but low-lying clouds obscured the moon, placing his route in almost total darkness. Several times he stumbled on the ties, almost sprawling headlong in the road bed.

Cursing the day he had chosen a clandestine profession, Siringo proceeded until he came to the tiny Wardner depot, with Justin Whitehead's imposing house further on. Mill Street was deserted so he wasn't observed when he went to the rear of the house and entered through the unlocked back door.

"It's all right," he told the startled servant girl who was making coffee in the kitchen. "Mr. Whitehead is expecting me."

In the sitting room, Frank Bromley, Walker Timmons and Justin Whitehead were ensconced with port and cigars. Mrs. Whitehead, with prescience nourished by experience, had greeted the dignitaries before retiring.

"Mr. Bromley, we're only talking about fifty cents a day," Whitehead said. "Maybe we should avoid trouble and give the union what it wants."

Timmons was shaking his head vigorously when Bromley replied, "Not yet. Every arriving train brings in men willing to work for Bunker Hill wages. Hungry families are a powerful weapon."

"You can only push men so far," Whitehead warned. "You heard what Haywood said."

"I'm not worried about a blowhard like Haywood," Bromley scoffed.

Siringo, standing in the dining room beside a very agitated servant girl, said, "He called all the shots in Colorado."

Bromley and Timmons craned their necks to see who had spoken. Whitehead rose quickly to greet Siringo. His face was flushed from several glasses of port.

"Charles, you scared me! What happened to your mouth?"

"I forgot to duck," Siringo said. "You know, your back door was unlocked. I could have been Harry Orchard."

Bromley and Timmons rose as Whitehead brought Siringo into the room.

"Charles Siringo, gentlemen," Whitehead announced. "Our Pinkerton man inside the union."

Bromley came forward to shake hands.

"Frank Bromley, Mr. Siringo. I admire your nerve, sir."

Siringo was surprised by the strength of Bromley's grip, coming from a man so pale and thin.

"I've had riskier jobs," Siringo said, hoping that Bromley wouldn't press him for a litany of his dangerous experiences. If he did, he could always tell him how he had once tracked Butch Cassidy.

"I presume you're armed," Bromley said.

"All the time, Mr. Bromley," Siringo said. "Even when I'm with a woman, my Smith hangs on the bedpost."

"You're late," Timmons said. "Mr. Bromley and I were getting ready to leave."

Siringo didn't like the tone used by this officious pink squid and wondered who he was.

"It couldn't be helped," Siringo replied calmly. "I was hoping to get some information from Haywood."

Bromley looked curiously at Siringo.

"You mentioned a name when you came in. Harry Orchard. What about him?"

"Orchard's a union killer and dynamiter," Siringo said. "He got off the train tonight. Get ready for some fireworks, gentlemen."

"Then Haywood isn't a blowhard?"

"Far from it," Siringo said, smiling reflectively. "If the talks fail, he'll tear things up. That's his style."

"Maybe you'll have to deal with this Harry Orchard, Siringo," Timmons said, in a commanding tone, meant to impress. "Dedicated union men can be very troublesome."

"I don't think I caught your name, sir," Siringo said.

"It's Mr. Timmons. I'm the Bunker Hill legal counsel. When I said 'deal with him' I wasn't talking about arrest."

"I'm afraid murder isn't in the Pinkerton charter, Mr. Timmons."

Whitehead directed Siringo to a chair and brought him a glass of port. The servant girl appeared with the coffee pot and cups on a tray. Siringo set his glass aside and took a cup of coffee.

He waited until everyone had been served before saying, "I hope you people have some sort of disaster plan, in case Haywood decides that he isn't going to get what he wants."

Bromley lighted a fresh cigar.

"It might surprise you to know, Mr. Siringo, that I have a plan in case, as you say, the union decides to tear things up. My plan calls for them to tear themselves up in the bargain."

"Oh?" Siringo sipped the hot coffee. From the expressions on Timmons's and Whitehead's faces, they didn't know any more about Bromley's strategy than he did.

Bromley rose to pace the sitting room. "I must admit, it sounds a bit unorthodox, maybe even a bit insane, but I've concluded that a major act of violence, like, say, the destruction of our mill, on the part of the union, would achieve certain objectives for us."

"Such as?" Siringo asked, when no one else spoke.

Bromley came to stand in front of him, seeming suddenly to be very tall.

"First, our Wardner mill is obsolete and will have to be abandoned shortly, in any event. We already have plans for a new concentrator, incorporating the latest processes, integrated with a smelter, to be built in Kellogg."

Whitehead nodded his head enthusiastically, as though he was beginning to see the wisdom of Bromley's plan.

Moving the operation to Kellogg, Siringo thought, would probably spell the end of Fatty Kincaid's saloon, depriving them of another conduit into the workings of the union.

"Secondly," Bromley continued, "I've discussed this with the other members of the Mine Owners Association and they'll back any move made by Bunker Hill. We have to get a firm and permanent upper hand with the union once and for all."

Siringo studied Bromley for a moment before he said, "If the union blows the mill to smithereens, that gives you the upper hand?"

"What follows does," Bromley said, dropping into his chair. "Before the last board hits the ground, my friend, Governor Steunenberg, will have the Idaho National Guard put the entire district under martial law. The men responsible for any acts of violence will be arrested and tried. By the time it's over, the Western Federation of Miners will be finished in the Coeur d'Alene." Behind his spectacles, Bromley's eyes had taken on an anticipatory glitter.

"And the shareholders and the insurance companies pay for all the fun," Siringo said, finding himself disliking Bromley.

"That's not your concern, Siringo," Timmons interjected. "Your job is to gather evidence which will send the union's top people to the Idaho State Penitentiary for long terms."

Siringo gave the lawyer a dry smile. "Considering something called union solidarity, I expect every union member from here to Burke can be convicted. The Idaho pen isn't big enough to hold them all."

"I'm not interested in the rank and file," Bromley said. "Just the men at the top; the ring leaders. And, of course, those involved in the actual dynamiting, like this Harry Orchard, if indeed, that's why he's here."

Siringo finished his coffee and got to his feet. "If you'll excuse me gentlemen, it's been a long day." He turned toward the door to the kitchen. "I'll go out the way I came in."

"Keep us informed, Mr. Siringo," Bromley said. "We need to be alerted to the first hint of trouble."

"Harry Orchard is the first hint. Goodnight, gentlemen."

"One moment, Siringo," Timmons said, glancing at Bromley. "I'd be very careful about communicating any of this to your Denver people. From what I've heard, we can trust nobody, including telegraphers and telephone centrals."

"That's right, Mr. Timmons," Siringo agreed. "Everyone in the Coeur d'Alene is up to something." He smiled at Bromley and added, "You know, Mr.Bromley, the union never forgets. If you sic soldiers on them, they'll come after you."

"I don't think so," Bromley replied calmly. "I live in San Francisco."

"You may wish you lived in Timbuktu," Siringo said. "Goodnight, sir."

# CHAPTER SIX

At Kate's dressing table, Orchard, in his shirtsleeves, used her brush to slick down his hair. He watched in the ornate mirror and could tell from the look on her face that she was enjoying the moment.

She was sitting up in her bed, with only a bed sheet covering her nakedness. When she leaned forward to take a cigarette from the package on the bedside table, one of her large breasts was exposed, now hardly enticing.

Her tone was mocking when she said, "You said you wanted to be with me for an hour."

She smiled at him as she lit the cigarette and blew a puff of smoke in his direction.

"I haven't been with a woman for a while," he told her reflection. "I'm out of practice."

He put on his coat and picked up his derby, anxious to get out of the room. Being made fun of by a whore was a new experience for him and he didn't like it. If she didn't have such a friendly relationship with Haywood he'd have slapped her silly.

"If you've got another three dollars you might beat your four-minute record," Kate said, lying back on her pillow, clearly amused by his discomfiture.

Orchard put on his derby and went over to stand beside the bed.

"If I wanted to beat you at your own game, Kate, I'd put my elbow in it and go all night."

"Whatever gives you pleasure, Mr. Orchard," she replied dreamily, blowing smoke at the ceiling.

Orchard turned on his heel and barged out of the room. In another second, he'd have strangled her.

He found Johnnie dozing in a chair in the deserted parlor and woke him without ceremony.

On the way back to Galena House, Johnnie had glanced slyly at him and asked, "How was that Kate, Mr. Orchard? I always wanted to try her but never had no three bucks to spare."

That was the trouble with fucking whores, Orchard thought. No matter how appealing they might seem at the time, one had to remember that those white legs had also wrapped themselves around the likes of scruffy Johnnie Neville.

"Just fine," Orchard said finally. "Mind your driving. I don't want any mud on me."

When they approached the hotel, Orchard saw that a buggy was tied to the porch rail and three men were talking on the porch. Even in the poor light of two kerosene lanterns, Orchard recognized Frank Bromley from a newspaper photo he'd cut out weeks before.

"Slow down," he told Johnnie. "You know any of those men?"

"The one with the fancy hair and mutton chops is Whitehead," Johnnie whispered. "He's the Bunker Hill super. I never seen them other two before, Mr. Orchard."

"My name is Hogan." Orchard told him. "That's what you call me in public. Think you can remember that?"

Johnnie nodded, but continued to stare at the men, prompting Orchard to alight from the buggy.

"Thanks for the ride," he told Johnnie. "I hope your mother's feeling better soon."

Before the puzzled Johnnie could respond, Orchard stepped up on the porch, gave Bromley, Timmons and Whitehead a friendly nod and entered the hotel. It was too bad Haywood hadn't given him the go ahead to do Bromley. It seemed to him that buckshot might be more effective than dynamite in this instance, to bring Bunker Hill around.

Siringo was on the porch of Mrs. Kessie's boarding house when Sheriff Thompson and one of his deputies came out of the shadows, pistols drawn.

"Allison? You're under arrest."

Siringo turned to face them, annoyed by this intrusion. He was tired and looked forward to getting into a lumpy bed to get some sleep.

"What the hell are you talking about, Thompson?"

"I got witnesses who seen Ed Shanks fighting with you and a jasper named Davis," the sheriff said. "They say Shanks hit you. Was that enough for you to kill him?"

"Shanks was on his feet when I left Kincaid's," Siringo said. "People saw me leave."

"He ain't on his feet now," the sheriff muttered, coming forward. "He's layin' in the back of the barbershop with his head stove in. I'm taking your weapon."

Very gingerly, the sheriff pushed Siringo's coat aside and removed his revolver.

"This would have done a neater job than the pool cue."

"I suppose you've got Davis in custody," Siringo said.

"Not yet, but he will be as soon as I find him. Do you know where he's at?"

"No, I don't. I've been with friends all evening."

"You can tell it to the judge in the morning, but tonight you're a suspect in a murder and you're sleeping in my jail."

"This is really stupid," Siringo growled, trying to think of ways to extricate himself from this mess. He probably should have left the saloon immediately

55

after the altercation with Shanks at the bar or made an effort to dissuade Davis, who was well known to the Pinkertons as a suspect in crimes ranging from mayhem to murder.

Well, he hadn't, and now he was going to get his sleep in the Wallace jail. Shit!

Hands clasped behind his head, Orchard lay in bed staring at the water stains on the ceiling of his room. Beside the bed, ticking noisily, was the sturdy, nickel-plated alarm clock he'd bought in Denver for ninety cents, expecting it to be a quality time piece. Unfortunately it had revealed itself to be less than that, waking him with its persistent bell at six-thirty, rather than seven, where he'd set it.

This was doubly annoying because he'd purchased it with double duty in mind. It could wake him at the proper time or it could set off a new-fangled electric detonator, should the need arise. It had proven itself incapable of performing either task accurately. If it didn't look so handsome he'd have thrown it out the window.

He was finishing with the chamber pot when it sounded like someone was pounding on Bromley's door, across the hall. Padding across the cold linoleum floor in his bare feet, he opened his door just a crack and peered out.

The man whom Johnnie had identified as Whitehead, the Bunker Hill superintendent, raised his fist to knock again when Bromley opened the door. His face was lathered with shaving soap and he had the brush in his hand.

He sounded irritable when he said, "Whitehead! What the hell is it?"

"Siringo's been arrested," Whitehead announced breathlessly.

"For what?" Bromley asked, looking up and down the hall. "Better come inside."

Orchard eased his door closed and waited until Whitehead had gone into Bromley's room. Then he tiptoed boldly across the hall to press his ear against Bromley's door.

"One of my watchmen was beaten to death last night," Whitehead was saying. "The sheriff's holding Siringo in the county jail at Wallace as a suspect. He just telephoned me."

Bromley asked, "Then, the sheriff doesn't know who he is?"

"No. We don't trust Thompson," Whitehead said.

"Damn!" Bromley exploded. "He said he'd been in a fight."

"Well, he can't stay in jail, even if he's guilty," Whitehead said. "If the union gets wind of who he is, they'll take that jail apart, brick by brick to get at him."

Down the hall a door opened. Orchard froze. A barefoot man wearing only pants and underwear and carrying a towel came out of a room and hurried toward the bathing room at the end of the hall.

Orchard put his ear against the door again. He was beginning to get nervous. He could hear stirrings in the room next to Bromley's. Probably the fleshy gent he'd seen with them on the hotel porch.

"I'll have Timmons contact the judge and tell him who Siringo is. That might be enough to get him released on bail." Bromley sounded like a military commander haranguing his troops. "A detective's no good to us in jail. When the judge sets bail, have your man, Kincaid, deliver the money so it won't look fishy. We have to get him out of there."

Orchard tiptoed back to his room and quietly shut the door. Bromley's words, "Your man, Kincaid" echoed in his head. The saloonkeeper was working both sides of the street. The fat son-of-a-bitch! Haywood will explode like giant powder when he finds out. And Siringo...who the hell was he? "A detective..." Maybe a Pinkerton detective posing as a union man? That was an onerous possibility. It had happened before. If he had to select a likely suspect in this case, it would be Allison, who had set off his personal alarm bells on the train last night.

In the middle of his breakfast in the hotel dining room, a scheme began to form in his head; one which could confirm Allison's true identity and keep him in jail if, indeed, he was a detective who had infiltrated the union.

He wolfed his greasy eggs, potatoes and coffee, deciding not to wake Haywood and Moyer. He didn't want to embarrass himself if he was all wet about Allison. By eight-thirty he'd bought a tickct at the Kellogg depot and was waiting to board the eastbound train, due at eight-fifty-five.

The plump man he'd seen with Whitehead and Bromley was also waiting. Orchard assumed he must be Timmons, whom Bromley had mentioned.

When the train pulled into Wallace, Orchard remained seated, observing Timmons's brisk departure. After a fifteen-minute wait, the train pulled out of the Wallace depot and began to make the laborious climb up the grade toward Mullan.

When the conductor entered the almost empty coach to collect the tickets, Orchard took a silver dollar from his vest pocket and dropped it into the man's outstretched hand.

"I want you to stop for a hot box when I tell you, so I can get off."

The conductor examined the coin nestled in his palm. His grin revealed several gold teeth.

"You just say the word, mister."

The smell of coal smoke permeated the car as the train struggled up the steep grade, enveloped in a pall of its own making. Orchard tried to calculate how long after leaving Mullan last night had the altercation with Alford Kildare taken place. It would be hard to determine the exact spot because the train had been traveling downgrade at a higher speed than the present agonizing pace.

"How far to Mullan?" he asked when the conductor passed through the car again.

The man consulted a large gold watch before announcing, "Twenty-two minutes, friend."

"I'll want off in ten," Orchard told him.

Fifteen minutes later he was standing alone in the middle of the Northern Pacific tracks watching the tail end of the train disappear around a sharp bend. The sky was threatening more rain so he commenced his search as soon as the train was out of sight.

First, he walked eastward, in the direction of Mullan, until he rounded the curve that had swallowed the train. Ahead was at least a mile of cut and fill, with no trees on either side. Retracing his steps, Orchard continued in a westerly direction until the thick stands of white pine and tamarack lined both sides of the right of way like soldiers at attention.

After almost an hour, Orchard found Allison's hat. Dusty, misshapen and covered with dry pine needles, it lay under some hazelnut bushes at the edge of the forest. Orchard picked it up, dusted it off and reshaped the crown, already beginning to enjoy the thought of returning it.

Turning it over, he found the name C. Leon Allison embossed on the sweatband. His second discovery was even more rewarding; a fifty-dollar bill, folded lengthwise in thirds, tucked under the leather band. This, he pocketed.

Amy Neville turned from the stove to stare angrily at her brother, sprawled in a chair at their rickety table.

"I don't want to hear you say scab ever again, John Neville. Poor Bella's up there waitin' for Ed's wife to die and him layin' on a plank in the barbershop and all you can think about is him workin' and you ain't."

She reached into the nearly empty wood box to put a couple of sticks into the stove.

"Ed Shanks wasn't no worse than half them union bums you run with. Have some respect for the dead."

Johnnie stared sullenly at the bread crumbs still littering the table from breakfast.

"I didn't mean nuthin', Amy," he muttered, "It's just at times like these, union men got to stick together."

Amy's blue eyes flashed another danger signal.

"I suppose they was stickin' together at Fatty Kinkaid's when they practically knocked Ed Shanks's head off his body."

Amy slammed the cast-iron stove lid into place so hard that her brother jumped.

"The union makes me sick!"

Johnnie pushed away from the table.

"I gotta go."

Amy barred the door.

"You ain't goin' no place 'til you fill my wood box."

"I don't think there's none left outside," Johnnie told her, trying to get by.

Amy stood her ground.

"What am I to cook with? You want we should burn the table? What's next after that? Go down the gulch to that shack that fell over."

"I'm supposed to be at the Galena House at ten with the rig to pick up Mr. Orchard," Johnnie said.

"And just who is this Mr. Orchard?" Amy said, hands on hips, looking like an angry child. "Another murderer?"

"Him and Haywood are plenty thick," Johnnie declared defensively. "Orchard's some kind of big mucky muck in the union."

"That says it all," Amy muttered. "I don't need to know nothing else. He's in the same bag with Haywood, Moyer and that ninny, MacNamara. Oh, Jesus, I just want all this trouble to end so's we can go back to leading normal lives again."

Suddenly overwhelmed, Amy buried her face in her dirty apron and began to sob.

Johnnie started to make his escape but paused in the doorway. It frightened him when Amy cried, which was damn seldom.

"Amy, don't cry. I gotta go, but..."

Amy's voice was muffled by her apron, but no less authoritative when she commanded, "The wood first. Take the ax."


"I believe you have my friend, Leon Allison, locked up in here, Sheriff."

Orchard stood respectfully just inside the front door of the squat brick jailhouse and sheriff's office. He was carrying Allison's hat in his left hand.

Sheriff Thompson was seated at a paper-strewn rolltop desk eating a large fried-egg sandwich. Some of the yolk was clinging to his moustache when he looked up, chewing methodically.

"That's right," he said, mouth full. "Who the hell are you?"

"Tom Hogan. We met at the Kellogg depot last night."

Thompson rose slowly, extracting a handkerchief from a back pocket to wipe his moustache.

"Oh, yeah. You're the one hit the special deputy," Thompson said slowly. "Broke his nose and crushed his sinus, the doctor said. You're damned lucky you ain't in here too. What do you want to see Allison about?"

"About him being locked up and what can I do for him," Orchard said. "Haven't you ever had a friend locked up in jail, Sheriff?"

"Not on a murder charge, I ain't."

"Come to think of it, neither have I," Orchard said. "Can I see him?"

"I reckon not," Thompson said, "unless you've got his bail. It was set this morning at five hundred dollars."

Orchard made a helpless gesture.

"Afraid not. Fifty dollars is about all I've got on me. I'd be much obliged if I could say a few words to him and return a hat he lost."

Thompson heaved a petulant sigh, which seemed out of character for such a big man.

"All right. Just stand over there and I'll have him brought out."

Orchard moved over beside the riveted strap-iron lattice separating the lockup from the office.

Thompson ambled to the door and shouted, "Lester, bring Allison down here. Fellow wants to see him."

"He's eatin' his dinner," came the shouted reply.

"Goddamn!" Thompson rattled the lockup door. "Bring him down here. He's got all day to eat his dinner."

Allison, in shirt sleeves and wearing leg irons, appeared at the door, followed by Lester, the hawk-faced deputy. He didn't seem as confident and debonair as he had on the train the night before. His gaze was unfriendly.

"Hogan? What do you want?"

Orchard affected an injured look. "I heard you killed somebody, Leon. I just wanted to see if you needed anything."

"I need to get out of here," Allison said. "I don't think you can help me there." Allison craned his neck. "Is that my hat?"

"It has your name in it."

"How the hell did you find it?"

"It was lying in the weeds behind Kincaid's saloon in Wardner," Orchard told him. "I knew you'd want it back."

"Gimme that!" Sheriff Thompson pulled the black slouch hat out of Orchard's hand and turned it over to check the hatband. He looked accusingly at Allison.

"It is yours, by God."

"Yes it's mine, but I didn't lose it at Fatty Kincaid's."

Allison's face was expressionless as he stared at Orchard. "You may have to convince a jury of that," Thompson said, fondling the handsome hat. "Take him back, Lester."

As Allison was being led away, the sheriff turned to appraise Orchard.

"I'm gonna need a statement from you, Hogan," he said. "As the law, I have to thank you for this, but I wouldn't want you for my friend."

Thompson tossed the hat on his desk where it half-covered the remains of the fried-egg sandwich, an atrocity Orchard was glad Allison or Siringo didn't have to see. It was almost two in the afternoon when Orchard got off the train at the Kellogg depot. He felt good about the day's work. The hat had clearly established that Leon Allison was an imposter, and a detective at that, and the statement Orchard had given Thompson might make it more difficult for him to be released on bail.

He went directly to the Galena house where Johnnie was sprawled in a corner of the small lobby. From his bloodshot eyes, it was evident that he'd not spent all his time in the imitation leather rocker with people stepping over his skinny legs and big feet.

"I been here since ten-thirty, Mr. um, Hogan."

"I told you ten o'clock."

Johnnie got unsteadily to his feet. "I don't see that it makes no difference," he muttered defensively. "You wasn't here nohow."

"Let's go outside," Orchard ordered, leading the way to the front porch, where he shoved Johnnie roughly against the wall.

"In my business, timing is important, sonny," Orchard said. "If I had been here and you weren't, I'd have had to kick your sorry ass. Are you able to drive? You're none too steady."

"I can drive." Johnnie regarded Orchard with sullen eyes. "Where to?"

"Take me to the Oriental Saloon. Then, find Haywood, Moyer and MacNamara and bring them there. Tell them it's important."

The normally docile mare that Johnnie had rented seemed to come off the ground with all four feet simultaneously when Johnnie laid into her with the whip. Eyes rolling fearfully, she dashed up the hill toward Wardner as though the buggy behind her was the devil himself. When she finally stumbled in a rut, almost going down, Orchard snatched the reins out of Johnnie's hands and stopped the horse.

"Put that whip back in the socket, boy, or I'm gonna stick it up your rear end!"

"You'll do no such thing!" Johnnie shot back. He made the mistake of raising the whip as though to strike Orchard with the butt end.

With one hand, Orchard snapped the reins against the mare's tender back. With the other he gave the youth a sharp jab in the ribs as the buggy lurched forward. Johnnie tumbled out of the buggy to land hard on the seat of his pants at the edge of the road.

"You'd better make up your mind, kid," Orchard told him. "You're either with me or against me. If you're against me, you can walk home and get your ma to wipe your snotty nose. I won't be needing you again."

Johnnie scrambled to his feet, brushing the mud off his pants. He was limping when he picked up the buggy whip and replaced it in its socket.

"I ain't against you, Mr. Orchard. I ain't."

He said no more until they'd arrived in front of the Oriental Saloon.

"I'll find them as soon as I can," he assured Orchard in a subdued tone.

"Where are you going to look for them?"

Johnnie seemed startled by the question.

"Well, I thought at Kate's or maybe Fatty Kincaid's."

"Try the union hall first," Orchard said, mounting the two steps to the saloon's front porch. "If you don't find them in an hour, come back here and get me."

The Oriental was a dimly lighted cave with a long bar and a stairway in the back. Behind the bar hung a huge and poorly executed painting of a naked, oriental girl struggling with two sword-bearing yellow men in long robes. Behind them, silhouetted against a greenish sky was a structure Orchard assumed to be China's Great Wall.

He ordered a schooner of beer and went to stand near a bowl of hard-boiled eggs on the bar. In the back, a quiet poker game was underway and a lone shooter perfected his game on the faded green felt of a pool table.

The strike had taken its toll on the saloons in the region; lack of business forced many of the smaller and less popular to close their doors. Orchard ate two boiled eggs while he thought about the days ahead and carrying out Haywood's plan.

If Allison, in his role of Wardner union secretary, knew anything about it, they'd have to abandon the entire scheme. It would be suicide to force entry into the Bunker Hill mill against Winchester-toting guards and special deputies, particularly if you were laden with dynamite and blasting caps.

Within the hour, Johnnie had returned with Haywood and Moyer. At Moyer's insistence, they took a private room in the back, ordering whiskey and cold cuts to be sent in. At the door, Orchard barred Johnnie from entering.

"Go watch the buggy, sonny. Apologize to the horse."

Johnnie gave him a wounded look and left the room.

In response to Orchard's question, Moyer explained that MacNamara was too sick to come. Probably too hung over to come, Orchard thought.

"If he'd been up to it, I was going to send him up to Burke to talk to the boys about getting the dynamite for Sunday," Moyer said, fixing Orchard with an accusing eye.

Orchard studied the dour Moyer. "I thought that was my job."

"It was," Haywood said, "but we couldn't find you this morning. Now what's this urgent meeting about?" He bit the tip off a cigar, spitting it toward the cuspidor in the corner. He sounded out of sorts.

"I had some business in Wallace. I wanted to see Leon Allison. He's in the county jail, you know."

Haywood sounded impatient when he said, "We know all about that. I've already sent a telegram to Denver for his bail."

"That may not be necessary," Orchard said. "Bromley is making arrangements to post his bond and make it look like a good will gesture from Fatty Kincaid."

Moyer scowled at him.

"How do you know that?"

"The walls are thin at the Galena House and I'm across the hall from Bromley," Orchard said. "Incidentally, Allison's real name is Siringo and I heard Bromley refer to him as a detective."

Moyer and Haywood stared at Orchard, surprised and perplexed.

"I'll bet he's a Pinkerton," Haywood growled.

"That's my guess," Orchard said, pouring himself a drink and waving the bottle invitingly.

Haywood allowed Orchard to fill his tumbler but Moyer shook his head irritably.

"If he is, he'll not leave that jail alive, if I have to pull the trigger myself."

"I'll take care of him," Orchard said, "as soon as we're sure."

Haywood downed his whiskey and poured another. "When we're through here, I'll wire Denver. We have people there privy to the Pinkerton roster."

"What do you want to do about Kincaid?" Orchard asked. "He's in Bromley's pocket."

"May that fat bastard rot in hell," Haywood snarled. "Goddamn, we trusted these people!"

"How much do Siringo and Kincaid know about Sunday's business?" Orchard asked, rocking back in his chair to fondle the brim of his derby in his lap.

Moyer was emphatic. "Nothing!"

"Unless MacNamara told him," Haywood said.

"If he knows anything," Orchard said, "it could be a slaughter for our boys. I think we're safer with him in jail but we'd probably be better off with him dead."

"That's my feeling, too," Moyer agreed. "The sooner the better."

"We'll know this afternoon if he's a Pinkerton," Haywood said. "If he is, we might want to have second thoughts."

"It makes no difference," Orchard replied. "We already know he's a spy for the mine owners. I'll kill him tomorrow on my way back from Burke."

Orchard got up, set his derby in his chair, and calmly made himself a sandwich.


Willi, the German girl, had brought dinner for Orchard, Haywood and Johnnie in Kate's private sitting room. Orchard, still smarting from his three-dollar bedroom disaster with Kate, had been relieved that as she flitted in and out, she seemed to have forgotten the incident.

Neither he nor Haywood felt up to partaking of Kate's wares and Johnnie was too broke and surly to be a target for any of the girls' wiles. Moyer hadn't joined them which was just as well. His dour personality would have put the kibosh on what had been a pleasant and relatively uneventful evening; uneventful until Kate had asked Orchard to get Johnnie out of the downstairs parlor, where he was having a loud, profane argument with a drunken teamster.

"Me and that jasper was just jawin' at each other," Johnnie muttered as they started down the steep Mill Street in the buggy. "I wasn't gonna fight him."

"Good thing," Orchard said. "He'd have kicked your ass so far up between your shoulder blades you'd have to take off your shirt to shit."

Haywood, passed out between them, opened his eyes, chuckled and closed them again.

Orchard was beginning to dislike Johnnie intensely. He was doubly annoyed because Haywood, his normal volubility enhanced by copious amounts of Kate's good Canadian whiskey, had expounded, in Johnnie's presence, on how devastating to Bunker Hill would be the destruction of their mill. Orchard wouldn't have trusted this nitwit with the address of the livery barn.

As though reading his mind, Johnnie muttered, "You don't like me. All you do is rawhide me."

"Didn't you learn anything this afternoon?"

"Like what?"

It was obvious that he hadn't.

"Like I'm going to knock you out of this buggy again if you don't drive me all the way to the Galena House with your trap shut. Do you understand me?"

"Mr. Haywood don't treat me like you do," Johnnie muttered.

"Then, by all means, you should complain to him," Orchard said. "You want me to wake him up?"

Johnnie shook his head and concentrated on his driving.

When they reached the hotel, Johnnie asked rather plaintively, "Do you want I should pick you up in the morning?"

Orchard shook his head.

"Mr. Haywood might need you. You can ask him when you get him up to his room."

With that, Orchard stalked into the hotel, leaving Johnnie to figure out how to get the two-hundred-pound Haywood out of the buggy.

He damned Haywood and Moyer both for neglecting to heed the basic axiom; trust no one.


After he had returned the rented horse and buggy to the livery barn, Johnnie headed to Fatty Kincaid's for some whiskey. A groggy Haywood had given him a dollar before he'd staggered into his room to fall across the bed.

After the second drink, he got involved in another argument, this time with a striking mucker from his own union. It was Fatty himself who grabbed him by the coat collar and the seat of his pants and had him out of the saloon into the night.

Now, stumbling across the tailing pile, he fell down, ripping the knee out of his pants and cutting a bloody gash on his shin. He dragged himself to his feet and let loose an anguished howl.

He'd walked only a few feet more when he stumbled again, not falling this time, but forced to run a few steps to maintain his balance. Sons of bitches! They were all sons of bitches. Orchard, ordering him around and treating him like a piece of dog shit. Fatty throwing him out of the saloon, after all the money he'd spent there, when he'd had it. Even Kate, that old big-assed whore, made him feel unwanted and unwelcome, the few times he'd been allowed inside her place. And it wasn't over. When he got home, Amy would light into him for spending the extra money on whiskey when she needed it for food.

As he wobbled by the Shanks house, he was attracted by the light from the kitchen window. He stood on an upturned bucket to peer in.

Bella, completely naked, stood in a galvanized wash tub in front of the stove, bathing herself. Her back was to him but he was transfixed by the golden glow of her skin in the lamplight. When she turned slowly to reveal rather large breasts and an impressive mound of reddish pubic hair between firm thighs, all the strength seemed to leave his body. He pressed himself against the house and ejaculated in his underwear. The spasm made him lose his grip on the window sill and fall noisily to the ground. The sound of the bucket clattering against the house was like a fire bell.

By the time Johnnie had dragged himself painfully to his feet, the kitchen door was flung open and Bella, draped in a blanket, came outside, holding the lamp.

"Who's out there?"

Johnnie stepped in the light and doffed his hat.

"It's Johnnie Neville, ma'am. Amy's brother. I was passing. I seen your light."

Bella held the lamp high so she could see him and also the tin bucket lying beside the house under the kitchen widow.

Her voice was full of loathing when she said, "You were watching me, you sneaky, peeping-Tom son-of-a-bitch!"

Johnnie made a clumsy gesture of appeasement, unable to think of anything he could say to calm her. But she wasn't done with him.

"I hope Bunker Hill runs all of you union bastards out of the district!" she screamed at him.

Johnnie wobbled up on the porch, forcing Bella to back into the kitchen.

"Yeah? If your scab brother hadn't got his head pounded in, come Sunday, he'd be flyin' over the mountains like a eagle."

Bella stepped forward and gave him a hard push. He staggered backward and dug a handful of loose change out of his pocket. He threw the coins past her into the kitchen where they rattled across the warped floor boards.

"That's fer lettin' me see them big titties," he told her.

Triumphant, Johnnie turned on his heel, took one step and fell off the porch, the sound of the slammed door assailing his ears.

# CHAPTER SEVEN

Orchard smoked a cigar on the porch of the Shamrock Billiard Parlor, next door to the Model Saloon. From this vantage point he had a clear view of Wallace's main street and the county jail. He and Klondike Davis had gone up Canyon Creek to Burke on the morning train to talk to the Burke union boys about the action planned for Sunday.

They had met with pale, blue-eyed Paul Corcoran, the president of the Burke union, and some of his most reliable lieutenants at the Burke union hall. It was agreed that the Burke men would commandeer the Sunday morning train before it made the return trip to Kellogg. The dynamite would be taken from the Frisco powder house. If there wasn't enough, they would get more at Gem, along the way.

Corcoran had obtained a rough drawing of the Bunker Hill mill from one of his members who had worked there. Studying the rendering, Orchard concluded that about a hundred boxes of dynamite would be enough to level the place and destroy the critical machinery.

In the middle of the meeting, Corcoran was called out of the room to take a telephone call from Haywood. When he came back to the table he asked Orchard to step outside for a minute.

"Haywood wanted you to know that Allison is a Pinkerton," Corcoran said, as they stood in front of the building. "Is he talking about Leon Allison, the Wardner secretary?"

"Yeah, the very same," Orchard told him. "Don't spread it around."

"I liked him," Corcoran said. "He always seemed like a decent, hard-working fellow."

Corcoran stared blindly into the street as the implications of having a spy in their midst became clear.

"He's going to be taken care of," Orchard assured him. "After it's done you can tell your men about it."

Orchard would have preferred not to share any of this, but presumed that Haywood trusted Corcoran or he'd have asked to speak to him directly. However, on the other end of the stick, Haywood had trusted Allison and Kincaid.

He left Klondike Davis to work out any further details with the Burke union and returned to Wallace on the noon train. Now he watched and waited. He'd learned from one of the Burke men that Sheriff Thompson usually journeyed across the street from his office to the Model Saloon for an afternoon drink, purported to be several ounces of bourbon and a schooner of beer.

Orchard had the advantage of knowing the jail's layout, so a plan was simple enough to formulate. Once Thompson was clear of the place, Orchard decided that he'd force the jailer to let him into the lockup and take him back to Siringo's cell where he'd kill the detective and lock the jailer in the cell with the body. If there were other deputies there, he'd lock them up too.

He was rehearsing the plan when Sheriff Thompson stepped into the street, stretched and headed for the Model Saloon. Halfway across the street, he saw Orchard and changed course to confront him.

"What's your game, Hogan?" He eyed Orchard warily.

"Hello, Sheriff," Orchard said. "I've come to take Allison off your hands."

"Not without his bail, you ain't."

"Got it right here," Orchard said, drawing his Iver Johnson and pointing it at Thompson's heart.

Thompson's startled expression told Orchard that perhaps no one had ever pulled a gun on him before. Thompson's reaction was no different from that of several other people Orchard had favored with this kind of attention.

He reached carefully under Thompson's coat to take his pistol out of the holster and toss it up on the roof of the Shamrock.

"How many deputies inside?" Orchard asked.

"Just Lester, my jailer," Thompson said, eyes glued to the short barrel of Orchard's pistol.

Two men came out of the billiard parlor. They looked curiously at Orchard and the sheriff.

Orchard slapped Thompson on the shoulder and exclaimed, "That's rich, Sheriff!" at the same time pressing his pistol against Thompson's rib cage with the muttered admonition to smile.

The sheriff gave Orchard a sickly smile as the two casual observers went on their way.

"Where are the rest of your men?"

"Down in Milo Gulch, doing some evictions for Bunker Hill, outta the company houses."

The sheriff turned suddenly and nodded toward the street.

"Here comes Allison's bail money."

Joe Gray Wolf rode toward the jail on a fine-looking horse. He led a second animal. Cold sober, he sat tall in the saddle, clad in a clean red shirt and a hat with a snakeskin band. He tied the horses in front of the building and went inside.

Orchard watched the Indian disappear into the jail.

"How do you know?"

"He's Fatty Kincaid's man. Fatty called me and told me he was bringing the bail."

That confirmed what Orchard had heard in the hallway of the Galena House. Bromley had referred to Kincaid as "your man" when speaking with Whitehead. He would have to be dealt with, but one thing at a time. Siringo took priority.

A three-seat surrey careened toward them from the opposite end of the street, throwing chunks of mud from its yellow wheels. It was driven by a grinning Klondike Davis and carried four other men with rifles. The surrey, with its fringed, imitation leather top looked like a vehicle which might have been appropriated from one of Burke's better whore houses.

Orchard pushed Thompson into the shadows when the surrey stopped in front of the Model Saloon, just up the street from the Shamrock. Its occupants surged through the front door, all in a boisterous mood. One man carried a coil of manila rope over his shoulder.

Somehow, the word had gotten out and Davis, true to his violent instincts, had organized a lynching party to solve the problem. This changed everything! For a moment, Orchard considered stepping aside and letting it happen. Lynched or shot, the end result would be the same for Siringo, but between here and the coroner's table would be a rough journey if he let the mob have him. He decided he wasn't going to let that happen.

"Christ," Thompson muttered, "that's a lynch mob."

Orchard dipped into his vest pocket for a fifty-cent piece.

"Go into the Shamrock and have a couple of beers on me. I'm going to attend to Allison before they do."

Thompson grasped Orchard's lapels, ignoring the pistol pressed against his chest.

"Look, Hogan," he pleaded, "if you're gonna kill him, you can't do it in my jail. They'd boot my ass clean outta the county. I've got a sick wife to worry about."

Orchard shook off the sheriff's hands.

"Do I look like a murderer, Thompson? I'm saving him from the rope. Get out of my way."

Orchard gave him a shove toward the Shamrock's front door and headed for the jail.

He entered to find Lester, the jailer, at Thompson's desk, counting the bills Gray Wolf had brought.

"I bring extra horse," Gray Wolf told him.

"Keep your feathers on. I have to write up a receipt," Lester said, at the same moment seeing Orchard, pistol in hand, standing inside the front door.

"You're going back empty handed, Geronimo," Orchard told Gray Wolf.

The Indian stared at him impassively.

Lester reached for his round-handled Colt, dangling butt-forward, high on his left hip. Orchard aimed at Lester's head. Gray Wolf took a step to the side to get out of the line of fire.

Orchard didn't want to shoot the jailer in the office because the noise might attract unwanted attention, but would have, without hesitation, if Lester did something stupid.

"Short life or long one, Lester," Orchard warned. "You're dealing."

Lester froze, pistol halfway out of the holster. Several seconds went by before he raised his left hand in a gesture of restraint. He pulled the old Colt slowly and carefully out of his holster and laid it on the floor.

"Now, get Allison out here, pronto," Orchard said. "You and this redskin stay put in the lock-up. Leave the money."

Lester tossed the bills onto the desk, and opened the lock-up. He pushed Gray Wolf into the enclosure and followed him back to the cells.

Orchard went to the front window to check the street. The surrey stood empty in front of the Model Saloon, the nervous horses tossing their heads and pawing the ground.

Orchard retrieved the bail money from Thompson's desk. The bills were wrinkled and dirty but they would spend as easily as new ones. He put them back into the brown envelope in which they'd come and stuffed it into his inside coat pocket.

Orchard noticed that the egg-stained dish from yesterday was still there, but Siringo's good hat hung from a nail on the wall. He was patting down the comforting wad of cash in his coat pocket when Siringo came out of the lock-up putting on his coat.

"Are you breaking me out, Orchard?" Siringo had a little half smile on his face.

Orchard didn't give him the satisfaction of seeing a surprised look on his face. He had a dart of his own to throw.

"Yup," Orchard said. "It's your lucky day, Siringo."

For a moment, the two men stared at each other. Then Siringo smiled and nodded knowingly.

"I guess the masquerade's over."

"Horses out front," Orchard said. "We'll walk 'em across the street and wait behind the Shamrock."

Siringo gave him a curious look.

"Let's go," Orchard told him. "Don't forget your good hat."

Siringo gave him an amused look as he exchanged his shabby fedora for the black slouch hat.

Orchard and Siringo stood beside the horses behind the Shamrock and waited. From where he was standing, Orchard could see the front door of the Model Saloon.

"What are we waiting for?" Siringo asked.

"You'll see in a minute."

Siringo gave Orchard a searching look. "How'd you get on to me?"

"I'm curious by nature," Orchard said, watching for the lynch mob to emerge.

"Me too," Siringo said. "I watched you plant a bomb in the shaft house of the Molly Ware in Telluride three years ago."

Orchard turned to look at him. "You are good. I never saw you. Why didn't you arrest me?"

"It never went off," Siringo said. "The watchman found it and cut the trip wire. Sloppy job for a man of your skills."

If Siringo thought he was going to make him feel guilty about one failure, he had another think coming.

"You know, Siringo, hindsight says I should have let that drunken Irishman on the train cut your head off."

"But you didn't," Siringo said. "Instead, you went to a lot of trouble to return my hat."

At that moment, the screen door on the Model Saloon banged open and the rowdy lynch mob spilled into the street. It had grown in size to a dozen by the time it surged across the street and rampaged into the jail.

Orchard and Siringo moved to the other side of the Shamrock where they could see the front of the jail. Siringo, serious now, exchanged a glance with Orchard.

"Looks like I owe you one."

"Never mind that," Orchard told him. "We'll just sit tight until the excitement dies down and then we'll ride out of here."

"To where?"

"Up Canyon Creek for a ways," Orchard said.

"Where you'll shoot me, right?" Siringo said, matter-of-factly.

Orchard jerked his head toward the jail.

"You'd have died harder with them."

Siringo seemed surprisingly calm for a man facing execution.

"What difference does it make? You shoot me or they do?"

"The difference is they wouldn't shoot you," Orchard said.

As though validating his words, a man came out of the jail and ran to get the surrey. He wheeled it around in the street and pulled up in front of the jail.

Two more men came out of the jail. They had Joe Gray Wolf between them, hands manacled behind his back. One of his captors had the Indian's hat perched jauntily on his head. They threw him down on his stomach behind the surrey.

Davis and the rest of the mob came out to stand on the porch to watch the rope being knotted around Gray Wolf's ankles and then tied to the surrey's rear axle. The Indian lay quietly on his belly, watching the men milling around him, too proud to beg for his life.

Davis and his men climbed into the surrey. Davis let out a wild whoop and laid on the whip. The horses reared and then the surrey flew down the street with Gray Wolf bouncing along behind it, red shirt flapping.

"Let's go," Orchard ordered as the rest of the mob scattered along the street or back into the saloon.

Orchard clambered aboard his mount uneasily. He disliked horses and rode them as seldom as possible, preferring the relative comfort of a buggy, or even a buckboard.

He was quick to see that Siringo had noted his unease and warned, "Don't try to ride off on me or you'll bleed all over that saddle."

They trotted down the main street to the railroad tracks where they turned and followed them to the Canyon Creek spur. Here, a narrow wagon road paralleled the tracks all the way to Burke. They had ridden about half a mile when two rifle shots sounded in the distance, from the direction of town.

"That must be the end of Gray Wolf's buggy ride," Siringo said, watching Orchard. "Unlucky bastard."

Orchard shifted his weight in the saddle. Already, the relatively short ride had made the insides of his thighs sore. He was riding the Indian's horse and the butt of a sheathed rifle kept interfering with the reins, making his handling of the animal awkward and tiring.

"Could have been the end of yours," Orchard told him.

"It would have been, if you hadn't saved me."

Siringo's tone was mocking.

Orchard was becoming annoyed. "You're pretty cocky for a dead man."

"I'm not sure you've got the sand to pull the trigger," Siringo said, still mocking him.

"It wouldn't be the first time, or the second, neither," Orchard said. He pointed to a pine-filled draw, thick with underbrush and fallen timber. "Head up that draw."

Siringo twisted in the saddle to look at him.

"The site of last rites?"

77

"Just ride."

The steep climb allowed them to look down through the treetops at Canyon Creek, a silver ribbon in the bright sunlight. The horses picked their way carefully.

"Is Orchard your real name?" Siringo asked suddenly, over his shoulder.

"What difference does it make who I am?"

Siringo took off his hat and ran his hand through his long, dark hair.

"I'd like to know the name of the man who kills me."

"If it's a comfort to you," Orchard said, "it's the name I'm best known by."

Siringo chuckled.

"I almost laughed out loud when you said you'd never been in Colorado. Before the Molly Ware, you were named in one of my bulletins as a suspect in another dynamiting in Telluride. The Polaris pump house. Remember that one?"

"Named, maybe, but never arrested."

The underbrush was becoming almost too thick to ride through without leather chaps. Already, Orchard had bloody scratches on his legs. He opened his mouth to give the order to dismount when Siringo let go of a branch he was holding. It snapped back, striking Orchard across the face.

The stinging force of the blow made Orchard pull back violently on the reins. His mount reared, lost its footing and fell heavily into a thicket, pinning him against the underbrush.

As Orchard struggled to free himself, Siringo wheeled about, jumped his horse over the struggling pair and headed back down toward the wagon road.

Orchard pulled himself free of the downed horse, avoided the flailing hooves and snaked the rifle out of the saddle scabbard. It was well oiled and in fine condition.

Orchard levered the action, ejecting a shell already in the chamber. Gray Wolf must have expected trouble. Dropping to one knee, he caught Siringo's back in the open buckhorn sight, keeping the bobbing figure neatly centered.

His finger closed on the trigger just as Siringo pulled up to look back. The rifle had a solid kick and made a lot of smoke. The heavy slug took off

Siringo's black hat, sending it spinning into the underbrush. Siringo bent low in the saddle and dug his heels into the horse's flanks.

Orchard levered another shell into the chamber but before he could take aim, horse and rider disappeared into the thickly spaced pines. When they emerged, the range was too great. Orchard rose slowly, staring after the retreating target. He watched Siringo plunge the horse into Canyon Creek, kicking up a cloud of spray. He forced the animal up the steep bank on the other side and vanished into the trees again.

Orchard lowered the rifle's hammer to half-cock, vaguely troubled by missing a clear shot. Had he subconsciously aimed too high? He'd never know, but tried to rationalize that the final outcome of the incident had achieved the desired results. It was unlikely that Siringo would pose any further threat to the union and that was what Haywood wanted. Killing him would have eliminated him as a threat forever, of course, but Siringo's death would have served no immediate purpose. However, Orchard's conscience wouldn't have been unduly burdened if the bullet had struck the detective squarely between the shoulder blades.

On his way back to the Burke union hall, Orchard stopped and dismounted next to a small stream which splashed into Canyon Creek. He dug the wad of bills out of his coat pocket and placed it under a flat rock, well away from the road. He and the horse stuck their faces into the clear, cold water and drank deeply before they resumed the ride.

He tied his horse next to the mud-spattered surrey with its heaving, lathered horses. Klondike Davis had obviously used them hard; probably dragging the dead Indian around for everyone to see, so they could either cringe or applaud in the face of the union's raw power.

"So where's the Pinkerton, Harry?" Davis asked when he entered the union hall. "Seems you beat us to him."

Davis and his cohorts all appeared to be drunk and several men he didn't know eyed him suspiciously. He was glad he'd taken the time to find his pistol and dig the dirt out of the barrel before starting back.

"He's been taken care of," Orchard said. "That was my job."

Paul Corcoran came forward. "You killed him?"

"If I didn't, there ain't a nigger in Georgia," Orchard told him. "I left him in the brush the other side of Gem."

"Where's the money at?"

The question came from one of the bleary-eyed lynchers.

"What money?"

Corcoran's tone was more conversational than accusatory when he said, "The jailer said Gray Wolf delivered five hundred dollars bail from Fatty Kincaid and you took it."

"The jailer is full of shit," Orchard said. "I took Siringo. If any money's missing, that's the sheriff's problem."

He raised his arms, keeping his right hand close to the butt of his revolver.

"Search me, if you think I'm lying."

The bleary-eyed man stepped forward to conduct the search but Davis stopped him.

"Whoa," Davis told the man. "If he says he didn't take it, well, he didn't take it. Shut your face."

The bleary-eyed man backed off, obviously intimidated by the hulking Davis.

"What happened to the Indian?" Orchard asked, eager to change the direction of the conversation.

"Last time I seen him," Davis said, "he was layin' in the weeds takin' a snooze."

"What are you going to do about Fatty Kincaid?"

Davis looked askance at Corcoran.

"His saloon burns down tonight," Corcoran said. "Haywood's got that handled."

# CHAPTER EIGHT

"Get around to the back if you're delivering." The servant girl's plain face and round eyes were unfriendly as she stared at Bella.

"I'm not delivering anything," Bella said. "I want to see Mr. Whitehead."

The servant girl put her hands on her hips. "What about?"

"None of your business, miss," Bella replied, feeling her cheeks getting hot. "Go tell him Miss Shanks is here with some information."

The girl closed the door abruptly, leaving Bella to wonder if she should wait or knock again. She decided to wait, though she was growing more ill at ease by the moment. She had procrastinated most of the day before she could summon the courage to come to the mine superintendent's home.

The door opened again.

"Mr. Whitehead will see you in the parlor, ma'am."

The girl's voice had lost its hostile edge. She led Bella through the vestibule into the parlor. It was a large room, furnished more elegantly than anything she's ever seen, with the possible exception of the Dewey Hotel lobby in Denver, which she had seen once.

Whitehead rose from his chair when she entered the room. A plump middle-aged woman disappeared through a draped doorway at the same time.

"What is your information, Miss Shanks?"

Before she could speak, he stepped closer to her.

"My watchman who was..." he began.

"He was my brother," Bella said. "I'm taking care of his wife and trying to make arrangements for Edward's burial."

"Oh, please sit down," Whitehead urged, pointing to a settee. "This must be a very hard time for you and Mrs. Shanks."

"Mrs. Shanks is dying," Bella said simply, sitting down. "It could happen any day now."

"You don't live here?"

"No, sir. I live in Goldfield, Colorado. I'm a dressmaker."

She mentioned her profession as a means of establishing herself as someone of substance in the presence of the mine superintendent, one of the most powerful people in the district.

"So, what is your information, Miss Shanks?"

Whitehead didn't sit down. Instead, he stood over her, hands in the pockets of his velvet jacket, as though to indicate her welcome was of limited duration.

"It's about the mill," Bella said.

The smell of food emanating from the kitchen was making her hungry and she thought she heard someone's soft giggle in the dining room, partially visible beyond the rope portiere.

"What about the mill?" Whitehead's tone was sharp.

"I know this union man," Bella said, searching for the right words. "He told me there's going to be some trouble on Sunday."

She heard the giggling again and saw the two young Whitehead girls watching her from the dining room. She felt suddenly as though she were going to burst into tears.

"What kind of trouble?" Whitehead asked impatiently, glancing over his shoulder at the simpering girls. That glance seemed potent enough to send them scurrying away.

"He said if my brother was still alive, he'd be flying through the air on Sunday," Bella said. "To me, that means dynamite. You see, in Colorado..."

"I know all about the problems in Colorado," Whitehead said, "and I think we're prepared to deal with similar trouble here, Miss Shanks, but I appreciate your coming to me."

On that note of finality, Bella got to her feet and allowed Whitehead to escort her to the front door. She didn't relish the long walk home, but had the satisfaction of knowing she'd done her duty.

As though reading her mind, Whitehead said, "Let me bring the buggy around and I'll drive you home. It'll be dark soon."


"Where do you think you're going with that?"

Amy Neville, carrying the sparse load of clothing she'd taken off the line behind the shack, regarded her brother suspiciously.

Johnnie, carrying the galvanized tin coal oil can, tried to step around his sister.

"I asked you a question," Amy said, barring the way. "I can always tell when you're up to no good. You sneak around like a back alley dog."

"I got some business to take care of," Johnnie said, trying to hide the can behind him.

"Not with my coal oil, you ain't!"

Amy made a grab for the can but he swung it away from her, causing some of the oil to squirt from the spout, splashing yet another stain on the cheap faded wallpaper.

He pushed her aside and made a dash through the door.

Amy stepped out onto the tiny sloping porch, yelling at his retreating back, "Whatever you're up to, hope you get caught and don't never come back."

She leaned against the wall for a minute before going inside and slamming the flimsy front door.

Johnnie slouched away into the gathering dusk, the bale on the can making little squeaking noises as he trod the worn path across the tailing dump.

Who the hell did Amy think she was, bossing him around, anyway? Since the strike, if it hadn't been for the few dollars the union paid him to do small jobs, he and Amy would have starved to death. He pulled his coat around him. He couldn't tell whether he was shivering from the damp night air or from the excitement created by tonight's task.

That afternoon at the union hall, MacNamara and Haywood had given him fifteen dollars to set fire to Fatty Kincaid's saloon.

"It's for the union cause," was all Haywood said as he handed him the bills. "It has to be done tonight."

When he reached Mill Street he decided he needed a little whiskey to bolster himself. He hid the coal oil can in the tall grass and made his way to Fatty Kincaid's, where he could look around for the last time before it burned.

The saloon was unusually quiet. None of the card players were in the back, the billiard tables were deserted and only three men stood at the bar drinking beer. The familiar figure of Joe Gray Wolf in his chair by the stove was missing, but Johnnie knew what had happened to him.

Fatty Kincaid eyed him from the end of the bar, his jaws working on a bite of an enormous steak sandwich, gripped in one fat hand.

"Where is everybody?" Johnnie asked when he eased up to the bar.

The three beer drinkers looked at him without comment. Two wore suits and derbies and had unfamiliar faces. The third, in a corduroy coat, was a mine boss from Burke, whose name Johnnie didn't know.

"Give Johnny a drink on me," Fatty ordered Baldy, the lone barkeep.

Baldy poured a generous shot. Johnnie raised his glass to Fatty.

"Thanks, Fatty. Yer good health."

"Drink hearty." Fatty waved his sandwich in acknowledgement.

Johnnie ordered another drink and when he paid, Baldy pushed his twenty-five-cent piece back at him.

"Mr. Kincaid's buying."

Johnnie had finished his fourth drink and was feeling a little light-headed when Fatty came down the bar to stand beside him.

"Gimme a beer and bring Johnnie another whiskey," Fatty told the barkeep.

"I shouldn't have no more," Johnnie told him. "I got some business to attend to."

"Union business, I suppose," Fatty said offhandedly.

Johnnie smirked.

"Woman business, Fatty. I'm goin' down to Kate's."

"Save your shoe leather," Fatty said. "I got one of Kate's girls upstairs. Have a go at her."

"Which one?"

"The yellow haired one. Pearl. Kate threw her out 'cause she was too pretty so I took her in."

Johnnie knew who Pearl was and he knew why Kate had thrown her out. Even as drunk as he was, he knew that if he were to pass out in Pearl's bed, the fifteen dollars in his pocket was a goner.

Johnnie shook his head. "She don't like me, Fatty."

"Well, then," Fatty said, "have one more whiskey, 'cause I want to ask you something."

"Ask me anything you want."

Fatty leaned close to mutter, "What's the union got against me all of a sudden?"

Johnnie spread his hands on the bar, almost knocking over Fatty's stein. He shook his head vacantly.

"Search me, Fatty. Nobody's said nothing to me."

"You heard what happened in Wallace today?"

Johnnie nodded.

"Too bad about Gray Wolf. He never meant no harm."

He really meant that, for he was appalled that the Indian had been killed for merely being a messenger. It made him consider his own role as messenger and errand boy for the union during the strike. If union men could murder Gray Wolf so casually, why couldn't Lyle Gregory or one of his toughs murder him for any offense, real or imagined?

"Neither did I," Fatty growled, leaning close to him and hunched on the bar like a huge bear in a striped shirt and brocade vest.

"I didn't know Allison was a Pinkerton," Fatty continued. "I was just trying to help a friend in trouble. Will you tell that to Haywood and MacNamara when you see them?"

"Why don't you tell them, Fatty?" Johnnie looked at him with bloodshot eyes. "You've always treated them good."

Fatty drew himself up. "Damn right I have, but I won't go down to the union hall. I'd never leave there alive. There's an ugly mood building. Something bad's about to happen. I can feel it."

"I can't feel nothing," Johnnie said, with a little trouble getting out the words. "I think I gotta go."

"Look around here," Fatty said, waving an outsize arm. You ever see my place this empty? It's the union's doing. Fatty Kincaid's been blacklisted."

"I wouldn't worry about it, Fatty," Johnny said magnanimously, as he wobbled toward the door. "They ain't gonna stay mad at you."

"You tell them what I said," Kincaid called after him.

The electric street lamps along Mill Street were burning when Johnnie came outside. He paused on the porch to rock unsteadily on the balls of his feet while he decided what to do. First, he'd have to find the coal oil. That might take a little doing, because now he couldn't remember where he'd hidden the can. When he did find it, he'd slip around the back of the saloon to find a good place to spread and light it. The dry wood frame building would go up like paper. He giggled to himself as he headed unsteadily back up Mill Street.

He was searching the tall grass when the sound of hooves made him crouch down out of view from the street. A buggy, driven by Justin Whitehead, the Bunker Hill superintendent stopped almost directly across from his hiding place. Bella Shanks was the passenger.

He heard Whitehead say, "I'll see that all the arrangements are taken care of, Miss Shanks."

Bella thanked him and climbed down from the buggy. Whitehead turned the buggy around and headed back up Mill Street. Bella took the path across the tailing pile.

She made no sound when Johnnie's arms encircled her and his weight bore her to the ground. She rolled over and tried to fight him off. Good God, she was strong! Johnnie pushed her hat down over her face and ripped away at her clothing. The buttons popped off her coat like grasshoppers and her cotton dress ripped from neckline to waist with one tug.

Grunting with exertion, he dodged her flailing arms and clawing hands by pressing his face against her. He tore the straps off her chemise and pulled it down until he could feel her hot breasts against his face. Suddenly all the fight seemed to drain out of her. Her half-hearted attempts to free herself served only to inflame him.

It was probably so long since she'd had a man who really wanted her that she might be willing to let him do anything he wanted. He managed to push her skirt up to her waist and was pulling down her drawers when he experienced an excruciating pain in his groin.

Jerking and twisting, he rolled away from her, frantically searching his screaming crotch for the source of his agony. Bella got up quickly, pulled her clothes together and was running away by the time he found the beaded end of a nine inch hatpin; a hatpin Bella had thrust through his trousers and scrotum, impaling one testicle and burying the point deep in the muscles of his thigh.

Locked in a fetal position, Johnnie lay on the cold ground, waves of nausea washing over him. His pain was less severe with the hatpin pulled from his flesh but the thought of where it had been was almost totally debilitating. By the time he dragged himself to his feet, gratified by the knowledge that he could still walk, he was completely sober.


Orchard had his bag open on the bed. He'd removed the two apothecary bottles and was wrapping them in a piece of newspaper when there was a soft rap on his door.

He grabbed up his revolver from the dresser and opened the door, keeping his foot against the bottom should the visitor try to barge in.

Johnnie sagged against the door frame, hunched over with gritted teeth. His face was dirty and his clothing, covered with dust. Orchard looked at him distastefully.

"What do you want?"

Johnnie held up a long hatpin and gasped, "I been stabbed—in the balls—with this."

Orchard flinched at the mere thought of it.

"That must hurt like hell. Whose hatpin is that?"

"I can't tell you, Mr. Orchard," Johnnie muttered, hanging his head. "Can I please come in?"

"I can't do anything for you," Orchard said. "I'm not a ball doctor."

"Haywood give me fifteen dollars to burn down Fatty's saloon, but I hurt too bad. I got to lay down."

"Well, you're not gonna lay down here," Orchard growled. "If you want me to do it, give me the fifteen dollars and tell me who skewered your gonads."

Johnnie pulled the crumpled bills from his pocket and handed them to Orchard.

"I got to get home," he moaned, turning to leave.

"Tell me who it was," Orchard said firmly.

Johnnie took a deep breath. "Bella Shanks. I...I tried to fuck her out on the tailing pile."

Orchard stared at this dirty, unkempt weasel. The thought of him putting his hands on Bella...

"On the tailing pile? That lady wouldn't fuck you in a bridal suite."

He pushed Johnnie back so hard that he almost fell down.

"Get the hell out of here before I put something in you that's permanent."

Johnnie whimpered and turned away. Orchard watched his painful, bow-legged departure before slamming the door closed.

He put the fifteen dollars in his pocket and put on his coat. He might as well get it over with as soon as it got dark. For a moment he wondered if it might be better to do it in the morning, as another distraction, but decided there wasn't time to recruit someone for the deed and he had a distraction of his own planned.

Orchard entered the saloon through the back door and took the staircase to the second floor. Three men stood at the bar, talking to the bald-headed barkeep. The barkeep glanced at him as he mounted the stairs, looked away and continued his conversation.

It wasn't hard to find who he was looking for. Attracted by the sounds, Orchard stealthily opened the door of the third room along the darkened hallway.

It was an eerie sight. Fatty, with his trousers around his ankles was mounting a young woman sprawled in front of him on a desk. Her long blonde hair reached halfway to the floor. Her legs, in black cotton stockings, rested on the rolls of blubber around Fatty's waist. He was thrusting and snorting like a copulating hippo. Orchard recognized the woman as Pearl, the blonde Kate had kicked out.

The flickering light of a lamp on the floor next to the desk created strange shadows on the papered wall.

Orchard paused in the doorway for a moment to watch this spectacle. It was made to order for his purposes. Neither of the participants seemed to notice when he stepped into the room, removed the key from the door lock, and kicked over the lamp.

He glanced back as he went out the door. A sea of flame spread across the floor. Pearl's hair was on fire. She and Fatty were both slapping at it while he, at the same time, was trying to pull up his trousers. Orchard locked the door and went quickly down the stairs.

Pistol drawn, Orchard stood next to the outhouse behind the saloon, looking up at flames licking the curtains of a window. A chair suddenly crashed through the glass and Pearl tried to climb out. Fatty pulled her away from the window and climbed out. He had given up on his trousers because he was wearing none.

He dropped to the steep porch roof, lost his balance, fell down, and rolled off, to land, dazed, in the mud. He struggled to his hands and knees, twisting his big head to look at Orchard.

"Why, for Christ's sake?"

"You picked the wrong side," Orchard said and shot him twice in the head.

Orchard looked up to see Pearl, hair still smoking, hanging from the window sill. She twisted around to look at him, lost her grip and slid down the porch roof, clawing at the shingles with bloody nails.

Ten minutes later Orchard was standing on the porch of the Shanks house. He looked back toward town. Flames were through the roof of the saloon by this time, a belching volcano of smoke and flame. A hastily assembled bucket brigade was tossing water at the conflagration but it was like pissing on Vesuvius.

Bella answered his knock but her attention was immediately drawn to the fire. To anyone who lived in the steep canyons of a mining district, fire was an implacable enemy which periodically gorged itself on everything within reach of its flaming tongue.

"My God, what's burning?"

She stepped out on the porch, hugging herself against the night air and her conditioned apprehension.

"Looks like Kincaid's saloon," Orchard said.

"Shouldn't you be helping?"

"Do I look like a fireman?"

Bella continued to stare at the fire which by now had spread to the next-door harness shop and the Yukon Ice Cream parlor.

"Bella, are you all right? I heard what happened."

She whirled to face him.

"How could you know about that? I've told no one. I thought you might have brought condolences about my brother."

Her lips were trembling and she seemed ready to lose her composure, but

Orchard persisted. "Did Johnnie hurt you?"

Bella shook her head and started to cry.

"Not like you mean." She raised brimming eyes to look at him. "Oh, I hate this God-awful place!"

Orchard put his arms around her. She didn't resist and buried her face against his chest.

"Maybe we should go inside," he said.

Bella disengaged herself and seemed embarrassed.

"You'd better go, Mr. Hogan. Death's waiting inside the house."

"I'm not afraid of death," Orchard told her. "Let me take you inside."

"You're a kind and thoughtful man, Mr. Hogan," Bella said, taking his hand and squeezing it. "I appreciate it. Go now, I have to get inside."

Orchard tipped his derby. "I'll be back."

# CHAPTER NINE

Klondike Davis, Tom Archer and Hans Vogel moved quickly toward the Northern Pacific locomotive. They had bandanas tied over their faces and each man carried a Krag-Jorgenson rifle issued by Paul Corcoran from the Burke union's arsenal. One hundred of these rifles, each carefully wrapped in oiled paper, had been hidden under the floor of the Burke union hall. They had been stolen from the National Guard during the last big trouble in 1892.

The narrow canyon was still in full shadow at six in the morning, stillness broken only by the barking of a belligerent dog and the sound of the fireman's shovel on the locomotive floor plate. By seven, the train would be on its way to Wallace with the empty boxcars which had accumulated all week on the sidings along Canyon Creek.

Davis was the first to enter the locomotive cab, covering the startled trainmen with his rifle.

"We're takin' this train, gents," he announced. "When'll you have enough steam to blow the whistle?"

The gaping engineer eyed the rifle distastefully, while the fireman, still stooped over a full scoop of coal for the grinning firebox, stared curiously at the masked men.

The engineer checked his gauges.

"I expect we got enough for that now."

"Then toot the son-of-a-bitch," Davis ordered, poking him with the rifle barrel.

The wail of the locomotive whistle reverberated up and down Burke Canyon. On this signal, Burke's main street was filled suddenly with running men. Some wore masks and carried the pilfered National Guard rifles, while others brandished an odd assortment of weapons, ranging from cap-and-ball relics to modern Winchesters.

There was much whooping and hollering from the elated men, acting as though they were participating in some kind of holiday celebration. They piled into the empty boxcars and when the last man was aboard, Davis prodded the engineer with his rifle.

"Down the canyon. laddie. Next stop's the Frisco powder house."

Reluctantly, the engineer threw the Johnson bar forward, released the brakes and eased back the throttle. A shiver went through the train as brakes released and couplings clattered.

"Then where?" he asked Davis, keeping his eye on the tracks ahead, where armed and masked stragglers waited next to the right of way.

"Don't worry about it," Davis told him, preoccupied by the sight of scrambling men being pulled into the moving boxcars. One slipped and fell, narrowly avoiding losing an arm to the train's wheels.

In minutes, they were approaching the Frisco powder house, a squat brick building with an iron door, hanging open now, its lock yielding to the sledges of the strikers.

More men were waiting alongside the track, each carrying a box of dynamite. One huge fellow carried two, one on each shoulder.

Ninety boxes were loaded into the boxcars under the supervision of Paul Corcoran, the Burke union president. At Gem, the engineer was compelled to back onto a siding to pick up two additional boxcars so that a group of fifty or sixty men and more dynamite boxes could be accommodated.

By the time the train rolled into the Wallace depot, it carried upwards of three hundred men and one hundred and twenty boxes of explosives, enough to make a noise that would be heard throughout the Coeur d'Alene district.

Setting the brakes and blowing excess steam, the engineer gave Davis and his cronies a triumphant look.

"End of the line, boys," he said, shifting the wad of tobacco against his cheek. "Can't go no further."

"The hell we can't!" Davis exploded. "We're goin' to Wardner."

The engineer shook his head. "Not on this Northern Pacific train you ain't. Right of way to Wardner belongs to Oregon Railroad and Navigation. I set one driver on them Oregon tracks and I've committed a Federal offense."

He pointed suddenly at the stationmaster, a fat old walrus of a man in shiny blue serge and brass buttons, who was waddling toward the locomotive.

With the train stopped, men were milling around the boxcars becoming increasingly restive, their excitement fueled by the daring nature of this adventure and more than a few bottles of cheap whiskey passed from hand to hand.

"Have to have written permission for unscheduled runs," the stationmaster explained, apparently comfortable in the belief that his authority negated the power of the dozens of armed men who crowded around him.

Davis pushed up to him aggressively.

"We're goin' to Wardner, stationmaster."

"Not without..." the stationmaster began.

Davis drove the butt of his rifle in the old man's stomach, sending him gasping to his knees. He ripped off the stationmaster's cap and planted it on his own head.

Turning on the engineer, Davis readied his rifle to give him the same treatment as the stationmaster.

"Get in the cab, mister, or your gut's gonna hurt for two weeks."

The engineer glanced at the stationmaster, still curled up on the station platform, trying to get his breath.

"Better do it, Al," Corcoran advised. "I can't be responsible for what happens to you if you refuse to drive us to Wardner."

"String him up!" someone shouted from the crowd. This triggered a rumble of assent from the impatient strikers.

The engineer spat disgustedly and climbed back into the cab.

"Hold up there!" Sheriff Thompson, unshaven, his suspenders draped over his union suit, hurried across the platform to confront Corcoran. As he spoke, he glanced at Davis several times, obviously remembering him as the leader of the lynch mob.

"What the hell's going on here, Corcoran?"

"What does it look like, Thompson? We're going on a picnic."

This brought a burst of raucous laughter from the observers, clearly unimpressed by the presence of the law.

"I haven't seen this many armed men since the war," Thompson growled, "and it's my duty to tell you that you're all subject to arrest."

Corcoran smiled easily and said, "You're going to arrest three hundred men? I don't think so."

"Then I'll arrest you for inciting a riot," Thompson said.

"You're not going to arrest nobody," Davis said, taking a position next to Corcoran. "Best you go home and get your old woman to fry you some flapjacks."

"I've gone along with you boys on plenty of unlawful shit," Thompson said, "but I can't allow no rioting."

"I don't see no rioting," Davis said, snapping the safety off his rifle. "I don't smell no gunpowder neither but I expect I might in just about a minute."

By this time the stationmaster had recovered enough wind to drag himself to his feet.

Emboldened by the presence of the sheriff, he said, "Do something, Thompson. These men want to use the Oregon tracks to Wardner."

95

Davis swung his rifle and hit the old man in the side of his head, knocking him down. He struggled to get up but was too dizzy to stand. He collapsed to the platform and sobbed. Corcoran and two of the strikers lifted him to his feet and helped him hobble toward the station office, still crying.

Davis jammed his rifle barrel into Thompson's belly, pushing him back. "Get on home or these boys are gonna string you up to an electric light pole. Right, boys?"

The roar of agreement was enough to cause Thompson to stalk away, suffering the taunts and catcalls of the excited miners.

"Into the cars, boys," Davis ordered. "Wardner's the next stop."

A cheer went up and the train began to roll, with men scrambling to get into the box cars. It headed down the canyon on the Oregon Railroad and Navigation right of way without permission—a federal offense.

Orchard's alarm clock jangled stridently at six-thirty, which was, by some miracle, the correct time. He rolled quickly out of bed and by seven had completed his ablutions and was dressed in overalls and a rough sweater. Before he left the room he gathered up the two apothecary bottles on his wash stand, wrapped in a copy of the Spokane newspaper.

With the lethal parcel under his arm, he left the hotel and walked up Mill Street at a leisurely pace, enjoying the fresh mountain air and the quiet of an early Sunday morning. While others with Christ in their hearts would trek to the little churches in Kellogg and Wallace, he would be doing the devil's business, but that bothered him no more than any other job for which he'd be paid. Right or wrong didn't enter into the equation when it came to union work. He accepted the assignments without question and was paid accordingly. Life was good, for the task at hand would command substantial remuneration.

He passed the still-smoking ruins of Fatty Kincaid's saloon and the adjoining buildings which had been embraced by the flames. He paused momentarily to examine the charred boards and broken glass.

96

The front porch and wall were still standing, though the structure leaned precariously.

He was sorry he didn't have a camera to record the spectacular remains, for he wanted a memento. Then he saw the relatively undamaged poster announcing the contest between Irish Paddy Delaney and Driller Jack Smythe.

Stepping gingerly on the porch's quaking boards, Orchard pulled down the poster, folded it and tucked it under his sweater. Thus rewarded, he continued up the street.

Justin Whitehead's house was a quarter of a mile from the Bunker Hill mill and concentrator. Though modern in every detail, with running water and an indoor convenience, it was painted barn red with white trim, as was the mill. It was as though Bunker Hill wanted the world to know that this fine edifice bore its imprimatur.

Orchard leaned against a telephone pole across the street and lighted a cigar. On an empty stomach it was not a savory smoke and he tossed it away after several puffs.

As was its custom, the Whitehead family sat down for breakfast promptly at seven-thirty. Justin Whitehead presided at the head of the table, with his wife at the opposite end. On either side sat their daughters, fifteen and seventeen.

When the hired girl had placed the platter of eggs and ham in front of Whitehead and had delivered the toasted white bread, the jellies and the coffee, he bent his head to say grace, aware of the tight feeling in his stomach which had destroyed his usually robust appetite.

"After church, we're going to take a ride down to the river," he announced, when he'd thanked the Lord for His blessings. "I think it'll be a nice day for an outing."

The younger girl looked at her sister. "But, Papa..."

"Not another word," Whitehead warned, glancing at his wife to solicit some support. "I want you to eat your breakfast and be ready to go by eight-thirty."

He placed dripping fried eggs and thick slices of ham on the plates and passed them around the table. He was anxious to get breakfast finished and

97

get his family into the buggy as quickly as possible. He supposed he should have warned Helga, the hired girl, that she should leave too, but he didn't want his wife and the girls to come home to a sink full of dirty dishes and crumbs on the table cloth.

His worries were probably for naught, he rationalized. The union surely didn't have anything against him personally. In fact, if the decision had been left up to him, he'd have given his crews the fifty cents they wanted and put the trouble behind him. It was Bromley who felt the union had drawn a line in the sand and he was adamant in his refusal to entertain their demands.

Head bowed, Whitehead stared at his plate for a moment after saying grace, wondering how many miners' families would have any breakfast at all this morning.


Orchard checked his watch when he heard the distant sound of the locomotive whistle. It was eight-fifteen. He estimated that the train should pull into the tiny Wardner depot in about ten minutes. Perfect timing.

Orchard tore the newspaper wrapping from the two apothecary bottles, loosened their stoppers and marched boldly across the street, carrying one in each hand. Mounting the Whitehead's porch, he hurled one bottle through each of the front windows. Inside, two muffled explosions were followed by sheets of flame and billowing black smoke boiling out of the broken windows.

As he hurried away, he could hear yelling coming from inside the house. He turned to look as the front door flew open and two screaming young girls, their middie blouses stained with soot, tumbled out of the house and ran toward the street. They were followed by Whitehead, half dragging, half carrying his hysterical wife. By the time they had cleared the front porch, flames were already visible through the windows at the rear of the house.

A stocky young woman burst through the back door. One of her sleeves was on fire. She fell to the ground, frantically rolling about and slapping at herself until she was able to put out the fire on one lobster-red arm.

Orchard picked up his pace, ignoring the curious who had turned out to see what was going on. He arrived at the depot several minutes before the train pulled in. A few sign-carrying pickets marched near the tracks of a spur which disappeared under the gates of the ten-foot-tall fence surrounding the Bunker Hill mill. At the sight of the train with its cargo of yelling and hooting strikers, they threw down their signs and cheered lustily, running to join the assault.

By this time a column of thick smoke was rising from the Whitehead house as it was being totally consumed in an inferno of unspeakable fury. The clanging of the town fire bell was drowned out by the sound of the train and its wild passengers.

Orchard joined the lone depot employee on the platform as the train pulled in. Corcoran and MacNamara ran up to Orchard. Corcoran pointed to the smoke.

"What the hell's that?"

"That's Whitehead's house," Orchard told him. "A little diversion."

Klondike Davis came over to give Orchard a slap on the back. "Slicker'n snot on a doorknob, Harry. What's next?

Men were pouring out of the boxcars. Those with dynamite were stacking their boxes on the depot platform.

"What's our best bet to get inside?" Corcoran asked. "They start shooting at us, somebody's going to get blown up."

"We'll ram the gates," Orchard said. "Let me have your rifle, Klondike."

Orchard ran to the spur switch and shot off the brass padlock. Then he threw the switch and beckoned to the engineer who was leaning out of the cab.

"Through the gates, bud."

The engineer shook his head. "I ain't goin' no further," he yelled back.

"Oh, yes you are," Orchard said, slamming another cartridge into the rifle's breech.

"No I ain't," the engineer repeated.

Orchard raised the rifle and sent a bullet into the locomotive cab, just missing the engineer's head and ricocheting noisily off a metal stanchion.

Blowing steam, the train began to move slowly toward the massive gates.

Orchard handed the rifle back to a grinning Davis and told Corcoran, "The cars'll give us some cover once we're inside."

Corcoran looked about nervously.

"I'm not sure how we should handle this, with the guards and all. We don't want to start a war."

"Why don't you just ride up with the engineer and make sure he minds his p's and q's," Orchard said impatiently.

Corcoran gave him a worried nod, ran over to the slow-moving locomotive to climb into the cab.

Davis, who seemed to have some talent for organization as well as mayhem, began bawling orders. "When we get in there, I want about twenty of you boys with rifles up on the ridge behind the mill. If the guards start shooting, you shoot back." At that moment, the locomotive cow catcher crashed through the tall gates, sending them flying open, even knocking one loose from its hinges.

Orchard mounted a pile of dynamite boxes to rally the mob. "Grab this gelatin and follow me," he shouted. "Put it where I tell you, but I'll light the fuses."

The men loaded up and walked beside the train. By this time many of them had allowed their bandana masks to slip off their faces and simply wore them around their necks. Other men with nothing specific to do remained in the boxcars, crowding around the open doors.

Orchard trotted alongside Davis, behind the group of designated sharp-shooters, when they entered the mill yard. Behind him came about a hundred men, each carrying a fifty-pound box of dynamite.

MacNamara caught up with him as they passed through the shattered gates. "Haywood left something for you at the union hall," he said. "Haywood's gone back to Denver."

"Of course he has," Orchard muttered, thinking that Haywood always protested to the press that his hands were clean when the union committed some atrocity at his behest.

The train stopped short of the hulking mill with its towering steel smoke stacks. The remaining men in the cars jumped down, milling around apprehensively, some pointing their weapons at the white framed windows of the big red buildings. It was eerily quiet when everyone stopped talking, puzzled and unnerved by the silence, by the total lack of opposition to their incursion.

Orchard, MacNamara and Davis took cover behind a stack of worn out conveyor buckets. They were joined by Paul Corcoran.

"There's something fishy about this," Davis muttered, raising his head to look around.

Across the yard, armed men, some masked, some not, waited for some kind of leadership. Others crouched over their dynamite boxes waiting for instructions.

"It's like having an invitation," Orchard said, "but we're here and we've got enough gelatin to level this place."

"I don't like it," Corcoran said. "I think we should pull out."

The situation was suddenly rendered irreversible when a drunken miner brandishing an ancient shotgun charged toward the mill. He was joined by a dozen others, hooting like Comanches.

From the ridge overlooking the mill came the crackle of gun fire. Bullets tore up the ground, bouncing off piles of equipment to go whining through the air.

A blond man in a red shirt rose from behind a lumber pile firing his rifle and yelling, "Shoot back, boys. It's a trap."

Men in the yard began to fire wildly toward the ridge until Davis jumped up, ran into the open waving his arms.

"Stop shooting!" he bellowed. "Those are our boys up there, for Chrissake!"

"They shot at us," the blond man protested, taking a final shot in the direction of the ridge.

"Well, they didn't hit no one," Davis said. He ripped the rifle out of the blond man's hand and threw it across the yard.

"The hell they didn't," shouted an elderly man waving a bloody bandana.

Driller Jack Smythe lay flat on his back, eyes wide open, staring at a mottled sky. His flannel shirt was soaked with blood which pumped out of a large hole in his chest.

"Jesus, dead center," Davis muttered.

Orchard knelt down next to Smythe to check for a pulse.

"He's still alive," he said, looking at Corcoran. "Paul, you and a couple of men get him back on the train."

Corcoran and three other men picked up Smythe and carried him toward the waiting boxcars, leaving a trail of blood in the dirt. His shooting had a sobering effect on the strikers, bringing with it a stillness which settled over the mill yard.

Orchard wiped some blood off his hand on his pant leg and joined the dynamiters. "Follow me, boys. We'll divide up when we get in the engine room."

They were only a few yards from the mill when John Cheyne ran out of the building, sprinting wildly across the yard toward one of the two-story boarding houses adjacent to the mill. Three shots broke the stillness. Cheyne threw his arms in the air to sprawl face down in the dirt.

"Jesus," one of the dynamiters muttered. "That was John Cheyne. Me and him won the billiard championship last year at Magnuson's."

"Looks like you'll be needing a new partner," Orchard said. "Let's get inside."

The engine room was dominated by a massive red and polished brass steam engine. While dynamite boxes were being stacked under its cylinder and flywheel, Orchard divided his men into teams.

"You, with the red bandana, take twenty men up to the top and plant your stuff where it'll take out the ore chutes and the stamp mill supports. Wait for me there." He waited until the first group was on the cleated walkway, headed for the top of the mill before issuing more instructions.

"Klondike, take another twenty men up to the concentrating area. Put your charges under the crushers and the vanners. The rest of you, down to the boiler room."

102

Orchard and his dynamiters were inside the mill less than twenty minutes, placing over ninety boxes of dynamite in half a dozen strategic locations. The huge stamp mill was mined below its supporting structure so it would topple into the mill's second level with the initial blast.

The second series of explosions would destroy the concentrating area, along with most of the mill's roof supports, bringing down the entire building. Finally, the lifter charge, consisting of thirty boxes of dynamite, stacked around the two enormous boilers, would turn the entire mass of wreckage into kindling and shattered iron.

In the boiler room, Orchard broke open one of the wooden boxes and spilled dynamite cartridges and their sawdust packing onto the cement floor. With his pocket knife he slit the cartridges. He crimped blasting caps to the fuses with his teeth, a trick which had taken off more than one man's head in the mines of the west. That done, he inserted capped fuses into a dozen cartridges. He placed one stick of dynamite between the stacked cases and shoved the rest into his pocket

"All right, everybody out," he ordered. "Tell the boys to get back on the train."

When the boiler room was clear, he cut the fuse for a five minute burn and lighted it. The boilers' banked fire boxes seemed to watch him with sullen orange eyes as he climbed the ladder to the engine room.

As he stooped to light the fuses in the engine room, Orchard glanced up at the glistening flywheel of the steam engine. He gave it a gentle pat.

"Sorry, old girl," he muttered as he struck a match on one of her massive spokes.

In the concentrating area, where the charges were more scattered, he had to hurry to place and light fuses so they'd all go off at once. He was breathing heavily by the time he had reached the upper level. He was dwarfed by the awesome mass of the stamp mill. Weighing as much as a hundred tons, it would probably drop all the way to the boiler room.

Only two of the dynamiters had waited for him by the stamps, a nervous elderly man and a rangy, redheaded kid.

Orchard surveyed placement of the boxes and shook his head. "I want to move some of these," he told them.

"Ain't time to move nuthin'," the man said. "This place is gonna blow in a minute."

Orchard grabbed up a box to relocate it.

"Then get the hell out before you wet your pants," Orchard snapped. "You too, sonny."

The nervous man departed in a hurry but the kid lingered.

"They's all scairt," the kid said, watching Orchard place capped dynamite sticks among the boxes. "Thought they smelled powder burnin'."

Orchard looked at him.

"What'd you smell? Baking bread?"

The boy's expression changed.

"You lit the rest?"

"Three minutes ago, laddie, and I'm touching off the last ones right now," Orchard said, striking a match.

"Them's mighty short fuses," the redhead said, backing away.

"About a minute," Orchard said. "You a fast runner?"

The redhead's departure was drowned out by the hiss of the fuses.

Klondike Davis was waiting in the mill yard when Orchard emerged from the mill.

"Jesus Christ, Harry," Klondike said, "I was about to come in and get you."

Orchard took his arm to pull him away from the building.

"Come on, it's gonna go in a minute."

They were halfway to the train when the charges under the stamps went off. There was a rumbling explosion. Smoke, dust, sheet iron and shingles erupted into the sky, followed by the horrendous sound of the stamps falling into the lower levels of the mill.

Klondike slowed to look but Orchard propelled him forward. "Don't stop or we'll be up to our ass in broken boards."

They were clambering aboard the train when dynamite in the concentrating area exploded. The sound was muffled by falling debris. The roof of the building undulated for a moment, like a crawling rattlesnake, before the entire structure collapsed with a roar. The two steel smoke stacks tottered for a few seconds before crashing down on the smoking wreckage.

Orchard and Davis stood in a boxcar doorway with a group of wide-eyed men, transfixed by the power of the explosions. The train was moving now. Behind them, on the floor of the car, lay the body of Driller Jack Smythe, the light heavyweight challenger from Sandon, British Columbia. He had bled to death before they'd gotten him aboard the train.

When the big lifter charge in the boiler room went off, the results were more spectacular than Orchard had imagined. The enormous pile of rubble rose into the air, spewing clouds of smoke and dust, seeming to hang there for an instant before crashing to earth again. One of the boilers landed at the edge of the pile, vomiting steam from its ruptured pipes.

Davis punched Orchard on the arm. "You always were a heavy loader, Harry."

Orchard winked at him.

"Nothing I blew ever got up and walked away."

He was sure that the blast had totally destroyed the Bunker Hill mill and concentrator but he was troubled by how easy it had been.

As though reading his mind, Davis said, "Where were the guards at? Why'd they let us do this?"

Orchard shook his head.

"I don't know, but whatever their reason, it's going to be hard on the union."

# CHAPTER TEN

Frank Bromley and a begrimed Justin Whitehead picked their way slowly through the great pile of shattered timbers and twisted steel that a few hours earlier had been the Bunker Hill mill and concentrator. They were accompanied by several mine bosses and a contingent of grim-faced armed guards under the supervision of Lyle Gregory.

Bromley stooped to pick up a piece of what had once been a door frame, one hinge still attached. It seemed to symbolize the total destruction of the mill at the hands of men skilled in the use of dynamite. Idly, he tossed it away.

"We have quite a mess to clean up here, Justin."

Whitehead, his hair disheveled, his clothing torn and ash-stained, seemed dazed by the magnitude of the destruction. He shook his head in disbelief.

"Why couldn't they have contented themselves with the mill? They didn't have to burn down my house. We've lost everything. Our poor hired girl will be scarred for life."

Bromley took out a white handkerchief to wipe his hands.

"They'll pay for everything, Justin. Oh, how they'll pay."

Bromley's anger suddenly boiled to the surface, a seething magma of hatred. "I won't be happy until there isn't a single union man working the Coeur d'Alene. I don't care if they and their families all starve to death. I've already called Governor Steunenberg to send the National Guard to put a lid on the district before anything else happens. Goddamn it! I won't be blackmailed."

His voice was so uncharacteristically loud that some of the others in the group gave him startled glances.

Frank Steunenberg was in no mood to discuss the affairs of the state of Idaho this Sunday. The big, affable governor had eaten a large dinner of roast duck, his favorite. The two glasses of port taken with a twenty-five-cent cigar on the wide front porch had made him relaxed and drowsy. Nonetheless, wrapped in a wool sweater and enjoying the vista of the greening countryside, he grudgingly admitted to himself that he must turn his attention to the brewing crisis in the Coeur d'Alene.

He watched his aide, Bart Van Cleve, open the front gate and approach the house at his usual brisk pace. They had spoken earlier by telephone, with Van Cleve relating Frank Bromley's adamant call for the National Guard. Reluctantly, Steunenberg had asked Van Cleve to take the afternoon train from Boise to Caldwell so they could plan a strategy which would placate Bromley without too much impact on the state's meager treasury.

He led Van Cleve into the parlor, which he had asked his wife and children to vacate to give them privacy for their meeting. Remnants of split fir logs smoldered in the fireplace.

"I swear, Bart, every time I come out here for a peaceful weekend there's a damn crisis of some sort," the Governor muttered, dropping into his favorite upholstered chair.

Van Cleve smiled briefly, revealing discolored teeth which seemed to be in need of dental work.

"If what Bromley said is true," Van Cleve replied, perching himself on the edge of a straight chair. "The lid has come off in the Coeur d'Alene."

Steunenberg rolled his cigar around in his mouth.

"The union boys blew up a mine you said."

Though he wouldn't confide his true feelings to Van Cleve, his sympathies were on the side of the miners who labored under deplorable conditions for wages that were eaten up by exorbitant charges at the company boarding houses and stores.

"Blew up the Bunker Hill mill, Governor," Van Cleve said. "Several people were killed. Hundreds of striking union men were involved. Bromley demands you send troops at once. He wants martial law. He wants to round up every union man in the district and bring them to trial."

"Oh, he demands, does he?" Steunenberg snorted. "Did you tell him that most of our National Guard units are in the Philippines? Doesn't he read the newspaper?"

Van Cleve nodded and said, "I told him that and he insisted that you call Washington to ask for federal troops. He said he was speaking for the Mine Owners Association."

Steunenberg stubbed out his cigar in an ash receiver made from an abalone shell.

"He's just full of demands, isn't he? Federal troops? Why doesn't he call McKinley? After he explains to our president where Idaho is, he can make his damn demands."

Van Cleve rose to stand in front of the fireplace where he could look down at the governor.

"We can't allow a thing like this to get further out of hand, Governor. An armed insurrection could tarnish your reputation in short order."

Steunenberg studied Van Cleve before responding. As able as he was, Van Cleve had an alarmist streak in his makeup and it was clear that he'd given little thought to the implications of a mass roundup of union men. The mine owners had been behind a similar effort seven years before in an attempt to break the back of the union. They'd failed to do so, but they had managed to break the will of some of the women who had to watch undernourished children die during the harsh mountain winter, while their husbands struggled on the icy picket line for a cause that was doomed to failure from the beginning.

"Did Bromley say there was an armed insurrection, Bart? Are pillaging mobs running through the streets of those dreary little towns?"

"He said they will be if troops aren't sent," Van Cleve answered. "He did say that armed gangs often meet the trains coming in with men who want to work. There's been violence on more than one occasion. I spoke with the sheriff and he confirmed that."

"I don't condone violence," Steunenberg said, "but I understand how desperate men can resort to it when their jobs are at stake. Sheriff what's-his-name. Did he have any inkling that this was coming? And what's he doing? Has he arrested anyone?"

"Governor, Sheriff Thompson is an elected official and probably has union sympathies," Van Cleve scoffed. "He made up the excuse that the union had threatened to lynch him if he interfered."

Steunenberg clasped his hands on his vest and leaned back in his chair. "I'm also an elected official, Bart. I'm in office because a strong union vote put me here." He raised his hand when Van Cleve tried to speak. "Have you ever seen one of those mining towns? Do you have any idea how those poor devils have to live?"

"No, sir."

"Well, I have, and I don't mind telling you, it's a dog's existence."

"But they can't disregard the law! That's anarchy. As governor, you can't permit it."

Steunenberg's eyes narrowed. "As long as I'm governor, I can permit or not permit anything I damn please. In this case, I don't have enough facts to warrant a request for federal troops."

Van Cleve sat down, pulling his chair closer.

"Send me out there to get the facts for you."

"Your mind's already made up isn't it?"

Van Cleve nodded.

"I believe Bromley more than I'd believe Sheriff Thompson. The union mob did blow up the Bunker Hill mill. He certainly didn't fabricate that story."

Steunenberg sighed. This was becoming tiring.

"I'm sure he didn't, but I choose to believe this could be the end of the trouble. The union and Bunker Hill can get back to the bargaining table and settle their differences. We don't even know what the strike is about, at this point."

"I do," Van Cleve said. "Fifty cents a day. For fifty cents, the strikers destroyed a mill Bromley said was worth over two hundred thousand dollars. He has no intention of reopening any talks with the union. He's going to starve them out. Send me out there, sir."

"You know, Bart, I get the distinct feeling that you're seeking a diversion from the tedium of the office."

He grinned at the intense young man to mitigate an accusation he believed to be correct.

"Take the morning train. Get up to the Coeur d'Alene district and see for yourself how bad the situation is. If, in your judgment, federal troops are required to maintain order, I'll wire McKinley for help."

Later, watching Van Cleve bounce through the gate and get into the waiting hack, Steunenberg wondered if he was doing the right thing or if he had set in motion a series of events which he would live to regret.

When he went back in the house, he found himself suddenly weary, as though resisting his duty as governor had taken all his strength. The thought of having to impose martial law on a free society was abhorrent to him and its aftermath would doubtless leave wounds which might never heal. He stirred up the fire and added more wood. The room had suddenly become uncomfortably cold.

# CHAPTER ELEVEN

The Gold Dollar and the Oriental Saloons seemed to have absorbed most of the trade enjoyed by Fatty Kincaid before his untimely demise. Both were unusually crowded this Monday because all the mines in the district had shut down following the Bunker Hill explosions the day before.

There was an air of apprehension over the drinkers lining the bar. The flush of Sunday's presumed victory had turned into worry about groceries for them and their families. This problem was exacerbated by the closure of all the company stores where the miners made their purchases on credit.

Orchard stood at the bar in the Oriental between John MacNamara and Klondike Davis. Cuddling his beer stein in two big paws, MacNamara spoke quietly out of the side of his mouth.

"We really did it, didn't we? Made a pile of kindling out of the Bunker Hill mill and they just knuckled under. Only the mine owners got together and shut the district down tighter than a bull's ass in fly time. There ain't a man on the street, scabs included, that's gonna have a dollar in his pocket come mid-May."

Orchard waved down the bartender to order three whiskeys to go with their beers. He'd have more than a dollar in his pocket by mid-May. In the safe at the union hall was two hundred dollars Haywood and Moyer had left for him, plus the bail money in the envelope under the pried-up floor board in his hotel room.

MacNamara downed his whiskey, grimaced and washed it down with the rest of his beer.

"Gotta go split some wood for the old lady or I'll be sleeping on the floor tonight."

Watching him go, Orchard thought that MacNamara sleeping on the floor might be a good idea inasmuch as he had three small children and another on the way. Of course, he was a good Catholic. Maybe Jesus would take care of him if the mines stayed closed.

He and Davis put away the whiskey and Orchard ordered a refill, enjoying the warm feeling spreading through his body.

"I didn't want to scare the shit out of MacNamara," Davis muttered, "but I heard they're already makin' lists of who took the train and who went into the mill."

He looked up at Orchard to add, "Deputy friend of mine said they know you done Fatty Kincaid."

"Is that a fact?"

"Yup. That blonde whore, Pearl Singleton, was fuckin' him. She told the sheriff she seen you shoot him."

Orchard drank his shot and set the glass down hard on the bar.

"Smart boys like you and me should haul our freight out of here, Klondike."

"Colorado?"

"That's where I'm headed."

They shook hands and Orchard left as Davis ordered another whiskey.

On the street, men were clustered on every corner, loitering on the wooden sidewalks and under the overhangs of other saloons and commercial establishments. On his way to the hotel he was hailed several times by men who recognized him. He returned the salutations with a grin and a wave but didn't linger to exchange pleasantries.

His instincts told him that things in the Coeur d'Alene were going to get a hell of a lot worse before they got any better. Whatever Haywood and Moyer had envisioned as the result of the Bunker Hill's destruction hadn't played out according to their plan. The mine owners had come together more quickly than they had imagined, striking back with their most potent of weapons, a complete shutdown. Punish everyone. Show them who was boss.

A pall was settling over the district, interrupted from time to time by flare-ups between union and non-union men. Roving deputies and mine police patrolled the streets to keep the peace and to prevent any further destruction, but this was probably only a prelude to the inevitable crackdown which was sure to come.

Orchard looked at his watch. He had plenty of time to pack up, stop by the union hall for his money and catch the eastbound evening train.


Amy Neville set a bowl of hot broth on the upturned soap box next to the bed where her brother, flushed and feverish, lay motionless, eyes tightly closed.

"Try to get this down, Johnnie," she urged. "You gotta eat something."

Johnnie opened his eyes. "Amy, I got to have a doctor. Jesus, my...I'm all swoll up something terrible and I feel like I'm on fire."

Amy, arms folded across her thin bosom, stared down at her brother. The nature of his injury, still unexplained, was such that she'd been unable to apply any of the standard remedies; a soak in a salt solution or the application of a poultice made with flaxseed or oatmeal.

Each time she had suggested that she examine him, Johnnie had drawn the bedclothes to his chin, adamantly refusing to allow her to peruse his testicles, one of which was the size of a large apple.

"We got no money for a doctor," Amy told him, "and after yesterday, there ain't a doctor between here and Wallace that'd do anything on credit for a union man."

"Why the hell not?" His voice was weak, even when he was speaking angrily.

"After what your union heroes done, ain't no one gonna take a chance on a union man. Most of you won't never work again—not in the Coeur d'Alene."

Johnnie closed his eyes again, his body stiffening from pain's onslaught.

"They had to show Bunker Hill what was what."

"No," Amy replied emphatically. "What they done was kill the union in this district forever. And now with you laid up, we can't even get out of here. Your friend, Orchard, and your other union cronies have fixed you real good, Johnnie." She waved her hands helplessly. "I don't know what we're gonna do."

"Maybe I can just lay here 'til I die," Johnnie blubbered. "Then you won't have no more problems."

Amy turned to leave. She wanted to run out of this stinking room forever and let him die. Damn the union! Damn Bunker Hill! Damn the fates which had brought them into the bleak confines of Milo Gulch, from which there seemed to be no escape.

The last thing Orchard placed in his canvas traveling bag before buckling the leather straps was Charley Siringo's black hat. He held it in his hands for a moment, his finger through the large bullet hole high in the crown. A couple of inches lower and the crafty Pinkerton's body would have provided dinner for the varmints in Burke Canyon. He wasn't sure why he wanted to keep the hat but did, nonetheless, cramming it into the bag atop his folded clothes.

He went to the window to look down on the street, observing the knots of men still lingering on every corner under the electric street lamps. A sense of foreboding, which he had started to experience earlier at the Oriental, returned, causing him to check the loads in this pistol. He poured the last of his whiskey into a tumbler as he waited for darkness to fall. Then, with any luck, he could make it to the union hall and down to the Kellogg depot unmolested. Once aboard the eastbound train, he'd kiss the Coeur d'Alene goodbye.

He was disappointed that he'd have to set aside his plans to get to know Bella Shanks, but it was now too dangerous to linger in the district. Perhaps their paths would cross again. Perhaps not. She wasn't the only woman he'd wanted, to no avail, and probably wouldn't be the last.

He was sitting on the bed sipping the whiskey and waiting for it to get dark when a sharp rap on the door startled him.

A woman's hushed voice said, "Mr. Orchard? I'm Amy Neville. Johnnie's sister. He sent me. I seen you at the Shanks's house with Bella. Remember?"

Her words seemed to come out in a rush, trying to include everything to win his sympathy.

Orchard opened the door to stare at the plain girl in the frayed shawl. He didn't recognize her, but whatever her business was, she was too skinny, too dirty, and too late.

"I was just leaving," he told her. "What does Johnnie want?"

Amy looked over her shoulder at the deserted hallway.

"Can I come in? I don't want to talk out here."

"We don't have anything to talk about."

"He needs a doctor." Her voice quavered. "He's got a terrible fever."

"Why me?" Orchard said. "I'm not a doctor."

"I know what you are, Mr. Orchard." She drew herself more erect. Her hostility was ill concealed. "We got no money for a doctor. We got no money for nuthin'."

"You need to see John MacNamara," Orchard told her. "He's in charge of taking care of sick union men."

"Johnnie's not sick. He got himself stabbed."

Orchard couldn't suppress a smile.

"Yes, I know, and in a pretty bad place at that."

"Then, you won't help?"

Before he could respond, his attention was diverted by loud voices in the street.

"Come in and close the door," he told the girl before going to the window.

A loud confrontation had occurred in front of the hotel. A large group of armed men wearing deputy badges and led by Lyle Gregory were engaged in a violent argument with fifteen or twenty miners in the middle of the street. Orchard raised the sash to listen, concealed behind the muslin curtains.

"Don't interfere with us," he heard Gregory warn. "We're all legally appointed deputy sheriffs of Shoshone County."

"You're all company finks!" someone shouted.

More voices were raised, all unintelligible until Orchard heard Gregory bellow, "Orchard's wanted for murder. This don't have nothing to do with the union."

Orchard lowered the sash and turned to find Amy watching him.

"Go home," he told her. "They'll be up here in a minute."

Amy opened the door while he unbuckled his bag to extract his shotgun. He could still hear the argument in the street and wondered how soon the shooting would start.

"Where do you live?"

"In the gulch below the dump houses."

"I'll be there as soon as I can," Orchard told her. "Get going. Don't speak to anyone."

Amy didn't move.

"What about the doctor?"

"Look," Orchard said, "If I don't get out of here, I'm gonna need a doctor."

"But you will get us one?"

Amy's stare was unwavering.

"If I live long enough," Orchard told her.

Roughly, he turned her around and gave her a shove to send her on her way.

Orchard put on his derby, grabbed his shotgun and his bag, going quickly to the opposite end of the hall. The back stairs terminated in the kitchen where two Chinese kitchen helpers hardly glanced up from their work when he passed through to slip out the back door.

He was annoyed with himself for waiting around Wardner until he had to make a run for it. Last evening he could have boarded the train and would have been across Montana by now.

He emerged from the alley, and headed up Mill Street toward the dump houses. He'd gone several blocks when six men staggered out of the Emerald Bar blocking his way. He approached them casually, shotgun in his free hand, ready to fill them with buckshot if they proved to be deputies.

"Where you headed, little man?"

They surrounded him, all drunk and fairly reeling. One of them, younger than the rest, came nearer to squint at him. His unshaven face cracked into a wide smile.

"Hey, it's the dynamiter!" He slapped Orchard on the shoulder. "We was with you yesterday. Ain't that right, boys? Whooee! What a blast!"

Now they were all grinning and patting him on the shoulders.

"Have a drink with us," several said at once.

"Sorry boys," Orchard said, extricating himself and adding with a wink, "I have some business with a lady."

The younger man was insistent.

"Just one. I'd be proud to buy it. I figure we owe you one."

"You could do me a favor," Orchard told him, glancing down the street for a sign of Gregory and the men. "Go find a doctor and send him to the Neville place."

He handed the man six dollars.

"Three's for the doctor and three's for you and your friends to have a drink on me."

"I'll go with him," one of the others announced in a Swedish accent. "I know where Johnnie lives."

"One more thing," Orchard said. "There's a pack of special deputies roaming town tonight. You haven't seen me."

They all shook their heads solemnly.

"We ain't seen you and if we see them, some heads is gonna get broke."

Probably yours, Orchard thought. He headed up the street wishing his bag wasn't so heavy. Darkness was falling rapidly in the steep canyon. He quickened his step, to put distance between himself and the deputies before the street lights were turned on.

An unsmiling Amy Neville admitted him to the evil-smelling shack, closing the rickety door behind him. He tossed his bag into a corner, laid the shotgun on top of it, and paused to check his good shoes. He'd scuffed one on something crossing the tailing dump. He spat on a finger tip and rubbed it on the shiny leather to heal the blemish.

That done, he looked around the room. A rusty stove, a pockmarked table and two chairs, powder boxes nailed on the wall to hold a few dishes, pots and pans and several indistinguishable parcels which might contain food. In one corner an iron bedstead with a sagging mattress and a dirty blanket was shoved against the wall. Clothing, what little there was of it, was hung on nails driven into the peeling wallpaper. A piece of faded cotton print strung on a wire served as the door to the only other room.

"It ain't quite as grand as the Galena House," Amy blurted, throwing him a challenging look.

"It ain't quite as grand as the shithouse behind Kincaid's saloon," Orchard growled distastefully. "And it stinks worse."

"You can blame Johnnie for the stink," Amy said. "I can't do nuthin' about that." Her voice broke a little, as though her tough exterior was about to collapse around her.

"Let's have a look at him," Orchard said. "I've got a doctor coming."

He pulled the cloth aside and entered the tiny bedroom, recoiling from the overpowering stench of infection.

A wan Johnnie stared at him with dull eyes and squeaked, "I'm glad you come, Mr. Orchard."

"I'm not." Orchard snapped. "Can we get some air in here? In a minute I'm gonna be sicker than he is."

"Window don't open," Amy said. She stood in the doorway, arms crossed on her small breasts, near tears.

Orchard went to the only window and drove his elbow through the glass.

"Go open the front door," he ordered Amy. "Get some ventilation in here."

When Amy left, Orchard pulled the bedclothes off her brother, exposing his distended scrotum and swollen thigh, scarlet with infection. The odor which rose from the damp bed where his wound was oozing made him turn away.

"Doesn't look too good." He tossed the bedclothes over Johnnie, eliciting a sharp groan. "Doctor's coming. He'll probably lance your leg and snip off your rotten balls. In a day or two you'll be as good as new."

Johnnie made a little whimpering sound and buried his face in his soiled, sweat-soaked pillow. Orchard looked at him and shook his head, marveling at the irony of the events which brought him here. He wouldn't have cared if this little piece of shit had died in agony for what he had tried to do to Bella Shanks.

He'd hardly given her a thought since the last time he'd spoken with her in the reflected light of the flames that were feasting on Fatty Kincaid's saloon. In that instant, as he stared at Amy, with her pimples and dirt under her fingernails, he could almost feel Bella in his arms; clean and full bodied with a mouth that wanted to be kissed.

"Make some coffee," he told the girl. "It might kill some of the stink in here."

"Got none," she said. "Got nuthin' but a piece of bacon and some potatoes, goin' bad."

"You got a neighbor you could get some from? I'll pay for it. Whiskey too, if they've got any."

Amy shook her head. "I don't know. Bella Shanks, in the company houses up the gulch is the only one I know good enough to borrow from. That's where I seen you, but you don't remember."

"Yeah, I remember, but I don't expect Bella'd be too keen on doing anything that might help Johnnie," Orchard said, searching his breast pocket for a cigar.

"And why is that?" Amy's spunkiness seemed to have returned.

"After what he tried to do to her," Orchard said, lighting his stogie.

"I don't know what you're talking about."

"No? He didn't tell you he jumped her out on the tailing dump?"

"Jumped her?"

"Yup. He was trying to screw her and it seems the lady didn't want to be screwed, so she jabbed him in the balls with her hatpin."

Orchard was enjoying Amy's shocked expression.

"Must have been a pretty long one, to do the damage it did."

Amy's shoulders sagged.

"Jesus."

"Never mind," Orchard said, "I'll go ask her myself."

"Don't go," Johnnie called hoarsely from the bedroom. "Don't let her know you're here."

Orchard poked his head into the bedroom. Johnnie was sitting up in bed, supporting himself on one elbow. His face was stark white from the pain and effort of his exertion.

"What the hell are you talking about?" Orchard demanded. Johnnie lay back down and lowered his voice.

"She's a fink for Bromley and his boys."

"Now you're being stupid," Orchard said, turning away.

"The night I...the night I seen her on the tailing dump," Johnnie continued, every quavering word an effort, "she was getting out of a buggy with Justin Whitehead."

"Don't lie to me," Orchard said, at the same time half believing what Johnnie said. He wasn't smart enough or devious enough to make up a story like that to justify what he'd tried to do. Bunker Hill did have some responsibility in the death of her brother and if she was with Whitehead, it was probably in connection with that responsibility. Still, he wondered.

"Maybe she and Whitehead were having a little fun together," Orchard replied lightly.

He turned to find Amy staring at him, shoulders back, hands on hips, ready for combat. Spunky little bitch.

"Her brother was murdered less than a week ago!" She spat out the words. "His wife is up there dyin'. 'Havin' a little fun!' Don't you men never think of nuthin' but your stomachs and your peters?"

"Right now, I'm thinking of my stomach," Orchard said. "If you're not too high and mighty to eat it, I'll beg some food from Big Ass Kate."

Amy backed off.

"I'm sure you're well known by her girls."

"Well enough."

"Johnnie's come home a few times stinking of their cheap perfume."

"That's a sight better then he smells tonight and Kate's girls take a bath now and again, which is something you might try sometime."

Amy's eyes widened. She flew at him, swinging and clawing. He grabbed her wrists and marveled at how strong she was as she struggled and screamed at him through clenched teeth.

"Don't you ever call me dirty, Orchard, you son-of-a-bitch!"

She tried to jerk away from him but he held fast, even though she was pulling him around the room.

"We got no money for food! How could I buy soap? I don't have no more wood. I couldn't heat a tub of water if I had all the soap in Wardner."

Suddenly she sagged against him, all fight gone, sobbing like a child. Her tears were staining the lapels of his suit.

He patted her thin shoulders awkwardly, hoping she'd calm down. He was in an arena where he had no skills. A truly helpless young woman with no prospects was something he was ill-equipped to deal with. She reminded him of the bird he'd found on the sidewalk as a child. With a badly broken wing it had been as helpless as she was now. Then, as now, his first instinct was to put it out of its misery, more as a service to himself, to be free of an unwanted obligation.

He'd stomped the bird to death.

Amy leaned back to look at him with red, streaming eyes.

"You ain't never lived like this," she sobbed. "You got no idea how it is to be as poor as dirt. We've never had nuthin.'"

Her eyes seemed to mirror the agony of this bleak existence as they searched his face.

Bereft of ideas on how he might get her under control, Orchard gave her a few more pats until she pushed him away.

"Don't you put your hands on me," she snapped, back in control.

"You needn't worry," Orchard told her. "I wouldn't touch you with a tamping rod."

He grabbed up his shotgun, went out the door and picked his way up the gulch, headed for Kate's. He kept asking himself why he was doing this and got no answers.

Kate wasn't glad to see him. He'd entered through the back door into the kitchen and had sent Willi, the German girl scurrying away to tell her of his arrival.

"Jesus Christ, Harry, they've come by here two or three times looking for you," Kate announced, a tower of disapproval in green velvet. "If they find you here they'll close me up."

Orchard went to her and pinched her rouged cheek, harder than if it were a simple gesture of affection. Kate winced and backed away from him.

"I'm not here to roll around with you or one of your whores, Kate," Orchard told her. "I need to buy some grub for a sick friend."

"You're not serious." Kate stared at him, still touching her pinched cheek. "This isn't a grocery store."

Orchard took out his pocketbook and removed a ten-dollar bill which he handed to Kate.

"Have your girl here put a basket together," Orchard said, "and bring me a bottle of good whiskey, not the panther piss you serve the trade."

He gave Kate a little push and took a seat in a chair against the wall where he would have a clear shot if someone unwanted came from the parlor or in the back door.

A nervous Kate brought him an unopened bottle of Irish Supreme and helped Willi select an assortment of tins, a bag of ground coffee beans, a large piece of ham, some cheese and two loaves of bread. These were tied up in a red-and-white checked table cloth and tucked into a wicker basket. At his request, Kate brought him a wool blanket.

"Will the tenner cover everything, Kate?" he asked as Willi handed him the bundle and the blanket.

"It's fine," Kate said. "Now, get out of here and don't come back. Union men aren't welcome."

"Careful, girlie," Orchard warned in a conversational tone. "Union peckers built this place. Union hands can pull it down."

Kate followed him to the back door.

"The union's finished in the Coeur d'Alene, Harry. You ought to get out while you can."

"Thanks for the grub, Kate. I'll be back the next time I need some free advice."

With that, he slipped into the alley, shotgun cocked and ready in his free hand.

The two drunken miners who had befriended him on Mill Street were lolling on the front stoop of the Neville shack when Orchard returned from Kate's. They were drinking from a bottle but seemed no drunker than they were before and acted like they were glad to see him.

"We brung Doc Stafford from Kellogg," said the younger man, giving Orchard a chance to decline the proffered bottle. "He didn't want to come 'til Oly picked him up by the seat of the pants."

The big Swede grinned happily. "Yah, I pick him up and he come."

"I had to give Chester Tavenier half a dollar to watch the doc's buggy," the younger man said, sober enough to hint that the venture was exceeding initial estimates.

Orchard smiled, found a dollar to give him and went inside. There was a fire in the stove and a pot of water boiling. A railroad lantern hanging from a rafter cast an orange glow. The shack was overly warm which seemed to accentuate the foul odor. Orchard laid his shotgun and the food parcel on the table, took off his coat and hat and placed them on top of everything. He could hear low voices in the other room.

Amy came out of the bedroom, her eyes flicking from him to the table cloth with its welcome supplies.

"Oh, it's you," she said. "I thought it might be one of those drunken bums on the stoop."

Next to the stove, Orchard noticed a pile of weathered fence pickets.

"You gather the wood, or did those drunken bums do it for you?"

"The doctor asked them to," Amy replied defensively.

The doctor, a youngish man with a neatly trimmed moustache came out of the bedroom carrying a lamp. As he spoke he couldn't seem to take his eyes off Orchard's revolver in its shoulder holster. Gingerly, he dropped a pus soaked towel into the stove.

"That man belongs in a hospital," he told Orchard. "Are you a relative?"

"I'm his uncle from Mullan," Orchard said, "and he's not going to the hospital."

"In that case," the doctor replied, still eyeing the revolver, "I'll have to lance his scrotum. I've gotten what I could out of his thigh."

"Have at it, Doc, it's been lanced before."

By ten o'clock it was over. Johnnie had exchanged over a cup of pus for nearly a third of Orchard's Irish Supreme and was asleep.

When the doctor had washed his hands and put on his coat, Orchard handed him five dollars.

"Those men gave me three dollars," the doctor said, as though the disclosure might spare him from being accused of overcharging.

"I know," Orchard said. "That was for the house call. The five is for the surgery. When we need you to come back, I expect you to do it. As far as this visit is concerned, it never happened, understand? One word to anyone and you'll have more holes in you than you've got fingers to plug them."

The doctor picked up his bag, nodding eagerly.

"You have my word, sir. Now, I must go. My wife worries."

Oly, the big Swede, standing beside the open door, grinned at the doctor and said, "Mine too, but she's in Minnesota."

When they were gone, Orchard untied the table cloth so they could survey the goods. Probably enough there to keep them going for three or four days, Orchard surmised. By that time things in the district would have settled down enough for him to leave. He was anxious to talk to Haywood to learn whether the explosions had softened the Bunker Hill position or hardened it. Eventually, the striking crews would go back to work as they always did, win or lose, and an uneasy calm would settle over the Coeur d'Alene—until the next time.

"Wash your hands," he told the girl, "and make us a couple of ham sandwiches and put on a pot of coffee."

"I never thought I'd be eating no whorehouse food," she said, pouring hot water into a chipped granite pan and finding a hard sliver of soap.

"You'll never know the difference."

By the time Orchard had finished his meal and two cups of strong coffee, he could feel himself getting drowsy. It had been a long day with more walking than he was used to. There was a painful tightness in the calves of both his legs.

"What are the sleeping arrangements in this here hotel?" he asked, eyeing the sagging bed. "Do we cut cards for the mattress?"

"That's my bed," Amy said. "Don't get no ideas. You got a better blanket than anything we got anyway."

True, he thought, and even with his clothes on, the dirty bed posed a threat which might deprive him of a decent night's sleep.

"So be it," he told her and spread his blanket against the wall. He placed his revolver under his rolled up coat which would be his pillow. From his bag he removed a wool overcoat which bore the welcome scent of camphor, to supplement the blanket and counter the vile odor of the shack.

"If you have to wake me, go easy," he told Amy, who was still eating. "Sudden moves in the dark get people killed."

Amy nodded and crammed the last of her sandwich into her mouth.

"Do them whores eat this good all the time?" she asked him, mouth full. "Maybe I'll try it."

125

"Forget it," Orchard said, rolling up in the blanket. "You got too many sharp points on you for that kind of work."

Amy tossed her head. "No, I ain't soft and round like Bella Shanks."

"No, you sure as hell ain't." He turned his back toward her, closed his eyes and thought about Bella Shanks's big breasts.

# CHAPTER TWELVE

Bart Van Cleve was at the head of the table, flanked on either side by Bromley, Whitehead, representing Bunker Hill, Charles Sweeney of the Frisco, Patrick Clark of the Vestal, and Will Cathcart who had taken over the management of the Tiger-Poorman mine after manager, Mike Teague, was badly burned in the fire which had consumed Fatty Kincaid's.

Owners and managers of lesser mines like the Last Chance, the Stemwinder, Black Bear and Union occupied chairs along the wall. All had acquiesced to Bromley's demand that he be the speaker for the group.

Van Cleve looked around the room. These were the members of the powerful Mine Owners Association, which controlled the destinies of thousands of workers in the Coeur d'Alene. He basked in the deference they had accorded him since his arrival in the district. Of course they all had their motives. Actually, not all. Some of the mines had accepted union demands and work there was progressing peacefully and efficiently. Those who had not, made it clear that they'd settle for nothing less than the utter destruction of the demanding union.

Van Cleve laid aside the sheaf of hastily prepared papers documenting the incursions of the union against the struck mines. Frankly, he was disappointed that many of the incidents that the Association considered threats to the entire community seemed little more than schoolboy pranks. A punctured pipe which supplied water to the Pelton wheel compressor at the Stemwinder; the sawing away of a tramway support at the Tiger-Poorman; the attempted arson at the Black Bear company boarding house. Countless fist fights between union pickets and non-union miners.

What Van Cleve had expected upon his arrival was a bloody insurrection. What he had found were streets filled with loiterers. Tent camps where men who had been kicked out of the boarding houses were sheltered and fed in a communal environment where everyone contributed. As much as he wanted to take the credit for the imposition of martial law, he could hardly justify sending bayonet-wielding soldiers against the unkempt, sorry-looking men who were supposedly the enemy.

Of course, there had been acts of violence in which men on both sides of the issue had been seriously hurt, and several killed. A mob of union men had stopped a Northern Pacific train near the Idaho-Montana border. They had gone through the train, car by car, to forcibly remove every working-age male who couldn't prove he wasn't entering the district to be scab labor. In several instances, they actually found flyers which the Association had sent as far as Kansas City, soliciting workers.

Blood had been shed by those who tried to resist the union's demand that they head back to Montana and points east on foot. One of the resistors had drawn a pistol and shot a striker dead who was allegedly prodding him with a pick handle. It wasn't clear in the report whether the pistol had misfired when the man attempted a second shot, or if more strikers' lives were saved by someone with a club. A day later, the badly beaten body of a man was found wedged between two boulders in Canyon Creek but the sheriff reported that it wasn't possible to determine whether this was the shooter or not. Case closed. Nothing here was black and white. Everything was delineated in confusing shades of gray, speckled with drops of blood.

"Gentlemen, these reports make interesting reading, but most of it is history, sordid history to be sure, but hardly the basis for a declaration of martial law."

Bromley leaned across the table. His fists were clenched.

"You've seen the Bunker Hill concentrator lying in ruins, Mr. Van Cleve. Do you need more than that? These men are capable of anything."

"You told me that plans were being formulated to arrest the ringleaders," Van Cleve said. "Has that happened?"

"Not yet," Bromley replied, looking around the table. "The County Council had to coerce Sheriff Thompson to deputize about a hundred men so we could begin to hunt them down."

Bromley's face was getting red.

"I take it no one's been arrested, then," Van Cleve said dryly. "Do you even know who the ringleaders are?"

Van Cleve leaned back to look unblinkingly at the group. These men possessed the infinite skills to wrest riches from the earth but they seemed incapable of dealing with a few rowdy union men. If he were in charge, those union troublemakers would be driven out of the district and safeguards established to keep them out.

Around the room, members of the Mine Owners Association exchanged wry glances, deferring to Bromley.

Bromley, lower lip caught between his teeth, seemed to weigh his words carefully before speaking.

"The ringleaders, sir, are the union officials in Wardner, Gem and Burke, primarily. They have been fanned to incandescence by the oratory of Bill Haywood and Charles Moyer, union leaders from Denver, who have fled the district." He took a sip of water. "You know about the exposure and escape of Pinkerton detective, Charles Siringo. Well, another conduit into the union was a saloon keeper named Fatty Kincaid. He was shot to death by a union assassin named Harry Orchard. We're after him. A man named Davis led the gunmen who took over the Northern Pacific train which carried dynamite and

129

dynamiters to Wardner to destroy our mill. We're after him."

"Are you having any luck?"

Bromley shook his head.

"Our spies tell us Davis has left the district and we don't know whether Orchard is still here or not."

"What about the union heads? They ought to be easy to find."

"We'd start a war if they were arrested," Bromley snapped. "That's why I want troops here so we can round up every union man in the district and sort out the bad apples."

Van Cleve stared at the agitated Bromley. Rounding up all the union men was a tall order and would require sound leadership which couldn't be placed in the hands of military officers unfamiliar with the terrain.

"Who would lead and coordinate an effort like that, Mr. Bromley?" Van Cleve asked. "You?"

Bromley threw him a sharp glance.

"I'm neither policeman or soldier, Mr. Van Cleve. I suppose the head of my company police."

"Gregory?" Will Cathcart spat out the name. "He's a head breaker, Bromley. That's a terrible idea." He scowled at Van Cleve. "Rounding up all the union men is another. My crews are working and we're paying union wages."

"Because you knuckled under," Bromley said.

"Because if we hadn't and the pumping crews had walked out, my lower workings would be full of water."

Cathcart pushed his chair away from the table and got up.

"I'd hoped we'd hear some ideas from Mr. Van Cleve," Cathcart said, "but he doesn't seem to have any neither."

Van Cleve raised his hands, seeking control of the meeting.

"We can work this out," he told them. "If necessary, I'll stay and lead the effort."

He paused to let that sink in.

"Assuming, of course," he continued, "that I can convince the governor of the need for the army."

In his heart of hearts, Van Cleve didn't believe the district needed martial law. It would be disruptive at mines like the Tiger-Poorman, which had settled its difference with the union. There would be the matter of finding facilities capable of housing hundreds of prisoners. There would be the matter of the army's reluctance to carry out the orders of civilian authorities. Martial law would require a brilliant leader. He knew just the man for the job.

Outside, some distance away, a steam whistle was blowing. Several of the men in the room got up to look out of the windows. Van Cleve joined them and was treated to the view of dozens of men running up Mill Street.

"What's happening?" he asked of no one in particular.

His question was answered when the door banged open to admit a hatless man with blood on his shirt. His wild eyes found Bromley.

"We got a big fight goin' at the concentrator, Mr. Bromley," he gasped. "There must be two hundred union pickets up there. They run the clean-up crew offn' the job."

Bromley catapulted himself out of his chair.

"Come on, Van Cleve. You can see for yourself what we're up against."

The upper end of Mill Street was filled with jeering union men by the time the buggy carrying Bromley, Van Cleve and Whitehead reached the mill site. Portions of the tall fence had been pulled down and the mill yard was strewn with debris. Huge piles of broken lumber were on fire, set by the cleanup crew for disposal purposes. The smoke and flames provided a backdrop for an area where a dozen or more bleeding men lay on the ground being tended by their comrades.

At the sight of the buggy, the hooting and shouting intensified, with a number of angry men running up to it to shake their fists and hurl curses at the occupants.

One man loosed a stream of tobacco juice which stained Van Cleve's

131

fawn-colored trousers. The mob allowed the buggy to pass, however, closing in behind it like a turbulent sea.

Van Cleve gripped the edge of the seat and tried to appear calm and un-ruffled, but he was more frightened than ever before in his life. Never had he seen such raw hatred. For a moment, he wondered if he would emerge from this maelstrom alive.

Lyle Gregory, grim-faced and hatless, gripping a bloody pick handle, stood at the apex of a group of perhaps fifty men with Winchesters who were holding a howling mob of striking miners at bay. On the ground, behind the phalanx of special deputies, lay more wounded men, some with badges pinned to their bloody shirts.

Gregory and his men waded into the mob to clear a path for the buggy. Van Cleve observed one of the strikers go to his knees, hands over his shattered mouth. He wasn't sure if he was a victim of Gregory's flailing pick handle or the rifle butt of one of the deputies.

"They jumped the crew about a half hour ago," Gregory explained when he could get close enough to the buggy to be heard. "When the powerhouse whistle started blowin', me and my boys got here quick as we could and broke up the fighting."

"Anyone killed?"

Bromley squinted against the blowing smoke at the downed men they had driven past and those who lay in front of them.

"A few broke heads on both sides," Gregory muttered, keeping his eye on the surly crowd which seemed to have lost some of its energy.

"One of the union fellers was stabbed, but they drug him away," Gregory continued. "One of the deputies got hit in the throat with a board. He ain't doin' too good."

Van Cleve studied Gregory. This was the oaf that Bromley thought capable of leading the cleanup of the district? He was obviously a man whose only tool was violence and which he used unsparingly. While some force would be required, it would take a great deal of finesse to avoid applying so much of it that the district and its output would be irreparably damaged.

Bromley looked over the yard where salvageable material, neatly stacked, was visible through the smoke of the trash fires. This was the only evidence that a cleanup crew had been working, for there was no visible activity.

"Where's the crew?"

"All that was able to walk away has quit," Gregory said.

He gestured toward the wounded men.

"Them would be gone too if they coulda made it under their own steam."

He smiled suddenly, as though the entire incident was amusing.

Bromley turned to look at Van Cleve.

"What do you think now, Mr. Van Cleve?"

"I'm convinced," Van Cleve said. "I'll wire the governor this afternoon. We need to get the army here as quickly as possible."

On the way back to the hotel, someone threw a railroad spike which struck the horse, causing him to break for a moment, but there was no further violence. The union mob was beginning to break up with men pouring down Mill Street, many disappearing into the saloons.

Van Cleve, fright replaced by resentment of those who had frightened him, was preoccupied with his plan to control the Coeur d'Alene.

# CHAPTER THIRTEEN

Siringo listened respectfully as the old man's voice rose and fell in a tide of recrimination and reprimand. James McParland was the head of Pinkerton's western division in Denver and though age was rapidly overtaking him, he was neither bashful nor reticent in dealing with what he considered inadequacies in his operation.

"I suppose you can thank Orchard for getting you out of the Wallace jail," McParland rumbled, "but you shouldn't have been in there in the first place."

Siringo toyed with his new hat, trying to be calm without being cocky.

"I don't think Orchard's motives were in my best interests," he drawled. "Clever scheme with my hat to keep me in there until he was ready to do me in."

"He played the sheriff, what's his name, Thompson, like a country fiddle," McParland snorted, "but we all know where his sympathies lie, don't we? No need to dwell on that. He'll be tossed out on his ass in a few days when the troops arrive."

"Troops? Are you sure?"

"Of course I'm sure." McParland's sharp tone reflected his dislike of having his pronouncements questioned. However, he smiled suddenly and his manner softened.

"Sorry, Charlie. I keep forgetting that you've been in transit, as it were."

He removed a cigar from a vest pocket and bit off the tip and spat it toward a spittoon by the door.

"Governor Steunenberg is going to declare a state of martial law affecting the entire Coeur d'Alene district," he continued. "I have a wire from Bromley confirming this. He wants us to send some operatives back there to help root out the rabid unionists and drive them out of the district."

"I'm not so sure troops are the answer," Siringo said.

He was thinking of some of the men he'd come to know in the Wardner union. They weren't firebrands bent on bringing the mine owners to their knees. For the most part, they were hard workers struggling to keep their families clothed and fed.

When McParland's search for a match proved futile, he heaved himself out of his chair to come around the desk to accept a light from Siringo.

"Of course they are," the old man exclaimed, shooting the words out with a puff of smoke. "If I'd had federal help in Pennsylvania instead of local police, we'd have had the bloody Mollies on the gallows months before we did."

Siringo kept his silence. He'd heard every chapter and verse of McParland's dismantling of the Irish terrorists, the Mollie McGuires. Though he acknowledged the skill and fortitude with which the old detective had executed that dangerous assignment, he didn't wish to trudge through the anthracite fields again at this time. He was tired from three days of traveling and the plaster on the side of his head covered the constantly aching crease in his skull put there by Orchard's bullet.

McParland stomped about the office leaving a trail of smoke.

"Bromley's out for blood, Charlie. He wants to bring all the union heads to trial and he wants people like this Harry Orchard and Klondike Davis convicted and hanged right there in Wardner."

He paused to beam at Siringo, savoring the thought.

"He wants to swing 'em from a tramway that's still standing where they blew up his mill, by God!"

"Have they been arrested?" Siringo asked, already sure he knew the answer.

McParland made a wry face and shook his head.

"No one's been arrested. Too many union men with guns. When the troops arrive, it'll be a different matter."

"When is that?"

"A few more days. They're coming from Montana," McParland said, studying the tip of his cigar and flicking ashes to the floor. "The union boys probably know but they're sitting tight, according to Bromley. No mass exodus from the district."

"Where would they go?" Siringo asked, a little annoyed with McParland, oblivious to the impending disaster of martial law.

Siringo had been through it in Colorado three years before and the suffering of the families was still fresh in his mind. He could still see the confused, pleading eyes of the hungry little children. There, the presence of the military in a struggle which many felt the miners won, had left deep wounds.

McParland sat down again to eye Siringo. There was a speculative glint in his eye.

"Bromley thinks Orchard's still there, but his people tell him that Davis headed for Colorado. He's offered a sizeable reward for each of them."

"Dead or alive?"

"He wants them alive. He really expects to have a public hanging as a warning to the union."

"Bromley'll be lucky if Orchard doesn't get him first."

"Pretty wily character, eh?"

"More than wily. I've met a lot of hard cases in the last ten years, but none like Harry Orchard. Gentleman one minute, brute the next. He'd piss in the Devil's lunch pail."

"Well, for the moment, we're not concerned with Orchard," McParland said. "I want you to find Davis and bring him in, alive, understand?"

"Yes, sir," Siringo said. "When do I start?"

McParland pointed to the door and made shooing motion.

"You've already started. I'll send your regards to the girls at the Bird Cage."

Gingerly, Siringo put on his hat.

"That's mighty thoughtful of you, but I intend to make my own goodbyes."

McParland slid an envelope across the desk. Banknotes peeked from the open flap.

"Tomorrow you can buy a horse and an outfit."

"Yes," Siringo said. "This afternoon I have other things to attend to."

"Of course you do," McParland said. "Good luck."

With a little bow, Siringo excused himself, leaving the greatest living Pinkerton with a half smile, twisting his drooping moustache.

# CHAPTER FOURTEEN

By nightfall Wednesday, Johnnie's condition had improved markedly. Another visit by a reluctant Dr. Stafford, combined with some decent food seemed to have had a positive effect. The only part of the treatment process in which Orchard participated, and disliked intensely, was the twice daily soaking of Johnnie's testicles in a basin of hot water and salts. If he'd been the doctor, he'd have snipped them off. The world would be a better place in the future, denied the presence of any of Johnnie's progeny.

This evening, for lack of anything else to do, Orchard helped Amy dry the crockery and clean off the table. He stayed in the shack during the day to avoid the ever-increasing number of special deputies roaming the district in packs. The fact that one of the more notorious deputized gangs was led by Lyle Gregory, seemed to give credence to the rumor which attributed the increase in special deputies to secret funding by the Mine Owners Association.

There had been a number of confrontations between deputies and strikers. Scabs had been pulled out of saloons and beaten. Pickets had been assaulted by company thugs. A shooting incident had taken place in the street in front of the Burke union hall which had left Tom Archer shot through the pelvis and a deputy dead.

"You don't have to do that."

Amy took the damp dish towel out of his hands.

"Sit down and have a cigar and some more coffee."

"I'm tired of sitting," Orchard told her, "And I don't mind helping you."

He was still annoyed that he'd been unable to slip away before the arrival and departure of all trains were overseen by the special police. The arrivals, to protect the non-union men coming to work; the departures to snare any union men believed to be implicated in the destruction of the Bunker Hill mill.

It had been revealed that a number of men who had invaded the Bunker Hill mill yard were actually company spies whose observations had placed many names on the Bunker Hill watch list.

Ironically, it was learned that one of the company finks, a mucker named Jervis Fedak, had actually lit one of the fuses in the mill boiler room and had run alongside Orchard and Davis, heading for the train, just before the blast.

"I've managed without no help for so long that I don't know what to do when I get some," Amy said.

She placed the last of the heavy dishes on one of the powder box shelves and gave him a troubled look.

"I don't even know what to say to you for what you done to help us."

She stared at him, biting her lip, tears brightening her eyes.

"You don't have to say anything," Orchard said.

He pulled a chair away from the table and sat down. He hoped she wasn't going to cry. In his time he'd made a few women cry for various reasons, none of which had anything to do with acts of charity. He supposed he didn't want her to cry because he'd touched something within her which she kept carefully concealed and it made him uncomfortable to have it revealed.

"I do have to say something, but I ain't got the right words," she said, picking up the dish towel and twisting it.

Amy took a deep breath and brushed tears from her cheeks with thin fingers.

139

"I don't know who you are or what you've done, Mr. Orchard, and I'm much obliged to you for helping us but...but what I'm trying to say is...I don't feel we can't never be, like friends, you in the union and all."

"Your brother's in the union."

"It ain't the same. He runs errands when he ain't working. You come in here to tear things up."

"You afraid I'm gonna tear up this shack? You invited me here. You don't think I'd stay in this dump if every deputy in the district wouldn't like to get his hands on me, do you? I don't want to be your friend neither, sweetheart."

Might as well get it out on the table, he thought, feeling himself getting angry. Cooped up in this shack with a worthless invalid and a woman who treated him like he was a charge that hadn't gone off, made him extremely uncomfortable. Maybe the girl's halting outpouring would make life easier for both of them until he could get away.

"I guess it's because of who you are," Amy said in a subdued voice. "I'm scared and nervous all the time, but I try not to show it. If I'm scared, then Johnnie'll be scared and that won't help the healing."

"What the hell are you scared of?"

Orchard was suddenly annoyed by Amy's concern for her brother.

Amy made a helpless gesture.

"Ain't an hour goes by that I don't expect Gregory and his bunch to kick down the door and drag you off to jail."

Orchard patted the butt of his pistol.

"I'd resist arrest. I don't think I'd like being in jail."

"Then we'd all be killed before the shooting stopped."

She sat down in the other chair, hands clenched in front of her, knuckles white, on the warped table top.

"Maybe only me, Amy."

He reached across the table to pat a rigid fist.

"With my dying breath, I'd will you my money and my shotgun."

"I don't want to talk about it no more."

140

"If you had my money you could buy yourself a pretty dress and with my shotgun you could put your sorry brother out of his misery."

From the bedroom came a muffled groan of protest.

"That ain't funny!" Amy said, unclenching her fists and flexing her fingers. "The first thing I'd buy with your money, Mr. Orchard, is a bathtub and some lavender soap."

"If I was dead, I couldn't wash your back."

"If you was alive, you couldn't neither."

Orchard rose suddenly and put on his hat and coat. Amy gave him a startled look.

"Where you going?"

Orchard reached for her hand.

"Come on. Get your shawl. We're going out for a while."

He picked up his shotgun and waited by the door. Hesitantly, Amy got up from the table and took her shawl off its nail.

"Where to?"

"I know a place that's got a bathtub."

"You ain't taking me to no..."

"Come on," he ordered. "You owe me a favor."

With Amy following halfheartedly and grumbling under her breath, they made their way out of the gulch and crossed the tailing pile to the upper end of Mill Street. Since the flaming demise of Fatty Kincaid's saloon, that section of the street was largely deserted.

Further on, they avoided the clusters of men on the wooden sidewalks in front of other saloons and congregated under the flickering electric street lamps, by ducking in and out of alleys and narrow back streets. Passage was difficult because Milo Gulch was so narrow that in several places, Wardner was only one street wide.

When they finally arrived at Kate's back door, Amy looked up at the brightly lighted house and balked.

"I ain't going in there."

Orchard grabbed her arm and pulled her toward the back porch.

"The hell you aren't."

Amy's hostile stare wavered as she glanced from him, back at the house, where piano music penetrated the clapboards. Her voice took on a wistful quality.

"God knows I'd love a bath, but in a whorehouse..."

"Nobody'll bother you," Orchard said. "I'll be sitting on the edge of the tub with my pistol in my hand."

She jerked away from him and he started to laugh.

"I'm only teasing. Come on."

Willi hurried out of the kitchen to find Kate. Orchard was amused by Amy's timid curiosity about the music, the laughter and the occasional squeal emanating from the parlor. Moments later, Willi returned with a highly agitated Kate. The servant girl stepped discreetly out of the way so Kate could train her big guns on Orchard.

"This isn't a goddamn hotel, Harry," Kate said, when he'd told her why they were there. "I told you last time it's too dangerous for you to come here."

"For you or for me?"

Orchard sat down and laid his shotgun across the kitchen table, leaving Amy standing rigidly by the stove, under the disapproving gaze of Willi.

Kate looked Amy over as she might have assessed the attributes of a new girl, rejecting her out of hand.

"I'm sorry," she said. "I don't have time for this."

Orchard shot a glance at Amy, rigid with embarrassment.

"Take time, Kate," Orchard said, his easy smile fading. "I'd take it as a personal favor. I could ask the boys in the parlor what you ought to do."

He reached for the shotgun and made a move to get up.

Kate took an angry breath, her large breasts rising in protest from their taffeta sanctuary.

"All right! Just this once. Follow me, you."

Amy drew herself up.

"My name's Amy."

"Oh, all right, Amy. Follow me. Stay out of the parlor Harry, as a favor to me."
Kate flounced out of the kitchen.

Orchard heard her bellow, "Willi! Goddamn it. Heat some water!"

Willi responded at once by putting two large pots on the stove and scurrying away, leaving Orchard to look around the kitchen, opening cabinets to peer at the contents. He found an unopened bottle of wine. He was searching for a corkscrew when Kate returned. She was carrying a bottle of Canadian whiskey.

"I left Willi in charge of the bath," Kate said, placing the bottle on the table and getting two glasses out of a cupboard.

Kate sat down and poured two drinks.

"She tells me you're living with her and Johnnie. Well, here's to love."

Kate downed the liquor with hardly a quiver.

"Love's something you and I don't know anything about, Kate. I happen to be sorry for the girl."

Orchard tossed down the shot.

"Sorry's something you aren't too well acquainted with, either, Harry," Kate said. "You'll really be sorry when the army gets here."

"I talked with MacNamara the other night," Orchard said. "He thinks that's just a rumor the mine owners are spreading."

"It's no rumor," Kate said. "I heard it from a customer who works for the governor."

"And who might that...?"

Before he could finish, a harried-looking Willi came into the kitchen for hot water.

"She don't want no help, that one."

She lowered her voice, giving Orchard an embarrassed glance, as though her pronouncement was unfit for his ears.

"Her things is terrible, Miss Kate. Her underwear is just rags."

"I saw," Kate said, rising. "Excuse me, Harry, I'll see if I can find something she can wear."

143

Orchard lighted a cigar, enjoying the warmth of the whiskey and the waves of heat coming from the roaring stove which Willi seemed to have stoked to capacity to heat water for Amy's bath.

Kate returned in a few minutes with a heavy woolen shawl which she draped over the back of a chair.

"We found some stuff," she told him. "Poor kid doesn't have tits or ass enough to fill out a decent dress."

"Or an indecent one, neither," Orchard observed dryly.

That made Kate smile.

"You're an odd duck, Harry Orchard. I've heard you've taken lives over trifles, but you risk yours for this scrawny girl."

"Never over trifles, Kate. Now, what about the army?"

"All I can tell you is that Mr. Van Cleve says they're on the way here and he works for the governor."

"Was he in your bed when he told you?" Orchard muttered. "Fucking you with the taxpayers' three dollars."

"He gave me five," Kate said. "That's my rate for special people. He didn't get winded as quick as you did, either."

"Holy Christ," Orchard muttered, ignoring the barb. "Nobody thought Steunenberg had the guts to declare martial law. Haywood'll have a shit fit."

"Lucky for him, he won't be here when it happens," Kate said airily.

"Any more good news?" Orchard asked, suddenly feeling strangely depressed.

As though rubbing salt in a raw wound, Kate said, "Bunker Hill's got a big crew cleaning up after what you boys did. They're paying them four dollars a day, which has been good for my business."

Orchard took a small notebook and a pencil stub from an inside pocket and scribbled some notes.

"I'll get someone to pass this along to Haywood in Denver."

"Keep me out of it," Kate warned. "I'm trying to make a living and I don't need to provoke the Mine Owners Association."

"I suppose a scab's dollar is as good as a union man's, isn't it?" Orchard said, putting away the notebook.

"I'm going to see how the girl is doing," Kate said, leaving the kitchen abruptly.

If federal troops were on the way, it was clear to Orchard that it was time for him to find a way out of the district despite the risks that entailed. He had money waiting for him in the safe at the union hall which he'd have to pick up before departing.

He was turning over his options in his mind when Amy appeared, followed by Kate and Willi. She wore a simple dark blue dress which seemed to accentuate the whiteness of her freshly scrubbed skin. Her hair, still damp, was tied with a ribbon behind her neck.

Amy came to him like a child seeking approval, her expression a mixture of embarrassment and pleasure. Orchard looked past her at Kate and Willi, who both seemed pleased by the transformation.

"You're a different woman, Amy," Orchard told her, trying not to sound too soft in front of Kate.

For the first time that evening, Amy gave them all a genuine smile. She turned suddenly to Kate.

"I thank you for letting me bathe, ma'am. When Mr. Orchard brung me here, I didn't want..."

Kate put her arm around Amy's waist to give her a reassuring squeeze.

"Don't say anything," Kate told her. "Just take Mr. Orchard and get the hell out of here before the deputies come by to check out my clientele."

She took the woolen shawl off the back of the chair and placed it around Amy's thin shoulders.

Willi opened the back door to peek into the alley. When she beckoned that it was clear, Orchard pressed a folded twenty-dollar banknote into Kate's hand. He held up the half-full bottle that he was taking with him.

"That's for the whiskey, Kate. I hope I won't have to bother you again."

"That makes two of us," Kate said, before closing the door behind them. "You hang around Wardner, you won't be bothering anybody."

145

Johnnie was snoring when they got back to the shack. Orchard hung his coat and derby on a nail, sat down at the table with the whiskey bottle, two glasses and a cigar.

Amy seemed unable to come to rest. She marched around the drab room, smoothing her blue dress; pausing to look at herself in the corroded, wavy mirror that was nailed to the wall above the tin sink. Her little whirling steps rustled the taffeta.

"Why don't you light, girl?" Orchard demanded somewhat irritably. "You haven't stopped moving since we got back."

Amy came over to grin at him.

"I can't help it. I ain't felt this clean and proper for so long I just can't be still." She went back to the mirror to study her hair.

"That Kate's a decent sort, ain't she?"

She was looking at him in the mirror.

"Kate's a business woman," Orchard said. "She does what she has to do to make money or to avoid a ruckus."

Finally Amy sat down at the table. Orchard poured two fingers of bourbon into one of the tumblers and pushed it toward her. Amy took a hesitant sip, made a face and set the glass down. Her ebullience faded when she looked at him.

"You can't believe the bad things that German girl said you done."

"Yeah," Orchard replied with a smile. "I kicked a dog once and I've been known to cheat at cards."

Amy picked up the glass and gulped the whiskey. A shudder went through her thin body. It took her a moment to get her breath.

"You know, it ain't easy for me to say this, but I'm sorry about the way I was 'fore we went down there."

She was blinking her eyes. Maybe from the harsh unaccustomed taste of the whiskey. She blushed suddenly, the rising color not unbecoming.

"You're a decent sort, too, Mr. Orchard. You got a good heart."

Orchard smiled at her and raised his glass.

"Tell your friends."

He got up suddenly to put on his hat and coat and to rummage through the food basket. He slipped two tins into his pocket.

Amy studied him with sudden suspicion.

"Where you goin' with those?"

"I'm going up to check on Bella Shanks," he told her.

"It ain't because you think she's hungry."

"Maybe I'm hungry."


Orchard slipped up on the porch of the Shanks house, cursing to himself when the toe of his shoe caught on a loose board on the second step. He knocked quietly, keeping his eye on the nearby houses. Most were dark but several windows emitted the orange glow of a lamp. The moon was high in the cloudless sky, giving him, as well as anyone bent on doing him harm, an advantage.

He was about to knock a second time when Bella opened the door. She peered at him and though her face was in shadow, he could tell she wasn't glad to see him.

He removed the tins from his pockets and held them out to her.

"Brought you something," he said, without preamble.

He raised one tin and squinted at the label in the dim light.

"Alaska pink salmon."

Bella made no move to accept the largesse from the Far North.

"Ed's wife died today."

Her tone was matter-of-fact with no hint of emotion.

"Not unexpected, was it?"

He pushed the tins toward her.

"I can't take anything from you," Bella said firmly. "Until I get them decently buried I have to depend on Bunker Hill. I'm almost out of money and Ed didn't leave anything." Her voice broke. "Somebody even stole his watch and his boots from where he was laid out in the barbershop."

"I'm sorry," was all he could think of to say.

"I've heard you led the gang that blew up the mill—Harry Orchard."

"Now you know everything, don't you? Well, I never claimed to be a choir boy." Orchard said. "Damn! Take these!"

Bella stepped out on the porch to take the tins. As he had earlier, she checked the neighboring houses and the path in front of them, a rutted scratch in the hillside.

"Why are you doing this? What do you want from me that you can't get from Amy Neville? The old woman in the next shack told me you're staying there."

That was disquieting. If Bella knew, then maybe the sheriff, Lyle Gregory or any other Bunker Hill thugs who might try to bring him in did as well.

"I'm getting nothing from Amy Neville. I'd much rather stay with you."

"Just long enough to get what you wanted?"

"That's a harsh judgment, Bella. As soon as it's safe for me to leave, I'm heading for Colorado. Would you go with me?"

Bella backed away from him.

"Let me tell you something, Harry Orchard, or whatever your name is. If I'm going to run off with a man, I want one with a future longer than fifteen minutes."

"I don't have much time then, do I?"

Orchard took Bella by the shoulders, pulled her to him and kissed her hard, than again gently, when her lips acquiesced.

A breathless Bella freed herself from his grasp, tears welling up in her eyes and running down her cheeks.

"I wish you hadn't done that," Bella muttered. "My life's hard enough without the likes of you dangling promises that can't be kept. Please don't come around here anymore."

Bella whirled away from him to plunge into the house. The door latch clicked with finality.

Orchard stepped toward the door to kick it in, cast the foolish impulse aside and took the path into the gulch.

Johnnie was still snoring and Amy was breathing evenly when Orchard slipped back into the shack. He undressed quickly, piling his clothes on the table, pistol on top.

Amy awoke when he crawled into her bed.

"What are you doing?"

"It's too damn cold on the floor."

Her body smelled of lavender.

"You didn't get what you was after, did you?"

"No, and I'm not after anything here, either. Turn over and go to sleep."

Orchard was awake long after Amy moved close to him and fell asleep. Somehow, he had to get out of the district as soon as he could.

# CHAPTER FIFTEEN

As soon as it was dark, Siringo left his room above Cripple Creek's Central Dance Palace to board the electric trolley for Victor.

At nine o'clock, in an unused back room at Sadie LaRue's, a brothel situated on a side street behind the Victor firehouse, he sat across a small table from Harvey Browne to share a pint of whiskey. Browne, a paid Pinkerton operative, worked as a miner in Altman, a few miles away, and belonged to the Altman union, where he was the secretary.

"Your man, Davis, is working for some leasers up on Bull Hill," Browne said, with a pleased expression on his unshaven face.

Siringo tossed down a shot of whiskey and winced as it burned all the way down. Sadie must have made this stuff herself.

"You're sure he's the same man?" Siringo said. "I don't cotton to a long ride up the mountain for nothing."

Browne poured himself another drink and seemed immune to its ravages as he gulped it down and wiped his mouth on the back of his hand.

He'd been easy for Siringo to recruit. He lived with his tubercular wife and two little boys in an isolated tarpaper shack he'd built himself. It was located on an old tailing dump that belonged to the Vindicator in Altman. The mine charged him five dollars a month to live there. Siringo had spotted him for a mark when the owner of the Union Saloon had loudly refused him more credit until he'd paid his arrears, which amounted to four dollars.

Siringo took care of the bill, bought him a few drinks, took him to Sadie LaRue's to get his ashes hauled, and after that, owned him, body and soul.

"Goes by the name, Klondike," Browne said. "He's been heard to brag about his work in the Coeur d'Alene. What more do you want?"

"I reckon that's enough," Siringo said. "I'll get an outfit together and start up there after him tomorrow."

Browne stretched his arms over his head and yawned loudly.

"If it was me, I'd save myself a long ride and get him when he comes into town. He hangs around Bessie Scrivner's 999 Dance Hall."

Siringo got up to put on his coat. He fished a five-dollar gold piece from his pants pocket and sent it rolling across the table. Browne slapped it down like one killing a cockroach and put it in his pocket.

"Too much chance of interference taking him in town," Siringo said. "I want to arrest him and take him down the back side of the mountain and lock him up somewhere until he can be extradited to Idaho."

Browne finished the pint, drinking directly from the bottle.

"You could have a problem up on the bench, Siringo. The leasers might not let you take him."

That possibility didn't trouble Siringo. He paused at the door to smile at Browne.

"They can come along, too, if that's their play," he told him. "I'll take an extra pack horse that isn't skittish about hauling carcasses."

# CHAPTER SIXTEEN

Colonel Mears, spectacles propped on the end of his long nose, read the orders aloud, glancing up at Major Bertram Hildebrand and Captain Jules Duschene at the end of each sentence.

"You are to proceed via the most expedient route, with the forces you deem necessary to place under martial law, the communities of Wardner, Kellogg, Wallace, Gem, Burke and Mullan, in the County of Shoshone, State of Idaho. Upon arrival, you will place your forces under the command of Brigadier General Theodore Merriweather to support Mr. Bart Van Cleve, the governor's appointee. Mr. Van Cleve will formulate those operations he considers appropriate to put down an insurrection by the local citizenry."

Mears stopped reading and took off his glasses. He turned in his chair to check the lenses at the window. From outside, the sound of hammers and saws carried into the building. A dozen black soldiers were visible repairing the roof on one of the log barracks buildings, dating back to the establishment of Fort Missoula in Montana Territory, some twenty years earlier.

"There's more to this," Mears said in a resigned voice, "but that's the gist of it. Union miners in the Coeur d'Alene district are defying authorities and the United States Army has been ordered to get them under control."

"Who's General Merriweather?" Hildebrand asked. "I never heard of him."

Mears fixed his troubled eyes on Hildebrand, a forty-five-year-old career officer who had distinguished himself in the final campaigns against the Sioux ten years before.

"He's an old hoss who's been put out to pasture down at Fort Sherman," Mears said. "While we were taming the frontier, Merriweather was shuffling from one staff job to another. I don't believe he's ever commanded an infantry unit."

"Good thing we're not going into battle then, isn't it, Colonel?" Hildebrand said.

"I doubt that he'll give you any problems," Mears said. "I've already made arrangements for a special train tomorrow morning at nine. You are to have A, C and D companies on that train and out of here by noon, understand?"

Hildebrand came to attention.

"Yes, sir."

Captain Duschene stepped forward. He spoke in a soft, southern accent.

"May I ask a question, Colonel? Occupying white communities with colored soldiers; is that a good idea, sir?"

Mears fixed Duschene with a look of pure exasperation.

"What the hell difference does it make what color the United States Army is, Captain? The men of this regiment are soldiers; well trained, disciplined soldiers. Carrying out these orders may be more difficult than keeping Indians on the reservation, but these men are up to it. You're dismissed, Duschene."

"One minute," Hildebrand said, turning to Duschene. "I want you to find Sergeant James and send him to my quarters. Then assemble the company commanders and the non-commissioned officers in the mess hall so we can plan this expedition."

153

When the door had closed behind a tight-lipped Duschene, Mears waved Hildebrand to a chair, leaning back to loosen the top buttons on his tunic.

"Do you think our young aristocrat has a point, Major?"

Hildebrand shook his head and smiled.

"He'll never get used to serving with Negroes, sir. The army should have kept him in a white regiment."

"Then, you don't anticipate any race problems in Idaho."

Mears swung his chair around to gaze out the window. There was some horseplay going on, but the work on the barracks roof seemed to be proceeding in an orderly fashion.

Hildebrand rose to stand by the window.

"The only problem I see is the business of reporting to a general who's dancing to a fiddle played by a civilian. This man, Van Cleve, could be one of those political zealots who believes the army can move mountains."

Mears snorted, "Or, God willing, he'll be a lazy good-for-nothing son-of-a-bitch who'll let you do your job without interference."

"Yes. God willing," Hildebrand said.


Failing to find Sergeant James, Captain Duschene confronted Corporal Isiah Plummer, who was supervising a group of soldiers bucking cedar logs into billets to be split into shingles for the barracks roof.

"Have you seen Sergeant James, Corporal?"

Plummer avoided his eyes, looking instead toward the mountains.

"No, suh. He was by here a while back to see how we was doing, but I ain't seen him since then."

"How long ago was a 'while back,' Plummer? And come to attention when addressed by an officer."

Plummer pulled his lanky body into the requested posture and adopted an expression of deep concentration.

"I reckon it was about the time we started making shingles, sir."

Duschene pulled out his pocket watch. It was a few minutes before nine. "You haven't seen James in three hours?" Duschene said accusingly.

"No, suh."

The corporal scuffed his boot in the damp grass, making little muddy scars. The others in the detail had either stopped what they were doing or had slowed the pace of their efforts to observe Duschene's rising anger and frustration.

Duschene put his watch away.

"Plummer, I want you to take a detail of four men and a wagon over to Berman's. Bring Sergeant James back to the post, even if you have to hogtie him. Got that?"

"What if'n he ain't there, suh?"

Plummer's eyes wandered around the post, never coming to rest.

"Then, I want five black asses back here by the noon meal," Duschene bellowed. "If he is there, make that six black asses. Now get moving."

Berman's Mercantile was housed in a rambling clapboard building on a knoll a half mile west of Fort Missoula. Most of each month it served as a general store and trading post for ranchers and cowboys in the area, doing a little whiskey business with the soldiers from the fort.

On payday, however, it was inevitable that several gamblers and half a dozen women, usually from Butte, were plying their trades in Berman's large back room or in the several lean-tos behind the building.

Since the first of the month, it had been common talk around the post that one of the women from Berman's last batch had remained behind and that Sergeant Augustus James was seeing her at every possible opportunity.

Major Hildebrand had finished giving orders to the lieutenants and non-commissioned officers and was coming out of the mess hall with them when Corporal Plummer's detail returned. Seeing Hildebrand, Plummer wheeled the wagon around and stopped it across the parade ground from where the major stood.

In the wagon box, face down, arms pinioned behind his back, lay Sergeant James, with two disheveled soldiers astride his body. One of the soldiers had

155

an eye which was swollen shut. Private Stubbs, the post boxing champion, was bleeding profusely from a deep scalp wound.

Duschene came to stand next to Hildebrand, an amused smirk on his face. Both officers strode quickly toward the wagon.

James was quickly untied and those holding him down exited the wagon in a hurry. James sat up, looked around and jumped to the ground, ready to commit mayhem on the nearest soldier. The tall, heavily muscled sergeant advanced on Corporal Plummer.

"Turn around and come to attention, Sergeant James."

Hildebrand's sharp command transformed beast into soldier. With a precise about face, James snapped to attention, every inch a proper non-commissioned officer of the Twenty-Fifth Infantry Regiment; this, despite the fact that he was hatless and naked to the waist.

"Who gave you permission to leave the post, Sergeant?"

Duschene stepped forward, hands on hips.

James gave Duschene a dismissive glance before addressing his reply to Hildebrand.

"I didn't have permission, sir. I wanted to see my woman friend before we left out of here for Idaho."

"How the hell did you know about Idaho?" Duschene demanded. "We just finished issuing travel orders."

"The telegram come last night, sir. I knew about it then."

"Goddamn!" Duschene exploded. "Reading that telegram is going to cost you your stripes, soldier! That wire was official..."

"I'll handle this, Captain," Hildebrand said. "You've got more important things to do, so I suggest you start doing them."

Duschene turned on his heel and stalked away.

"Get into uniform, James," Hildebrand ordered. "I'll wait."

"Yes, sir!"

Sergeant James trotted toward one of the barracks buildings. He returned almost immediately, buttoning up a blouse that was tight across his big shoulders and bore no First Sergeant chevrons. His hat was nondescript and dirty.

"Mine are hanging on a nail at Berman's," he explained, coming to attention in front of Hildebrand.

"I'll send someone to fetch them, Sergeant. I need you here."

"In the guardhouse, sir?"

"Not unless you go back to Berman's. You've got a woman over there, eh?"

James raised his head, his eyes unwavering.

"Yes, sir. She wants to marry me. She's a white woman."

There was an unmistakable note of pride in this announcement.

"She wants your money, James."

Hildebrand sighed, meeting the sergeant's steady gaze.

"She's a whore. I can't think of a quicker way for you to ruin your career in the army than marrying a whore."

James stiffened. A spark of rebellion flashed in his dark eyes.

"Major, the army's got no call to mess with a soldier's personal life."

"I'm just giving you an opinion, Sergeant," Hildebrand said. "When we finish our business in Idaho, you can do what you damn please. Let's go. I want you to make sure the quartermaster is loading enough grub for at least two weeks."

Halfway across the parade ground, Sergeant James asked, "Does it rile you that I been keeping company with a white woman, Major?"

Hildebrand looked sidelong at James, giving him a slow smile.

"Your woman doesn't interest me, James, but I'd suggest you don't discuss her with Captain Duschene. I can't afford to have one of my officers die of apoplexy."

Sergeant James's grin displayed white, even teeth.

"You won't have nothing to fear from me, Major. All I say to that one is yes, massa, and no, massa."

# CHAPTER SEVENTEEN

From his vantage point behind a rocky outcropping, Siringo studied the area of the prospect through his field glasses. It was obvious that substantial progress had been made by Davis's employers. A sizeable dump already marred the mountainside and the maw of the tunnel was dark enough to suggest considerable depth. Pieces of rock strewn about the area, some far from the workings, seemed to suggest that these users were heavy loaders when it came to the use of dynamite.

Morning mists were still hanging in the aspens on the upper elevations of Bull Hill. The narrow draw in which the lease was located still waited for the sun. Smoke rose straight up from a fire where Siringo observed a man making coffee. Nearby, a dirty white tent, set on uneven ground, probably contained the camp's other occupants.

Some distance away, two mules grazed in the damp grass, creating a peaceful scene. Siringo eased a shell into the chamber of his new rifle, a powerful Winchester which used smokeless powder. He'd wanted one since they came on the market in 1895 and had used his Pinkerton expense money to buy it; a purchase justified by the potential hazards of the assignment.

Harvey Browne hadn't been sure whether Davis was working for two or three other men so Siringo decided to wait for the rest of the crew to stir before he approached their camp. In a few minutes two men emerged from the tent. Siringo raised his glasses again. Neither of them was Davis. One splashed water on his face from an enameled pan, the other went to the edge of the dump to urinate. It was cold enough that his piss steamed as it hit the ground.

Siringo leaned back against the ledge yawning sleepily. He'd traveled most of the night so he could reach the prospect by first light. The horses he'd rented were raw-boned, sure-footed beasts who seemed unfazed by negotiating mountain trails by moonlight. He could smell the coffee now and his stomach tightened with pangs of hunger. He found the bacon sandwich he'd tucked in his coat pocket and devoured it quickly, wishing he had some of the leasers' coffee to wash it down.

Davis appeared suddenly, coming up out of the bottom of the draw with an armload of firewood which he deposited next to the cook. Siringo waited patiently while the four men had their breakfast. When two of them finally climbed up the dump and disappeared into the tunnel, Siringo made his move.

Staying high, he circled the campsite, emerging from behind the tent where he would have a clear shot in case any or all of them tried to give him any trouble. Davis, squatting by the fire, finishing a cup of coffee, had his back to him when Siringo stepped into view.

"Klondike Davis, I've come to take you in. You're under arrest."

He made the announcement in a loud voice so there would be no misunderstanding about his sudden presence.

Davis spun around, mouth open, momentarily speechless. The other man lunged toward an old Springfield rifle lying across some pack frames near the fire.

Siringo thumbed back the hammer on the Winchester and placed him in his sights.

"This rifle'll knock you all the way back to Victor, friend. Don't push your luck."

"He's got me cold, Maloney," Davis blurted. "Don't get us both killed."

Davis dropped his tin coffee cup and rose to face Siringo. The sullen Maloney didn't move.

"Sorry we missed you in Idaho, Allison—Siringo."

Siringo smiled amiably and said, "I'm not, but that's where you're going for trial."

"Trial? For what?"

He affected a wide-eyed innocent expression which, on his hard face, was almost comical.

"Murder. Mayhem. Inciting a riot. Arson."

Siringo paused, swinging his rifle to cover the two other men who stood at the edge of the dump staring at him.

"Just sit down where you are, boys," Siringo told them. "Davis and I'll be leaving in few minutes."

The two sat down, curious, but not hostile.

"What's he wanted for?" one of them asked.

"Spitting on the sidewalk in Altman," Davis replied good naturedly.

"Ain't no sidewalks in Altman," the other man said.

Siringo motioned to the one called Maloney.

"You. I've got two horses up behind that outcropping. Bring them down here."

"Go fuck yourself," Maloney muttered, reaching for the coffee pot.

When he picked it up it exploded in his hand and the canyon was rocked by the report of Siringo's rifle. Maloney jumped up, a compact, startled man, covered with hot coffee and coffee grounds. He blinked furiously, trying to get it out of his eyes.

"You son-of-a-bitch!" he screamed at Siringo.

Siringo levered another cartridge into the breech.

"The next one goes in your brisket, Maloney. Get my horses."

Muttering to himself, Maloney scrambled up the steep slope. When he was gone, Siringo placed manacles on Davis, hands behind his back. He made Maloney help Davis into the saddle when he returned with the horses.

Davis tried one final threat to dissuade Siringo from carrying out his assignment.

"The union never forgets, Siringo. You take me in and you'll have to sleep with one eye open for the rest of your life."

"I do now," Siringo said. "Better mind your riding. You fall off with a foot in the stirrup, I'll drag you all the way to Florence."

He turned to look at Davis's former employers.

"This bird owe you any money? Where he's going, he won't need any."

They all shook their heads and watched him ride off, leading the second horse bearing his prisoner.


Florence was a dusty farm town chosen purposely by Siringo for its subdued atmosphere and the absence of impassioned, drunken miners on its streets. What he hadn't expected was a mob of impassioned farmers like that which was milling about in front of a hay and grain barn, across the street from the jail.

A tall man in faded bib overalls was standing in the back of a wagon, haranguing the crowd. A fat man with a full beard stood beside him, brandishing what looked like a goose gun.

Siringo kept the horses to the far side of the street.

"Looks like you've got a reception committee, Klondike."

"I been on one of those," Davis replied, "but the guest of honor skipped."

Siringo and Davis were greeted at the jail door by two rifle-toting deputy marshals. He presented his credentials and his warrant and was annoyed when they were snatched out of his hand by the taller of the two, who seemed openly hostile

"What's going on across the street?" he asked the shorter deputy, who seemed to have a more agreeable demeanor.

"They want two rapers we got in the clink," the deputy said. "Don't know why anyone would have to rape..."

161

"Shut up, Shorty," the taller deputy snapped. "Let's get inside."

As they were ushered inside, Davis grinned at Siringo and said, "All the things I done, I never raped no one."

"Be sure and tell the judge," Siringo replied, distracted by the presence of two more deputy marshals at the windows watching the lynch mob across the street.

City Marshal Terhune, a burly red-faced man, rolled away from his desk in a rush when Siringo and Davis entered.

"Whatcha got here, Bud?" he asked the taller deputy, ignoring Siringo.

Bud jerked his head toward Siringo.

"Pinkerton detective with a prisoner."

"I need to park him here for a day or two, Marshal," Siringo explained. "You can bill the State of Idaho when they pick him up. He's wanted for murder."

Terhune got out of his swivel chair and shook his head.

"I can't guarantee your prisoner's safety, detective. You're gonna have to take him up to Canon City. They can hold him at the penitentiary."

Siringo looked around the room and pointed across the street.

"Why not? Four rifles ought to stop that bunch in their tracks."

The city marshal looked pained and made a fluttering gesture with his hands that wasn't in keeping with either his office or his physique.

"Half of them people are my friends," he said. "I can't very well shoot them."

"Friends!" Siringo scoffed. "That's a lynch mob."

Terhune wiped his face with a blue bandana.

"Well, look at it this way," he said. "Them two back there don't deserve to live no how, for what they done to Emma Hetherton."

"Did they kill her?"

Terhune shook his head reluctantly, as though the victim's survival unfortunately weakened his argument for giving in to the mob.

"No, but they grabbed her off the street and dragged her into an empty box car and raped her. She said the old man done her twice."

The deputy called Bud stifled a snicker.

Siringo shot a glance at Davis whom the deputies had seated on a bench next to the bars of the lockup. He followed the conversation but didn't appear to be particularly worried.

Siringo strode over to the lockup and looked into the first of four small cells. Two sorry-looking suspects; a grizzled oldster and a frightened boy, barely out of his teens, sat disconsolately side by side on a wooden bunk in the vomit-fouled cubicle.

"Did your prisoners confess?" Siringo asked Terhune over his shoulder.

Terhune and the suspects all shook their heads in unison.

"They claim they paid her four bits," Terhune said. "She ain't too bright."

"God's truth!" the oldster exclaimed.

Shorty winked at Siringo.

"She give it to Bud for nuthin' at the turkey shoot last summer."

"Lock this man up tonight," Siringo told Terhune. "I'll take him up to the prison tomorrow. If I hear any shooting, I'll come back and help you."

"Well, I don't know..." the Marshal whined.

Siringo leaned into the Marshal's face.

"If I had your job and wanted to keep it, I'd mosey over there and have a talk with my "friends." I'd tell them that the population of Florence will get a lot smaller if they try to rush my jail. Where's the hotel?"

Siringo lay back in the tin bathtub trying to enjoy the bath. The water was cooling and the untrimmed wick of the lamp on the shelf above the tub was stinking up the small room. He was tired after the long ride out of the mountains and the muscles of his legs ached from gripping the horse to stay aboard on the steep trail.

The young boy, to whom he'd given a quarter to tote hot water, knocked lightly and appeared with a steaming bucket.

"Sorry it took so long."

He sounded a little breathless.

"Cook went to the hangin' and let the fire go down."

The hanging! Siringo came out of the tub in such a rush he almost tipped it over. He dove into his long johns, threw on shirt, pants and boots, grabbed his rifle and was out the door, almost knocking down the boy in his haste.

The first thing he saw in the gathering dusk when he burst from the hotel was a photographer's magnesium flash lighting up the front of the hay and grain barn.

The hanged bodies of the two rape suspects and Klondike Davis dangled from the upper window. A few gawking spectators stared up at them.

City Marshal Terhune and the tall deputy marshal called Bud observed from a distance. There was no sign of the instigators.

"I didn't hear any shooting," Siringo said.

The Marshal licked his lips and looked uncomfortable. Bud adopted an aggressive stance with his hand near the butt of the large pistol on his hip.

Finally, the Marshal said, "There wasn't any shooting."

Siringo restrained himself from punching the puffy red face.

"You just let those farmers waltz into your jail and take your prisoners—and mine? You are one sorry excuse for a law man."

Siringo ripped the Marshal's badge off his coat and threw it into the street.

Bud reached for his pistol but Siringo put the barrel of his rifle in the deputy's belly button and shook his head.

"How old are you, deputy?"

"Twenty-eight."

"Pull that iron on me and you'll never make it to twenty-nine."

Terhune picked up his badge and put it in his pocket. He didn't make eye contact with Siringo.

"Come on, Bud," he said in a tired voice and headed across the street to his empty jail.

Bud walked stiff-legged beside him, looking back once before disappearing into the jail.

Siringo took a last look at Klondike Davis's dangling body. Of the three, he was the only one who deserved the rope.

# CHAPTER EIGHTEEN

Major Hildebrand stood with General Merriweather and Bart Van Cleve on the platform of the Wallace depot, watching his troops debark from the Northern Pacific Train. This was something they had done on numerous occasions and they accomplished unloading of the heavy supply wagons and horses without incident.

It was three in the afternoon and though he'd met the general and Van Cleve less than an hour before, Hildebrand had already formed strong opinions about both of them.

It was obvious that General Merriweather, with his tailor-made uniform and well-trimmed beard, had formulated no plan for the occupation of the district. He strutted back and forth on the platform, outfitted with a cavalry saber which required his constant attention so it wouldn't drag on the boards, because of his short stature.

On the other hand, Van Cleve could scarcely contain his enthusiasm for martial law. He spoke glibly of wholesale incarcerations, military tribunals and mass deportations of union men. The man's fervor made Hildebrand worry about what was happening to America. But then, there was the destruction of the Bunker Hill mill. Somebody had to pay for that—but you couldn't convict everyone.

"Your Negroes are very good at unloading those wagons," Van Cleve said. "I'm sure we'll be able to keep them busy with construction and guard duty."

Hildebrand held his tongue, but some of the leering white infantry men mingling with the curious crowd of Wallace citizens begged comparison. General Merriweather had arrived the day before from Fort Sherman in Coeur d'Alene City, to the east of the district. His command consisted of two hastily assembled companies of garrison soldiers who were not sufficiently trained for duty in the Philippines with either the Idaho National Guard or the balance of Fort Sherman's regular army regiment already there.

Captain Duschene crossed the platform to give General Merriweather a snappy salute while favoring Van Cleve with a gracious bow.

"The troops are ready to move to the bivouac area, sir," he told Hildebrand.

Merriweather and Van Cleve exchanged a quick glance.

"The Fort Sherman troops have pitched their tents in the town baseball diamond," Van Cleve explained. "Your men, Major Hildebrand, have been assigned to a reasonably level area behind the laundry."

He waved his hand in the general direction of a brushy hillside which abutted the outskirts of the town.

"Of course, it's only temporary. Tomorrow, I want two of your companies to march to Kellogg and set up a permanent camp. General Merriweather's men will stay in Wallace to conduct their operations in Gem, Burke and Mullan."

Hildebrand looked at General Merriweather's florid face and uninterested eyes.

"Doesn't the train run to Wardner?"

Merriweather made a clucking noise.

"Come now, Major, your men look fit enough for a short march. How far is it, Mr. Van Cleve, five or six miles?"

"No more than that, General," Van Cleve said.

He turned his uncompromising eyes on Hildebrand.

"I want the people of the district to be fully aware of a military presence here, Hildebrand. That's why your men will march. Assign your best officer to command them. I want you to remain here as part of my staff."

My staff! Hildebrand bit down on a sharp retort.

"Yes, sir. If someone will direct us to the bivouac area, we'll set up camp. My men haven't eaten since breakfast at six o'clock this morning."

When one of the special deputies had been assigned to guide Captain Duschene, the men of the Twenty-Fifth Infantry regiment shouldered their rifles to march in precise formation through the mud of Wallace's main street.

Hildebrand, Van Cleve, General Merriweather and Lyle Gregory, representing the Mine Owners Association, adjourned to the barroom of the Carter Hotel to plan a strategy against the Western Federation of Miners and its members.

Though Van Cleve eschewed hard liquor, he stood for a round, ordering a sarsaparilla for himself.

"The first step, gentlemen, is to round up all the union men—union sympathizers and the like—in the district," Van Cleve declared, sucking noisily on his soda straw. "Once everyone is locked up, we can sort out the thugs and the agitators and bring them to trial."

He pushed his glass aside with a flourish.

"This will be the beginning of the road to the penitentiary for many of these union hotheads."

Hildebrand sipped a cold beer, secretly appalled by the complexity of the task ahead as envisioned by the governor's appointee. He wondered if the governor had any inkling of what he had turned loose on the hapless miners of the Coeur d'Alene. He tried to stifle the impending sense of doom which was engulfing him.

"You contemplate the arrest of how many people, Mr. Van Cleve?" Hildebrand asked.

Van Cleve was vague. He made a couple of gestures with his hands before speaking.

"Five hundred. A thousand, maybe. What's your estimate, Gregory?"

Gregory shrugged massive shoulders and spat something into the nearest cuspidor.

"Maybe a thousand. Plenty of them'll light out, now that the sojers is here."

"Where do you expect to house and feed a thousand prisoners?" Hildebrand asked Van Cleve.

He was thinking of the trouble he'd had ten years before taking care of two hundred renegade Sioux at Fort Keogh.

Van Cleve reddened and he banged a bony fist on the table for emphasis.

"Damn it, Major, this is martial law. I'm having copies of the governor's proclamation printed up right now so it can be posted where everyone can read it. If we need a building for a prison, we take it. If we need food for the prisoners, we take that, too. Isn't that the way you see it, General Merriweather?"

The general cleared his throat and fiddled with the buttons on his tunic.

"I would hope the townspeople will cooperate for a good cause before we're forced to confiscate any private property." he said.

"I'd hope the whores'd give it to me for free," Gregory said. "It ain't gonna happen, General. As soon as the roundup starts, you walk under a second story window in Burke or Wardner, somebody's liable to throw a bucket of shit on your nice blue uniform."

General Merriweather adopted an expression of genuine shock as he seemed to form a mental picture of such an indignity.

"Surely, everyone doesn't condone murder, mayhem and the destruction of property, Mr. Gregory."

Gregory stretched, leaning back in his chair to crack scarred knuckles.

"Maybe not," he told Merriweather, "but your sojer boys are gonna have to jab a lot of asses with them bayonets before this party's over."

They talked for another half hour when Van Cleve looked at his watch, telling them he'd promised to wire Governor Steunenberg when all the troops had arrived.

"I'd like a more precise definition of my duties here, General," Hildebrand said, as soon as Van Cleve was gone. "I'm sure we weren't brought from Montana for construction and guard duty.

General Merriweather cleared his throat.

"I'm sure Mr. Van Cleve was speaking in generalities, Major," Merriweather said. "God knows my own duties are less than clear. I'm afraid all of us will have to make up some of the rules as we go along. Eh?"

When Hildebrand had taken his leave of General Merriweather, who, like Van Cleve, seemed to have little to offer, other than generalities, Gregory volunteered to direct him to the bivouac area.

"It ain't that Wallace is so big you couldn't find two hundred niggers," Gregory chortled, giving Hildebrand a friendly punch on the arm.

Hildebrand stopped abruptly and turned to face him.

"They're not niggers, Mr. Gregory. They're soldiers of the Army of the United States. They may be the wrong color to pitch their tents with General Merriweather's lily-white troops, but if there's any real trouble, you'll be damn glad they're here."

Gregory backed away in mock fright.

"Hold it, Major. I got nuthin' against nigger sojers. No call to get worked up."

Hildebrand stalked away, feeling Gregory watching him. That made it unanimous. He didn't like any of them.

Captain Duschene's orders from Major Hildebrand were to set up a bivouac near the Kellogg railroad station while awaiting the arrival of Lyle Gregory and a group of special deputies who would arrive by train later that afternoon.

By the time he and his troops reached Kellogg, Duschene and his lieutenants had two companies of tired, disgruntled soldiers on the their hands. The distance, which Hildebrand had told him was six miles, was closer to ten and the march had taken over three hours, with full packs. The men's dissatisfaction grew when the word spread through the ranks that railroad tracks they marched beside actually carried trains which could have accommodated them. Duschene heard little of the grumbling from his seat on one of the quartermaster's wagons at the rear of the column.

Duschene directed the soldiers to establish their camp in a field adjacent to a large barn which served as a grain and feed warehouse. They had just begun to unload the wagons when Duschene was accosted by a portly middle-aged man wearing a canvas apron. He was accompanied by two teen-age boys.

"I'm Nels Grinstad," he told Duschene. "I own this here property."

Duschene stared at the man while trying to think of something to say. He was aware that Sergeant James, who had been supervising the hasty preparation of a noon meal, was watching him and, for some reason, seemed to find the confrontation amusing.

From inside his blouse, Duschene produced a copy of the governor's declaration and handed it to Grinstad.

"By the authority of Governor Steenberg," Duschene told him, "the Twenty-Fifth Infantry regiment, United States Army is confiscating this property, including your barn."

Grinstad's mouth dropped open before he said, "Our governor's name isn't Steenberg and what the hell do you want my building for?"

"To house military prisoners, Grinstad. If you have personal belongings or animals in there I suggest you remove them at once."

He turned to Sergeant James who was dispatching soldiers to rustle up some firewood for the company cooks who were unloading field stoves from the wagons.

"Sergeant, take a detail and secure the building."

"You got no right to do this, Captain," Grinstad muttered as he watched Sergeant James post a pair of soldiers with fixed bayonets at each of the building's entrances.

"I have every right, sir," Duschene said, turning his back on the perplexed merchant to walk stiffly away.

Grinstad followed him, trailed by the two angry-looking boys.

"Well, goddamn it, I got a right to know how long your prisoners'll be in my building."

"It's my understanding they'll be kept here until they can be brought to trial."

Duschene's attention was diverted by hooting and catcalls from a growing group of spectators, men, women and children. A sorrier looking lot he'd never seen, if you didn't count reservation Indians.

"Then, I expect your darkies will be sleeping and shitting in my yard until then," Grinstad growled.

"Let me tell you something, sir," Duschene snapped. "My darkies have fought Indians and renegades to make this country safe for fat worms like you."

He surprised himself to be defending his troops to another white man, but from what he'd seen of the Coeur d'Alene, they were beginning to look good despite their color.

"I meant no offense," Grinstad said in almost a whisper.

"I might add," Duschene said, adding a pinch of salt to the wound, "they aren't here by choice. What sane person would want to be in this shit hole?"

The train carrying Gregory and three dozen special deputies didn't arrive until early afternoon. It had been halted near the village of Osborn, three miles west of Wallace, by railroad ties piled on the tracks. While the deputies were clearing the obstruction, a force of angry union men surrounded the train, pelting it with stones and railroad spikes, breaking the windows in the coaches. The locomotive fireman suffered a serious wound after being struck in the head with a spike. One of the deputies had to shovel coal.

All of this was related to Duschene by an angry, red-faced Gregory, as his men stumbled off the train.

"We should have shot them sons-of-bitches," Gregory snarled, "but some of them was armed so I didn't want to start no war without the sojers."

"If my men and I had been permitted to ride the train, you wouldn't have had any trouble," Duschene said, watching the rough-looking men coming off the cars. In addition to firearms, many of them carried large wooden clubs tucked in their belts.

171

He didn't tell Gregory that the same group of union men had hurled racial insults and epithets at the soldiers when the column passed through Osborne at nine that morning.

"What's the plan, Cap'n?" Gregory demanded. "My boys want to get this roundup started so's they can bust some heads."

Gregory towered over Duschene, fixing him with a belligerent stare. Several of the deputies, bearing cuts and abrasions, seemed ready to advance on the crowd of onlookers so they could try out their bludgeons.

Duschene drew himself up to within several inches of Gregory's full height.

"There's to be no violence, if it can be avoided. Your job is to identify the union men, nothing more. You or your men break any heads and I'll place you under arrest."

Gregory turned to grin at his grim-faced crew of special deputies. He stepped closer to Duschene.

"Union trash gets its shit kicked today, sojer boy." Involuntarily, Duschene took a step backwards. He was aware that he and Gregory were the center of attention, not only from the deputies, but from his soldiers as well. He hated the skimpy hand he'd been dealt, but as a good officer, he had to play it out.

"I said no violence, Gregory. If you or your men start any trouble you'll be locked up with the unionists where you'll get your shit kicked, I'm sure."

"You don't lock up my men!" Gregory bellowed.

Before he could say anything else, the sharp point of a bayonet on a rifle in the hands of Sergeant James pressed into Gregory's meaty chin. He made a gasping sound and tilted his head back to avoid being impaled.

"Give the captain some room, mister," James ordered, keeping pressure on Gregory's chin.

"You black bastard!" Gregory roared.

He was almost on tiptoe, his head tilted so far back that his hat fell off.

"That's quite enough, Sergeant," Duschene ordered.

Duschene tried to appear unruffled, but could feel his heart pounding. Out of the corner of his eye he saw the deputies advancing. They stopped abruptly when Corporal Plummer slammed a magazine into the Gatling gun his detail was placing in front of the warehouse.

"If one of them men raises his piece agin the captain or the sergeant," Plummer told the gunner, "you be crankin' this piece 'til I orders you to stop, hear?"

Never mind that the Gatling's .50 caliber slugs would have mowed down the deputies and the gawking townspeople as well, Duschene felt he now had the upper hand.

"What about it, Gregory? Do you cooperate with the army or do I place you under arrest."

Gregory, rubbing the tender spot under his chin, stooped down to pick up his hat. His smile was obsequious.

"Aw hell, Cap'n. We got a job to do. We don't want no trouble with the army."

"Very well," Duschene said. "When my men have been fed, we'll organize squads to cover specific areas and begin a sweep of Kellogg and Wardner."

When Duschene had turned his attention to his junior officers to plan the roundup, Gregory sidled up to Sergeant James.

"I'm gonna stick a bayonet up your ass, nigger."

James smiled and put his hand on his crotch.

"Do it whilst I'm givin' Big Josh to your sister and I won't even feel it."

Several of the deputies who were standing nearby, snickered. Gregory, red-faced and furious, pushed them roughly out of the way.

It had been decided in Wallace that the initial sweep would concentrate on union men who had worked for Bunker Hill. Those who could be identified by Gregory and his deputies would be sorted out from the crews of the mines which had accepted union demands and were working.

It was Duschene, who fancied himself as a master tactician, who decided that the troops would quick-march the length of Mill Street to impress the populace. Gregory and his deputies would follow in commandeered wagons. After all, it was martial law, and as he understood it, he, as the man in charge of the effort, could do pretty much what he had to do to make it a success.

173

# CHAPTER NINETEEN

Amy and Johnnie watched Orchard pack his bag. John MacNamara had come by that morning to warn him that the army had arrived in Wallace the night before. He seemed oddly unperturbed. Orchard was annoyed that the big Irishman hadn't brought with him the envelope Haywood had left for him.

"Long as we go about our business and don't cause no trouble, I can't see them doing nothing to us," MacNamara had said by way of assurance.

He had also mentioned that many of the union men in the district had taken the trails over the mountains into Montana, where they'd remain until this blew over.

"MacNamara didn't seem very worried," Amy offered hopefully. "He ain't leaving, is he?"

"He's got a wife and four kids," Orchard said as he fastened the straps on his bag. "How could he go anywhere?"

"Well, what about us?"

Orchard placed his bag in a corner and laid his shotgun on top of it. Ever since he'd announced his intention to leave the district, he feared that Amy was going to place some kind of responsibility on his shoulders for her and her brother's welfare. That was the trouble with women; one fuck and they thought they owned you.

"The Army won't bother you," Orchard told her. "I'll give you some money before I go."

"What about Johnnie?"

"What about him?"

Johnnie, hunched over the table gnawing on a piece of stale bread, flicked his eyes from one to the other. This was the second morning he'd washed and gotten fully dressed. If his appetite was the sign of recovery, he was out of the woods, for he ate everything that was placed in front of him and rummaged through their meager larder between meals.

"If they start looking for union men, he'll be arrested for sure." Amy's voice had taken on a quavering note.

"Maybe he could hide under Bella's skirts," Orchard said.

"The army don't scare me none," Johnnie muttered.

He got up from the table and limped outside to sit down on a box in the sun.

Amy came to Orchard, putting her hands on his lapels. She was wearing the blue dress that Kate had given her and she'd taken care to wash her face and tie up her hair. It was as though she was presenting herself to him for his approval before proposing some kind of fragile partnership in which she felt she had earned a place by cleaning herself up.

"You're not gonna just run away and leave us, are you?"

Amy's desperation was making him very uncomfortable. He wanted to push her out of the way and escape the gritty confines of the shack. He hadn't determined how he was going to get out of the district but he was sure of one thing. He was going alone.

"Can't you say nuthin' to me?" Amy whimpered, tears filling her eyes.

He felt suddenly trapped and had to get out of there.

175

"I have to go to the union hall," Orchard told her. "We'll talk when I get back."

"You are coming back?"

"I can't very well go without my things, can I?"

Orchard gently pried her clinging hands off him. Outside, he opened his mouth to say something to Johnnie but closed it again. Nothing he could say would get through to him. Apparently, Johnnie felt the same way. The ungrateful bastard didn't even look up at him. To hell with Johnnie Neville.

Orchard slipped in the back door of the union hall. Fortunately, it was on a nameless street and backed up to a brushy mountainside which, though stripped of trees, provided some cover. Earlier, as he cut across Milo Gulch, well beyond the end of Mill Street, he heard what sounded like a bugle. That sound seemed to make it official. The U.S. Army had arrived, and as far as Orchard was concerned, the district would never again be the same for the union.

A few men loitered in the barren union hall, several playing checkers on an upturned barrel. One or two acknowledged him with a smile or a wave, but overall, the atmosphere was somber, as though they were waiting for the unknown.

He found MacNamara in the small office digging through a pile of papers. The Irishman jumped when Orchard opened the door.

"I was goin' through Allison's records," he explained sheepishly. "Wanted to make sure there was nuthin' here to do harm to any of our boys."

"Siringo's records, you mean," Orchard corrected. "I'm sure he passed any damaging information to Bunker Hill through Fatty Kincaid. You find any membership rosters, you should get rid of them, though I'm sure Frank Bromley's already got them."

MacNamara frowned and shook his head in a gesture of puzzlement and disbelief.

"How can a man do such a thing? Set himself up as a friend, burrow into the Wardner union like a wood tick and leave us at the mercy of Bunker Hill."

Orchard sat down in a rickety chair next to the desk. He noticed that the safe door was open.

"He was doing his job," Orchard said. "Just like the rest of us. I need what Haywood left for me, John."

MacNamara bent down to retrieve a manila envelope from the safe. He also dragged out a tin box and set it on the desk top.

"Dues money the boys paid in," he explained. "Don't know what to do with it."

Orchard was counting and didn't respond until he was finished. Haywood had left him two hundred dollars and had agreed to give him two hundred more when he returned to Denver. Even so, it seemed like a picayune sum for leading the charge that leveled a mill worth at least a quarter of a million. He'd have to ask for more on the next job.

He still had most of the bail money he'd taken the day he'd sprung Siringo from the Wallace jail, so he was going to be all right once he got to Colorado.

"I don't know what to do with the dues money," MacNamara repeated, tapping the tin box.

"How much is in there?" Orchard asked, wondering if there was some way he might get the simple Irishman to give it to him for safekeeping.

"About eighteen dollars," MacNamara said. "We already paid for the beer and the food for the May Day celebration and we had to give Duffy Hammond's widow forty dollars after he was crushed."

"Don't look like you'll be celebrating May Day, unless you do it with the army," Orchard said, "and you won't be collecting dues while men are on the picket line. If you don't want to leave it here, take it home."

At the sound of the front door banging open and loud voices, Orchard stuck his head out of the office door. Two breathless men stood just inside the hall, struggling to speak.

"We run all the way," one of them said. "They was quick-marching up Mill street."

"They got bayonets on their rifles," the other man gasped.

"What are they doin' with our boys?" MacNamara shouted.

"Nuthin' yet, but I heard they's gonna arrest the whole Bunker Hill crew and lock 'em up somewheres."

"Better get everybody out of here, John," Orchard said, making sure the Haywood envelope was tucked securely into his inside coat pocket.

The hall was emptying quickly. Orchard moved toward the back door. He would return via the same route he'd used to get there. He didn't want any company.

"It ain't fair!" MacNamara bellowed.

He stomped back into the office and plopped into his chair.

"I ain't goin' nowhere! I'm a officer of the Wardner union. They got no call to even come in here."

"Bad move, John," Orchard said, and was out the back door.


Before the troops had reached the end of Mill Street, which was up-hill all the way, they had attracted a hostile crowd of men, women and children who lined the wooden sidewalks and voiced their welcome in loud, vile language. This, in addition to fatigue, had a negative impact on their morale and attitude. On several occasions, individual soldiers had kicked at scruffy little boys who had run into the street to throw mud balls at their uniforms.

The deputies, who had trouble finding enough wagons to transport their numbers, were nowhere in sight. Since Duschene and his officers had elected to ride with the deputies, it fell to Sergeant James to maintain discipline. This he did with an iron hand, having the advantage of being respected by the soldiers. When some of them wanted to stop union men fleeing the Wardner Union hall, he kept them in check, not wishing to take on any responsibility which wasn't specifically assigned to him.

His orders were to quick-march the troops to the end of Mill Street and that was what he'd done. The order for the arrest and incarceration of white men would have to come from Captain Duschene.

Orchard could feel the sweat soaking through his coat by the time he reached a place where he felt safe. It was the site of an old mining prospect which overlooked Milo Gulch and gave him a clear view of almost the entire length of Mill Street.

He sat down on a thick timber which was entwined in a piece of rusty cable, peering out from behind a huckleberry bush. He lighted a cigar but his thirst made the taste rather unpleasant so he stubbed it out, saving it for another time.

By the time he'd arrived at his perch, the blue-clad army troopers had jogged past the ash heap that was Fatty Kincaid's saloon and were resting on the tailing pile at the end of the street. It looked to Orchard like a force of at least a hundred men. They had stacked their rifles in a series of shiny pyramids and were squatting or lying on the ground. Many were smoking, some were pissing and several had moved away from the main body to shit.

A few minutes later, the first wagonload of deputies came into view. The movement of the horses pulling the wagon was erratic as spectators lining the road threw an occasional missive at them or at the deputies.

The wagon stopped in front of the Wardner Union hall to disgorge its occupants. Orchard could observe arguments taking place between army officers and deputies but only fragments of their raised voices carried to him.

While he watched, a group of deputies charged into the building and emerged moments later, dragging a wildly struggling MacNamara. One of the deputies struck him on the head with a club and had raised it to strike him again when two army officers intervened. They helped him over to the wagon and assisted him to climb in, where he sat, head bowed and bleeding.

Two more wagons arrived and Orchard recognized Gregory in one of them. The men in these wagons paused only long enough to break all the windows in the union hall before moving on.

When the deputies and the soldiers converged, there was a brief discussion between Gregory and the officers before the soldiers formed ranks and began their march down Mill Street. Orchard observed squads of soldiers entering saloons or heading up side streets to the boarding houses. Men were dragged into the street, some docile, some fighting authority. More than once, soldiers stood by while deputies used their clubs to subdue the most violent of the prisoners.

Felix Magnuson's Billiard Palace was the site of the initial confrontation between the U.S. Army and the union. Captain Duschene directed Sergeant James and a detail of twenty men to be responsible for the arrests. Gregory and five of his special deputies would make identifications.

"Are you gonna be with us when we go in, sir?" James asked Duschene.

"I have too many things to do, Sergeant, to help you do your job."

With that, Duschene joined his lieutenants who were waiting for orders.

This was good and bad, James surmised. Good, because it was obvious that Captain Duschene had no idea how to conduct this operation, but bad, because James would be paired up with Gregory. He tolerated most white men, civilians and officers alike, but Gregory was a glaring exception. If there ever was a man who needed killing it was the head of Bunker Hill's special police.

James divided his detail into two squads of ten men each. Ten would accompany the deputies inside and ten would remain in the street, facing a hostile crowd of onlookers. They would be responsible for chasing down anyone who managed to escape the building and to keep any arrestees under control.

Captain Duschene marched the rest of his troops down the street, to send another detail, under the command of a second lieutenant, into the Oriental Saloon.

Magnuson's, a barn-like structure, was a favorite lounging place for the Wardner miners. It was busy when James and his troops entered, followed by Gregory and the deputies. Games were in progress at all four billiard tables and the bar was lined with beer drinkers.

Conversation ceased when the soldiers appeared. One could hear only the clicking of the ivory balls for a moment as the two groups stared at each other. James licked his lips and motioned to his men to take up positions at the front

180

and back doors. Surprisingly, the patrons gave way for the movement of the troops within the building with little more than curiosity.

Gregory's growl broke the silence.

"Them three at the bar."

James approached the men. This was the first time in his fourteen years in the army he had ever so much as given an order to a white man. He could feel sweat running down his back.

"You men are under arrest," he said in a firm voice. "Put down your beer and step outside."

A young man with tousled hair and a straggly moustache giggled nervously. "We ain't done anything."

Gregory rushed up to the men and bellowed, "You joined the Wardner union; that's what you done! Get outside."

He reached for the man's shirtfront to drag him away from the bar but James knocked his hand aside and blocked him with a hard shoulder.

"Leave us do our job, mister, and you do yours," James said. He blocked Gregory from any further advance.

The three men put down their beers and left meekly, escorted by two soldiers.

A tall man wearing a colorful vest and a derby hat came out of a back room. Gregory's presence in his establishment was obviously disturbing to him and from his expression, he clearly had never seen a black soldier before.

"I'm Felix Magnuson," he told Sergeant James. "This is my place. What's going on?"

"Martial law," James told him. "We're arresting all the Bunker Hill union men."

"Good God!" Magnuson exclaimed. "That's most of the men in Wardner."

"Tough luck," Gregory said. "Let's get on with this."

He swept the room with an accusing finger.

"Them two at the second table. That one settin' by the stove. Them four at the back table."

181

One of the men at the back table hurled his billiard cue at the advancing troop and bolted for the back door. There was a short scuffle with two soldiers guarding the door before he was marched with the others out of the building and into the street.

"Anyone else?" James asked Gregory, who was scanning the room with narrowed eyes.

"Yeah. Him."

Gregory nodded toward Magnuson, standing behind the bar, a look of outraged disbelief on his face.

"You can't take me," Magnuson protested. "I'm not in the union."

"You're a goddamn union sympathizer, Magnuson," Gregory said, enjoying the moment. "I seen the orders. We can lock up union sympathizers and that's what you are."

"Get going," James ordered. "Everything's gonna get sorted out later."

"Who's going to run my business? I'm here alone today."

Magnuson looked appealingly at James and glanced at Gregory and the deputies before he was escorted out.

"Drinks on the house, boys!" Gregory shouted.

One of the deputies ran to the cigar case and helped himself to a handful of five-cent cigars.

At the door, James paused to look back at the seven or eight who hadn't been arrested. They seemed to be waiting for the door to close behind the soldiers. Two of the deputies were heading for the bar.

"All right, everybody out!"

James unbuttoned the flap on his holster for emphasis.

"Right now!"

With more disappointment than hostility, the remaining men filed out of the pool hall. James went to the back door to throw the heavy bolt. Outside on Mill Street, he beckoned to Magnuson, standing with the growing group of prisoners, surrounded by soldiers.

"Everybody's out. Lock the place up. I threw the bolt in the back."

Magnuson searched his pocket for his key.

"Thank you, soldier. Those fellows would have put me out of business. Every dime I've got..."

"Just lock the door and get back in the street," James ordered, embarrassed by the proprietor's gratitude.

He turned to find Gregory staring at him.

"You're pretty big fer your britches," Gregory muttered.

"Big enough," James said.

He watched Gregory walk away. Yup. That man needed killing. James had killed half a dozen renegade Indians and had badly wounded a freighter who'd pulled a knife on him at Berman's, but he'd never killed a white man. Lyle Gregory might be the first.


Orchard ate a few green huckleberries to quench his thirst and re-lit his cigar. He found a more comfortable seating position and settled down to wait for nightfall, when he could return to the shack to get his things. He didn't relish the thought of hiking over the border to Montana, but the presence of so many soldiers made it imperative. It appeared that the Army had sent a force large enough to contain all of Wardner and everyone in it, and there were probably more in the other towns.

He was turning over his options when a crackling in the brush made him draw his pistol and crouch in a defensive position. In a moment Amy, sweaty and bedraggled, staggered out of the bushes. Her prized blue dress was ripped and there were scratches on her arms and legs. She ran to Orchard, threw her arms around him and sobbed.

"Oh, God, Mr. Orchard. I thought the soldiers had got you, for sure. They're goin' through town arresting everyone."

Orchard patted her back without enthusiasm.

"I know," he said. "I've had an orchestra seat. How did you find me?"

"A friend of Johnnie's was hiding under the union hall. He seen you come up here. What's gonna happen now? I'm so scared."

Amy continued to cling to him. He could feel every rib when he put his arms around her, hoping he could make her calm down without committing to anything that he couldn't easily renege on later.

"Look," he said, trying to sound sincere, "maybe I can scrape up a buggy tonight. The three of us can leave together."

Yes, of course. A buggy. Even better, Jesus might show up and pin wings on all of them so they could fly over the Bitterroots.

Amy leaned back to look at him.

"You're not just sayin' that?"

"Nope. That's what we'll do. Honest injun."

Her arms tightened around his neck and she kissed him hard on the mouth.

"Honest injun?"

"Yup. Now, you'd better get back. I'm staying here 'til dark."

Amy kissed him again.

"You won't be sorry, Mr. Orchard."

He watched her begin her trek down the mountainside, already sorry that he'd made her a promise he had no intention of keeping. He owed her brother and her nothing and would have been long gone if he hadn't responded to her initial plea for help.

He sat back down and buttoned his coat. The green huckleberries he'd eaten had declared war in his stomach, their muted battle cries heightening his overall discomfort.

The scene at Magnuson's was repeated dozens of times that afternoon until Mill Street was filled with shambling union men being marched to their new quarters.

As they neared Kellogg, Captain Duschene, dusty and perspiring, was comparing prisoner head counts with Sergeant James when their attention was diverted by a commotion further down the street.

"See what's happening down there, Sergeant," Duschene ordered.

John MacNamara had been pulled from the wagon in which he was being transported and was held upright by two deputies who had pinioned his arms. Gregory, almost nose to nose, was screaming at him. Soldiers stood by watching silently.

"Where's Orchard at?" Over and over.

James arrived on the scene in time to hear MacNamara say, "I told you, I don't know no one by that name."

Gregory backed off, exasperated and out of breath. One of the deputies lurched forward to kick MacNamara in the groin. The big Irishman dropped to his knees and rolled over on his side, drawing up his knees in agony. The deputy raised his rifle to smash its butt in MacNamara's face.

"Stick him, Stubbs," James commanded, shoving Private Stubbs toward the deputy.

Without hesitation, Stubbs put five inches of steel into the deputy's right buttock. The deputy yelped and levitated, throwing away his rifle. Stubbs's fellow soldiers lowered their bayoneted rifles to a ready position and faced an angry group of deputies.

Two soldiers helped MacNamara back into the wagon but when the limping, white-faced deputy tried to get in, James jerked him away.

Gregory picked up the flung Winchester and charged up to James.

"You'd let union scum ride and my man has to walk?"

Duschene pushed his way up to the wagon, staring at the writhing MacNamara, his face in a puddle of vomit.

"What's going on here?"

"One of the deputies kicked the prisoner in the balls, sir," James said, eyeing Gregory and the deputy warily.

"One of these black bastards stuck my man in the ass with his bayonet," Gregory protested, pointing to the deputy who had lain down on the wooden sidewalk, a large bloodstain spreading across the seat of his pants.

"The deputy was trying to kill the prisoner, sir," James said. "Private Stubbs done what I told him to do."

James braced himself for a reprimand. Captain Duschene rarely sided with him on matters of discipline.

Duschene nodded and turned to Gregory who looked like he was expecting justice, considering the respective colors of victim and the soldier.

"I don't want that man around anymore," he told Gregory. "Get him up to Wallace for medical treatment and then discharge him. We don't need his kind."

"We don't need your kind, neither, sojer boy!" Gregory said, pushing Duschene back with a big hand.

James stepped between them, hand on the butt of his revolver.

"Captain, permission to shoot this here white trash if'n he don't move down the road straight away."

Gregory backed off. He stalked over to the wounded deputy to help him to his feet.

"That won't be necessary, Sergeant."

Duschene turned quickly away but Sergeant James thought he detected a smile.

By six o'clock, there were two hundred and thirty-two men confined in Grinstad's warehouse. Outside, under the barrels of two Gatling guns, an unruly crowd of two or three hundred had gathered. They were mostly wives and children. Many bore parcels of food and blankets.

At first, Captain Duschene refused to allow the passage of any food into the warehouse until he was advised by the quartermaster that insufficient rations were available on the regimental supply wagons. Later, after a telephone call to Captain Hildebrand had revealed that the special train carrying additional supplies would not arrive until morning, Duschene relented again and allowed blankets and overcoats to be passed to the prisoners.

A large woman in a mended dress, carrying blankets and a basket of food, had screamed at Duschene, "My husband was in the army when you was a snotty-nosed brat, Captain. You really ought to feel proud of what you done today."

Mrs. Flaherty's outburst had precipitated the eruption of a prolonged torrent of abuse from the relatives, joined by the prisoners themselves. The men of the Twenty-Fifth went about their duties, trying to ignore the curses and epithets hurled at them from every direction, but many of them were hurt and confused, for this was like no other hostile engagement they'd ever experienced.

The last group of men, who were flushed out of several boarding houses, was herded into Grinstad's warehouse, after their names were recorded by Corporal Plummer.

Gregory came over to Captain Duschene who was fluttering around the company cooks, worried about the evening meal. Sergeant James, counting the names on Plummer's list, watched unobtrusively.

"I'll be thinkin' about you boys sleepin' on the ground tonight whilst me and my boys are rollin' around with Ellie Freshette's plump little gals," he told Duschene.

"White men gets fucked there for a dollar," he added, grinning at James.

"Ellie Freschette." James mumbled to Plummer. "Remember the name, Corporal."

He'd wondered about Wardner's sporting houses. He'd observed several female onlookers who seemed a bit too gaudy to be miner's wives. There could be no one here who could compare to the woman he'd left behind at Berman's, but there might be one who could ease the ache in his heart

# CHAPTER TWENTY

"Just what the hell do you think you're doin', John Neville?"

A bedraggled Amy stood in the shack's doorway, eyeing her brother. She could feel blood soaking her stocking from the scraped shin she'd suffered coming down the mountain, but that was minor compared to this. Her brother stared back at her with dull, drunken eyes. On the table in front of him was Orchard's open bag, clothing spilling out. In Johnnie's hand was a nearly empty bottle of Irish Supreme.

Amy couldn't believe what she was seeing.

"You'd steal from the only man in this damn town who might be able to help us get out of here?" she screamed at him. "Did you take his money too?"

"Only enough to have a little fun," Johnnie replied airily, taking a pull on the whiskey bottle.

"Fun?"

Amy gave him an astonished look.

"How can you have fun when every bum you know is probably locked up by now?" Amy took a breath. "What a stupid fool you are!"

She dragged a battered valise from under her bed, opened it and began gathering up her meager belongings from the box which held them all.

"We're getting outta here tonight," she warned her brother. "Soon as it gets dark and Mr. Orchard comes, we're leavin'. He's gonna get a buggy."

"I ain't goin' nowhere tonight," Johnnie declared stubbornly, lying back in the chair and holding the bottle to the light to check its contents.

"The hell you ain't," Amy shrieked at him. "You go out in the street, the army's gonna grab you. Tomorrow they'll be kickin' in the door."

Johnnie rose unsteadily and wobbled toward the door.

"No!" Amy flung herself at him, trying to restrain him.

"Leave me be, goddamn it!"

He shook her loose and when she charged him again, he struck her hard on the side of the head with the whiskey bottle. Amy collapsed at his feet and lay still, her body against the door. He stared stupidly at her for a moment before grabbing her ankles and dragging her away from it.

"Glad you ain't heavy" he muttered as he opened the door and stumbled outside.


Despite his drunken condition, when Johnnie Neville reached Mill Street he was immediately aware of the profound change which had taken place in Wardner in a single day. The street was deserted, without the usual clusters of men in front of the saloons. A number of places, like the Emerald Bar, were closed. Even the popular Oriental Saloon was unusually quiet, without the sound of the player piano which normally tinkled all day and into the night.

He was able to reach Ellie Freshette's without being apprehended. He had slunk along back streets which had no electric illumination and took advantage of a fist fight taking place in front of the Elite Grill to slip across Mill Street and into the Antlers Hotel. He was halfway up the stairs leading to the rooms occupied by Ellie and her girls when the door banged open and a group of men came in.

He rushed up the stairs and rapped urgently on Ellie's parlor door. If he could get inside, give Ellie a dollar to slip into one of the rooms with Bertha or Mae, he could go down the back stairs when he was finished. The sound of Lyle Gregory's voice made his heart jump.

"Well lookee here!"

Rough hands dragged him away from Ellie's door to slam him against the wall in the glare of the single electric light bulb dangling from the ceiling.

"If'n it ain't John Neville," Gregory exclaimed triumphantly. "MacNamara's errand boy."

Gregory looked down at him, amused, yet menacing.

"Guess the net didn't catch all the small fry."

The parlor door opened to reveal Ellie Freschette, a wiry brunette, tough as a sailor, hard as a wedge. She wore a loose-fitting negligee and was holding a cigarette in a long holder.

"Are you boys coming in or are you just gonna stand out here and cause a ruckus?"

Then she recognized Johnnie against the wall.

"You'd have been better off with the army, sonny."

"Close the door, Ellie. We'll be in shortly."

Gregory pushed her roughly back into her parlor. While she watched, he grabbed Johnnie by his coat lapels and threw him headlong down the stairs. They could all hear his collar bone snap when he landed, arms outstretched, in the doorway below.

"Gawd, you must have kilt him," one of the deputies breathed, running down the stairs.

Johnnie was trying to get up. His head hurt where it had struck the doorjamb. His right shoulder and upper arm were getting numb. The numbness turned into burning pain when the deputies, seeing that he was alive, picked him up and dragged him outside. They propelled him through the opening between the Antlers Hotel and the Miners Supply Company and sat him down on an upturned nail keg behind the hotel. His shoulder was beginning to throb now and he could feel a peculiar protrusion under his right lapel.

"Orchard wasn't arrested today," Gregory said, leaning close. "Where is he?"

Johnnie gritted his teeth against the pain. His body had begun to shake. "I ain't seen him."

A hard blow to the belly knocked him off the barrel to lie gasping in the accumulated trash on the ground.

"Where's Orchard at?"

The question was accompanied by a kick which caught on the left ear.

"God, I don't know," he screamed. "I don't know!"

Another kick. Another question. Another kick.

"Gone," Johnnie whispered. "Left the district."

"Get him up," Gregory commanded.

The deputies sat him back on the nail keg, head hanging, spitting blood and broken teeth.

Gregory grabbed his right arm and twisted it behind his back, clamping a big hand over his mouth to stifle his scream.

"I want Orchard. Where's he at?"

Johnnie raised his swollen head and nodded. Gregory released his arm and uncovered his mouth.

"He's been stayin' with me and my sister. He should be there now."

Johnnie's head dropped to his chest while sobs wracked his entire body.

"Take this bastard down the hill and turn him over to the army," Gregory said. "I'm goin' after Orchard."

Instead of returning to the shack by trying to negotiate the mountainside in the dark, Orchard took a trail high on the side of Milo Gulch which terminated just below the Bunker Hill workings. From here, pistol in hand should he encounter a watchman or a deputy, Orchard stayed in the shadows and worked his way down the hill, emerging behind the Wardner union hall.

The front of the hall was a mosaic of light and shadow, painted by a lone electric street light. The front door sagged open and shards of glass from the smashed windows glittered on the wooden porch. Inside, the place was a shambles, the floor littered with papers and broken furniture. A chair, tossed through one of the front windows, dangled crazily from the sill.

Orchard slipped across the street and took another path leading across the tailing dump. As he approached the company houses, he noted that light was coming from the Shanks house and that the front door was standing open. As curious as he was, he felt he had no time to investigate.

Halfway down the gulch below the company houses, he noticed the light in the Neville shack and could see people moving about inside. A queer alien feeling of impending disaster assailed him; so strong it caused him to stop to catch his breath.

Drawing his pistol again, Orchard moved quietly toward the shack. As he drew closer, he could see that the front door had been kicked off its hinges and lay on the floor.

He recognized Bella, though her back was to him. She was talking to a woman who was nearly bald, who held a kerosene lamp. They were joined by another, much older woman, who was crying.

When he spoke Bella's name from the darkness, she gave a small, startled exclamation, watching apprehensively, along with the others, as he stepped into the light.

"Oh, my God, Mr. Hogan, you scared me," Bella cried out. "I thought they might be coming back."

Orchard mounted the stoop, pushing past Bella and the other women. The stove lay on its face in a corner, soot and ashes tracked across the bare floor. The table leaned against the wall, two of its legs torn off. His bag and its contents were scattered about the room. He recognized a piece of the envelope which had contained the Siringo bail money. Then he saw Amy's blue dress wadded into a ball.

"Amy? Where is she?"

Nobody answered. Orchard took the lamp away from the bald woman, pulled the cloth aside which separated the two rooms and stepped inside.

Amy lay on the bed covered with a blanket. Shreds of her undergarments were strewn about in the tiny room. From the doorway, he knew she was dead.

"I heard her screaming," Bella whispered, "but there was nothing I could do. Three of them had her."

She turned away, shoulders shaking.

"I hid outside. I could hear the bedsprings creaking and them yelling and hurting her. Oh, God, it was awful."

The old woman put her arms around Bella and they cried together.

Orchard bent over the bed to look at Amy. Her head was misshapen from heavy blows which had left gaping, jagged wounds. Probably from one of the table legs. Blood spattered on the walls attested to the fury of the attack.

He raised the blanket and recoiled from the ugly sight of what they'd done to the rest of her. He turned away quickly to join the cowering women in the other room.

"Didn't anyone else hear her screaming?" he shouted. "Where were all the men; the scabs who weren't arrested today? Wouldn't they help her?"

Rage was becoming an inferno inside his body. He felt like he was going to explode. It was a strange feeling to be this angry.

"Wouldn't nobody come," said the old woman who was holding Bella's shoulders with gnarled hands. "My old man's terrible afeared of Gregory. Some of the others told Bella, here, that union folks got what they deserved."

"Gregory did this?"

The man was a bullying brute, but rape and murder? It was hard to believe, even of him.

"Him and two others," the bald woman whispered.

Bella looked at him, devastated, her face wet with tears.

"I tried to get help. I tried, but nobody would do anything. There are men living in the company houses after Bunker Hill evicted the union people, but they wouldn't come."

Orchard went to the door to look up at the lights burning in the company houses.

"I'll be goddamned," he muttered. "I'll be goddamned."

Something shiny lay in the sparse grass near the stoop. Absently, he went over to pick it up. It was his pump gun. A piece of the stock was broken off. He pumped out five shells and reloaded it. Without another word to the women, he headed up the gulch to the path across the tailing dump which led to Mill Street.

Kate was horrified to find him in her kitchen when Willi, the German girl, fetched her.

"Good God, Harry, are you crazy? The place is full of soldiers."

Orchard had seated himself at the kitchen table, the pump gun lying in front of him. He eyed Kate calmly.

"You entertaining colored boys now, Kate?"

"Of course not!" she said. "Do you want a drink? I need one."

"Not tonight," Orchard said, "but don't let me stop you."

Kate took down a bottle and a glass from one of the cupboards and poured herself a stiff drink. Orchard kicked a chair away from the table but she shook her head.

"There's two companies of white soldiers in Wallace," she told him between sips. "Some of them sneaked down here."

"How about Lyle Gregory? I'm looking for him."

"He never comes here," Kate said, pouring herself another drink. "I'd think he'd be the last person you'd want to see."

Orchard rose and picked up his shotgun.

"He and two of his deputies killed Amy Neville tonight. Tore her up pretty bad first. They were looking for me, I think."

"Oh, dear God! That poor girl. What's happening to this place?"
Kate sat down.

"Are you going to kill him?"

"If I find him and he doesn't kill me first."

"Try Ellie's place," Kate said forlornly. "I've heard he goes there."
Orchard handed Kate a crumpled wad of bank notes.

"Last favor I'll ever ask, Kate. I'll need a horse tied up in back in about half an hour. Send the German girl down to the livery barn."

Orchard opened the back door to check the alley. Before Kate could protest, he gave her a little salute and slipped into the darkness.

When the alley terminated abruptly because of the mountainside's intrusion, Orchard slipped through the space between two buildings to Mill Street. He stayed in the shadows, out of reach of the flickering street lamps. The street had never been this quiet since it was scraped out of the floor of Milo Gulch, years before. By the time he reached the Antlers Hotel, he was feeling less vulnerable and marched boldly in the front door.

Near the top of the stairs, Ellie's parlor door opened and three white soldiers pushed past him on the way out. They were too drunk to notice the shotgun he was holding close to his side. However, the hard-faced woman at the door saw it and started to close the door.

"Ellie? I need to talk to you."

Ellie shook her head and tried to close the door. Orchard placed the gun barrel in the doorjamb.

"Come out here," he whispered, "or I'll blow this goddamn door off the hinges."

Startled, she glanced over her shoulder before slipping into the hall and pulling the door shut behind her.

"Is Lyle Gregory inside?"

Ellie shook her head, her eyes darting to his shotgun.

"Him and two deputies was here earlier."

She took a breath and a shudder went through her tough little body.

"They grabbed Johnnie Neville and threw him down the stairs. Sounded like he broke some bones. I don't know where they went after that."

"I know where they went," Orchard said, turning to leave.

"If you find Gregory," Ellie muttered, "put one in him for me."

Back on the street again, Orchard was forced several times to step between the buildings to avoid confrontation with the occasional passerby who either

195

hurried or staggered along the raised wooden sidewalk.

He was debating whether to hide the shotgun somewhere to avoid looking so conspicuous, when a bald-headed barkeep at the Oriental Saloon came out on the porch carrying an empty beer keg. Orchard laid the shotgun on the window sill of Mother Atkins Luncheonette two doors away and stepped into the light.

"Would Lyle Gregory be inside, friend?"

The barkeep squinted at him.

"You're the fella I seen go upstairs at Fatty's the night of the fire."

"Is Gregory inside?"

"Him and a couple of others. You want I should unbar the back door fer you?"

"Can I trust you?"

"I ain't said nuthin' yet."

"That's why you're still able to carry a keg."

Orchard waited near the Oriental's back door until he heard the sound of the bolt being thrown. He gave the barkeep time to get out of the line of fire before he opened the door and went inside.

Gregory and his two deputies shared a bottle at one of the tables. Gregory saw him as he came through the door. Orchard fired twice as the three of them dove for the floor. Some of the pellets hit one deputy in the face. Blood spattered the wall behind him.

Gregory and the second deputy crouched behind the overturned table, opening fire with rifles. A heavy slug tore into the doorjamb near Orchard's head, sending splinters flying.

At the bar, the few patrons were climbing over each other to get out the front door. Baldy, the barkeep, watched, chin on the bar, half-empty beer mugs for protection.

Orchard fired again. Buckshot splintered the table top. Someone yelped with pain. Encouraged, he stepped closer and fired again into the welter of tables and chairs.

Suddenly a pain like a burn from a hot poker seared his side and the impact of a rifle bullet drove him backwards out of the door. He tripped over his own feet on the rear stoop and rolled into the mud of the alley.

Gregory and the bloodied and limping deputy stumbled out of the saloon's back door to peer cautiously into the dark alley. The deputy's left trouser leg was soaked with blood and a trail of it followed him.

"We got the son-of-a-bitch," the deputy croaked.

He seemed to be having trouble keeping his balance on one undamaged leg and was leaning heavily on Gregory, who seemed to be unscathed.

Orchard dragged himself to his knees, pumped and fired. The deputy took most of the buckshot and was propelled back into the saloon to fall among the furniture. Enough of it hit Gregory to drop him to his knees. He raised his rifle, fired a wild shot and crawled back into the saloon.

Orchard's pain didn't prevent him from savoring the thought of the damage his next load was going to do to Gregory's ass and balls. He pumped the shotgun. Empty.

He reached for his pistol but he was suddenly conscious of the sound of running feet and raised voices. Soldiers. Their lanterns bobbed like fireflies. Bayonets glinted in the lantern light.

Orchard dropped his shotgun and crabbed away, sliding into a mine drainage ditch running parallel with the alley. The murky effluent was neck deep and scalded the wound in his side, taking his breath away.

He moved down the ditch until the detail of black soldiers had pushed into the saloon. He dragged himself out of it and began to wend his way back to Kate's. Several times he had to stop where he could support himself and rest. He felt like a complete failure but conceded that only the soldiers' unforeseen appearance had prevented him from executing Gregory. He wondered if their paths would ever cross again.

Kate had a scrawny mare waiting for him, tied to the back porch railing. He'd given her enough money for a better horse and saddle than this one, but there wasn't time to complain. So she'd made a few dollars on the deal.

He didn't make it into the saddle until his third attempt and was getting

197

so weak from pain and loss of blood that he wasn't sure he could stay there.

He walked the horse, his head down, his legs dangling, pointing her up Mill Street toward the tailing dump.

# CHAPTER TWENTY-ONE

When Orchard opened his eyes he was conscious of only two things; a terrible burning in his left side and a strong, unpleasant smell. He tried to pull himself up to see where he was but the pain drove him back into the pile of straw he was lying on.

He rolled his head from side to side to assess his surroundings. He was in some kind of rough shed made out of weathered boards haphazardly nailed together. Afternoon sun penetrated cracks in the structure. He appeared to have found his way into someone's pig pen, but that didn't explain the blanket that was covering him.

He raised it to look at his wound and found himself heavily bound with strips of muslin bed sheet. Some blood had seeped through but he didn't seem to be gushing.

"Detail halt!"

The sound of the distant voice made him try to raise himself again to see who was outside. Soldiers obviously, but were they looking for him? The pain was too much. He fell back on his pallet with a groan and an involuntary exclamation.

"Holy Christ!"

A hand was clamped over his mouth and Bella Shanks was leaning over him. He could feel her breasts against his shoulder.

"Shh," she whispered. "Soldiers out front."

"Where the hell am I? Smells like pig shit."

"In the shed. I found you this morning. Your horse ran off. I couldn't catch her. Why did you...?"

"I wanted to see you."

"You're lucky you didn't bleed to death. Who shot you?"

"Gregory and his deputies. They lost some blood too."

Bella pushed her hair back from her face.

"I don't want to hear about it. I don't know what's happening. I think the soldiers are searching the houses looking for men without permits."

"What permits?"

Orchard pulled himself up on his elbows, despite the searing sensation.

"All the non-union men are being issued permits. Without a permit, you go to Grinstad's."

"Grinstad's?"

"That's where they're locking up everyone."

Orchard lay back to stare at the cracks in the roof shakes. Permits. It sounded like the ball game was over for the union.

Bella peeked through a crack to look for the soldiers. Orchard looked at her, admiring the color in her cheeks and wondering at the same time how she'd managed to drag him into this foul-smelling hiding place. If the army was searching for union men, smell and all, this was a safer place than the house.

Somehow she'd gotten him out of his coat and shirt and had unbuttoned and pulled down his underwear to bandage him.

To do that, she had to remove his pistol and shoulder holster. His pistol! He reached out to touch her arm.

"Do you have my revolver?"

Bella removed his Iver Johnson from her apron pocket, handling it like it was a dead rat. She laid it on his chest.

It would be small comfort against army rifles.

"Lie still," she told him. "I'll try to deal with the soldiers."


On the second day of mass arrest and detention, the men of Wardner and Kellogg were joined by several hundred members of the Gem and Burke unions. These prisoners had been arrested the day before and had been held at the Wallace ballpark, where the Fort Sherman troops were bivouacked.

Most of them hadn't eaten anything since the noon meal the previous day and brought bitter tales of sullen disregard by white troops for the prisoners and mismanagement of the Wallace encampment under the watery eyes of General Merriweather.

The army had employed the same technique in the Canyon Creek towns as it had in Wardner; a saloon-by-saloon search culminating in a sweep of all the boarding houses, company and private.

As each new group arrived, the prisoners huddled in corners, out of earshot of the black soldiers standing guard, to speculate on who had escaped the district and who lingered, as yet not apprehended.

It was noon, after some of the wives had been permitted to leave parcels of food, that word of the shooting of Lyle Gregory and his deputies reached the prisoners. John MacNamara heard about it from Jake Yancy, the rawboned, tobacco-chewing president of the Gem union.

"One of them deputies near bled to death," Yancy said. "'Nother one's blind in one eye and lost most of his tongue's what I heard. Gregory's in the hospital up to Wallace with buckshot in both legs."

"A more decent man it couldn't happen to," MacNamara growled.

He still bore bruises and abrasions from his rough handling of the day before. "Do they know who done it?"

"Fellow named Orchard," Yancy said. "Gregory says he was shot too.

Leastways, John, any more shooting and they can't hang nothing on us."

Bella faced Corporal Plummer between the house and the shed.

"Don't go any farther, soldier," she said, nervousness making her voice a little shaky.

"My orders is we search ever' house," Plummer said. "The sheds, too, ma'am."

"You take your men and get away from here," Bella told him. "My pig's got swine fever. People get it too. Makes them crazy."

"I ain't afeared of no swine fever," Plummer said, standing tall in front of his detail.

Before the soldiers could move toward the shed, Bella made a face and a growling sound.

"I think I've got it already," she gasped, advancing on the soldiers with her head lolling about on her shoulders. She twisted her face into a terrible scowl.

Plummer and his soldiers stared at her, wide-eyed.

"Don't come no closer, ma'am," Plummer warned, backing away.

He turned to his demoralized detail.

"Detail. We get's the hell away from here!"

He and his men moved off. When they were a safe distance away they all began to grab at each other and act crazy. Much shoving and laughter marked their departure as they moved down the narrow, rutted track in front of the company houses.

Bella watched them leave with considerable relief. She prayed that no one else had witnessed her performance.


Orchard, who had watched Bella and the soldiers through the space between the boards, lay back down. Despite the pain and his overall weakness, he was forced to chuckle to himself over her portrayal of a lunatic. There was even more to this woman than he could have imagined.

Bella returned in the late afternoon, bringing a bowl of bean soup, some coarse white bread and a half-empty bottle of whiskey.

Orchard dragged himself into the sitting position, the movement pulling a groan out of him which he couldn't suppress.

"Is that whiskey?"

"It's not to drink. It's for disinfectant. The bullet went all the way through, thank God. I wouldn't know how to get one out."

Bella held the bowl for him while he ate the soup and bread. It wasn't until he smelled it that he realized how hungry he was. When he was finished he held out his hand for the whiskey bottle. Bella gave it to him but he could see that she was displeased with him. He took a long pull on the bottle and handed it back to her.

"You didn't leave much."

"You could buy more. You took my money."

"Your money's in that feed sack you're using for a pillow. You were bleeding all over it."

Her tone and eyes were reproachful. Damn! Now he'd offended her.

"I'm sorry, Bella," he said, trying to sound contrite. "I wasn't accusing you of stealing it. My God, how can I ever repay you for what you're doing?"

"Keep your voice down," Bella warned stiffly. "I'm not doing this for money."

"Then why? You know, you're taking a big chance helping me."

Bella looked at him and pushed her hair away from her face. She bit her lower lip and shook her head.

"I don't know why, but I am," she whispered. "Now let's see to that hole in you."

Sweating profusely, eyes closed, teeth clenched, Orchard submitted to the cleansing of the bullet holes just below his rib cage. He couldn't help but marvel at how lucky he was that they weren't a couple of inches higher, where the heavy bullet would have gone through a lung.

Bella worked efficiently, glancing at him from time to time when he flinched. Her hands were quick and sure when she bandaged him with fresh strips of bed sheet. She even allowed him to finish what was left in the whiskey bottle.

"Mr. Orchard? Can you hear me?"

His eyes popped open.

"Honey, I'm perforated, but I'm not deaf."

"You have to leave tonight. The soldiers'll be back for sure. People are trying to sneak back into some of the houses and the men are being arrested."

Orchard reached out to touch her hand.

"Will you go with me?"

"No. I have to bury Ed and his wife before I can go home. That's where I was this afternoon. Making arrangements."

"When'll that be?"

"I'm hoping tomorrow. They tell me the graves are dug. There won't be any service." Bella paused, tears in her eyes. "I asked them to take care of Amy Neville, too."

"Bunker Hill's going to bury Amy? Her brother a union man and all."

"I asked for a favor," Bella said. "How much work is it to dig a grave?"

"Not as easy as filling one," Orchard said. "Have you heard what happened to her brother?"

"I heard he's in Miners Hospital in Wallace," she said, "but I don't know if it's true."

"You know, I think he told Gregory I was staying at the shack."

Bella gave him an alarmed look.

"You aren't going to...?"

"Kill him? No, they probably beat it out of him."

He closed his eyes to think about what he was going to do. He kept seeing Amy in her blue dress smiling at him. He pulled a bloody envelope out of the feed sack and removed some bills.

"I'm going to need some more whiskey for the road. Do you think your brother has any clothes I could wear?"

"I'll see," Bella said. "He was bigger than you."

"I'm not going dancing," Orchard said.


By late afternoon Grinstad's barn contained more than five hundred men.

The living conditions, overlooked initially by prisoners and troops alike, were becoming intolerable. Once inside the building, no prisoner had been allowed to leave for any reason. Only two meals had been served in thirty-six hours, both of which had consisted of sow belly and beans, eaten out of mess kits belonging to the soldiers. In both cases it had taken over three hours to get everyone fed, including the soldiers.

One end of the barn which had once contained stalls for horses, had a dirt floor. This had been designated the latrine area where the prisoners had dug shallow trenches and erected plank seats supported by boxes and barrels. It hadn't taken long for a sickening stench to penetrate the entire building.

The prisoners slept on the wooden floor, spreading the hay which was left in the loft to soften the splintered planks. A number of the men were in shirtsleeves, having been taken unaware by the fast-moving dragnets. The few blankets the wives could spare from the family beds were woefully inadequate for such a large number. Some had taken to emptying feed sacks on the floor so they could be used for bedclothes.

Finally, John MacNamara, Jake Yancy and Paul Corcoran presented themselves to the guards at the door.

"We want to see the officer in charge," Corcoran told them.

A private, his rifle at port arms, eyed the miners uneasily.

"You ain't comin' out an' Cap'n Duschene ain't likely to come in there, so's best jus' go back and lay down."

The other guard nodded his head in a gesture of affirmation.

"We want to see the officer in charge," Corcoran repeated firmly.

"And if you don't fetch him here, we're gonna burn down this here barn," Jake Yancey drawled.

"And it'll be your fault," MacNamara added.

The guard called to a passing soldier, "Go git Sergeant James. These mens goin' to burn down the barn."

The soldier took off on a dead run. The union men waited, without further threats to antagonize or unnerve the guard. Within five minutes the soldier was back, whispering something in the guard's ear.

"Then go find Cap'n Duschene," the guard ordered. "Don't say nuthin' about Sergeant James. Hear?"

It turned out that Ed Shanks was a lot bigger than Orchard. Bella had found a pair of rough woolen trousers, a flannel shirt and a canvas coat. Since Ed was to be buried in his only suit, these things would have to do.

Orchard was able to exchange his sodden trousers for the woolen ones unassisted but had to wait for Bella's return before he could get into the shirt and coat. The trousers smelled of camphor and the shirt of sweat. He had to turn up the trousers and gather the waist with his belt, but they felt good against his skin.

He was saddened that he'd have to leave his eight-dollar Sears Roebuck suit behind but it was a sodden mess. Worsted wool with a fine stripe, it always made him look particularly natty, he thought. However, sartorial elegance was low on his priority list, considering the hazards which lay ahead.

Bella returned with bread, cheese and a quart of Duncan and Duncan. She had also purchased a roll of heavy bandage material and a bottle of disinfectant.

Short of breath and perspiring, she was out of sorts when she slipped into the shed and tossed everything down on the straw beside him.

"I think I should disinfect your bullet holes one more time," she said, "and I don't want to waste any of your precious whiskey."

"I'm sorry to be such a damn burden," Orchard growled as he opened the Duncan and Duncan. "Maybe you should have just left me in the weeds."

"I hate it when grown men start feeling sorry for themselves," Bella snapped. "Sit up so I can take off your bandage."

Orchard watched her work, peeling away the matted muslin, careful not to hurt him. Well, she was hurting him but he was damned if he was going to let her know it. Bella had good hands, strong and efficient. A good woman with good hands. A gem indeed.

On second thought, his wonder at her goodness was a product of his own experience. He'd known a few women in the course of his travels, but none who would have done for him what Bella had. The "whore with a heart of gold" was a popular myth, but most of them whose beds and bodies he'd rented would have picked him clean and left him where he lay.

Others with whom he'd forged brief relationships—servant girls, store clerks, and one piano teacher—never expected to see him again, nor he they, so little concern was squandered on character. They used him as he used them until their paths arced away from each other. Neither goodness nor badness had time to flourish in the barren soil of these encounters.

"This is going to hurt."

Bella's warning pulled him out of his reverie. The sting of the disinfectant kept him there, eyes closed, muscles rigid. She patted the evil-smelling stuff on the entrance and the exit wounds, the latter twice as large and ugly as the round hole where the bullet had entered. Strangely, the fluid seemed less volatile than the cheap, unbranded whiskey of his earlier medication. He wanted to think that he was starting to heal but knew he'd be lying to himself if he tried to believe it. If he could avoid infection until he could find proper medical care, he'd be satisfied.

"Raise your arms, Mr. Orchard," Bella ordered as she prepared to bandage him.

He complied obediently and held his breath as she bound his torso with yards of gauze. Several times, when her hair brushed his face, he fought the impulse to put his arms around her. Partly because he didn't want to make her angry and partly because he realized that he must look like a gutter rat, hardly the guise for a momentary show of gratitude and affection.

"There," she said finally. "I hope that's not too tight."

"No," Orchard lied. "It feels fine."

Actually, when he tried to move, the pain was so severe that it took his breath away. To complicate matters, the tight bandage constricted his breathing so much that he feared he might suffocate if he had to run for it.

"I was watching you," Orchard said, trying to expel as little air as possible. "You have good hands."

"Seamstress hands," Bella said, extending them, fingers apart. "Not good at much else."

"Don't sell yourself short, Bella."

She helped him into the shirt and coat, buttoning him up as one might a child, before sending him off to school.

"I'll see if I can find a hat," Bella told him, "and I'll make something for our supper."

"I'm not very hungry."

He was anxious for her to go into the house so he could take a couple of serious drinks of the whiskey she'd bought for him, hoping they would numb the burning in his side.

At the shed door, Bella demonstrated that she could count clairvoyance as another of her skills.

"Go easy on the liquor, Mr. Hogan," she told him. "I'm going to help you walk but you have to be able to move your legs."

Orchard put the cork back in the bottle and laid it aside.

"Fair enough," he told her. "Helping a drunk across the tailing pile in the dark is too much for anyone to ask."

"It's all right, Mr. Hogan," she said.

"Bella, would you do one more thing for me?"

"I need to know what it is."

"Call me Tom."

For the first time that day, she smiled.

"I'll try, Tom."

While she was gone, Orchard checked his revolver, making sure there was no mud in the barrel. He broke it open to extract all the cartridges and clean them, using a piece of the bloody bandage Bella had replaced. If he made it to the livery barn and could rent a rig, anyone who got in his way would have to kill him to keep him in Wardner.

Captain Duschene wrinkled his nose distastefully. The rank odor coming from the barn was overpowering. He had just started his dinner when Private Daniels had summoned him. At first he'd refused to be coerced until Daniels repeated the miners' threat to fire the structure. Having observed the awesome destruction wreaked on the Bunker Hill mill, he knew his prisoners were capable of almost any violent act.

Duschene stood rigidly on the slanting wagon ramp at the side of the barn while Corcoran, MacNamara and Yancey were led outside, under the bayonets of four soldiers.

"Which one of you men is threatening arson against this stockade?"

Corcoran stepped forward.

"We wanted to be sure you'd meet with us, Captain."

Duschene's soft mouth became a thin line.

"You men had better understand something right now. Under conditions of martial law I'm empowered to shoot anyone who incites a riot or commits any unlawful act against the U.S. Army or its property."

He took a deep breath.

"Do you want to be shot?"

"We want to be treated like human beings," Corcoran said. "You've got five hundred men penned up in here like animals."

"From what I've seen," Duschene sniffed, "you are animals."

"Do your orders call for you to starve us to death? Did your superiors tell you to make us drown in our own shit?"

Corcoran took a step toward Duschene. Four bayonets were leveled at his belly.

"You brought this on yourselves. I'm only doing my duty," Duschene replied defensively.

"How long we gonna be locked up in your 'stockade'?" MacNamara demanded, ignoring the tense soldiers. "We got families."

Duschene turned away and the soldiers prepared to escort the miners back into the barn.

"I have no idea," he said. "That's up to General Merriweather and the powers that be."

"And who might they be?" Corcoran said. "The Mine Owners Association?"

"Maybe we need to talk to General Merriweather," Jake Yancey said. "Bet he don't know you're starvin' us."

Duschene's tone reflected his own frustration.

"Nobody's going to starve, damn it! It takes time to work out the details."

"You done all right with your own details," MacNamara said. "We see those black fellers sloppin' up sow belly and beans."

"They aren't prisoners," Duschene muttered, before ordering the guards to escort the miners back into the barn.

Back in his tent, Duschene found that he had lost his appetite for the rest of his cold dinner. He summoned his orderly to take it away while he rummaged in his campaign chest for a bottle of sherry. He wanted to have a cup or two before he walked over to the O.N.&R. depot to telephone Major Hildebrand in Wallace.

Sergeant James and Corporal Plummer, conspicuous for their black skins rather than their blue uniforms, drank whiskey with a beer wash at McFee's Double Eagle. They had slipped away from the encampment in the late afternoon, after the last batch of union men had been placed in the stockade.

They had gone up Mill Street to a point where Milo Gulch widened enough to accommodate a second narrow street, lined with dingy saloons, secondhand stores and several cribs, all squatting against the mountainside. Now, two hours later, they were gloriously drunk.

Several of the special deputies, whom James recognized, were lounging at McFee's bar. A few others played cards in the back of the dimly lighted room. No one had spoken to them since their arrival. McFee had served them with studied indifference.

"What you think, Sarge? We gonna ask about that whorehouse or not?"

Corporal Plummer hunched on the bar, on folded arms, yellow eyes staring at nothing.

James downed his whiskey with a restrained shudder and took a deep swallow of beer to neutralize the burning sensation.

"Plenty of time, Plummer. I'm waitin' fer one of these brave deputies to buy us a drink."

Plummer snorted, finding the remark particularly amusing.

"Gonna be Christmas day, Sergeant, 'fore anybody in this place buys you a glass of water."

James rotated his body so he was facing the room, elbows on the bar. McFee and his patrons reminded him of the white sharecroppers who used to drive their wagons into Tuscaloosa on a Saturday morning. He felt the same contempt for these vacant-eyed men that his father, a houseman and butler all of his life, had felt for poor whites in Alabama.

"Vultures," James muttered to himself, "picking at the dead meat."

"You say somethin', Sarge?"

James shook his head and faced the bar again. Plummer's glass was still empty and McFee was engaged in quiet conversation with one of the deputies.

"Don't seem eager to serve us, does he?" James said, jerking his head in the direction of the man.

He picked up Plummer's glass and dropped it behind the bar, where it clattered noisily on the duckboards.

McFee bustled toward them, stooping to pick up the glass on the way.

"Another round, my man," James told him, "and a clean glass for the Corporal, if you please."

"I ain't your man," McFee said, placing the glass in front of Plummer. "You want another drink, it's outta this or nuthin'."

James looked at him, half amused. The stocky, unshaven McFee, jaw outthrust, returned his stare.

"Corporal, this fat little man here needs a shave. You got your razor?"

211

Plummer grinned, displaying a gold incisor.

"Do a bear shit in the woods?"

He reached into his boot to produce a folding straight razor with a mother-of-pearl handle. He slapped it into James's outstretched palm.

McFee's eyes were glued to the shiny blade when it was revealed in a quick flash. James leaned toward him, took him by the shirt front and pulled him against the bar. Several of the deputies were watching but made no move to interfere.

"Now, mister, you bring us a clean glass and hustle us some drinks or I'm gonna shave you, with just your sweat for lather."

McFee pulled away, causing a shirt button to pop off and land on the bar.

"Don't threaten me, nigger. I'll have these deputies throw you two out in the street."

James gave Plummer an astonished glance.

"Did you hear that, Plummer? This gentleman called me a nigger."

Plummer gave McFee a long, appraising look.

"This ugly little horse turd?"

James nodded, unbuttoning the flap on his holster.

"Says he's gonna sic these brave deputies on us."

At the card table, one of the players reached for a Winchester standing in a corner. James waggled a finger at him.

"Just keep playin' your hand, friend. You touch that rifle and I'll kill everybody in the room."

McFee raised his hands in a placating gesture.

"I don't want no trouble, soldiers. Drinks comin' right up."

When McFee returned with two whiskeys in clean glasses and two fresh schooners of beer, James gave him a pleasant smile.

"Now my man, a question. We've heard of a place where two lonely soldiers could find a woman. Ellie Frenet's?"

"Naw," McFee said. "Ellie Freschette's. Up the street to the Antlers Hotel. Her rooms is upstairs. Buck a ride, I'm told."

"Well then, them grateful ladies'll take us for free."

James tossed down some coins for the drinks, leaving an extra nickel.

"A little something for your hospitality, Mr. McFee."


Duschene could feel his face growing hot. Major Hildebrand's responses were curt and impatient, as though he had far more important things to worry about than Duschene's problems.

"I've been trying to conserve my supplies, Major. I have barely enough rations for my men."

Hildebrand's irritation crackled in the receiver.

"Conserving your supplies! For Christ's sake, Duschene, you're camped next to a railroad track. General Merriweather's detachment has enough supplies for a regiment. You have the authority to requisition from the company stores. After all, they're the ones who wanted martial law. Do I have to wipe your ass for you? Your prisoners are to be fed at least two times a day and three, when you have enough rations, understand?"

"Yes sir. I have another question. Are the prisoners to have latrine privileges?"

"What the hell are latrine privileges, Captain Duschene? You mean are they allowed to move their bowels?"

"I mean, we only have enough latrines for the troops."

There was a long pause before Hildebrand replied.

"Where...what are the prisoners doing? Carrying it around in their pants?"

"They're doing their business in the barn, sir."

Duschene experienced a strange sensation. It was as though he was becoming physically smaller the longer he spoke with Hildebrand.

Another pause. Then...

"Duschene, you're a Captain in the United States Army. Can't you summon enough imagination to deal with that problem, Goddamn it? At daybreak, you turn out some prisoner details to dig latrines. Those men know how to dig. That's how they make their living. Can you handle that?"

"Yes, sir. One more question."

"If you find any silver while you're digging, you can keep it, Duschene."

With that, Hildebrand hung up.

Sergeant James and Corporal Plummer found the Antlers Hotel without difficulty, mounting the stairs two at a time. In the second-floor hallway, Ellie Freschette's uneasy appraisal took some of the edge off their appetites. She had popped into her small parlor the moment they'd stepped inside. Hands on hips, dangling cigarette, in a flowered kimono, she presented a formidable obstacle.

"I reckon you boys are just as much entitled to a good time as anyone else," she told them, "but some of my girls might not feel that way."

The soldiers faced her awkwardly, hats in hand. Plummer yawned and put his hat back on.

"Come on, Sarge. We ain't wanted here no how."

James didn't move.

"Why not ask the girls, ma'am?"

"All right, I will."

Ellie shrugged her bony shoulders.

"They should get used to seeing a few of you colored boys around here, now that the whole district's locked up."

James stepped around her to take a seat on a plush settee and lean back like a pasha.

"Who knows?" he said. "We might even be more welcome than white men before this here martial law's over with."

"I'm just trying to keep everybody happy, honey," Ellie said. "You boys do take a little getting used to. I'll get Bertha for you."

"Come on in here, Plummer," James ordered.

Corporal Plummer, who had remained in the hall, came into the parlor. He didn't sit down, but stood at the side of the room, pocketbook in hand.

Ellie returned with a large, bovine young woman in tow. From her expression it was apparent that she wasn't keen on servicing members of the Twenty-Fifth Infantry Regiment.

"This here's Bertha, boys," Ellie announced, giving the girl's upper arm a friendly pinch which made her wince. "The price is three dollars."

The girl pulled away from Ellie, her coarse features twisting into a petulant frown.

"Why pick on me, Ellie? Why not Pearl? She ain't even earning her keep."

"Go get her," Ellie ordered impatiently, clearly eager for this transaction to be concluded as soon as possible.

Bertha and Pearl were preceded by their breathless voices as they came down the hall. Ellie stepped out of the parlor to add some weight to the argument. She had taken the girl in after Fatty Kincaid's saloon had burned to the ground and it was time she showed some gratitude. Most of Pearl's hair had burned down to a frizzy mat on her head and she'd suffered bruises and abrasions escaping the fire. Now with a silk scarf tied around her head and her scrapes hidden under a coating of powder, there was no reason why she couldn't begin to earn some money to pay her way.

James and Plummer watched the confrontation in the hall.

"She got somethin' wrong with her haid," Plummer whispered when Pearl came into view.

The white scarf around her head did resemble a bandage.

When Ellie pushed the girl into the parlor, James took a long look and shook his head.

"This one don't have no hair," he told Ellie. "For my three dollars, I want one with hair on both ends."

"I ain't screwin' no niggers!" Pearl yelled and flounced out of the parlor with Ellie at her heels.

James bit the end off a cigar, lit it and sat back on the settee in a cloud of smoke. Plummer remained standing.

"You still of a mind, Plummer?"

"I reckon."

Ellie returned, red-faced and breathing hard.

"Pearl's changed her mind, boys. Who wants to go first?"

215

"Go ahead, Plummer," James said, stretching his legs out in front of him. "I'm gonna finish my seegar."

Orchard leaned heavily on Bella as they stood in the shadows, across the street from the livery barn. If it hadn't been for the whiskey and Bella's strong support, he knew he would have never made it across the tailing dump.

There were few people on the street and they had hidden between two buildings when a squad of soldiers passed, led by a young and very angry-looking Captain. Orchard was less worried about the army than he was about the special deputies, some of them drunk, staggering in and out of the few open saloons. All armed. All dangerous.

"Bella, I can make it from here. They catch us and you'll go to jail."

"I'll help you across the street," Bella whispered. "Pull your hat down."

Bella had found a shapeless felt hat for him, so large that he'd shimmed the sweatband with newspaper so it would fit. She reached up and tugged at the floppy brim until it was so far down over his eyes that he couldn't see anything. Orchard pushed her hands away, trying to be gentle, but annoyed that she thought he was so dependent on her that she had to fix his attire.

"No. I'll be fine."

He pushed away from her to stand, unaided. His side burned as from a saber thrust. He was a long way from fine.

"You're a hell of a woman, Bella. I hope we'll meet in Colorado."

Bella closed her eyes and shook her head. She looked like she was about to cry.

"It's the wrong time for us, Tom."

"Maybe I'm just the wrong man for you."

"Maybe."

"Then why are you helping me?"

"I'm doing it for Amy Neville. Maybe you'll get the bastards who killed her."

"Might have gotten one already. Listen, I left some money for you in the shed. It's under a feed sack."

"You didn't have to do that."

"You didn't have to help me."

Orchard leaned over and kissed Bella on the cheek.

"Goodbye for now, Bella."

He moved off the sidewalk and into the street. His gait was unsteady but he made it across and entered the livery barn. Once inside, he looked back. Bella was gone.

Between the copious amounts of liquor he'd consumed and the heat in the parlor, James could feel himself getting sleepy as soon as he was comfortably seated. He dropped his cigar into the nearest cuspidor so it wouldn't burn a hole in his uniform should he drift off. And drift off he did, waking when a perplexed-looking Plummer entered the parlor, followed by Ellie Freschette.

James stretched his arms toward the ceiling.

"You're next, soldier," Ellie said. "You can pay me."

"How was it, Plummer?"

"Like a horse collar," Plummer muttered, "and that whore done stoled my pocketbook and now she say she don't know nuthin' about it."

"My girls never steal nuthin'," Ellie said. "Are you going or not?"

"Which room is she in?"

James was on his feet, wide awake.

"I don't want any trouble," Ellie shouted. "The two of you, get the hell out of here!"

"In a minute, madam," James said. "Which room, Plummer?"

"I'll show you, Sarge."

With Ellie following them down the hall, Plummer led James to the locked door of Pearl's room. James knocked loudly. No response. James kicked the door open, splintering the doorjamb.

Pearl sat on the bed retying her head scarf.

James stuck out a big hand and wiggled his fingers.

"Get out!" she screamed. "He got what he paid for."

217

"Hand over Plummer's pocketbook," James demanded.

"I don't know nothing about it," Pearl said, concentrating on tying the scarf.

James slapped her with an open palm, so hard it knocked her off the bed, causing her to bang her head against the wall.

"Hand it over, you goddamn white trash bitch!" James roared. "I'll twist your sorry head off and throw it at your dyin' ass."

Pearl scrambled to her knees, a shocked look on her face, as though no one had ever struck her that hard. She reached under the edge of the mattress.

"All right! Here it is!"

James was momentarily diverted by Plummer's shouted warning. When he looked back at Pearl Singleton, her derringer exploded in his face. The heavy bullet struck him in the chest. He stumbled backward as her second shot missed Plummer, tearing into the door frame next to his head.

James sat down hard, pinning Ellie Freschette against the wall. He rolled on his side, drawing his revolver almost by reflex alone. Pearl covered her face with both hands to try to stop the bullet which passed between her fingers, splattering the wallpaper behind her with blood and brains.

Orchard leaned against a stanchion to watch the elderly stable hand put the horse between the shafts of a small buckboard. His shirt was sticky to the touch in spite of the heavy wrapping around his torso. If he could make it into the buckboard's seat he'd be all right, he told himself. Somehow, sitting down was less painful than standing.

The stable hand had just finished when Orchard heard the shots. Three of them, from somewhere fairly close by.

"Somebody won't see mornin'" the old man said, looping the reins around the whip socket. "What you aimin' to haul in this here wagon?"

"A casket," Orchard told him.

He slipped his bottle into a coat pocket and dug some bills out of his pants which he handed to the old man.

"More'n one day is extra," the stable hand warned.

"Yes, dad, you told me," Orchard said. "There's an extra dollar there for you. Now, give me a hand up."

He braced himself on the old man's shoulder to hoist his body into the seat. Sitting down hurt to beat hell, but once in position, with his feet against the floor board, the pain seemed to diminish. He took out the bottle and had one for the road.

He drove slowly down the strangely quiet Mill Street. A few armed men were in evidence here and there, but no one gave him so much as a second look, much to his relief. Though his pistol was handy, he hoped he wouldn't have to use it. Sitting high in the buckboard made him an ideal target for only a fair shot, armed with a Winchester.

The four soldiers and the young captain came out of the Oriental saloon a few yards ahead of him. Orchard debated with himself over the wisdom of whipping the horse and galloping past the detail or proceeding at an unhurried pace. He elected the latter.

As he came abreast of the soldiers, the captain raised his hand in a restraining gesture.

"You, there. Halt and identify yourself."

Orchard stopped the buckboard. He held the reins in his left hand, his right inches from the butt of his Iver Johnson.

The captain had started toward him when one of the soldiers pointed up Mill Street.

"Yo. Here come Plummer."

Over the pounding of his heart, Orchard heard the running footsteps behind him. Before he could turn to see who it was, a breathless Corporal Plummer rushed up to Captain Duschene.

"Where the hell have you been, Corporal?"

"Suh," the corporal gasped. "A whore done shot Sergeant James. Dey both daid."

The captain gave Orchard an impatient wave of dismissal and turned his full attention to the corporal.

"Where?"

Orchard flipped the reins and steered around the soldiers. Some anonymous whore had been his guardian angel.

Major Hildebrand, speechless with anger and numbed by an overwhelming sense of loss, stared at Sergeant James's sprawled body. The room was heavy with the odor of blood and gunpowder. There was no sound, save the breathing of the soldiers. The blonde whore, shot between the eyes, lay between the bed and the wall, one black stockinged leg pointed toward the ceiling.

Several hours had elapsed since the shooting. After he'd received the telephone call from a rattled Captain Duschene, Hildebrand had commandeered a railroad hand car, propelled by two sweating soldiers. Since it was downhill most of the way, he'd arrived at Kellogg station less than half an hour after leaving Wallace. A quartermaster wagon had delivered him to the Antlers Hotel, where Duschene and his detail were waiting. He was soon followed by a platoon of soldiers under the command of one of Duschene's lieutenants.

Hildebrand backed out of the room, trying to decide what to do. The best soldier in the regiment had been murdered by a common prostitute over Corporal Plummer's pocketbook which, it turned out, contained four dollars. He glanced at Duschene, standing shocked and silent beside Ellie Freschette in the narrow hallway. Had the fancy-pants son-of-a-bitch been capable of imposing discipline on his soldiers or, at least, winning their respect, Sergeant James would still be alive.

"Get the sergeant's body downstairs," Hildebrand ordered in a tight, unnatural voice.

He waited stiffly for three soldiers to pick up James's body and carry it out. Next, he confronted the brothel madam.

"I'm closing you up," he told grim-faced Ellie Freschette. "I want every woman, every douche bucket, every rag and shoe out of here in ten minutes. My troops will escort you to the Kellogg station and see you aboard the next train leaving the district."

"That ain't fair," Ellie protested, her face turning red. "Pearl done the shooting and she's dead. You can't run me out of town for that."

Hildebrand gave the woman a powerful shove. Her body felt as hard as a pick handle.

"Captain Duschene, take this slut out of here at once. If she gives you any trouble, throw her into the stockade with the union men."

Hildebrand turned his eyes on the platoon leader who stood at attention every time the major looked at him."

"Lieutenant, get this place emptied out. Pile everything in the street. When it's empty, post guards front and back."

The mound of clothing, shoes, utensils and bric-a-brac grew in front of the Antlers Hotel to the accompaniment of screams and curses of the displaced prostitutes. Some had been rousted so hastily that they were nearly naked beneath their thin wrappers. A few surly customers struggled into their clothing; testimony to the fact that business had continued after the shooting took place.


The lone nurse stared at Orchard's revolver. Her eyes drifted to his bloody shirt. He had to give her credit. She wasn't intimidated.

"Mr. Neville can't be moved," she told him. "He has a broken clavicle."

Orchard leaned heavily on the counter.

"Want yours broke too, nursie?"

For emphasis he pushed over a jardinière containing a plant. It shattered noisily when it struck the floor.

"Take me to him."

Tight-lipped, the nurse led him into a darkened ward. A dozen beds. Half of them occupied. Johnnie lay on his back, his raised arm immobilized by a plaster cast. Orchard leaned close to him.

"Johnnie, can you hear me?"

Orchard struck a match.

Johnnie opened his eyes. He stared at Orchard blankly for a moment

221

before he recognized him.

"Oh, God," he whimpered. "Kill me and get it over with."

"They killed your sister."

Johnnie began to sob, his body shaking.

"I told her I'd get you out of here," Orchard said, "so stop your blubbering."

He turned to the nurse with her disapproving eyes.

"Got a wicker casket?"

"With that cast, he won't fit."

"Get it. Let me worry about the cast."

When the nurse had gone, Orchard gripped the cast with both hands. Johnnie screamed when it broke and then fainted. Several heads in adjacent beds rose up to see what was happening and then fell back.

The nurse helped him slide the casket from the trolley into the back of the buckboard. When it was done, he gave her a five-dollar gold piece.

"I can't take this," she muttered, turning the coin over in her hand. "It's like a bribe."

"Would you rather take a bullet?"

Orchard hauled himself onto the buckboard's seat.

"You're going to bleed to death before you get where you're going," the nurse said, "so you probably won't need this, anyway."

"Looks like I paid in advance for medical advice," Orchard said.

Before she could respond, he slapped the horse's back with the reins. It trotted off smartly with Johnnie crying and moaning inside the bouncing casket.

The soldiers watched amusedly as the women fought like alley cats over the disputed ownership of various articles of clothing, deposited by the armload or tossed out of second-floor windows. At six in the morning, Ellie Freschette and her six bedraggled prostitutes were loaded aboard the Oregon Navigation and Railroad train headed for Spokane.

When the train pulled out, the whores leaned out of the windows to shake their fists at the soldiers. One raised her dress high enough to reveal that she wore no underwear.

Hildebrand took Duschene to the far end of the platform, away from the lounging soldiers. The captain, white-faced and nervous, stared straight ahead as Hildebrand spoke in measured tones.

"I blame you for what happened last night, Duschene. We've lost a good soldier because you weren't capable of keeping your men under control."

Hildebrand paused to regard his subordinate with an expression that bordered on loathing.

"Do you have anything to say for yourself?"

Duschene swallowed and said, "These nigras are hard to handle, Major. They all lie to protect each other. I wouldn't have had any way to know that James was missing, even if I'd asked."

"Even if you'd asked?" Hildebrand spat out the words. "You're a mighty sad example of an officer, Duschene. I have half a mind to request a replacement for you."

Duschene appeared to be on the verge of tears.

"That would finish my career, Bert. You know that."

"And that might be best for the army," Hildebrand said. He was beginning to regain control of his anger and disgust. "All right, I'll give you one more chance, but if I don't see a marked improvement in performance and attitude, I'm sending you back to Fort Missoula."

"Oh, thank you, Bert," Duschene gasped. He extended his hand. "You'll see a marked improvement in my men, too. I promise. I know I've been too easy on them."

Hildebrand ignored the hand.

"From now on, you'll address me as Major, understand?" Hildebrand said. "And as far as your men are concerned, improvement doesn't mean a flood of harsh disciplinary measures, Captain. You may have to drag yourself down to their level to win them over."

223

"Yes, sir," Duschene croaked, staring at his boots.

"Now, get the hell away from me before I change my mind."

Hildebrand watched him stalk across the platform. How could the army have permitted him to rise to the rank of captain? He thanked his stars that he'd had better men than Duschene under him when the Twenty-Fifth was rounding up the Sioux.

# CHAPTER TWENTY-TWO

Twice that day, Siringo saw men on the streets of Telluride whom he recognized from the Coeur d'Alene. However, sporting a full beard and wearing overalls and a workman's cap, he doubted that anyone would recognize him.

It seemed that the recent violent history of the Coeur d'Alene was in the process of recreating itself in this mountain fastness. Of course, the embers of that last big conflagration which had pitted miners against owners in Telluride had never been fully extinguished.

Charles Moyer and Bill Haywood were in town to renegotiate the eight-hour day which had been abandoned by many mines in the district, after once being the norm throughout the state. So far, the Western Federation of Miners seemed to have the upper hand. Some of the lesser mines, intimidated by acts of violence, ranging from suspicious fires to the merciless beating and forced deportation of non-union men, had closed. Others remained open, grudgingly agreeing to the eight-hour edict of the union. However, the giant Smuggler-Union mine, the largest employer in the Telluride area, had refused to knuckle under to the union. It was operating two ten-hour shifts with non-union crews.

Groups of surly, brooding men clogged the streets, and the saloons were filled with unemployed union men drinking up the last of their pay. It was the same oppressive atmosphere Siringo had escaped in Idaho. It caused him to be guarded in his conversations and casual associations.

At the depot, he waited for the train that was to transport Moyer and Haywood back to Denver. They had failed in their negotiations with the Smuggler-Union, creating an anticipatory atmosphere throughout the district. Union and non-union men alike didn't expect the Western Federation to take the rebuff without striking back in some way.

The depot platform was crowded. A number of well-dressed women and children, presumably families of Telluride's commercial community, waited with heavy baggage. Men in shabby clothes accompanied by their washed-out wives and pallid children, miners headed for greener pastures, made up the majority of the would-be passengers.

Siringo watched the milling groups with interest. Such an exodus was an indication of the fear and uncertainty that was gripping the community. Union and non-union men alike were constantly buffeted by the winds of discord and discontent that swept through the camps.

The commotion between the union men following Haywood and Moyer and an escorting group of special deputies hired by the Smuggler-Union, began in front of the New York Music Hall, a block from the depot.

Siringo moved up the street to observe the Western Federation President and Treasurer in the vortex of a violent, yet only vocal disturbance. Union men on both sides of the street were shouting epithets and waving fists at the armed deputies. The inevitable physical clash was triggered when one of the deputies shoved Haywood, who responded by dropping the man with a large fist to the jaw.

Miners poured off the wooden sidewalks to attack the deputies with their fists. The deputies, apparently under orders not to fire, used their rifles as clubs. Haywood and Moyer were among the first to go down, both bleeding from head wounds.

More deputies were coming down the street on the run while, at the same time, union men were spilling out of Telluride's twenty-odd saloons. As the battle widened, it moved away from Moyer and Haywood, leaving them lying in the street, dazed and bloody. They were being guarded by two deputies with Winchesters.

The scene presented an opportunity Siringo couldn't resist, though he had specific instructions to avoid all confrontations. Spurred by the sound of the approaching train's whistle he accosted a group of men on the periphery of the fray. Several of them displayed swollen faces and bloody noses.

"Let's get Haywood and Moyer to the train."

The two guards were instantly engulfed by a mob of fist-swinging miners. Their Winchesters were pulled from their hands and used on them like baseball bats. Siringo, with the help of several burly union men, hoisted Haywood and Moyer to their feet and half carried them to the depot. Siringo tried to stay out of Haywood's line of sight.

They forced their way through the frightened crowd on the depot platform, boarding the nearest coach almost before the train stopped moving. Siringo backed away as soon as the two officials were muscled into their seats. Moyer seemed to have taken the worst of the beating. He sat slumped over, his face in his hands.

"Ask him what he wants us to do," Siringo mumbled to the big man who had helped Haywood into his seat and was now standing over him.

In response to the question, Haywood, eyes still glazed with shock and pain, took a small notebook and a pencil stub from an inside pocket and began to scribble. A drop of blood spattered the ruled paper. He ripped out the page and handed it to the man.

"Get this to Mike Harmon. Destroy it if the deputies try to pick you up."

Harmon, the President of the Telluride union, was one of the men Siringo had under surveillance. At that moment, he happened to be at home where he was recovering from food poisoning after eating some venison from an animal which had been hanging in the sun too long. Thus, he hadn't participated in the Smuggler-Union negotiations.

Siringo followed the big man off the train.

"I'll take that note to Harmon," Siringo told him. "He's at home sick."

"I never see you before," the big man said. "What your name?"

"Dawes," Siringo said easily. "Charlie Dawes. I've been working in Cripple Creek."

"How you know big Mike sick?"

Siringo made a face.

"Because I ate some of the same deer meat that Mike did. I want to see how he's doing today."

The big man laughed.

"God, he blessed you with strong stomach."

He slapped Siringo on the back and handed over the note.

"I'll tell Mike what you did for Haywood and Moyer," Siringo said. "What's your name?"

"Kovac," the man said. "Jan Kovac."

"Mike'll want to thank you when he's feeling better," Siringo said, before hurrying away.

By the time he was in the street again, the melee had degenerated into a shouting match as both sides tended their wounded. The special deputies were retreating up the street in a compact body, carrying two unconscious men. Others were helped along by their comrades.

The union men had several of their partisans stretched out on the sidewalk in front of the San Miguel Saloon and were trying to revive them with whiskey. They were so badly beaten they looked like they had fallen down a mine shaft. It seemed unlikely that the eighty proof medications would produce any positive results.

Siringo crossed the street quickly and slipped between the buildings, the shortest route to his boarding house. He waited until he was safely inside his room before he opened Haywood's note.

Haywood's handwriting was atrocious and splotches of blood had rendered portions of the note almost illegible but its message was crystal clear.

> *Mike—handle Burgoyne as we said. Do you need Orchard?*
> *Available 3-4 days.*
> *H*

Siringo lay back on his bed to stare at the note. David Burgoyne was the Smuggler-Union general manager, obviously marked for death. He would have to be warned at once. But the mention of Harry Orchard—that was what fascinated Siringo.

# CHAPTER TWENTY-THREE

"The doctor in Missoula said Johnnie's probably lost some use of his right arm," Orchard told Haywood, who still bore battle scars from the violence in Telluride. "I've got him holed up in a cheap rooming house on Sycamore until he's able to get around. They really worked him over."

He sat across the desk from the Western Federation Treasurer, hoping the union didn't want to send him to Telluride, at least not until he felt better. His wound had become infected during the long drive over the Bitterroots to Missoula, a drive which had almost killed the horse and Johnnie Neville.

Once in Missoula, Orchard had found a doctor for himself and Johnnie and a livery barn which had accepted the horse as a gift, with a promise of good care, and had paid him fifteen dollars for the buckboard. That worked out well for Johnnie. If Orchard had been compelled to choose between saving only one of them, the loyal horse would have been the winner.

The doctor ran a small clinic out of his home and that was where Johnnie had been ensconced until he had strength for the train ride to Denver.

Now that he was here, Orchard felt he had no more responsibility for his welfare. The union would decide what to do with him. He knew too much about the union's activities in Wardner to be shunted aside and yet didn't know enough to be killed. A common problem in troubled times.

Haywood rolled an unlit cigar around in his mouth. He sounded impatient.

"I don't want to talk about Neville, Harry. We'll find a safe nook for him once he's healed."

Haywood leaned forward, massive jaw outthrust, ham-like hands spread on the desk top.

"I was going to send you to Telluride," he rumbled, "but there's no need now. Our boys blew up the hoist works at the Smuggler-Union yesterday. Burgoyne the general manager and a shift boss were in the cage."

He smacked his lips like a man who'd just enjoyed a fine meal.

"Probably still in it," he continued. "It's at the bottom of the shaft under twelve hundred feet of cable."

"So, do you have anything for me, Bill?"

Orchard was relieved that the problem in Telluride had been resolved and he was anxious to get out of Haywood's office and walk around Denver. He wanted a good steak and he needed to buy some new clothes. Then, perhaps, a turn at the poker table, and some time with a woman. One who had some soft meat on her bones, like Bella Shanks.

"You ever hear of Judge Gabbert, Colorado State Supreme Court?" Haywood asked. "He's been a thorn in our side on every union case that's come before his court. Damn near got Moyer put in prison."

"The Mine Owners Association influences the Supreme Court?"

"Of course," Haywood snorted.

Orchard found this assertion very troubling. If the judges on the State Supreme Court weren't impartial, where could a working man seek justice? Of course, the union overstepped its bounds in its dealing with the owners, but it had little choice and little money. However, killing a Supreme Court

Judge was a tall order and could be very dangerous, if indeed that was what Haywood was leading up to.

"The old fool walks to work," Haywood said, as though he'd read Orchard's mind. "Early in the morning, I'm told. Getting him should be easy."

"Bill, killing someone in broad daylight is never easy."

Haywood rolled his swivel chair over to the open safe. He rolled back to his desk and tossed some banknotes on the desk in front of Orchard.

"Here's a hundred for some decent clothes and whatever you need to do the judge. When it's done, I'll have some more for you."

"You still owe me two hundred for the Bunker Hill," Orchard reminded him.

Haywood returned to the safe for the money.

"Why didn't you remind me before I gave you the advance?" Haywood said. "You could use your own damn money for a new suit."

"Now I can afford a better one," Orchard replied with a grin. "A man's got to look his best to deal with a judge."

By the end of the second week, following his meeting with Haywood, Orchard felt he was ready to carry out his assignment to assassinate Judge Gabbert. In addition to new clothes and a stout canvas traveling bag, he'd bought himself a lightweight Ithaca twelve-gauge pump-action shotgun and a box of double-ought buckshot. He paid a blacksmith fifty cents to cut twelve inches off the barrel. Back in his room, he sawed off most of the stock so he now had a weapon easy to conceal under a coat and compact enough to fit in his bag, without disassembly.

He'd found the friendly atmosphere of the Elite Saloon, near his rooming house, to his liking, where he won and lost at the poker table. He called it pretty much a push for the two weeks. His wounds were almost healed and save for an occasional twinge, bothered him little.

Haywood had made arrangements to ship Johnnie off to Altman when he was fully recovered. He would do what work he could for a saloon keeper who was friendly to the union.

Orchard had watched Judge Gabbert walk to work on three consecutive mornings and had found him to be a creature of habit, following the same route daily. At first, he'd toyed with the idea of simply putting a load of buckshot in the judge but rejected the idea as too risky. Denver was a civilized city and had a large and efficient police department. A simple bomb, hidden along the route the judge took to the courthouse would do the job nicely with a minimum of personal hazard to the bomber.

"I hope this pleases your wife," the smiling saleslady said as she wrapped the forty-five-cent lady's purse.

Orchard had decided that the purse would be an attractive triggering device. In his mind's eye, he could see the judge bending over to pick it up. By the time he'd discovered it was attached to the bomb with a piece of strong cord it would be too late.

Assembling the bomb wouldn't be difficult because he'd built several similar devices in the past, including the one which had failed to demolish the shaft house of the Molly Ware in Telluride.

Back in his room, Orchard opened his trunk, which had been stored at the union hall, and examined the contents, a veritable war chest for a man in his profession. Dynamite, giant caps, sulfuric acid and a roll of stout surveyor's string were stowed between several changes of work clothes, boots, a billed cap, underwear, shirts and a miner's tin coat and pants. He'd accumulated the clothing over the years to disguise himself while he carried out various tasks at hand. The contrast in physical appearance between him dressed as a laborer and the Harry Orchard in a stylish suit and derby, would, in his mind, render identification virtually impossible.

For the judge, Orchard used a wooden cheese box that would hold six sticks of 2X dynamite, caps and a small bottle of sulfuric acid. The bottle was positioned to dump its contents on the caps when the stopper was pulled by the string tied to the purse.

Judge Gabbert always cut across a vacant lot on his morning journey, so it was here that Orchard decided the judge's life should end. It was raining lightly when he arrived at the site before seven in the morning. It annoyed him that he was getting his two-dollar derby wet, so he worked hurriedly to place the bomb in a thicket and the purse where it was visible at the edge of a well-defined path.

He didn't choose to wait nearby to observe the results of his handiwork, but he did hear it go off when he was several blocks away. He hoped the bomb had been detonated by the judge and not by someone else who might use the same shortcut. His hope was in vain.

According to the story that appeared the next day in the Post, a store clerk with a large family had crossed the vacant lot to save precious minutes because he was late for work. A shaken Judge Gabbert was able to tell newspaper men that the clerk had rushed past him moments before being blown to bits.

Moyer was furious. In Orchard's presence, he castigated Haywood for authorizing an attempt on the judge's life without his sanction.

"Haven't we got enough trouble in Telluride and Cripple Creek without stirring things up on our very doorstep?"

He glowered at Haywood who stared sullenly out the window.

"If you want to tear things apart, for Christ's sake, send Orchard into the Cripple Creek district where there's going to be a real need."

"We agreed to get Gabbert a long time ago," Haywood said, sounding strangely contrite

"But we didn't get him!" Moyer shouted. "Orchard, here, managed to blow up an innocent citizen and ran the risk of getting all of us indicted for murder."

Moyer came to stand in front of Orchard.

"You've done some good work for us, Harry, but you made a mess of this one."

"I guess I was in too much of a hurry," Orchard said, lamely.

Moyer stomped to the door of Haywood's office, where he paused to stare at the union Treasurer.

"Bill, as long as I'm president of the Western Federation, I call the shots, understand?"

Haywood, face averted, gave no sign that he'd heard.

"Do you understand what I said, Bill?"

Moyer's voice was shrill with irritation.

Haywood's head bobbed affirmatively.

"You're the boss, Mr. Moyer. What do you want Harry to do?"

"Get yourself situated in the Cripple Creek district," Moyer told Orchard. "Sign up with one of the smaller unions—Altman, maybe, and go to work. We'll let you know what we want you to do when the time comes."

Orchard was philosophical. So it was to be blisters again for the Western Federation of Miners. Well he'd done it before and unlike the stiffs he'd be working with, he knew he could count on Haywood for a little extra money from time to time, with a big payday for special jobs. He was a qualified driller and had no reservations about working underground. He supposed he might even consider a stint of hard work as the penalty for his recent failure.

When Moyer was gone, Orchard chuckled.

"Seems like you need permission to wipe your ass these days, Bill. You and Moyer have a falling out?"

Haywood rose abruptly to go to the safe to take out two hundred dollars in small bills. He tossed them unceremoniously onto Orchard's lap.

"What goes on between Moyer and me is none of your business, Harry. You just get down to Cripple Creek and go to work."

He went to the office door to open it, signaling that he was finished with Orchard for the time being.

"Incidentally, I think Moyer's suggestion is a good one. Join the Altman union. They're more aggressive than some of the others when it comes to dealing with scabs. Joe Wyatt is the president."

For the first time that morning, Haywood smiled suddenly.

"He'll greet you with open arms."

Back at his rooming house, packing his bag, Orchard reflected on the meeting with Haywood and Moyer. Many in the union considered Haywood to be a bombastic loudmouth, heavy on style, light on substance. However, Orchard's relationship with him had always been positive, their business conducted in

235

an atmosphere of mutual respect. It troubled him to see Haywood chastised by Moyer but more unsettling was Haywood's admonition to mind his own business. He'd made it clear to Orchard that he was standing on the outside looking in when it came to the top-level workings of the union.

Somewhere in his head, his alarm bell was ringing. It warned him that he probably couldn't depend on Haywood, and certainly not Moyer, to throw him a life line if he was ever apprehended. Troubling thoughts kept him awake well into the night. Finally he drifted off to sleep as he wondered if he'd see Bella Shanks again.

In the morning, he arranged to have his trunk shipped back to the union hall where it could repose until he needed it again. He'd never told Haywood or Moyer that it contained all the makings of a powerful bomb but concluded that what they didn't know wouldn't hurt them, as the saying went. In any event, he wasn't sure what awaited him in Cripple Creek but he didn't wish to be encumbered with too much baggage should he have to move in a hurry.

# CHAPTER TWENTY-FOUR

By the third week in May, it seemed to Major Hildebrand that martial law in the Coeur d'Alene had accomplished its purpose. The six hundred men, still held in custody, represented the dedicated union members, including many of the troublemakers. Numerous others had been arrested, held briefly until interrogation by special prosecutors appointed by Governor Steunenberg had absolved them of participation in any acts of violence.

In that same period, Hildebrand had observed General Merriweather mutate from a vaguely uninterested commander to an autocratic martinet who reveled in his newfound powers. It was at his direction that dozens of men with no visible connections to mining or the miners' union were swept up and held for days before they could prove their innocence.

This dictatorial policy had resulted in the death of one innocent man, a Wardner storekeeper named George Greavey. Outraged by his incarceration, Greavey pried loose a board on the floor of the Grinstad barn and escaped. He was observed running away from the building by Private Andrew Jefferson and shot dead when he refused to halt.

The loss of an innocent man's life infuriated Hildebrand but he was powerless to do anything about it. He did, however issue a general order to the troops of the Twenty-Fifth Regiment, prohibiting the discharge of weapons unless the bearer was personally attacked. He also apprised Colonel Mears at Fort Missoula of the tragedy and confided his lack of confidence in General Merriweather.

Greavey's death had caused great unrest among the prisoners in the stockade, to which Duschene had responded by recommending that Jefferson be court-martialed.

"Throw one nigra to the wolves to keep them quiet," he'd suggested to Hildebrand, the day after the incident.

"Maybe I'll throw you to the wolves, Duschene," Hildebrand told him. "You're in charge of the stockade. That makes you responsible."

"It was only a joking suggestion, Major," Duschene said, turning pale and breaking into a sweat. "I didn't mean..."

"Then keep your stupid suggestions to yourself."

The discontent may have continued to simmer but was no longer overt when Hildebrand put the prisoners to work near the detention site. Their task was to construct a building one hundred and fifty feet long, which they already had named "The Bullpen."

This rambling structure, with its three-tiered bunks, would house the prisoners until all the investigations were completed and indictments handed down. When Hildebrand had suggested the construction to General Merriweather and Bart Van Cleve, both gave it thumbs down. They reversed themselves a week later when it was learned that a group of journalists from Portland, Seattle and Denver would be arriving in the district. They wanted a firsthand look at a segment of America's civilian population held against its will, under the bayonets of the U.S. Army.

General Merriweather issued requisitions for lumber from mills in Coeur d'Alene City and authorized the recruitment and hiring of skilled carpenters from Spokane. Subsequently, to Hildebrand's profound annoyance, General

Merriweather accepted the plaudits of the press and was proclaimed by several western newspapers to be a great humanitarian, whose compassion ranked with duty and honor.

Shortly after the journalists departed the region, Hildebrand received a wire from Colonel Mears at Fort Missoula. The message was cryptic and concise.

"People in high places share your views."

Signed, Mears.

Within days, Hildebrand was summoned to Bart Van Cleve's office.

"Don't sit down, Major," the seated Van Cleve told him. "What I have to say will take only a moment. General Merriweather and his troops have been ordered back to Fort Sherman, which means that you'll be the senior military man in my command."

Mentally, Hildebrand flinched. Thus far, General Merriweather had acted as a buffer between him and Van Cleve, whom he'd grown to detest.

"As you are aware," Van Cleve said, "I believe in using strong medicine to deal with this insurrection."

Hildebrand drew himself up and took a deep breath.

"I think we've used strong medicine, Mr. Van Cleve. We've placed over a thousand men under arrest and we are presently holding over six hundred in confinement. Hundreds more have left the district rather than obtain work permits. Special deputies, paid by the Mine Owners Association, have practically destroyed the union halls in Wardner, Gem, Burke and Mullan. They have committed similar atrocities on the homes of many of the prisoners, putting families at the mercy of the elements."

He paused to catch his breath, feeling his face growing hot.

"Efforts to provide some relief to the prisoners' families have been undone by gangs of hoodlums who destroyed or stole foodstuffs intended for women and children who are starving. I would characterize the measures used as harsh, sir."

Van Cleve seemed surprised.

"You're not allowing your sympathies to incline themselves toward the union radicals, are you, Major?"

"My duty takes precedence over my personal feelings, Mr. Van Cleve."

Van Cleve withdrew a gold watch from his vest pocket and glanced at it.

"That's good," he said. "I have General Merriweather's assurance that you're a good soldier. Now, I have a meeting with the prosecutors. I want to see you at eight in the morning, Major. There's a problem developing in Burke that's going to require the army's attention."

Van Cleve rose to signify that the meeting was over.

"Will I be taking General Merriweather's place in the meetings with the prosecutors?"

"I'll let you know when I want you in attendance," Van Cleve said, moving toward the door. "At the moment, I'm the only one who can get them back on the track. They're proposing the release of the rank and file and sending only a few bigger fish to the penitentiary."

Hildebrand returned to his office with a queasy feeling in his stomach. Earlier he'd cheered to himself that General Merriweather was leaving but now realized that he'd been spared much direct contact with Van Cleve, which was going to be burdensome.

"I want to have a word with you, Major."

General Merriweather stood in the doorway.

Hildebrand rose and came to attention but felt exceedingly awkward.

"Please come in, General. I was hoping I'd see you before you left."

General Merriweather came in and closed the door behind him.

"I've come by to give you some advice," General Merriweather said, sitting down. "You've suddenly become Van Cleve's whipping boy and I can't say I'm sorry to be relieved of that assignment. I know you've resented some of the orders I've given you, Major Hildebrand, just as I would have resented them, had they come from you to me. But we're soldiers and we follow orders."

General Merriweather pulled himself closer to Hildebrand's desk and leaned across it. Hildebrand thought he caught the odor of alcohol.

"Carry out Van Cleve's orders to the letter and say a prayer every night that the Sioux break out of the reservation so you can get the hell out of here."

Merriweather lowered his voice.

"Van Cleve fancies himself as a combination of Napoleon and Solomon. He's very dangerous."

Merriweather rose and stared down at Hildebrand.

"Perhaps the same angel who has rescued me, will come back for you, sir. I hope so."

The general turned to walk stiffly away, without saying goodbye. Hildebrand watched the door close behind him and thought of what he'd told Colonel Mears about Merriweather.

"God, what have I done?" he asked himself.


Bart Van Cleve didn't care for James Hawley or William Borah, the special prosecutors appointed by Governor Steunenberg. For one thing, he didn't understand their legal jargon, and for another, neither of them exhibited a whit of awe in his presence.

The windows of the jury room in the Shoshone County courthouse were open and both lawyers were in their shirtsleeves when Van Cleve came in. Neither rose nor put on his coat in deference to Steunenberg's top aide.

Hawley, spare and sharp featured, waited for Van Cleve to seat himself.

"Bill and I think we've finally made a case against some of the Western Federation people and are ready with the indictments."

Van Cleve stared at Hawley over a tent of fingers.

"How many?"

"I have the list and the charges here," Borah said.

He riffled through a pile of papers.

"Here we are. Paul Corcoran, charged as an accessory to the murder of John Cheyne, a non-union employee of the Bunker Hill Mining and Concentrating Company."

Van Cleve signaled his impatience with an angry gesture.

"Just the names and charges. I don't want to hear all the other mumbo-jumbo."

The unsmiling Borah, bulldog jaw outthrust, exchanged a glance with Hawley and read on.

"John MacNamara, accessory to murder. Thomas Archer, conspiracy to incite a riot. There are also Federal charges pending against him and others who commandeered the Northern Pacific train."

Van Cleve smiled and nodded enthusiastically.

"Jacob Yancey," Borah continued. "Conspiracy to incite a riot."

Additionally, twenty-one men were to be indicted for their participation in the dynamiting of the Bunker Hill mill. Seven more were charged with felonious assault on non-union men. Four others were charged with lesser offenses, ranging from vandalism to malicious mischief.

Van Cleve bolted forward in his chair when Borah's deep drone ceased.

"That's all? What about the shooting of Lyle Gregory, Bromley's man, and the attempted murder of one of his deputies? Then there's that Fatty Kincaid, Bromley's pipeline into the union. Who killed him? Who burned down his saloon? Who helped John Neville, reportedly Bill Haywood's confidante, escape from the hospital?"

Van Cleve lay back in his chair, biting his lip in frustration.

"You fellows and a coroner's jury have interrogated union miners for two weeks and these are all you've got? Surely we can bring more to trial than what, thirty?"

"Afraid not" Hawley said. "These men are very loyal to one another. We're lucky to have enough evidence to bring anyone to trial."

"The list does not include certain fugitives who are no longer within the reach of the Idaho courts," Borah rumbled.

"Like Harry Orchard. Even the Pinkertons knew he was here and it appears that he led the mob which destroyed the mill, but no one can tell us where he is."

Van Cleve rose abruptly.

"Maybe when Gregory gets out of the hospital, he can help with the questioning. Some of the miners might be willing to tell him what they know."

Borah rose to face Van Cleve across the table.

"We have testimony from two women who implicate him and his deputies in the rape and murder of one Amy Neville," Borah growled. "That incident falls outside our purview, otherwise I'd work to indict him for murder and would cheer at his hanging."

"Well, I can tell you, the Mine Owners Association isn't going to be happy with what you've presented," Van Cleve said, ignoring the accusation against Gregory.

Hawley looked surprised.

"I wasn't aware that Borah and I are here to make the Mine Owners Association happy, Van Cleve. We're representing the people of this state and are charged with prosecuting those guilty of violating the law."

"If you have some other understanding with Governor Steunenberg, you'd better spit it out right now," Borah said.

"I'll be speaking with him by telephone this evening," Van Cleve said. "I'll apprise you of his comments."

Van Cleve slammed the door as he left the jury room.

Each time Major Hildebrand visited the town of Burke at the bottom of a steep canyon, he was stricken with a feeling of near claustrophobia. The railroad track ran down the center of the main street and under the overhanging second and third stories of the Tiger Hotel. Horses tied in front of Burke's stores and saloons had to be led to safety when a train passed. A buggy wouldn't have fit between the boxcars and the storefronts along the right of way.

The problem that was developing in Burke, as Van Cleve related it, had to do with the Tiger-Poorman Mine's pump crews. They had been released from custody at the urging of the Mine Owners Association and had gone back to work manning the Tiger-Poorman's steam-driven pumps. However, all of them had refused to denounce the Burke union, nor would they apply for state permits.

Van Cleve's instructions to Hildebrand were simple and to the point.

"They can't work without permits. Take a detachment of soldiers to Burke and arrest them."

"I'll assign this to one of my platoon leaders, unless I can use some of General Merriweather's troops," Hildebrand said.

"General Merriweather's soldiers are packing up to return to Fort Sherman," Van Cleve said. "Besides, I want you to handle this personally, because it could get a bit sticky."

"In what way?"

Hildebrand felt like a man about to step into quicksand.

"The Mine Owners Association wanted these men released," Van Cleve said, "but martial law cuts both ways. After all, we aren't here to make the Mine Owners Association happy."

Will Cathcart, the Tiger-Poorman manager, greeted Hildebrand and his ten-man detachment at the entrance to the mine property. He had a large wad of tobacco in his cheek.

"Mr. Van Cleve telephoned to tell me you were on the way, Major."

Cathcart paused to spit and wipe his mouth on a stained blue bandana.

"I tried to explain to him that I need these men and they want to work, but not under any kind of permit system."

"Then, sir, I have to arrest them and return them to the stockade," Hildebrand said.

"But I don't understand this permit nonsense, when workers and management have a working arrangement," Cathcart said. "I'm paying them union wages. Always have. Even now, with a non-union crew, everybody gets union wages. There was no call to shut us down."

Cathcart's urgent appeal was embarrassing to Hildebrand and there was no way he could justify anything so illogical as shutting down a mine because a few key employees wouldn't sign a piece of paper.

"I have my orders, Mr. Cathcart," Hildebrand said.

"Look, Major, my lower workings will be flooded in twenty-four hours if the pumps are shut off. Would you be willing to see for yourself what I'm up against here? Then maybe you could telephone Mr. Van Cleve and explain to him how critical it is for me to retain these fellows until I can find some qualified replacements with permits?"

Hildebrand had never been inside a mine before and the descent of almost a quarter of a mile in the swaying cage was a unique experience. Wearing a gum rubber coat and with his trousers tucked into rubber boots, Hildebrand followed Cathcart along the low tunnel, where miners drilled and shoveled. The tunnel was illuminated by small electric bulbs dangling from wires in the ceiling.

They followed the narrow gauge rails, hugging the wall to allow mud stained men pushing ore cars to pass. Water dripped from the ceiling and, in certain places, gushed from the walls. Hildebrand could feel sweat running down his rib cage as they moved toward a pumping station. Steam leaked from fittings and the clatter of the reciprocating pumps drowned out all other sounds.

Cathcart leaned close to him to shout into his ear.

"We collect water in a sump at this level and boost it up to a sump on the sixth level. Takes four stations to get it to the top and out at about six hundred gallons a minute."

Hildebrand was aware that the men of the crew were watching him. He didn't know how to respond to Cathcart, so he nodded as though he understood. Actually it had been apparent to him on the surface that the Tiger-Poorman had a water problem. He'd observed the muddy cascade shooting from a discharge pipe into Canyon Creek upon his arrival.

Now that he had seen the problem at its source, Hildebrand didn't feel he was any better equipped to dissuade Bart Van Cleve from enforcing the permit edict. In Van Cleve's mind, defiance of authority, not water, was the problem at the Tiger-Poorman and with the dictatorial powers which the governor had conferred upon him, he wouldn't negotiate with dissidents.

While his soldiers lolled in the sunshine on a stack of timbers outside the mine office, Hildebrand went inside to telephone Van Cleve at the Carter Hotel in Wallace. His uniform was damp with perspiration and his trousers were wrinkled and muddy. He didn't feel that he cut a very commanding figure at a time when he needed to be assertive.

When Van Cleve came on the line, Hildebrand attempted to explain the Tiger-Poorman mine's dilemma. He used the mine manager's rationale to justify his failure to place the pump crews under arrest.

When he had finished, Van Cleve exploded.

"Goddamn it, Major Hildebrand, I gave you specific orders and I expect you to carry them out."

"Carrying out those orders creates a greater problem than sixteen men working without permits," Hildebrand said. "I respectfully suggest that you see this mine for yourself, Mr. Van Cleve."

There was a long pause before Van Cleve spoke.

"Major, I want you to wait right where you are with your troops. I'm dispatching Captain Duschene at once to relieve you. When you get back to Wallace, you report to me at once, understand? I will be contacting your superiors at Fort Missoula with a report of your insubordination, sir."

Hildebrand placed the receiver carefully on the hook. He got up from Cathcart's desk and shook his head in a gesture of frustration.

"I'm to wait here until I'm relieved," he explained. "Captain Duschene will take charge of my detail and will, I'm sure, carry out Van Cleve's orders."

"Damn politicians!" Cathcart exclaimed. "Excuse me, Major, if I have to shut down my pumps, I have to relocate some of my crews. Thanks for trying to use common sense."

Captain Duschene arrived by special train at mid-afternoon, accompanied by twenty more soldiers. When they marched across the mill yard, the sunlight flashed on their fixed bayonets. Above-ground laborers in the yard stopped what they were doing to watch their arrival.

"I have orders to relieve you, Major Hildebrand," Duschene announced stiffly, barely able to conceal his eagerness.

Duschene adopted an aggressive stance, as though expecting Hildebrand to take issue with his newfound authority.

"Yes, I know, Duschene." Hildebrand said.

He went out on the covered porch and sat on the railing. For the first time since his enlistment, he was sorry to be a soldier. To be placed under the thumb of a civilian like Bart Van Cleve was an affront from which he was sure he'd never recover.

Over the next several hours the Tiger-Poorman's pumps were shut down and the pump crews lined up in the mill yard. In groups of four, under the bayonets of the soldiers, they were marched into the mine office where Duschene waited at Cathcart's desk. In front of him was a stack of work permits, a pen and an inkwell.

Cathcart joined Hildebrand on the porch and offered him a chew of tobacco which the major declined.

"This Van Cleve fellow has some queer ideas," Cathcart muttered, jaws working on a large piece of cut plug. "My men are never going to trust me again, and that's too bad because the mines on Canyon Creek aren't like Bunker Hill. We've always been fair with our boys and have gone along with the union. Things won't be the same after this."

"Things won't be the same for most of us," Hildebrand replied.

He wondered what was in store for him when he returned to Missoula. The army had little use for officers who refused to carry out orders.

At five o'clock the special train went back down the canyon to Wallace. Duschene and his detachment had sixteen men in custody. All members of the pump crews had refused to sign either applications for work permits or a statement repudiating the union. One, in manacles, had thrown the contents of the inkwell on Duschene's tunic.

# CHAPTER TWENTY-FIVE

By the time Orchard had settled in at Maggie Graeme's boarding house, using his preferred alias, Thomas Hogan, word of the infamous bullpen in the Coeur d'Alene had spread throughout the Cripple Creek district. During his first few nights in Altman, the main topic of conversation at the bar and gaming tables of the Gold Dollar Saloon, a union hangout, was the violation of men's rights in the mountains of Idaho.

Joe Wyatt, the Altman union president, was built like a beer keg and had black powder marks on his face from a premature explosion twenty years before. His manner was hearty, and as Haywood had predicted, greeted Orchard enthusiastically.

"I can get you on as a driller at the Vindicator on Bull Hill," Wyatt told him. "Superintendent McCormick is a friend of mine. All the Cripple Creek mines work with the union."

"The way Haywood and Moyer were talking, it sounded like the lid was about to come off down here," Orchard said.

He wondered if they simply wanted to get him out of Denver. He wouldn't have expected that kind of treatment from Haywood, but he didn't trust Moyer.

"They might be up to something," Wyatt said with a shrug of big shoulders. "The smelter in Colorado City sticks in Haywood's craw, I know that. They fired nine of our boys a couple of weeks ago, like they was weeding out union men. The rest of them hunkies don't care about the union and never will."

The mostly non-union Colorado Refining and Reduction Company in Colorado City had long been a source of irritation to the Western Federation of Miners. The last time Orchard had been in Colorado, Haywood was fulminating about the smelter men, who were mostly central Europeans. They had always been opposed to paying dues to anyone for the privilege of working. It didn't seem to Orchard to be an issue worth worrying about, but Haywood was like a bulldog once he got his teeth into a problem.

"Moyer sent a letter to all the big mines around here telling them not to ship no more ore to Colorado City," Wyatt said. "Some of them told him to pound sand up his ass."

"That would tend to make someone with Moyer's short fuse upset," Orchard replied. "If we're waiting for something to happen, I'll be in no hurry to go to work. I want to nose around the district a bit and renew old acquaintances."

Orchard was thinking of Bella Shanks, wondering if she'd returned to Colorado. He was annoyed with himself for failing to ask her for a specific address when they'd parted in front of the Wardner livery barn. However, he'd been in so much pain that he probably wouldn't have remembered it anyway.

Bella had mentioned that her fiancé had died at the Gold King, which was near the town of Goldfield. He'd make a few inquiries there as he traveled about the district.

That evening, dressed in a new suit, Orchard took the electric trolley from Altman to Victor. He craved a woman, and one of the men at Mrs. Graeme's had suggested he visit Sadie LaRue's place.

"Her gals are a little older and more experienced," the boarder had whispered across the dinner table while Mrs. Graeme was bringing more potatoes from the kitchen.

Orchard found the place on a narrow street behind the Victor firehouse. He spent some time with a tall woman who called herself Elizabeth. She had an English accent and claimed royal birth. She also had some movements which she obviously hadn't learned in the Queen's court.

He was leaving Elizabeth's room when two men appeared in the dimly lighted hallway. Force of habit made him back into the room, watching them through the door's crack.

One was Harvey Browne, the secretary of the Altman union. Wyatt had introduced him shortly after Orchard's arrival. The other man, a slim, easy moving chap with a full beard, seemed familiar. As they passed the door, inches away, Orchard recognized Charlie Siringo. He waited until he heard their feet on the stairs before leaving the puzzled prostitute with her rotating hips and clipped accent.

His first impulse on his return to Altman was to tell Wyatt that his union secretary was hobnobbing with a Pinkerton. On further consideration, he decided to take his time with Browne to figure out his play. Siringo had fooled everyone in Wardner and he might be playing the same game here. Browne may have simply thought he'd found a friend. That wasn't something which should call for a death warrant. That night he couldn't sleep, his mind a kaleidoscope of the past few weeks. Amy Neville was there, along with Lyle Gregory and Charlie Siringo. When he finally went to sleep, he dreamed that Siringo put a bullet in him as he stood over Fatty Kincaid behind the burning saloon.

The next night and the next, Orchard waited behind the Victor firehouse observing those entering and leaving Sadie LaRue's, but recognized no one. On the third night of his vigil, Siringo entered the establishment at eight-thirty, with Browne following a few minutes later. They were inside for about half an hour before Siringo appeared at the front door, alone. Orchard followed him to the trolley line, watching from the shadows as the detective boarded the car for Cripple Creek.

Seated across from Wyatt the following night, at the Kansas City Steak House in Victor, Orchard asked, "How often do your boys get arrested for beating up a scab when there were no witnesses to point a finger."

"More often than we should," Wyatt said, with his mouth full. "Wonder sometimes if we've got a spy on the inside."

"I'd keep an eye on Harvey Browne," Orchard said. "He has a friend in Cripple Creek who's a Pinkerton. They meet at a whorehouse here in Victor."

"Are you sure?" Wyatt pulled off the napkin which he'd stuffed into his shirt collar. "He ain't given me no call to suspect him of double dealing."

"The Pinkerton's name is Siringo," Orchard said, sawing away on a very tough steak. "He wormed his way into the Wardner union as the secretary, like Browne."

"How come nobody killed him when he was found out?" Wyatt asked.

"That was my job," Orchard stated frankly, "but he got away from me before I could put a bullet in him."

"Now, maybe you'll get another chance."

Wyatt pushed his chair back from the table and got up. He dug a fifty-cent piece out of a vest pocket and dropped it on the table.

"That's my share of the dinner, Tom. I'm going back to Altman. I think me and some of the boys need to have a little talk with Harvey Browne. If he's a Pinkerton spy, he'll wind up at the bottom of a mine shaft on Bull Hill."

Orchard tossed his knife and fork into his plate.

"I'll go with you. I'd like to hear what he has to say."

From the Altman depot, Orchard and Wyatt went first to the Gold Dollar saloon. Wyatt acknowledged several of the drinkers but didn't seem satisfied with the pickings.

"We'll try the Colorado Belle," he told Orchard. "Steve Adams is usually there."

"Adams? Redhead? Hot temper?"

"That's him," Wyatt said. "You know him?"

"We've done a little business," Orchard said. "I've been wondering if he was around."

As Wyatt had predicted, Adams was at the bar with a fellow Altman union member, Jake Schultz. They made an odd pair. The furtive Adams was tall and lanky; the squat Schultz, open and outgoing. Orchard and Wyatt joined them and Orchard stood for a round.

Adams, who had known him as Harry Orchard in Telluride, didn't miss a beat when Wyatt said, "You remember Tom Hogan, Steve."

Behind the bar, above the mirror was a painting of the Colorado Belle. The naked woman, full breasted, large of ass and pink of nipple, reclined on a red settee. She was draped with a gauzy garment which failed to conceal her ample feminine attributes. Even after the introductions, Schultz seemed to be mesmerized by the painting.

"Good to see you again," Adams said in a surprisingly high voice, offering his hand. "What are you up to?"

Wyatt lowered his voice. "Tom thinks Harvey Browne's been talking to a Pinkerton.

"A Pinkerton?"

It seemed to take a minute for Adams to comprehend what Wyatt was telling him.

"The Pinkerton's named Siringo," Orchard said. "I know about him from Idaho."

"Siringo?" Adams said. "That ain't a name you'd forget too easy. Yup. I know where I seen it."

Adams took out his pocketbook, found a folded newspaper article and smoothed it on the bar. He pushed it over for Wyatt and Orchard to read. The piece had been torn out of the newspaper so the heading and introduction were missing.

Orchard read it aloud.

"The two suspects, along with Davis, were taken from the jail by a mob of fifty men and hanged from the upper windows of a nearby building. Davis, wanted for murder in Idaho, had been arrested by Pinkerton Detective Charles Siringo. He had been placed in the Florence jail for safekeeping until transportation arrangements could be made."

"Knew I'd seen that name," Adams repeated. "I wonder if this is the same Davis who was with us in Telluride."

"Yeah," Orchard said. "He's the one who killed the constable. Hung by farmers. Sweet Jesus!"

Revisiting the Florence debacle seemed to energize Adams.

"Let me go get my rifle," he told Wyatt. "If Browne's a fink, I'll kill the bastard myself."

"I've got a better idea," Orchard said. "Let's feed Browne some bum information and see what happens."

Schultz seemed confused by anything other than direct action.

"How do we do that?"

"When we find him, let me do the talking," Orchard said.

In agreement with the plan, the four of them left the Colorado Belle to find Harvey Browne.

Browne's thin, consumptive wife answered their knock, moving awkwardly aside so they could enter.

"Harvey's sleeping," she told them, pausing to cough a glob of phlegm into a crumpled handkerchief. "You want I should wake him?"

"Get him up," Orchard ordered. "We want to talk to him."

He stood by the open door to allow the night air to dissipate the unpleasant closeness of Browne's living quarters. It made him think of the Neville's shack in Wardner, except that Amy made an effort to keep that place reasonably clean. Here, bits of food lingered on the unswept floor and the scant furnishings were draped with pieces of canvas tarpaulin to keep them from falling apart like lepers.

Sour smelling wash dried on a rope stretched near the stove. For an instant he felt sorry for anyone who had to live in such squalor, but only for an instant.

253

Browne appeared in the bedroom doorway, pulling up his trousers. His black hair stood on end and his eyes were puffy with sleep. He regarded them suspiciously when he came into the kitchen parlor.

"Go back to bed," he ordered his wife, closing the bedroom door behind her.

"What's up, Joe?" he asked Wyatt. "It must be past midnight, ain't it?"

He stretched his arms over his head and yawned. It seemed to Orchard that Browne was making an elaborate attempt to appear unruffled.

"Tom Hogan, here, wants to talk to you, Harvey," Wyatt told him in a loud voice.

Browne frowned at Orchard and thrust his hands into his pockets.

"Yeah? About what?"

"I've gotten word that there's a Pinkerton detective operating in the district, Harvey," Orchard told him. "I thought you might help us find out where he's living."

"Why would I know?"

Browne looked angrily from Orchard to Joe Wyatt.

"What's the idea, Joe? This fellow's been around here three or four days and he's asking me about Pinkertons?"

Orchard shrugged and smiled benignly.

"Well, Harvey, you're the union secretary and you know all the men. One of our union operatives out of Denver tells us there's a Pinkerton spy in the Altman union."

"Union operative? What the hell's a union operative?"

Browne rubbed his unshaven jaw and swept the room with a belligerent glare.

"We've got a man in Cripple Creek," Orchard said. "He's posing as a Pinkerton, with full credentials. His name's Siringo."

Browne pulled out one of the chairs and sat down heavily at the kitchen table. He stared at his stocking feet.

"I know him, but not as a Pinkerton," he mumbled.

He raised his head to give Wyatt a desperate glance.

"That's the God's truth, Joe."

"How'd you meet him?" Wyatt asked, stepping forward to stand over him.

"I run into him in a whorehouse in Victor."

From behind the closed bedroom door, a fit of coughing erupted.

"He tells me different," Orchard said, enjoying Browne's discomfiture. "He says you're giving him information."

"I haven't told him nothing," Browne protested, casting stricken eyes on each, in turn. "He's just a friend, I swear."

"When are you planning to see him again?"

"Dunno. We don't have regular meetings."

Steve Adams lunged across the table. His voice was shrill with anger.

"How do you get word to him, Harvey? Tell Hogan what he wants to know or, by God, I'm gonna nail your balls to the floor and set this shack on fire."

"I telephone where he rooms in Cripple Creek," Browne said, in almost a whisper.

Orchard patted Adams on the shoulder to calm him down.

"You're going to telephone him again in the morning, Harvey, and set a meeting for tomorrow night," Orchard told him.

He turned to Wyatt, who seemed ready to explode.

"I think he needs to be locked up somewhere tonight, Joe."

"Let's take him to the union hall," Wyatt growled, "though I'd like to plant the bastard."

They hustled Browne out the door, still in his stocking feet, leaving behind the sound of his wife coughing, interspersed with the querulous voices of the children, wondering what was happening to their father.

At the union hall, Adams volunteered to stand guard until morning but Orchard insisted that Schultz, who didn't seem to have any homicidal tendencies, share the burden. Leaving Adams alone with the shaken Browne could mean that they'd have a body to dispose of in the morning.

Orchard arrived at the union hall at nine o'clock in the morning to find that Browne had survived the night. Adams grumbled that Schultz had slept most of the time, but other than that, the plan was still on the track.

Orchard sat across the table from Browne and listened while he arranged a meeting with Siringo that night at Sadie LaRue's. He used the bait they had agreed upon, the revelation of a plan to foment violence at one of the small, non-union mines on the fringes of the district.

By noon, Browne, his wife and two scared and hungry little boys, waited on the platform of the Independence depot for the Florence and Cripple Creek train which would take them away. Everything they had been able to carry was stuffed into two canvas sacks. Orchard and Adams escorted the Brownes to the depot. Jake Schultz stayed behind in Altman to set fire to their house.

That evening, Orchard and Adams waited in the shadows behind the Victor firehouse for Siringo to arrive at Sadie LaRue's. Orchard carried a large paper sack.

"That's him," Orchard whispered, when Siringo came down the street and entered the establishment. "When he comes out, just hand him this sack and tell him Browne had to leave the district."

Siringo came out of the bawdy house a few minutes after entering. He stood on the porch surveying the street, dimly illuminated by electric street lamps.

"Now," Orchard whispered.

"He ain't gonna shoot me, is he?"

Somewhat reluctantly, Adams took the sack from Orchard.

"Naw. He wouldn't hurt a flea."

Orchard watched Adams cross the street at a brisk pace, step up on the porch to hand Siringo the sack. As they had agreed, Adams was to proceed on down the street and would meet up with Orchard later at the Colorado Belle in Altman.

Orchard watched Siringo open the sack and remove his rakish black hat. He looked around again, as though searching for his benefactor. Then he put his finger through the hole in the crown and wiggled it, pointing toward the firehouse. Even in the poor light, Orchard could tell that he was smiling.

# CHAPTER TWENTY-SIX

Toward the end of July, Orchard, who had either drunk or gambled away most of his resources, took a job as a driller at the Vindicator. Joe Wyatt, who had a good working relationship with Virgil McCormick, the superintendent, had vouched for him.

He hated the mud, the noise and the vibration of the big air drill, which made his side ache, but the pay was three dollars and fifty cents a day and he needed the money. Ironically, the job brought an unexpected benefit. It played a role in reuniting him with Bella Shanks.

Moyer and Haywood had visited the Cripple Creek district twice since his arrival there. They were still militating for a boycott by the big mines of the Colorado City smelter. On neither visit to the district did they seek him out, though he heard they'd had discussions with Wyatt. He was more angry than hurt to be excluded from discussions about possible future actions to bring the mine owners to heel. He admitted to himself that he'd hoped to be summoned by Haywood, for no reason other than the chance the union treasurer would give him some money for future business, but it didn't happen.

Johnnie Neville, his right arm severely compromised, showed up in Altman in August and was given a job as a swamper at the Gold Dollar. Despite his handicap, he was able to sweep and mop as well as help behind the bar when the need arose.

He told Orchard in confidence that the Western Federation had given him two hundred dollars to compensate him for his ruined right shoulder and to help him get started in a new town. Orchard was sure the union had another motive; keeping him quiet about what he knew of union activity in Wardner.

Men arriving in the district from the Coeur d'Alene brought news of the Idaho bullpen where over two hundred men still languished. Paul Corcoran had gone to trial, charged with complicity in the murder of John Cheyne. He was found guilty and sentenced to seventeen years in the Idaho state penitentiary. John MacNamara was found guilty of conspiracy to incite a riot and received a two-year sentence. On the charge of being an accessory to murder, he was acquitted.

One highlight of the MacNamara trial had been the note his wife and a number of other women had received from Captain Duschene, who was in charge of the bullpen. The captain had solicited Mrs. MacNamara and the others to assist in the recruitment of a "sufficient number of women and young ladies willing to do their duty for the United States Army by entertaining the troops of the Twenty-Fifth Infantry Regiment."

It was reported that a near-riot occurred in the bullpen the day the contents of the note were made public. The prisoners, many with wives and daughters in the district, set fire to their bedding straw before rampaging into the exercise yard. There, they were quelled by shots fired over their heads from a Gatling gun.

Steve Adams had made several forays to Cripple Creek in search of Charlie Siringo, without success. It seemed that Harvey Browne's forced deportation might have destroyed any viable link the detective had with the union, forcing him to suspend operations. In a way, Orchard was relieved that the volatile Adams hadn't found him. The Pinkerton had earned a new lease on life the day he'd outsmarted Orchard up on Canyon Creek. Thus, it seemed to Orchard that he should have the say on whether Siringo lived or died, and if killed, by whom.

At the end of August, the Western Federation of Miners called out the union mill and smelter men in Colorado City after failing to convince Colorado Reduction and Refining to accept a union shop. Orchard thought little about it inasmuch as only a few men were involved. Working conditions all through the Cripple Creek district were at their peak, particularly at the Vindicator, where the management hierarchy appeared to be fair and decent men. Virgil McCormick, the superintendent, and Mel Beck, the day shift boss, never failed to have a friendly word of encouragement for the underground crews when they came down into the workings to check on progress.

Orchard was teamed with Jake Shultz on the drill and it was Jake who was responsible for enabling him to improve his standard of living.

They had finished lunch one day, a week after Orchard started, when Schultz took a piece of quartz out of his lunch bucket to show Orchard.

"This is worth about two dollars," he said. "Tomorrow during lunch I'll show you a ton of it that's easy pickings."

"Isn't that risky?"

"It's on the seventh level. Nobody's working there."

"How'd you find it?"

"I was stealing dynamite to sell to some leasers," Schultz explained, a mischievous expression on his round face. "The roof of a stope caved in. Scared the hell out of me but when I took a look at what fell, I thought I'd found the Lost Dutchman."

The following day, instead of eating lunch, Orchard and Schultz followed a crosscut on the sixth level, where they were drilling. Climbing down a rickety ladder to the seventh level, they navigated by candlelight until they came to the caved-in stope.

On their hands and knees, they pawed through the fallen rock and decomposed quartz which was seamed with gold. Pockets bulging, they made their way back to their drill just in time to go back to work before being missed.

That night, Shultz took Orchard to an assay office in Victor.

"Yours is worth four," the elderly assayer told Orchard, handing him two silver dollars. "I get half for my risk."

"That seems high as hell for the little risk that fellow takes," Orchard told Schultz when they were back on the trolley.

"Oh, he runs some risk, all right." Schultz replied with a chuckle. "Last winter in Victor and Goldfield, four or five of them little assay shops was blasted to hell."

Orchard began to look forward to each new day, for he and Schultz had discovered an abandoned tunnel which had never been closed. Now it was possible to bring much larger amounts of the high-yielding ore to the surface at lunch time, recovering it at night. On some days, Orchard made as much as ten dollars and was compelled to open a savings account at the Victor First National Bank.

By mid September he'd deposited over two hundred dollars, had paid off his accumulated gambling debts and was beginning to feel particularly well off. He still smarted from the implied rebuke in Moyer's and Haywood's indifference to him, finding some comfort in the knowledge that they'd need him again. When they did, the price would be high.


Orchard rode the electric trolley every day between the Vindicator and his rooming house on the far side of Altman. The trolley line happened to pass the substantial McCormick home, which towered above the street and always caught Orchard's eye. Early on a Friday evening, as he returned to his rooming house, he observed a young woman standing on the McCormick's front porch, apparently waiting for someone to open the door. He was almost certain it was Bella Shanks. By the time he could get off the trolley, she had gone inside.

He had planned to join Schultz after dark at the mouth of the abandoned tunnel to retrieve their spoils, but this was more important. Orchard parked himself across the street from the McCormick house, lit a cigar and waited. He had washed and changed clothes in the Vindicator changing room at the end of his shift but wished that he was more presentable to renew his acquaintance with Bella, if indeed, the woman he'd seen was her.

He had waited well over half an hour and was beginning to lose patience when McCormick's front door opened and Bella came out. She was carrying a parcel and lingered on the porch for a moment to talk to a stout middle-aged woman whom Orchard assumed was Mrs. McCormick.

When Bella came down the steps, Orchard waited, until Mrs. McCormick had closed her front door, before speaking.

"Bella?"

Bella was startled. She hugged the parcel to her breast as though it could protect her. She didn't relax until Orchard stepped into the light cast by a nearby street lamp.

"Oh, my God! Harry Orchard!"

"Sorry if I scared you," Orchard said, coming closer. "It's Tom Hogan, Bella. I'm using my real name here."

The skeptical look which flashed across her face told him he'd better have a good explanation.

"I'm working as a miner," he told her. "I'd never get hired as Harry Orchard."

"You're actually doing honest work?"

"Every day."

Bella looked thinner than the last time he'd seen her but it didn't make her less attractive.

"I was wondering if I'd ever see you again," Bella said.

Orchard smiled and nodded.

"Yeah, me too."

"What are you doing here? I mean, right here. How did you know I was inside?"

"I was on the trolley," Orchard explained. "I saw you go in."

"That explains it," Bella said.

She stood there looking at him, as though unable to think of anything else to say. Her manner was reserved, almost indifferent to his reappearance.

"I'm glad I found you," Orchard said, feeling a little like a schoolboy talking to a girl he fancied. "I'm able to properly thank you for helping me get out of Wardner in one piece."

"You don't owe me any thanks," Bella said, hefting her parcel and glancing toward the trolley stop. "I really should be getting along," she added, stepping away from him.

"Bella, are you unhappy to see me?"

Orchard stared hard at her. He wanted her to say something which might indicate that there was a chance to renew their relationship, if they'd ever really had a relationship. Even a nod would do. He didn't expect her to fall into his arms.

Bella met his gaze.

"I don't know. You and I lead two different lives. I'm just a dressmaker, but I create things. You're a dynamiter who tears things down."

Bella paused to catch her breath, color rising in her cheeks. At that moment, the McCormick's front door opened and Mrs. McCormick came out on the porch. She gave Orchard a suspicious glance.

"Is everything all right, Miss Shanks?"

Bella smiled and nodded, though she seemed a little flustered.

"Yes, thank you, Mrs. McCormick. This gentleman's wife is one of my customers."

"Very well, dear," Mrs. McCormick said and went back into the house.

"So you've married me off to get rid of me," Orchard said, amused by her quick response.

"Do you know who she is?"

"I believe she's the wife of Virgil McCormick, the man I work for. I'm a driller at the Vindicator."

He held out calloused hands to prove the declaration, disappointed that

Bella didn't seem to be impressed that he was properly employed.

"I suppose you heard a lot of bad things about me before you got out of Wardner," Orchard said.

"I heard that Tom Hogan isn't your real name. I've met Harry Orchard. How many other people are you?"

"This is the real me," Orchard said. "Thomas Sylvester Hogan. Named after my grandfather who was a sea captain."

Sometimes he surprised himself with his glibness.

"Here comes the trolley," Bella said, either unimpressed or not caring one way or the other.

"Can I ride along with you? I'm living in Altman."

"I have a house in Goldfield," Bella said.

Orchard was pleased that she hadn't resisted his proposal to join her. However, the trolley was crowded with men from some of the other mines in the area and there was little opportunity for the kind of conversation Orchard would have preferred: thanking her for helping him in Wardner, and playing on her sympathies by telling her that his gunshot wound still gave him painful twinges from time to time.

Goldfield was at the end of the trolley line, a mile or so past Altman. Bella's little house was several blocks from the depot and though unpainted, did boast a lilac bush in full bloom near the front door.

"Bunker Hill gave me a small settlement," Bella said. "Enough for this house, a little furniture and a new sewing machine."

Orchard walked her to the front door. Something told him that Bella wasn't going to invite him in, just as she'd never invited him into the house in Wardner. The only place she'd made him feel welcome was the vile-smelling pig shed, where, bless her, she'd dressed his wound.

The first doctor who'd examined him assured him that had she not disinfected him with the whiskey he would probably have died from infection.

"Why are you smiling?" Bella looked sharply at him. "I didn't say it was very grand, now, did I?"

263

"What are you talking about?" Orchard asked, pulling himself out of his reverie. "I was thinking about something that happened in Idaho."

"I thought you were laughing at my house," Bella said meekly.

"No such thing," Orchard said. "It looks very sturdy."

He took out his watch to check the time.

"Look," he said, "let me get cleaned up and come back for you in an hour. We'll take the trolley into Cripple Creek and have dinner at the Palace Hotel."

"The Palace Hotel! Dinner for two is a day's wages."

"With good wine, nearer two," Orchard said airily.

"I don't want you spending your blood money on me," Bella said, stepping up on her tiny porch.

"I gave all the blood money to the Orphan's Fund," Orchard drawled. "All I have now is what the Vindicator pays me. Can I come back in an hour?"

Bella shook her head.

"I can't go anywhere tonight."

She hefted her parcel for emphasis.

"I have to finish this dress for Mrs. McCormick."

"Well, all right then," Orchard said, backing off. "Maybe I'll see you again sometime."

He was disappointed that she'd expressed no enthusiasm about seeing him again but he was damned if he was going to press her. He'd go by himself and look up Birdie, the redhead at Molly Tucker's place. She had a few tricks up her skirt that would put Bella Shanks out of his mind.

Bella started to open her door. She paused to look at him as he headed for the trolley line.

"There's a church picnic on Sunday."

Orchard turned to look at her. She was smiling.

"Maybe you'd like to go with me."

"Maybe."

"If you're busy..."

"No, I'm not busy," Orchard said. "I just had to think about it for a minute.

I haven't been on a picnic since I was a kid, or in a church ever."

"It should be a nice day," Bella said. "Give yourself a chance to relax under the trees."

"It sounds better all the time. Can I bring anything?"

"Just bring yourself to the Goldfield Methodist Church at ten o'clock. The wagons leave at ten-thirty."

"What if I could get a buggy?"

"You don't have to do that."

"I want to. I'll be here for you at ten."

"You are persistent."

"You knew that in Wardner. I'll see you Sunday."

Orchard turned abruptly and walked away. He was pleased with himself. Though he didn't look forward to a picnic with a church group, he might have Bella to himself for a time. He would impress her by emphasizing how hard he was working and convince her that his frugality was alone responsible for his bank account.


The picnic was held in a mountain meadow surrounded by aspens. It was apparently a popular gathering spot and boasted half a dozen plank tables and a fire pit. Nearby was a spring, emerald-like, in the tall grass. An array of droppings indicated that animals drank there when the area was free of people eating and singing praises of Jesus.

The food was simple fare but plentiful. Bella had been responsible for a cabbage salad which Orchard felt had too much vinegar in it. Someone else had brought a platter of deviled eggs. These, Orchard found particularly tasty and admitted to himself that he'd taken more than his share. The pie was tolerable, with a pleasant-tasting filling, protected by an almost impenetrable crust. The large woman who was serving the slices offered him a second piece which he declined, pleading a lack of further capacity.

Orchard was disappointed that there was no beer and none of the men, even those whose gnarled hands and ropy arms identified them as miners, produced a bottle. Thus, he kept the flat pint in his coat pocket and drowned his urge for spirits with strong hot coffee.

The attendees were a diverse group which included several merchants and their families, a number of miners from the various works, though no one who claimed to be a Vindicator employee. When Bella introduced him to her fellow churchgoers as Tom Hogan, he was greeted courteously. One young man, whom he was to learn later was the minister's son, didn't seem happy that Bella had invited him to the gathering. Too bad, Orchard thought, assessing the pale face and pink hands. If he and Bella ever made it into bed, Orchard was sure she'd be better off with him between her sheets than with the surly Christer.

After the meal, he and Bella found a comfortable spot beneath a tree where they could rest their backs and watch the dozen or so children frolic while the parents visited.

Her shoulder was firm and warm against his until a breeze picked up and she had trouble keeping her skirt over her ankles.

"I should have worn britches," she said laughingly when a gust exposed her calf above her high-topped shoe.

"I'd like to see that," Orchard said, picturing her in tight pants. "You said it might be breezy."

"My fiancé and I used to come up here."

"He was killed, you said."

As soon as the words came out of his mouth, Orchard was sorry he'd uttered them. He felt Bella contract and draw away from him. She bit her lip and stared silently at the towering mountaintops.

"At the Gold King," she finally said. "The cage fell four hundred feet. With him, two others and a mule."

She shot a glance at him with tear-filled eyes and looked quickly away to dab at them with her handkerchief.

"He's the reason you've never married?"

He wanted to reach out and put his arms around her but restrained himself, sensing he could do little to lift her out of her sudden grief.

"He was the love of my life," Bella whispered.

Orchard reached out to touch her hand. She gave his a little squeeze and got to her feet.

"I think it's time you take me home, Tom. I still have some sewing to finish."

They waved goodbye to those at the tables and made their way to the buggy. Orchard took Bella's arm to help her into the seat. The effort brought a sharp twinge to his side which caused him to wince. Bella looked closely at him.

"Are you all right?"

Orchard didn't answer until he was in the seat beside her, reins in hand.

"Where I got plugged. Still hurts sometime."

"Of course you've been to the doctor."

"Of course, and you know what he told me?"

Orchard turned to smile at her.

"He said you probably saved my life."

"Oh, I don't know about that," Bella said, fiddling self-consciously with her shawl. "I just did what anyone would do..."

"...if they found a gut-shot stranger lying next to their house." Orchard said. "Well, Bella, I intend to make it up to you, whether you want me to or not."

When Orchard stopped the buggy in front of Bella's house he turned to her and said, "My offer's still open about the Palace Hotel. Maybe we could go next Saturday."

"Don't you work on Saturday?"

"Not when I'm sick. If you say yes, I'm sure I'll come down with something."

Orchard hopped out of the buggy and reached up to help Bella down. His hands lingered on her arms after her feet touched the ground.

"Yes or no for Saturday?"

Bella stared into his eyes as though she were trying to see what was going on in his head, trying to assess his motives. Finally, she smiled.

"I'd like to go. I've heard it's quite grand."

"We'll be the grandest couple there."

Bella extricated herself from his grip.

"Thank you for going to the picnic with me. I had a reason for asking you."

"Yeah, I saw him," Orchard said. "Were you trying to make him jealous or did you want him to think the claim was already staked?"

Bella laughed.

"I wanted to dampen his ardor, as they say. He's the minister's son. I think he feels that gives him an advantage with the unmarried ladies. I'm not the only one he's taken a shine to."

Bella extended her hand.

"Thank you for a nice afternoon."

Orchard took her hand and pulled her to him, gently, but firmly. He kissed her on the lips.

Bella didn't pull away when she said, "Once, you apologized for doing that."

"Another state. Another me."

Bella leaned back in his arms to study his face.

"Yes," she said. "I wonder if I'll ever know who you really are."

He kissed her again and she kissed him back.

# CHAPTER TWENTY-SEVEN

Siringo felt good to be on the hunt again. After the startling discovery that Harry Orchard knew he was operating in the Cripple Creek district, he'd gone back to the Denver office. Without Harvey Browne, his only contact inside the union, and with Orchard lurking in the shadows, he and McParland had concluded that the assignment wasn't worth the risk; particularly when a generally peaceful atmosphere prevailed.

Now, back in Telluride, he was assisting Jim Clark, the city marshal, in the apprehension of the murderers of David Burgoyne. The Smuggler-Union manager had thanked Siringo for his warning and assured him that he was maintaining a high level of security at the mine. Sadly, it hadn't been enough.

As always, the trail led directly to the Western Federation of Miners' union hall, only to vanish behind the locked front door. A suspect had been arrested, however, and was lodged in the Telluride jail. He was joined in the lockup by a bearded and scruffy Siringo, representing himself as one Charlie Dawes, hellraiser extraordinaire and bearer of a Cripple Creek union card. He had been arrested, he told his cellmate, for beating the daylights out of a special deputy employed by the Mine Owners Association. Thus credentialed, he was welcomed as a kindred spirit in the working man's struggle for justice and equality.

Late that night, in a whispered conversation, the suspect, a miner named Oliver Brighton, admitted to Dawes that he had lighted the fuses in the Smuggler-Union shaft house as the cage carrying Burgoyne descended into the mine. According to Brighton, the union had paid the hoist engineer and his assistant each twenty dollars to look the other way when the charges were placed and to make themselves scarce when fuses were sputtering before the blast.

Siringo tried to appear appreciative but was churning inside as he listened to Brighton's tale. That life could be valued so cheaply that the Western Federation of Miners could kill Burgoyne and a shift boss for forty dollars was beyond belief.

Brighton was close-mouthed about the other union participants and Siringo didn't press him for fear of arousing suspicion. He did, however, lay personal claim to a number of dastardly deeds from Butte to Cripple Creek to build on Brighton's confidence. Some of the miner's reticence seemed to dissipate when Dawes admitted to killing two men; a crime, he said, for which he'd never been charged. It was then that Brighton became more voluble.

In the morning, Siringo sat on his cot and waited for Jesse, the jailer, to unlock the cell door. The large, stooped man with a walrus moustache arrived at seven o'clock.

"Charges agin you been dropped, Dawes," the jailer muttered as his key rattled in the lock. "Since you're leavin', ain't no sense givin' you a free breakfast, the marshal says. Outta there, now."

Brighton waved goodbye and said, "Go break some more heads for the union, Dawes. Show them scab bastards."

Siringo winked at Brighton and smacked a fist to a palm.

"I'll get one for you, Oliver."

Sitting with Jim Clark in the marshal's office, Siringo carefully outlined Brighton's role in the Burgoyne murder, as well as naming two other

Telluride union members, not yet in custody, whom Brighton had identified as accomplices.

"If there are any more," Clark said, cracking his knuckles, "we'll get the names out of him one way or another."

Brighton was in for some rough days and nights ahead, but that didn't bother Siringo. He'd come to hate the union murderers and dynamiters, so he didn't care what the marshal did to him.

"I'm sorry you won't be around to help us," Clark continued, "but McParland wants you back in Denver. He telphoned me last night. Things have busted loose at the smelter in Colorado City. National Guard's been called out and the Mine Owners Association's afraid the trouble'll spread to Cripple Creek."

Clark pulled open his desk drawer to retrieve Siringo's Smith and Wesson. "There's a train at eleven."

Siringo stood up to take off his coat so he could put on his shoulder holster. Before he stowed the Smith he broke it open to make sure it was fully loaded.

"I'm of no use in Cripple Creek," Siringo said. "My only informant was run out of the state by the union, damn lucky to be alive."

"Seems like McParland's got some fellow in Altman who wrote him about a reward," Clark said. "One of them Idaho boys. Willing to finger union men for a price."

That changed everything. Returning to Cripple Creek would be extremely risky, but with a new informant who was motivated by money rather than hatred, Siringo felt he could make real progress in blunting the tip of the union's spear.

# CHAPTER TWENTY-EIGHT

A pall of uncertainty hung over the Cripple Creek district. Pickets were still at the gates of the smelter in Colorado City and negotiations were going nowhere. Those close to the situation reported that the only reason the smelter would ever capitulate would be the lack of available non-union manpower, which seemed to be plentiful.

Once again, Haywood and Moyer were in the Cripple Creek district, attempting to wrench an agreement from the major mines in the district to boycott the smelter until the Colorado Refining and Reduction Company agreed to operate with union smelter men.

It was late September and Orchard was hoping that Haywood would be successful without calling for a strike. Though Haywood hadn't sought him out for as much as a drink this time, Orchard harbored no resentment. His main concern was that a strike would curtail his nightly high-grading activity, an enterprise which netted him five to ten dollars a day with extremely low risk.

He found himself that fall with money in the bank, a job he'd learned to tolerate and a good woman with whom he enjoyed keeping company. He tried to analyze his feelings toward Bella. He was sure it wasn't love, though he wasn't sure he'd recognize love if Cupid's arrow ever penetrated his tough hide. All he knew was that his life seemed more complete, now that he was seeing her on a regular basis. Thus far, he'd been unable to lure Bella into the bedroom, but her willing lips seemed to convey the implied promise that paradise might not be much further down the road.

How far, he'd attempted to determine on the Saturday evening he'd taken her into Cripple Creek and treated her to a steak dinner at the Criterion, a restaurant patronized by the local swells. Perhaps it was because Bella had been self-conscious about her appearance, but she drank a good deal more wine than she was able to handle.

Orchard had assured her repeatedly that she looked every bit as nice as the other lady diners. Though her dress lacked some of the lavish embroidery and elaborate tucks and lace, it was, nonetheless, made from a fine silk taffeta which Bella had proudly told him she'd ordered from San Francisco.

As far as he was concerned, they made a fine-looking couple, she in her silk dress and he in a twelve-dollar gray vicuña suit, which he had told her cost only nine at "Sears And Sawbuck." It annoyed him that anyone would look down on them because they worked with their hands. His hands had performed some tasks which would have a more lasting effect than anything most of his fellow diners would ever achieve.

He had to help Bella on the short walk from the restaurant to the trolley. In the car, she sat close to him and held his hand. Once, when he thought she was snuggling closer to give him a kiss, she belched, giggled and fell asleep.

The kissing came later, after he'd helped her onto her front porch and waited for her to unlock her front door. When she turned to him, still unsteady on her feet, he took her in his arms, intent on sealing the deal in her bed. Instead, she pushed him away and waggled a warning finger in his face.

"It's been a wonderful evening, Tom," she said, slurring her words. "You're a generous man. Dinner was del...delissus, but now it's time for me to go to bed—alone."

"Bella, you saved my life," Orchard reminded her. "I want to show my gratitude."

That annoying waggling finger again.

"I know what you want to show me. Goodnight, Mr. Hogan."

With that, Bella kissed him on the nose and went inside.

Orchard stood alone in the cool night air, angry, disappointed and feeling a little sorry for himself. He bit the tip off a cigar and spat it angrily into the street.

Orchard pulled on his pants as the woman, who said her name was Alice, squatted nude over her douche pan to wash herself. The room stank of vinegar.

"I hope you'll come back again, love," she said over her shoulder, intent on the task at hand.

Orchard threw on his coat and clamped his derby on his head.

"I will, the next time I need more than a kiss on the nose."

Not bloody likely, he told himself. The woman's feeble attempt to simulate unbridled passion was a poor substitute for the real thing.

Haywood greeted Orchard warmly by his alias when he entered the Altman union hall, followed by Charles Moyer, the Western Federation president. Moyer was more reserved but did acknowledge Orchard with a cursory hand shake.

Orchard sat in the front row with Schultz and Adams. Haywood and Moyer took two of the wooden chairs to the front of the room to sit facing their audience as they waited for the hall to fill. When the last union men straggled in, Moyer rose to address the crowd.

"I have some good news for a change," he said, with a tight smile. "The smelter in Colorado City has agreed to start hiring some union crews. They won't agree to operate as a union shop, but we've called off the strike, because this is a good start."

Some whistling and stamping of feet followed this announcement but stopped abruptly when Haywood got to his feet.

"The reason they knuckled under," Haywood boomed, "is because we've gotten the big mines in this district to agree to use the smelter in Idaho Springs if the union-busting in Colorado City doesn't stop."

More hooting and stamping filled the room.

"Mr. Moyer and I want to avoid a strike at all costs," Haywood continued, "but we're ready to shut the district down if our agreements fall apart, even if we have to kick some ass."

"What if they kick back?" Schultz asked.

"Then, we get their attention."

Haywood looked meaningfully at Orchard, as did Adams.

"You can count on us, Big Bill," Adams declared enthusiastically. "Right, Hogan?"

He punched Orchard on the arm.

"If it comes to that," Orchard said.

"What the boys done in Idaho sent a few men to prison," Schultz reminded Haywood.

"That's right," Haywood growled, "and the people who sent those men to prison have a hearing with the devil coming up."

When the meeting ended and the hall had cleared, with Moyer returning to the hotel, Haywood invited Orchard to join him in the back room for some whiskey and a smoke.

"I don't share Moyer's confidence that these so-called agreements are worth the powder to blow them to hell," Haywood confided, after pouring two generous drinks and waiting for Orchard to get his cigar going. "You're going to have to be ready with some kind of Harry Orchard handiwork if things go to hell."

"Don't deal me into anything too heavy, Bill," Orchard told him. "I've met a lady who might become part of my future."

"That's wonderful, Harry, but if the music starts in Cripple Creek, you'll have to be ready to dance. You're the one man I can depend on. Incidentally, I may want to send you to San Francisco. We still owe Frank Bromley for what he did to us in the Coeur d'Alene."

Orchard sipped his whiskey and puffed on his cigar.

"Bromley doesn't seem as important to me as he once was."

Haywood stiffened, his good eye glittering with anger.

"I suppose you don't remember the humiliation of running from the bayonets of nigger soldiers."

"No, I don't. Do you?"

Orchard finished his drink and rose to leave.

"Harry, you're in a good position to bring some grief to the Vindicator if they start to backslide on us."

Orchard nodded and put on his hat.

"Do you need any money?" Haywood asked as he corked the pint and put it in his coat pocket."

Orchard shook his head.

"I've got money in the bank, Bill."

"A man of means!" Haywood's tone was mocking. "Money in the bank and a good woman in your bed. No wonder you're lukewarm about doing your duty for the union."

"Just money in the bank," Orchard said. "I'm working on the other."

Indian summer prevailed into October with unseasonably warm days and balmy nights. On the second Sunday of the month, Orchard rented a buggy, packed a blanket, chilled bottles of beer, assorted cold cuts and breads he'd been able to purchase in Cripple Creek, and drove Bella to a high mountain meadow bisected by Commander Creek.

Sated after the bountiful picnic lunch, Orchard stretched out on the blanket, propped his derby over his face and closed his eyes. Bella leaned back against a tree, totally absorbed by the beauty and tranquility of their surroundings. The only sounds were the calls of two hawks circling lazily overhead and the music of water splashing against the boulders in the creek bed.

Orchard opened his eyes and peeked at Bella from beneath the brim of his hat. She wore a candy-striped shirtwaist and had her hair pulled up under a straw hat adorned with a red ribbon. He couldn't recall ever seeing her so relaxed and serene. Shadows played on her face, making her truly beautiful.

"Are you happy, Bella?" he asked lazily, rolling onto his side to look at her.

"Yes, Tom, I think I am—now that I have a fella."

Orchard went to her and took her in his arms. When they kissed, her mouth was hot and she responded eagerly.

"I didn't want this to happen with you," she murmured, pulling her lips away from his, "but I think I'm in love with you, Tom. Are you scared?"

Orchard smiled and said, "Only of being reformed."

"You've reformed yourself," Bella said. "I want to think you've done it for me."

"You can think whatever you want," Orchard said, "but you have to remember, I'm a good actor."

Some of her earlier serenity departed as Bella searched his face, a frown tugging at her eyebrows.

"You mean this is all a pose?"

"What's all a pose?"

It pleased him that she cared for him and he warned himself not to push his independence to the point of alienating her or hurting her feelings.

"The honest working man," Bella said. "The good provider."

She encompassed the ample remains of their lunch with a sweep of her hand.

"I want to think that you've made a complete change from the man I knew in Wardner," Bella told him, adding thoughtfully, "though I must admit I wonder sometimes about the money you spend."

"I've always been a frugal sort," Orchard said. "It's nice to have some money saved so I can spend it on my girl."

He leaned forward to kiss her again, which seemed to ignite something within her. He didn't reach paradise with her that Sunday afternoon, but she permitted him to touch her hot, plump thighs above her stocking tops, fully concealed by a rustling petticoat.

277

As soon as the door closed behind her, when they had returned from the picnic, Bella began to cry. She was experiencing such inner turmoil that she surrendered to tears. Only she knew how lonely and devastated she'd been with the loss of David Gaines, her late fiancé. She'd confided in no one and had pressed forward with her life as best she could, with a pain in her heart which she believed she'd bear forever.

Then this man, who called himself Tom Hogan, but who might have been someone else, had kissed her. It was the first kiss from a man in almost three years. Bella had convinced herself that no man would ever want her again and she tried to ignore the stirrings within her, brought about by memories of David's urgent lips and impatient hands. As much as she wanted what he wanted, she'd made him agree to wait until they were married before he took her virginity.

Now, with virginity intact, but seriously at risk, Tom Hogan was back in her life. Bella sagged against the wall. She could taste his lips and feel his hands on her. She wondered if she should have abandoned herself to her passions there beside Commander Creek, and allowed Tom Hogan, or whoever the hell he was, to have his way with her.

Bella lurched to the front door and yanked it open. Orchard was turning the buggy around on the narrow street and, thank heavens, the horse was balky and not responding well to his tugging on the reins.

"I want a word with you, Tom Hogan," Bella said as she stepped out on the porch. She was embarrassed by how loud her voice was.

He gave her a surprised look and climbed down from the buggy, coming to face her with a quizzical expression.

"I want to know something, right now," Bella told him, trying to keep her voice from quavering. "I told you I loved you and all you did was try to take off my bloomers. I want you to know that I wasn't telling you that to give you an invitation."

"I didn't think you were," Orchard said.

"Is that all you have to say to me?"

278

"What else would you like me to say?"

"You could tell me you feel the same way."

"Well, Bella, I do feel the same way."

Bella fixed him with a probing stare.

"You can't say the word, can you?" Bella said, holding back her tears. "Well, I want to tell you something. I love you, but no man, who isn't my husband, takes off my bloomers."

Bella turned to go back in the house when she felt his hands on her arms. Gently, he turned her to him. He placed his hands on her face and wiped the tears from her cheeks.

"I've known that from the beginning, Bella," he said, "and I accept your terms."

"What does that mean?"

"I want to marry you."

"Then, you do love me."

"Set the date and you'll find out."

"Say it, if you want an answer."

"I love you, Bella."

Bella threw her arms around him and pressed herself close.

"Oh, my dear, as soon as possible."

On the twenty-first of October, with Jake Schultz and his semi-invalid wife as witnesses, Harry Orchard and Bella Shanks faced a Methodist minister in Bella's living room and exchanged their vows, becoming Mr. and Mrs. Thomas S. Hogan.

That night, surprised by the pain, embarrassed by the bleeding, but amazed by the strength of her response, Bella gave herself to her husband with complete abandon. The barrier with which she had surrounded herself, was washed away in a sea of passion more turbulent than anything she could have imagined.

Later, they lay side by side, holding hands and staring at the ceiling.

"Did I hurt you?" Orchard asked.

"A little, at first," Bella whispered, squeezing his hand.

She turned suddenly to bury her face against his chest.

"I'm embarrassed."

"About what?"

"About liking it so much."

Orchard gathered her in his arms.

"I'm glad you like it as much as I do."

Bella wriggled out of his arms to raise herself on one elbow and look down at him.

"Oh, Tom, this is a wonderful new beginning for both of us. You have steady work. I'm earning some money. In a few months we might have enough for a new kitchen range."

"Got it all figured out, haven't you, sweet thing?"

Orchard rolled onto his side where he could see the bedroom door and the small window, the tiny room's two avenues of escape. The thought of saving to buy a stove was so alien to him that it gave him pause to consider what he'd gotten himself into.

When Orchard gave up his room at Mrs. Graeme's boarding house, it meant that he had a much longer trolley ride at the end of his shift each day. However, his new life had its compensations. Bella was a good cook and homemaker whose cries of delight in the bedroom drowned out any discordant notes generated by the institution of marriage.

Even the normally obtuse Johnnie Neville seemed to sense the change which was taking place in Orchard's life.

"You act like you ain't even interested in the union no more, now that you're married and settled down."

Johnnie, in a soiled apron, was behind the bar at the Gold Dollar, where Orchard often stopped on his way to the trolley.

"Right now, I've got more important things to think of than the union," Orchard said, sipping his beer.

"There's still plenty of non-union scabs that needs taken care of," Johnnie observed, picking up a glass to dry it.

His right arm hung peculiarly from his ruined shoulder, but he'd retained enough use of it to perform simple duties around the saloon.

280

"As long as there's jobs for every union man," Orchard said, "I'll let you and Wyatt and Adams worry about the scabs."

Johnnie leaned confidentially on the bar facing Orchard and spoke in low tones.

"I heard Adams shot a soldier in Colorado City. Is that true?"

Orchard finished his beer and picked up his dinner pail.

"Why don't you ask him?"

Adams was sprawled across a billiard table in the back of the room, spurning the bridge for a shot at the far end.

"Him and me don't get along," Johnnie replied sullenly and went back to drying glasses.


Bella came to give him a kiss when Orchard walked in, setting his dinner pail on the kitchen table.

"I'm glad you're not too late, Tom," she told him. "I want you to ride into Altman with me after supper."

She went to the sewing machine to pick up the brown dress with black lace trim which she'd been laboring on for over a week.

"It's finished," she announced triumphantly. "I promised Mrs. McCormick I'd bring it by tonight."

"Why can't Mrs. McCormick come and fetch it herself?"

Orchard wasn't happy that Bella had continued with her dressmaker's trade now that they were married. It didn't seem fitting that his wife should work when he had money enough for both of them.

Bella ignored him and continued with her dinner preparations.

"Wash up and sit down, dear," she ordered. "I have a nice treat for you."

Orchard patted her bottom.

"Before supper, or after?"

"Pot roast with onions and carrots. Your favorite."

She raised the lid on her Dutch oven, filling the kitchen with the aroma of her art.

281

"You're my favorite," Orchard said, "and I'll ride into Altman with you. I suppose Virg McCormick'll want me to wait on the porch, though. I don't imagine he entertains many of his drillers."

"Only the good ones," Bella said, as she placed their dinner on the oil cloth table cover. "You'll see. He's a very nice gentleman."

As usual, Bella was correct. The genial McCormick invited Orchard into the parlor for a glass of port while Bella helped Mrs. McCormick with her new dress.

"You've got a good woman there, Mr. Hogan," McCormick said, settling back in his chair, big hands clasped on his ample belly.

"Yes, and I intend to keep her," Orchard agreed, sipping his port.

After Mrs. McCormick had modeled the dress for her husband and had received compliments from him and from Orchard, McCormick walked them to the front porch.

"Don't take much to make these women happy," McCormick observed while Bella and his wife paused to discuss the latest fashions. "You a long-time union man, Mr. Hogan?"

"Since I was big enough to hold a candle," Orchard replied.

McCormick laid a friendly hand on his shoulder.

"Don't let the union poison your heart. It does that to some. We'll never have the problems you boys had in Idaho."

"I'm surprised you hired me, knowing I was in Idaho."

Orchard wondered how much McCormick knew about what had happened in Wardner. Haywood had mentioned seeing a Pinkerton bulletin which had identified one Harry Orchard as one of the ringleaders in the dynamiting of the Bunker Hill mill and concentrator. Fortunately, it would have borne no photograph, because he had never been arrested. For some reason, the Idaho prosecutors hadn't charged him in the killing of Fatty Kincaid, so one bulletin was all Haywood believed existed.

"Do your job," McCormick said. "Don't cause any trouble. That's all I ask of you and the union. In return, you'll be paid top wages in a safe mine."

"Fair enough," Orchard said, as they shook hands.

Bella joined him and he took her arm possessively to help her down the steps to the street.

On the trolley, Bella sat close to him and held his hand.

"What were two talking about?"

"He wanted to know if I was an old union man. He knows I'm from Idaho. I told him I was surprised he'd hired me."

"What did he say?"

"Do your job and don't cause trouble and things'll be peachy."

Bella twisted in her seat to look at him.

"That's fair, isn't it?"

"That's what I told him."

"You have your job and he has his," Bella said. "He has to keep the mine running and the union in check."

"We'll see how well he does, if things go to hell in Colorado City."

Bella sat up very straight and moved away from him.

"You know something you haven't told me."

"I know a lot of things I haven't told you," Orchard said.

He picked up her hand, kissed her palm and gently closed her fingers.

"Keep that with all our secrets, yours and mine."

That night, lying beside a sleeping Bella, after they'd made love on their return from Altman, Orchard thought about Virgil McCormick. It was difficult to reconcile the union-bred hatred for management when the class included a man like McCormick who had extended his unguarded hospitality to a dedicated union man.

Dedicated? As long as the price was right, he was dedicated. Orchard made no bones about his loyalty to the Western Federation of Miners. It was bought and paid for. That was not to say that he'd turn his back on the union and become a Pinkerton fink if he was offered a financial incentive, as some did. Even he, who had pulled the trigger a few times for the union, had to draw the line somewhere.

# CHAPTER TWENTY-NINE

On the second week of November, the Colorado Reduction and Refining Company began laying off union men, in violation of the agreement reached with Moyer and Haywood less than three weeks before. It was learned that they had been able to recruit scab labor from Montana, as the result of efforts which had been taking place during the strike.

A new strike was called against the company but only nine men responded. It seemed that the threat of winter was a powerful incentive to stay on the job, even at reduced wages, in defiance of union edicts.

A week later at the Palace Hotel in Cripple Creek, a grim Charles Moyer gave the Mine Owners Association an ultimatum. No more ore was to be shipped to the Colorado City smelter or a district-wide strike would be called. Moyer's flung gauntlet prompted Joe Wyatt to call an emergency meeting of the Altman union, which Orchard attended.

"There ain't any good reason for a strike in the district," Wyatt told the assembled miners, "but if headquarters calls one, we're going out."

The announcement was greeted by an undercurrent of grumbling and several demands that the membership vote on it. However, Wyatt remained firm and the meeting concluded on a depressing note.

For the next week, union men in the district labored above and below ground speculating uneasily on the Western Federation's decision. It seemed to Orchard that opinion was almost unanimous against a strike among the men of the Vindicator, as well as others with whom he spoke on his tours of the saloons of Victor, Altman and Goldfield.

However, on the last week in November, with snow flurries chalking the slopes, Moyer issued the call. Thirty-five hundred loyal union men threw down their tools and walked out of almost all of the mines in the Cripple Creek district. Most, including Orchard, felt the mine owners would quickly give in and agree to a boycott of the Colorado City smelter.

The single men hung around the saloons while the married men busied themselves laying in the winter's wood or fixing up the houses and shacks which sheltered their families. Orchard whiled away his time at the poker table at the Gold Dollar, leaving town for several days to go deer hunting with Jake Schultz.

When he returned to Goldfield with ten pounds of venison steak wrapped in a newspaper, Orchard stopped at Nesbitt's Mercantile, where he and Bella had a charge account. He wanted to surprise her with some apples and raisins for mincemeat.

"That'll have to be cash, Mr. Hogan," the elderly clerk advised apologetically. "Mr. Nesbitt's orders. No more credit 'til the strike's over."

"That's a little tight-fisted, isn't it?" Orchard said, tossing a silver dollar down on the counter. "Some of the boys won't have any cash until they go back to work."

Stanley Nesbitt, the bearded proprietor, came out of the back carrying a case of evaporated milk, in time to hear Orchard's comment.

"You fellows brought this on yourselves, Hogan," Nesbitt said. "Considering the issues, this strike seems pretty damn stupid to me."

Orchard picked up his dollar and dropped it into his pocket.

"Here's an issue for you to consider, Nesbitt. Shove these apples and raisins up your sorry ass. I'm gonna see to it that no union man ever sets foot in here again."

"You do that," Nesbitt said. "Now, get the hell out of my store!"

Bella was upset when Orchard told her what had happened.

"Do I have to go into Altman to trade, Tom? I've been going to Nesbitt's for ages."

"Well, you're not going any more, Bella," Orchard told her. "I won't be put upon by a goddamn storekeeper."

"You can't blame him for wanting to be paid."

"He'll get every dime when the men go back to work. He's made a bloody fortune in that store."

"Well, I'm not riding the trolley car every time I need ten pounds of potatoes," Bella muttered as she picked up the bloody venison bundle.

"You'll not go to Nesbitt's, Bella, or I'll have the boys give him a coal oil christening," Orchard shouted.

He paced angrily, sensing that he might have less control over his wife than he was willing to admit.

Bella stopped abruptly and turned to look at him as though seeing him for the first time.

"You would do that, wouldn't you? Isn't that what always happens when someone offends the union? I saw it in 1894, right here in Goldfield. Bricker's saloon burned to the ground one afternoon and union men just stood around and laughed. Mr. Bricker had a seizure and died the next day—murdered by the union."

Bella began to cry, lifting her apron to cover her face.

"I should have known what you were like when I found your revolver under your pillow on our wedding night."

Bella sank into a chair at the kitchen table, laid her head on her arms and sobbed.

Orchard slammed out the front door and took the trolley to Altman. This was a good night to get drunk.

Siringo found the ramshackle rooming house where Johnnie Neville lived, perched against a hillside, the front supported by stilts. The space beneath the building was crammed with stacked firewood, visible in the grey light of a new morning. Siringo had chosen dawn to confront Neville, for several reasons. One, awakened from a sound sleep, he wouldn't have his wits about him and two, if anything went wrong and he had to shoot someone, he wanted to be able to see his target.

Siringo climbed the steep stairs leading up to the building. Snow had melted and refrozen into ice on the steps making headway hazardous, inasmuch as there was no railing. He wondered how many drunken miners had broken their necks trying to return to their rooms after a night on the town.

McParland had been pleased when Siringo acknowledged that he knew who Neville was; sometimes miner, but mostly a union errand boy. He'd seen him often around the Wardner union hall, especially when Haywood and Moyer were in the district butting heads with the Mine Owners Association.

"In his letter, he says he knows who placed the dynamite in the Bunker Hill mill," McParland had explained. "That's old news but we want him to think the reward's at his fingertips. He may know nothing about union activities in Cripple Creek, but we know some of his former associates are there."

"Yes," Siringo had replied with a wry smile, "Harry Orchard."

"Well, I'll keep him on the hook until we need him, and then I'll have you look him up."

Inside the rooming house, the air was fetid, compared to the crisp fresh air outside. The room he was searching for was up another flight of stairs and down a hallway so narrow it would have been difficult for two people to pass one another.

He tried the porcelain doorknob but the room was locked. Siringo looked up and down the hallway and knocked softly.

On the third knock, Johnnie Neville opened the door. His eyes were full of sleep, his hair tousled and his thin, uneven shoulders hunched under a blanket with several moth holes. He squinted at Siringo without recognition.

"Yeah?"

Siringo held up Johnnie's crumpled letter.

"You sent this to us."

At the sound of Siringo's voice, Johnnie's eyes widened and he backed away from the door.

"Holy mother! Leon Allison."

"The name's Siringo."

He pushed his way in and closed the door behind him. Faint light, entering through the small window, revealed a room cluttered with dirty clothes, soiled bedding and copies of newspapers and gazettes scattered randomly about.

Johnnie collapsed onto the bed and pulled the blanket around him.

"I heard you was killed," Johnnie mumbled as he tried to get himself oriented.

"Do I look like I was killed? I'm here to talk to you about the reward we offered for Harry Orchard."

"I don't know no Harry Orchard," Johnnie said, staring with great concentration at his big, bare feet.

Siringo waved the letter in his face.

"You said in here that you could give us the names of the Bunker Hill dynamiters."

"I don't know nothing," Johnnie whispered. "I was drunk when I sent the letter."

"Do you know what would happen to you if the union saw this letter?" Siringo asked leaning close.

He wrinkled his nose at the sour smell of the bedding.

Johnnie nodded but didn't answer.

"For openers," Siringo said, "they'd probably cut off your pecker. After that, a couple of bully boys'd go to work on you with pick handles before they threw you down a mine shaft."

Johnnie made a little squeaking sound and tried to make himself smaller under the blanket.

"We're no longer interested in what happened in Idaho, Neville," Siringo continued. "We're keeping tabs on the union here."

"I ain't in the union no more," Johnnie gasped. "I don't know nothing."

"I know where you work. Popular place with the union boys, right? Keep your ears open and you may earn that reward."

Johnnie shuddered.

"They'll kill me."

Siringo slapped his face, twice, as hard as he could swing. Johnnie fell over on the bed to lie sniffling, his head covered with his blanket.

"You work for me now," Siringo said. "I'll be in touch."

He tossed a five-dollar gold piece on the floor and was gone.

The strike was two weeks old when the El Paso mine, with a ten-foot-high board fence around the property, reopened with a crew of seventy-five non-union men. Two days later, the Gold King began to erect a similar fence, while rough-looking imported deputies patrolled the area and exchanged insults with union pickets.

The final blow fell when the Vindicator announced that it was reopening with a scab crew. On a snowy afternoon, Orchard, Wyatt and Adams huddled with bundled-up pickets to watch workmen erect a tall fence and post a large sign beside the gate.

HELP WANTED–ABOVE AND BELOW GROUND
UNION WAGES
Strike Conditions

While they were reading the sign, McCormick and Mel Beck came out and seemed to be waiting for someone or something. When McCormick recognized Orchard, he came over to him.

"I'm sorry you're involved in this, Mr. Hogan."

"I go where the union goes, Mr. McCormick," Orchard said, "I'm sorry, you're sorry."

"Your union's broke its pick at this mine," McCormick growled and rejoined Beck, who regarded Orchard with an unfriendly scowl.

"We'll see whose pick is broke," Orchard said, but McCormick didn't hear him.

A few more minutes passed before a large group of non-union miners, laden with baggage and bedrolls, trudged up the road through the snow toward the mine gate. They were accompanied by a number of grim-faced men carrying Winchesters who had met them at the train. More armed special police appeared inside the gate to herd the men inside.

Wyatt spat a stream of tobacco juice into the snow.

"If the Vindicator gets going, all the other mines'll start up too, as soon as they can find crews," he told Orchard. "I'm gonna telephone Moyer and Haywood. We got to do something."

When Wyatt was gone, Adams muttered, "Them boys look scared. Shouldn't take too much to run 'em off."

Indeed, many of the newly hired workers cast apprehensive glances at the surly union pickets as they passed. They were an odd lot. Young men, hardly more than boys. Elderly miners, stooped from years in cramped tunnels. A smattering of dark-skinned foreigners who seemed oblivious to the hostile environment they were entering. McCormick and Beck were going to have their hands full getting full production from this bunch, Orchard thought.

"Bet if I was to shoot off my pistol, they'd run like rabbits," Adams said.

"Good way to get us all shot," Orchard warned. "A snowball might be better."

"By God, you might be right!"

Adams bent quickly to scoop up a double handful of wet snow which he packed into a hard ball. He hurled it at the scabs, striking one on the ear, almost knocking him off balance with his heavy load.

Other pickets began to throw snowballs, causing the laden men and their armed overseers to bob and weave to avoid being struck by the icy missiles.

The non-union men threw down their baggage and began to throw snowballs back at the pickets. When someone threw a rock, sending one of the pickets to his knees with a wound on the side of his head, a wild melee developed. Men attacked each other with bare hands, sticks and rocks.

Orchard and Adams found refuge behind a lumber pile, neither wishing to engage in the bloody free-for-all. The fight went on for over ten minutes when it was ended abruptly by a series of gun shots.

At the gate, several of the special police were firing their weapons into the air. They were joined by McCormick and Beck.

"These men have orders to shoot anyone who tries to damage this property or harm my crew," Beck yelled at the pickets. "Back off. You're on private property."

Beck was a big man with a booming voice. He walked toward the assembled pickets, clearly not intimidated by their numbers. The pickets began to move back from the gate.

"This dispute ain't going to be settled out here in the snow," he said.

Everyone's attention was suddenly diverted by the sight of another group of non-union miners coming up the road. They, too, were accompanied by armed men.

Orchard watched from behind the lumber pile. One of the escorts caught his attention; a big man, who walked with a limp, and carried a shotgun. It was Lyle Gregory.

Orchard pulled his head down so Gregory wouldn't see him when he passed. A sudden sharp twinge went through his side. He could feel his face getting hot and cold sweat ran down between his shoulder blades. Up until that moment, Orchard had stifled any inclination toward acts of violence against the Vindicator, but suddenly felt that Virgil McCormick and Mel Beck had betrayed him. It was infuriating to think that they could hire a murdering scum like Gregory.

"I'm gonna find Wyatt," Orchard told Adams and headed down the road without further explanation.

Wyatt wasn't at the union hall, nor at either the Gold Dollar or the Colorado Belle. Orchard stopped in several other union hangouts before giving up the search and returning to the Gold Dollar.

"I just saw the jasper who killed your sister," Orchard told Johnnie Neville, who was filling in for a sick barkeep. "The bastards at the Vindicator hired him as a guard."

Johnnie poured him a whiskey but didn't take his money.

"What are you gonna do?"

"I don't know yet, but something," Orchard said. "If you see Joe Wyatt, tell him I'll be back later."

He made his way home through drifting snow and found Bella at her machine busily stitching up a dress.

Bella looked up from her work. Her expression told him she was angry.

"You might have told me you wouldn't be home for supper," she said. "There's a plate in the oven for you. I won't join you because I have to finish this."

Orchard went to her and put his hands on her shoulders. She wriggled away from his touch.

"What are you sewing?"

"I'm making a ruffle for Mrs. McCormick."

"Bella, I don't want you doing any more work for that old sow."

Bella whirled around to face him.

"What are you talking about?"

"Her husband's hired some of the worst strikebreakers in the country, including the son-of-a-bitch who shot me in Wardner."

Bella's shoulders slumped.

"Oh, my God!"

Just as suddenly, she drew herself up to confront her husband.

"What did you expect, Tom? Mr. McCormick has to keep the mine open any way he can, no matter what your damn union says."

Orchard stared at her with mock disbelief.

"You sound like you're on his side."

"I'm not on anybody's side. Don't try to drag me into this."

"You're on my side," Orchard growled. "You're my wife and you'll do what I say!"

"Tom, you're drunk," Bella said, getting up. "Let me put your supper on the table."

"Well, thank you, wife," Orchard said. "Let me put this in the stove."

He ripped the fabric out of the sewing machine, jerked open the stove door, burning his hand, and stuffed it into the flames.

Bella watched him with a stricken expression as he jerked open the front door and plunged into the night.

Wyatt was waiting for him at the Gold Dollar. The place was quiet. The billiard and card tables were deserted. Johnnie was hunkered down at the end of the bar talking to a pair of beer drinkers. Orchard declined Wyatt's offer of a whiskey and they took seats at the empty poker table in the back corner.

"I talked to Haywood," Wyatt said. "He's really worked up over the Vindicator opening."

"Well, all is not lost," Orchard said. "There's plenty of gelatin stored in that mine, Joe. If it was to blow up, those scabs would be on the next train out of here. I'd have a go at touching it off, if the price was right."

"You're talking about killing a lot of people," Wyatt said.

Orchard shook his head.

"I'm talking about making a lot of noise. The stuff's stored on the seventh level where no one's working."

Wyatt seemed relieved by that.

"I could talk to Haywood. See what he says."

"Tell him I'd need a hundred dollars," Orchard said.

The next day, in the Altman union hall, Wyatt told him in confidence that he had Haywood's blessing.

"Remember," Wyatt cautioned, "for now, we just want to scare off the scabs."

That night, after supper with a solemn, unspeaking Bella, Orchard put on his coat and left the house. He told his wife he was off to collect a debt.

Jake Schultz was waiting for him at the Colorado Belle. They each had a hot rum to ward off the evening chill before taking a path up Bull Hill toward

293

the Vindicator.

"You didn't say anything to Johnnie Neville about what we're up to, did you, Jake?"

They had paused to catch their breath. The lights on the Vindicator shaft house were a few hundred yards away.

"Naw," Schultz replied. "I ain't ever trusted him. I know he's one of your Idaho boys, but he asks too many questions. That goddamn Adams tells the son-of-a-bitch everything when he's drunk."

"Which is often," Orchard said.

He found Schultz's comment interesting. It seemed to him that Johnnie had become increasingly inquisitive in recent weeks. Though he himself confided nothing in him, it made him wonder, nonetheless.

"Down," Schultz whispered, pulling Orchard off the trail.

They lay on their bellies in the dark while two mine guards trudged by, rifles in their hands.

"Plenty of them bastards around," Shultz warned as they resumed their climb toward the unused tunnel mouth where they could enter the Vindicator workings undetected. It was here that they had stored their daily glommings from their high-grading efforts.

Once inside the tunnel, Orchard and Schultz lit the candles they'd brought, picking their way through fallen debris to an abandoned shaft. Here, they doused the candles so they'd have both hands free, before commencing a downward climb of several hundred feet in total darkness. The rungs of the old ladder, some broken, others missing, were familiar to them for their high-grading forays before the strike.

Following a crosscut which had been their high-grading route, they emerged into the main tunnel on the seventh level, pausing to relight their candles. The dynamite boxes were stored along one side of the tunnel, several hundred yards from the active shaft where the elevator descended into the mine.

"There's enough here to take the top off of Bull Hill," Schultz whispered gleefully. "You just want to cut a long fuse and light it when the first shift shows up in the morning? It'll still be dark. We'd be able to get away."

"Too risky," Orchard said. "I've got a better idea."

Actually, it had come the night before as he sat across the kitchen table from his sullen wife.

"We'll take a few boxes and stack them near the elevator shaft," he explained to Schultz. "I'll rig it so the first person comes down here for some gelatin'll set it off."

By flickering candle light, Orchard and Schultz stacked eight boxes of dynamite near the elevator shaft. Orchard took a roll of copper wire from his pocket and lashed his Iver Johnson to an upright timber, so it pointed directly at the boxes. Then he ran a piece of wire from the revolver's trigger to the gate which had to be raised to get in and out of the elevator cage. After he'd made sure that raising the gate would pull the pistol's trigger, Orchard carefully pulled the hammer back to full cock.

"Let's get out of here."

Bella was asleep when he slid into bed beside her. She made a little sound when he put his arms around her and didn't pull away from him as she'd done the night before. That was a good sign. Maybe tomorrow they could ride the trolley to Cripple Creek and have dinner at the Criterion. Good food and wine might put a smile back on her face. If not, he'd have to wait for time, the great healer, to do its work—provided it didn't take too long.


Virgil McCormick and Mel Beck rode the cage down to the sixth level to check on work being performed by their new crew. Many of the men who had been brought back into the district as strikebreakers were relatively inexperienced and progress was painfully slow.

"Some of these fellows are coal miners," Beck explained. "They're lost in hard rock."

McCormick and Beck reentered the cage and told the operator to ring for the seventh level.

"Maybe we can use some of these men for clean up down here," McCormick said "They sure as hell aren't good for much else."

The cage stopped. Beck had ordered the electric lights turned on at this level, in anticipation of McCormick's inspection tour.

"There's a stope back here, we could start them on," Beck said, reaching to raise the gate. "Some of the ore looks..."

Some body parts were never found and investigators at the scene counted as a miracle the fact that two hundred boxes of dynamite stored nearby hadn't gone off.

A few scraps of copper wire and a shattered Iver Johnson pistol led investigators to conclude that the blast had been a deliberate act of sabotage.

The day following the blast, an aura of gloom hovered over the district. The atmosphere in the Gold Dollar Saloon was particularly somber. Many of the men who frequented the place had worked at the Vindicator before the strike and knew McCormick and Beck to be friendly, thoughtful supervisors.

Orchard, Jake Schultz and Steve Adams sat at a table with a copy of the Victor Record spread out in front of them. On his way from the union hall, Orchard had picked up a copy of the special edition, which was being hawked by raucous little boys on the streets of every town in the district.

The Record's headline blared, VINDICATOR BLAST NO ACCIDENT. There were photographs of McCormick and Beck, the latter obviously a wedding picture. They were captioned, MURDERED BOSSES. There was also a photograph of Orchard's revolver with some copper wire still wrapped around the grip.

"We're in deep shit, boys," Schultz muttered as he stared at the newspaper.

"It was an accident, Jake," Orchard said.

He was annoyed that Schultz and Adams were both quite drunk by the time he'd joined them. He wanted to discuss possible ways to spread the word that the explosion had been an accident caused by the Vindicator's scab crew.

Even tough Joe Wyatt had been shaken by the Vindicator explosion. Almost grudgingly, he'd handed Orchard the promised hundred dollars.

"Virg McCormick and Mel Beck were both friends of mine and friends of the union," Wyatt told him. "This is a terrible thing."

Orchard carefully put the bills in his pocketbook.

"I understand a bunch of their fellows quit right after it happened," Orchard said. "That's what we wanted, wasn't it?"

He disliked being put on the defensive over something which had Haywood's sanction.

"I told you what I wanted, Hogan, but you must not have been listening," Wyatt said. "I talked to Haywood this morning and he's none too happy about this, either."

"He was happy enough yesterday."

"That was before he'd heard that Governor Peabody was calling out the National Guard," Wyatt said. "You see, we got a good bit more than we bargained for."

"Unintended consequences," Orchard said airily, going to the door. "I have things to do."

Now at the Gold Dollar, Adams picked up the bottle and refilled their glasses. He set it down hard on the table and grinned at Orchard.

"I heard there's a big crowd at the train depot," he said gleefully. "Scabs headed back to Montana and Utah and maybe even Roosha,"

He drained his glass and blinked his eyes like a happy toad.

"Wyatt says the governor's calling out the National Guard," Orchard said. "If that happens, some of us are going to have to lay low for a while."

"I can't go nowhere," Schultz protested. "My old lady can't walk but a few steps at a time."

"Well, better put in some supplies and stay off the street 'til this blows over," Orchard advised.

If Adams hadn't been present, he'd have given Schultz twenty-five dollars to cover his needs but he could wait until he and Schultz were alone. No sense in letting Adams know he was flush with cash.

Orchard went to the bar to buy some cigars, hoping to avoid any conversation with Johnnie Neville, who was still filling in for the absent barkeep. No such luck. Johnnie set the box in front of him and leaned close.

"I heard they found McCormick's shoe, with his foot still in it, on the sixth level."

"Must have been a hell of a blast," Orchard said.

Johnnie whispered, "Adams says that Schultz done it."

Orchard leaned close to grip Johnnie's thin wrist, causing him to wince.

"I didn't get you out of Idaho to spread rumors, Johnnie. Best you just keep your mouth shut about what you hear."

Johnnie swallowed hard and nodded solemnly when Orchard let go of him and returned to the table.

It was snowing again by the time Orchard got off the trolley in Goldfield. A young boy was selling newspapers in the depot and seemed to be doing a brisk business in spite of the bad weather. Orchard was hoping that Bella hadn't seen the Vindicator story when he stepped inside and knocked the snow off his derby.

She was sitting at the kitchen table with her back to him when he came in. She made no movement to indicate that she knew he was home.

"On my way home, I bought two tickets to Denver," Orchard said, trying to sound cheerful.

Then he saw the Victor Record on the table in front of her.

Bella pointed at the photographs and turned to face him. Her eyes were red and her cheeks were wet with tears.

"Who did this, Tom? Your murdering union cronies?"

"Bella, the union wasn't involved," Orchard said. "It had to be an accident, caused by a green scab crew."

Bella rose to face him. She was trembling and her voice had a strange guttural tone.

"The union's always involved when the bosses are killed. If it ever turns on you, you'll be as dead as they are."

"The union won't turn on me."

She took a step toward him, fists clenched.

"I want you out of my house and out of my life, Tom," Bella screamed. "The union stands between us like another woman. I must have been mad to think you could give her up for me."

Orchard reached for her but she backed away from him and slapped at his hands.

"If I have to choose between you and the union..." Orchard began lamely.

"You've made your choice. Just get out. Get out! Get out!"

Bella collapsed, sobbing, into her chair, her head on her arms, covering the photo of his Iver Johnson.

# CHAPTER THIRTY

Orchard moved back to Mrs. Graeme's boarding house but in less than a week there, he began to feel hemmed in. Governor Peabody had declared that Teller County was in a state of rebellion and had dispatched the National Guard, under Adjutant General Ben Sheridan, to occupy the district and impose martial law.

Encampments were established in Cripple Creek, Victor, Altman and Goldfield. In Altman, union men were being seized on the street, held incommunicado and interrogated by National Guard officers and special police. Some of the interrogations were such bloody affairs that several subjects lay near death in the Cripple Creek hospital. When the Victor Record protested the suppression of men's rights, the entire staff was arrested and held overnight in the Victor Armory.

Since it was too risky to try to see Bella in Goldfield and with undisciplined soldiers roaming the streets of all the towns, Orchard decided to spend a few days in Denver. He made it to the depot and boarded the train unmolested. The soldiers seemed more interested in people entering the district than those leaving.

Orchard registered at an inexpensive Denver hotel, not far from the Western Federation headquarters. After he'd deposited his bag in his room he went directly to a hardware store to purchase the latest thing in firearms; a Colt eight-shot automatic pistol, chambered for .38 caliber high-pressure cartridges. The pistol and a box of fifty shells cost him almost twenty dollars, but the comfort it brought, tucked in his waistband, seemed worth the extravagance.

Orchard entered the Western Federation offices with some trepidation, unsure of the reception he'd receive. Wyatt had made it sound as though Haywood was angry and totally dissatisfied with the Vindicator outcome.

Moyer was out of town and Haywood, after keeping him waiting for over an hour, greeted him with modest enthusiasm.

"Too bad about getting the bosses instead of the scabs," Haywood rumbled, "but after all, Harry, we shut down the mine. That was the goal."

Haywood waved him to a chair. Orchard noted that he'd been reading the Denver Post, whose front page was plastered with stories of martial law in the Cripple Creek district.

"Joe Wyatt isn't too happy about it," Orchard said, sitting down and shifting the automatic so it wouldn't dig into his stomach.

"Why not?" Haywood demanded. "Two enemies of the working man and a scab blown to bits. Good job, I say and I'll tell Wyatt the same thing."

Haywood paused to look at him.

"How do you feel about it, Harry? Are you sorry?"

"I'm never sorry, Bill," Orchard replied. "Beck and McCormick were nice enough fellows but they were on the wrong side. After I saw they had Lyle Gregory on the payroll, I'd have bombed the gates of heaven. Looking back, the only thing I'm sorry about is not killing more scabs."

Haywood chuckled appreciatively.

"You are a cold-blooded devil, Harry. I wish I had a thousand like you."

They discussed the Cripple Creek strike and the possibility that it, like the one in the Coeur d'Alene, might fail. At the mention of Idaho, Haywood's face darkened and his manner changed.

"I'll never be happy until we've paid back Bromley and Steunenberg for their treachery."

Haywood's teeth clamped down on his cigar, threatening to sever it in two.

"Those two are walking around while better men rot in jail."

Haywood was getting so agitated that he had to pause to catch his breath.

"They're both dead men, Harry, as sure as we're sitting here. You and I'll live to piss on their graves."

The ringing telephone ended his tirade. Haywood picked it up to carry on a conversation with the caller which consisted of little more than a few angry grunts before he slammed down the receiver. "That was Wyatt. The Findley mine just reopened with a scab crew."

The Findley, near Independence, was not as big an operation as the Vindicator, but its reopening diminished the effect of the Vindicator shutting down.

Haywood mashed out his cigar in a gold pan he used for an ashtray.

"He said the National Guard soldiers stood by while special deputies beat the shit out of our pickets at the Independence Depot where the scabs take the train."

Haywood stared into space, apparently speechless with anger that such an outrage could occur. His feigned indignation always fascinated Orchard. Haywood could issue a death warrant on a high-ranking official with one breath and get totally worked up over a few black eyes and broken noses with the next.

"That might be a good place to do up some scabs," Orchard said. "A few boxes of gelatin under the platform when the shifts change..."

Haywood didn't answer immediately, but finally said, "Do you think you could pull that off?"

"Probably," Orchard said, "but it's risky with the soldiers and company thugs all over the place."

Haywood got up and went to the window. When he turned to look at Orchard, his left eye twinkled with good humor.

"Harry, it's me, Bill Haywood. You aren't talking about risk. You're talking about dollars."

Orchard shrugged, amused by the banter.

"I could put that depot up in the air for a hundred and fifty dollars, Bill.

"Could you put it up higher for two?"

Haywood was grinning now.

"I want to close the Findley, Harry, just like you closed the Vindicator. We have to hit them again to show those people that martial law means nothing to us. Two hundred dollars. Half now and half when the smoke clears."

"I think I'd like to have all of it now," Orchard said. "I don't know where I'll be living after I pull this off. Colorado's going to be a dangerous place for me."

"Maybe you could go to San Francisco."

Haywood made it sound like a casual suggestion but Orchard knew immediately what he was talking about.

"For business or pleasure?"

"It would be my pleasure to have you take care of Frank Bromley, Harry."

"That's a tall order," Orchard said. "You'd really have to make it worth my while." He smiled reflectively. "You know, Bill, I'm almost forty years old and I know more about murder than I do about mining. It has to end sometime. I'd like to live the rest of my life with a good woman in a quiet town."

"Would five hundred dollars make it worth your while?"

Five hundred dollars! Enough to buy an interest in a saloon somewhere. Enough for a fresh start.

"When I'm finished in Cripple Creek I'll let you know where to send my trunk and the money."

"There's another five for Steunenberg, Harry."

"Plus expenses."

Haywood stuck out his big paw.

"Plus expenses."

Johnnie Neville had just deposited a box of trash in the alley behind the

Gold Dollar when two hands seized him by the shirtfront and slammed him against the building. In the dim light emanating from the saloon's back door, he recognized Siringo.

"Jesus, you scared me," he told the detective. "What do you want?"

"I want the names of the men who blew up the Vindicator."

"I only got one," Johnnie said, "but I ain't too sure he's the one."

"Was it Harry Orchard?"

"I told you, I don't know no Harry Orchard."

"Then who?"

"The union finds out I told you, I'm a dead man."

"You don't give me a name, you're a dead man anyway."

"If I had some money I could get out of here. Go somewhere safe."

"The owners of the Vindicator have put up a five thousand dollar reward," Siringo said, dangling the bait.

"Would I get that, if I give you the name?"

"Like the poster says, 'upon arrest and conviction.'"

"Shit. That could be years."

"Suit yourself. I can have your letter delivered to Joe Wyatt in the morning and you'll never see another sunrise."

Siringo turned as if to leave.

"Wait!"

Johnnie checked the half-open door to make sure no one might come looking for him.

"It's Jake Schultz."

Johnnie's whole body seemed to sag, as though all the vitality had left it.

"I've never finked on no one," he whispered to Siringo before he reentered the saloon and bolted the door.

Jake Schultz was arrested and dragged from his home in Altman at seven in the morning by a young National Guard lieutenant and two special deputies, Walter Kenley and an ex-convict known in the district as Dumps Benton.

In the scuffle which preceded the actual arrest, Benton struck Schultz's semi-invalid wife with his fist, breaking her cheekbone and knocking her unconscious. They left her lying in the snow when they hauled Schultz away. Frightened neighbors came to her assistance after everyone had gone.

Schultz was hustled aboard the electric trolley and taken to Victor where he was lodged in the city jail. His cell mate was a slim, bearded man, charged with tearing down a posted declaration of martial law. He told Schultz his name was Charlie Dawes. It was a risky assignment and had to be concluded quickly. He was sure that Lyle Gregory, now employed as the Vindicator's head bully boy, would probably recognize him, beard or no beard. That wouldn't have been fatal because they were both on the same side, but could be if Gregory shot off his mouth about it.

Schultz, one eye swollen shut and with blood oozing from a badly split lip, sat disconsolately on his cot staring at the heavy wood door with its barred window.

"That bastard, Benton, hit my old lady hard as you'd hit a man," he muttered, as though talking to himself. "And her, hardly able to walk."

Siringo didn't reply. He hadn't liked the looks of Kenley or Benton when he'd met with them and a National Guard major the night before, to give them Schultz's name. Both of the deputies, paid by the Mine Owners Association, like most of the others, were hard cases. They were useful only in the kind of emergency situation which was developing in the district, where desperate miners were resorting to acts of vandalism and arson. He wouldn't have been surprised to find Pinkerton bulletins on both of them.

At ten o'clock, the cell door was opened by a jailer who ordered Siringo out.

"Soldiers want to talk to you, Dawes. Get a move on."

In the office, the major, the lieutenant, along with Kenley and Benton, awaited his report.

"I couldn't get a word out of him," Siringo said. "He's worried about his wife." He gave Benton a long look.

"He said she was beaten up when you men arrested him, and her a cripple."

305

The major sat up a little straighter to look askance at the lieutenant, who made a helpless gesture.

Benton, big and raw-boned, reddened.

"All I done was shove the old bitch out of the way."

"Well, he's not talking," Siringo said, "and I don't intend to spend all day waiting for him to change his mind."

He could feel himself becoming irritable. He hadn't had much sleep and his mood wasn't improved by the company he was forced to keep.

A breathless National Guard corporal burst into the office to confront the officers, giving them a hasty salute.

"They's a fight goin' on in a sporting house over by the fire station," he blurted. "Unionists got the place surrounded and are tryin' to set the place on fire."

The major glowered at the corporal.

"Why would the fools want to burn down a whorehouse?"

"Well, sir," the corporal said, exchanging a sly glance with Siringo, "some of our boys is trapped inside."

"But they're on duty," the shocked major protested, jumping up. "Come on, Lieutenant."

The jailer was getting Siringo's revolver when Kenley said, "Gimme your keys, Roy. Me and Benton are gonna mosey down and have a little chat with Mr. Schultz."

The jailer took his ring of keys from a nail on the wall and tossed them to Kenley, a muscular man of medium height, who caught the ring and entered the lockup. Benton followed.

The jailer had just handed over Siringo's weapon when both he and the jailer heard the sounds of a scuffle, punctuated by grunts and squeals of protests. Then Schultz screamed; the long, desperate howl of a man who was either terrified or in great pain.

Siringo made a move to enter the lockup but the jailer stepped in front of him.

"I'll see to this, Siringo. Stay put."

Siringo hurriedly put on his holster and checked the rounds in his revolver. He was dropping the weapon into leather when Kenley and Benton came out of the lockup, followed by the white-faced jailer. Benton was wiping his hands on his pants.

Kenley's thin lips twisted into a smile when he said, "We're looking for a fellow named Tom Hogan in Goldfield."

Siringo felt his heart jump. Hogan had to be Harry Orchard, using the same alias he'd used in Idaho! Of course, Johnnie Neville had lied about not knowing him, but he could be dealt with later.

"Schultz says they pulled it alone," Kenley continued, "and I believe him."

He and Benton exchanged an amused glance. The jailer seemed to be growing increasingly agitated.

From the lockup came the sound of Schultz sobbing and moaning.

Siringo asked, "What did you do to him?"

Kenley drew a clasp knife from his trouser pocket and flipped it open to reveal a heavy blade.

"I showed him this. We pulled down his pants. Benton grabbed his balls and I told him we was gonna make a steer out of him." He paused to grin at Benton. "That's when he started to beg and spill his guts at the same time."

Benton was still wiping his hands on his pants leg.

"Peed all over me."

Siringo stared at the two grinning thugs. He would have enjoyed putting a bullet into each of them. It was always the same in these struggles. Each side, bent on outdoing the other, resorted to unspeakable mayhem.

"Did you cut him?"

"I might have knicked him a tad," Kenley replied. "He'll be good as new by the time the strike's over."

"Not if he don't see a doctor, he won't," the jailer blurted and grabbed up the telephone.

Siringo didn't wait for the outcome. Schultz's health wasn't his concern. He wanted to find the major and get a detail of soldiers to assist in the apprehension and arrest of Harry Orchard.

It was early afternoon before Siringo and his contingent arrived in Goldfield. Because of Orchard's importance, Sheriff Aiken of Teller County wanted to be involved and had to come from Cripple Creek. Despite the overlying power of martial law, Aiken wanted to obtain a no-bail warrant from the County Prosecutor's office so, as he said, "There can be no slip-ups." Apparently, past experience with lawyers representing members of the Western Federation of Miners had taught him that the law could be circumvented by well-paid sharp minds.

The committee approach to law enforcement annoyed Siringo and had been instrumental in his choice of the Pinkerton Agency to pursue his career. As a detective with a private organization, he had much wider latitude in carrying out his duties.

He was doubly annoyed when Aiken finally showed up, accompanied by two of his own deputies as well as Walter Kenley and Dumps Benton. Siringo had learned, subsequent to leaving the Victor jail, that Jake Schultz had almost bled to death and was now lodged in the hospital in Cripple Creek.

One thing was certain, he told himself, despite Orchard's murderous misdeeds, neither Kenley nor Benton would lay a hand on him, if he had to shoot them both to prevent it. He expressed this to Sheriff Aiken, who assured him that the two special deputies were there only to represent the Mine Owners Association

After a few inquiries, Bella's house was located and the squad of soldiers surrounded it. Sheriff Aiken bustled up to the front door to knock loudly. Siringo placed himself behind Aiken and in front of Kenley and Benton, who had moved ahead of Aiken's own deputies.

Bella opened the door and was obviously startled to see such an array of armed men standing in the snow in front of, and around her house. For an instant, Siringo didn't recognize her. She was thinner than she'd been the last time he'd seen her on Mill Street in Wardner. It was apparent that she didn't recognize him either as her eyes swept the group before returning to stare quizzically at the sheriff.

"Yes?"

"I have a warrant for the arrest of Thomas Hogan," Aiken said in his official voice. "Is he here, ma'am?"

"No," Bella said, shaking her head nervously, "I believe he's in Denver. On business."

"Are you Mrs. Hogan?" Aiken asked.

Bella nodded but said nothing. She was clearly intimidated and unnerved by such a show of force.

"Excuse me, Sheriff," Siringo said, pressing forward.

He could tell by the way Bella was looking at him that she was trying to place him.

"Hello, Bella," he said. "You probably don't remember me from Idaho."

"Yes, I think I do," she said. "Mr. Allison?"

"That's right," Siringo told her, "but my real name's Siringo. I'm a Pinkerton detective."

Bella frowned and she pushed her hair away from her face. She gave him a nervous little smile.

"Seems everyone has more than one name these days."

"I'm afraid so," Siringo said. "The man you know as Thomas Hogan is actually named Harry Orchard."

Bella took a deep breath.

"What's he wanted for?"

Siringo suspected she might already know the answer to that question.

"He's wanted for the Vindicator mine explosion," Aiken said, reasserting his authority. "We're gonna have to search the house, Missus."

Bella said nothing as she stepped aside to allow Aiken and Siringo to enter her living room. Siringo, already impressed by Bella's composure, was further taken by her clean, well-furnished home. His eyes traveled around the room, taking in the tufted sofa, the sewing machine, and finally coming to rest on a small, carved sideboard. There, in a silver frame was a photograph of Orchard and Bella. He picked it up to examine the faces. Orchard, sitting stiffly with his derby cradled in the crook of his arm, looked just the same; neither smiling nor frowning. Inscrutable. Poor Bella. She looked happy.

Sheriff Aiken gave the bedroom and kitchen a cursory look before asking, "Where's your husband staying in Denver?"

"I don't know," Bella said. "We're no longer living together."

"I'll have to take this, Bella," Siringo said, holding up the photograph he'd taken out of the frame.

He tried to sound matter-of-fact, but a picture of Harry Orchard was a priceless treasure. His face would soon be adorning reward posters plastered all over the Cripple Creek district.

"I'm sorry," he told her.

"I understand," Bella said. "You're doing your job."

# CHAPTER THIRTY-ONE

After a week in Denver, Orchard, wearing a pair of stage glasses he'd found in a curio shop, arrived at the Cripple Creek train depot in the early evening. In addition to his automatic pistol, he was armed with fresh business cards introducing him as H.S. Thomas–Triangle School Supplies–Chicago, Ill.

As he debarked from the Colorado Short Line and crossed the depot to board the Florence and Cripple Creek train, he was acutely aware of the profusion of National Guard troops, some armed with rifles and fixed bayonets.

Men in working garb who were traveling alone were being singled out for interrogation. It seemed that neither men accompanied by their families nor the scattering of well-dressed business travelers like himself were troubled by the soldiers.

In Denver he'd listened to a diatribe by Haywood on the dangers inherent in having the Mine Owners Association reimburse the state for the mainte- nance of the National Guard, as was the case in Colorado. He'd thought little about it at the time, but now, observing these sometimes raucous, often rude and bullying young citizen-soldiers in what amounted to a private army, the potential for abuse was clearly evident.

He was waiting to board the train when he saw Steve Adams approaching. He didn't recognize him at first because Adams was wearing a trainman's striped overalls and had an FC&C brakeman's badge pinned to his billed cap. He shook his head when Orchard opened his mouth to speak and squatted down beside the coach to check the packing in a journal box.

Orchard took out a cigar and searched his pocket for a match. Apparently finding none, he approached Adams, indicating he needed a light.

Adams, burning match cupped in his hands, leaned close to mutter, "Get off at Victor. Soldiers watching your house. Schultz talked."

"How'd they get on to him?"

"I think Neville turned him in."

The engineer blew two sharp blasts and the train began to move. Orchard tipped his hat to Adams and climbed aboard. He took a seat in the almost deserted coach across the aisle from a major and a captain, both of whom ignored him.

He settled back to stare at the copy of the Denver Post he removed from his coat pocket. It was hard for him to believe that Shultz had given him away voluntarily. The man was as solid as the granite of Bull Hill. Maybe they'd bought him. Orchard knew he was short of money and had never given him anything after they'd done the Vindicator. He was still puzzling over this when the train pulled into Victor.

There was less military presence in the Victor depot than there had been at Cripple Creek. A few troops lolling on baggage carts were the only evidence of martial law. He was trying to decide where he could stay when he saw Adams get off the last car, cross the platform to lean against a stanchion to light a cigar.

Orchard stopped near Adams to rummage in his pockets as though he might have lost a key or a baggage check.

"King George Hotel," Adams hissed. "Room twenty. I'll meet you."

With that, Adams was gone, disappearing into the darkness beyond the lights of the platform. Orchard picked up his bag and prepared to follow when he was halted by a sharp command.

He found himself facing a boyish-looking National Guard captain and a hard-eyed special deputy. The captain was blond and had a wispy moustache which reminded Orchard of George Armstrong Custer. Probably why the kid wore it,

"Hold up there, Mister. All persons entering Victor are required to state their business and provide identification."

Smiling easily, Orchard set down his bag again and extended his business card.

"Horace Thomas, school supplies. The latest thing in fountain pens."

He hoped the captain didn't ask him for a sample because the fountain pen embellishment had been the first thing to cross his mind.

The captain studied the card.

"You're not from Colorado, then?"

"No sir," Orchard said, ignoring the captain's apparent stupidity. "Can't handle the altitude for more than a day or two."

"This man look familiar to you, Mr. Kenley?" the captain asked the deputy.

Walter Kenley looked over the fountain pen salesman from Chicago and shook his head.

"Never seen him around here," Kenley said. "Maybe Siringo ought to have a look at him."

Orchard continued to maintain a pose of conviviality but unbuttoned two buttons on his overcoat. Odd, he thought, it could all end right here on the depot platform. He had eight shots. Siringo. The captain. The man called Kenley. He directed a glance at the lolling soldiers on the baggage carts. Maybe a couple of them before they recovered their wits and shot him.

"Siringo's in Goldfield," the captain said.

He handed back Orchard's card with a shrug and a smile.

"You may proceed, sir. You look all right to me."

Adams was waiting in room twenty at the King George Hotel. On the bed, Orchard recognized his work clothes and his shotgun.

"Soon's I heard they was after you," Adams explained, "I grabbed what I could at your boarding house."

"Glad you did," Orchard said. "I'll need that stuff for a job Haywood wants you and me to do. Now, tell me what happened."

"I think it was my fault," Adams said. "I told Neville Schultz done it. I was drunk and he was asking questions."

Orchard started to speak harshly but Adams held up his hand to stop him.

"After that, people told me they seen Neville talking to a gent that fits Siringo's description."

Orchard felt like shooting Adams right there, but he needed him for the Independence Depot. Maybe later. Maybe never. It depended on the outcome of the next job.

"I'm disappointed in old Schultzie," Orchard said.

"He's in the hospital," Adams said. "After he was arrested, the Vindicator's special police got hold of him in the jail. A deputy named Kenley tried to castrate him."

As he listened to Adams's account of Schultz's ordeal, Orchard felt a chill. He would have spilled too if they'd done that to him.

"I met Kenley in the depot tonight," Orchard said. "I'll put him on my list, along with Lyle Gregory."

"Want me to help you with them bastards?" Adams asked. "I could find out where they hang out and we could wait for them."

"You find out and get back to me here," Orchard said. "I'll do the waiting. After I'm done with them, you and I are going to put a train station up in the air."

Orchard took out his pocketbook and handed Adams fifty dollars in ten-dollar bills.

"Nose around and find us a couple of boxes of dynamite," Orchard told him. "We're going to need a place to lay up for a few days, too."

Orchard slept well that night and in the morning he put on his glasses and ventured out boldly to acquire some items for the Independence Depot job. He could have bought sulfuric acid in Denver but he feared it would eat up all his clothes if the stopper came out.

Adams thought he knew where he could buy some dynamite and he sometimes used an abandoned prospector's cabin on Grizzly Flat, where they could go afterward. The money Orchard had given him would cover the gelatin as well as the supplies they'd need while they waited for things to die down in the district.

Orchard was conflicted about trying to see Bella again. He knew he'd have to leave the district when he'd finished his assignment, perhaps never to return. As soon as he was done here, he'd be off to San Francisco to exact the union's revenge on Frank Bromley. He wondered if the lure of California might be enough to persuade Bella to come with him. A voice inside him declared that it was wishful thinking, but male ego persuaded him to try to see her one more time. Maybe the memory of how good they were together in bed might be the tipping point. He shoved some graphic images aside as he loaded his shotgun.

# CHAPTER THIRTY-TWO

Orchard was surprised to find that Sadie LaRue's brothel had burned to the ground in his absence. He passed the pile of charred sticks on his way to the Divide Music Hall. According to Adams, it was the National Guard watering hole in Victor and was also frequented by many of the Vindicator's special deputies, including both Lyle Gregory and Walter Kenley. The saloons in Altman had proven to be too dangerous for any non-union drinkers, forcing many to make the trek to Victor where the union held less sway.

The frozen snow crunched under his feet and a sharp wind caused him to turn up the collar on his mackinaw. Beneath wool gloves, the metal of the shotgun was cold to the touch.

The night was eerily quiet, the silence broken occasionally by sounds of laughter coming from the Divide as he approached.

With a heavy scarf covering much of his face, Orchard felt relatively immune to being identified. He stepped up on the saloon's front porch and peered in through the front window. He saw Gregory hunched over a beer stein at the bar but couldn't recognize Kenley among the twenty or so patrons seated or standing around the room. The small stage at the back of the room was dark, indicating that either business was bad or the entertainers, such as they were, had fled the violence.

He was about to turn away, concluding that someone else could do the hard case another time, when Kenley suddenly entered the room through the back door, buttoning up his trousers. He joined Gregory at the bar to claim the stein hidden from Orchard's view by Gregory's bulk.

Before he could get off the porch, two drunken soldiers staggered through the front door. So intent were they on laughing and shoving each other that they didn't see him standing in the shadows.

When they had gone, Orchard crossed the street and entered a small church which seemed to be located like a spider web to entrap the drunken sinners as they stumbled out of the Divide. A single light bulb dangled from a cord in the cramped vestibule. Behind rough-hewn double doors, Orchard could hear muted voices.

A notice tacked on the wall announced that bible study would be conducted Monday through Thursday from seven to nine in the evening. Well, old or new testament, this would have to do. If he had to wait out in the wind and cold, his fingers would be too stiff to pull the trigger when his quarry appeared.

Orchard reached up to unscrew the light bulb and settled back against one wall to begin his vigil. If anyone came out of the church before he was finished he'd have to come up with some kind of excuse for being there. He'd jump over that porcupine when he came to it.

He'd waited perhaps twenty minutes when the double doors opened and a small group of middle-aged men and women pushed into the vestibule. They clutched their bibles to their bosoms like Roman shields.

"Watch your step," Orchard cautioned. "Let me hold the door for you. The light's burnt out."

A woman's voice called out, "Again?"

Keeping his shotgun at his side, Orchard held the outer door until everyone was outside. As the last woman stepped into the snow, he saw two men emerge from the Divide Music Hall. He wasn't sure who they were until they passed under a street light. Their sizes should have told him they were Gregory and Kenley and the light on their faces confirmed it.

Gregory carried his ever-present shotgun. They headed for the trolley line while the church group went in the opposite direction, breaking up and disappearing down side streets to the accompaniment of cheerful goodnights.

Orchard followed Gregory and Kenley at a safe distance, flexing his cold fingers. As the voices of the churchgoers faded, the street became very still. Somewhere in the distance a woman was singing off-key, in a high pitched, tremulous voice.

When a lighted trolley car appeared ahead, Orchard made his move. He increased his pace until he was well within range and put a load of buckshot into Gregory's broad back. Gregory seemed to be suspended in a rigid upright position for a moment before falling forward and rolling on his side, arms and legs flopping and great wheezing sounds coming from the bloody holes in his lungs.

Orchard pumped the shotgun and covered Kenley. The deputy reached for something under his coat and his hand came out with a heavy pistol dangling from his fingers. He dropped it into the snow and stepped away from it.

"Whoa, brother. I ain't armed," Kenley declared breathlessly. "You got no reason to shoot me. I don't even know you."

"Well, I know you, Kenley," Orchard said, "and I do have a reason. His name is Jake Schultz."

"Oh, Jesus," Kenley panted. "I didn't mean..."

Orchard never would find out what it was that Kenley didn't mean to do. He shot him between the legs, just below the bottom of his coat. The force of the charge knocked him backward several steps before he fell down and drew his knees close to his body. A crimson stain spread beneath him as the big arteries in his thighs pumped blood. The shock was so intense that he made no sound for half a minute. Then came a series of hoarse moans as he writhed in the bloody snow.

Orchard bent over Gregory, who was still alive. Gregory nodded his head.

"I knew it was you in Telluride."

Orchard pumped the shotgun and placed the end of the barrel under Gregory's bloody chin.

"Go ahead," Gregory gurgled. "I'd do it to you."

Orchard pulled the trigger.

# CHAPTER THIRTY-THREE

Orchard and Adams arrived in Independence a little after ten o'clock at night. Adams led Orchard to a brushy gulch near the depot where he'd hidden dynamite he'd bought from some leasers on Bull Hill. It consisted of three boxes of 1XX and an opened box of 2XX, old and leaking. Nitroglycerine oozed through the oiled paper.

Angrily wiping his sticky hand on his pants leg after handling one of the sticks, Orchard muttered, "This damn stuff could get us blown to hell instead of the scabs. Don't drop any of it or we'll all go together."

"Best I could do on short notice," Adams said, sounding aggrieved. "I didn't buy it at the Miners Supply, you know."

"I know," Orchard said. "You did the best you could. Better let me carry it, though."

The village street was deserted and dark as a coal mine, too poor for electric street lamps. They walked down the railroad tracks to the depot. In his pocket, Orchard carried a carton of giant caps, a small vial of sulfuric acid and a fishing reel containing several hundred yards of line.

Adams, grunting under the weight of the fifty-pound box, muttered, "Slow down, for Chrissake. We got two hours before the train comes."

The depot platform was nearly deserted when it came into view. A baggage man was repairing a wheel on the lone baggage cart under the eyes of two yawning soldiers. Orchard and Adams left the tracks and moved stealthily through the weeds toward the pilings which supported the structure.

A cutting wind had sprung up, making Orchard grateful for the shelter afforded by the platform's underpinnings when they slipped beneath it. The sound of the baggage man's hammer drowned out the thud when Orchard tripped over a wooden support and dropped the opened box of dynamite.

Cursing under his breath, he gathered up the cold, sticky cartridges in the dark. He should be praying, he thought suddenly, because the stuff hadn't gone off. Carefully, he and Adams crawled to the space where Orchard felt the blast would do the most damage. While he prepared the charge, Adams made two more trips to bring the other two boxes. Had silence not been mandatory, Orchard was sure Adams would have grumbled that he had to do all the work.

A little light from the depot's few electric bulbs filtered down through the cracks between the planks overhead, making the task of rigging the bomb only slightly less dangerous. Orchard twisted a screw eye into the vial's stopper and pulled some fishing line off the reel before handing it to Adams.

"Head up the hill," he told him. "Give me a tug when you're out of line and I'll tie this end."

Adams was shivering and his teeth were chattering.

"Only tug it once," Orchard warned. "Anything after that means business."

Adams crawled away, careful to see that the line didn't entangle itself on any of the platform's supports. Orchard sat next to the dynamite boxes, keeping a firm grip on the end of the fishing line. Bella crossed his mind and he thought about her soft, warm body against his in their bed. Best to forget that, he told himself. After tonight, if all went well, reconciliation would probably be impossible.

321

The sudden tightening of the line brought him back to reality. He tied the end to the acid bottle's stopper and joined Adams on the windswept hillside.

They took turns walking around to keep warm. One walked while the other held the reel to avoid any mishap in the dark which might set off the blast before the midnight shift ended at the Findley mine.

"How many do you think we'll get?" Adams asked through chattering teeth.

Orchard glanced down at the depot where a few men in muddy overalls and carrying dinner pails were beginning to appear, indicating that it must be just after midnight. Joe Wyatt, on instructions from Haywood, had pulled off all the union pickets the day before, which was a blessing.

"I don't know," Orchard said, "but I reckon it'll be a fair bunch."

By the time the railroad locomotive's headlight pierced the darkness, the number of men milling about on the platform and inside the building had tripled. Orchard could see the two soldiers, standing on the baggage cart, hugging their coats around themselves.

"You gonna do it?" Adams demanded impatiently. "I'm freezing my ass off."

"As soon as the train stops," Orchard said.

He was sure he was just as cold as Adams but he could hold out for a few more minutes, for maximum effect.

Bell clanging, steam blowing, the train rolled to a stop beside the depot platform. The waiting men moved across the platform toward the cars. Orchard could hear the clanking of their dinner pails when he pulled hard on the fishing line.

He and Adams held their breaths. Half a minute passed.

Adams kicked at a clod in the snow.

"Shit!"

The flash which accompanied the thunderous explosion lit up the entire canyon. The platform rose into the air, heavy planks spreading like a giant fan. Men could be seen running in mid air before disappearing into the smoke and debris.

322

The concussion blew out the windows in the railroad coaches, shredding the men inside. The locomotive stayed on the tracks but the engineer must have grabbed the whistle cord to steady himself because the whistle's eerie wail almost drowned out the screams of injured and dying men.

"Holy mother," Adams whispered.

Orchard reeled in the fishing line. No sense in leaving anything behind which could be used as evidence, no matter how trivial it might seem.

# CHAPTER THIRTY-FOUR

On the third morning in the cabin at Grizzly Flat, Orchard awakened with an overwhelming feeling of uneasiness. His legs ached from being drawn up all night in an attempt to get warm. He and Adams both slept in their clothes and shared Adams's two thin blankets in the creaking rope-sprung bed with its moldy straw ticking.

Beside him, Adams lay on his back, snoring loudly, freckled hands crossed on his chest, like a corpse on display, Above their heads, slivers of gray sky were visible through cracks between the hand-split shakes; cracks which had admitted copious amounts of snow during the night.

Orchard rolled out of bed and pulled on his boots. Shivering uncontrollably, he squatted in front of the rusty stove to get a fire going. His mouth was dry and his head throbbed, heightening his unrest. When the fire was assured, he took a pull from the bottle sitting on the table next to their tin plates with the congealed remains of their dinner.

He and Adams had finished Orchard's Duncan and Duncan the first night, in a drunken requiem for the Independence Depot. Then, the whiskey had been warm and reassuring. Now, the cheap swill which Adams had laid in tasted like cold cow piss.

While he waited for the coffee pot to boil, he stepped outside to piss in the snow a few feet from the cabin. The air was so cold that he was surprised his stream didn't freeze before it hit the ground.

He looked up from buttoning his pants to catch a glimpse of a man watching him from a thicket fifty feet away, half-hidden by the tumbledown remnants of a wooden flume.

Humming to himself, despite the cold sweat dampening his armpits, Orchard went back into the cabin. When he woke Adams, he put his hand over his mouth to stifle any outburst.

"We've got company," he whispered. "Grab your rifle and cover me from the window. I'm going back outside."

Orchard cocked his automatic and tucked it into his waistband. Outside, he foraged for scraps of wood among the old sluice boxes and placer paraphernalia littering the cabin site. When he was closer to the spot where he'd seen the intruder, he pulled his pistol and fired two shots into the thicket, the sounds reverberated in the stillness of the Aspens.

"My Gawd, boys, don't shoot!" a voice bawled. "It's Kildare!"

Hands raised, a tall man in a dirty gray mackinaw with a black stocking cap pulled over his ears, tumbled out of the brush. Adams came out of the cabin, rifle raised.

"What the hell are you doing here?"

Orchard moved around behind the man, covering him with his pistol.

"This is the jasper what sold me the gelatin," Adams said.

"Sneaking around in the brush is a good way to get your fool head blown off," Orchard said.

When the man turned to face Orchard, there was a moment of silence before his eyes widened and he blurted, "You're the feller was gonna shoot me on the N.P. train!"

Orchard went to him and pulled off the stocking cap, freeing a heavy thatch of stiff gray hair. Indeed, this was Alford Kildare, the Irish scab Siringo had clubbed off the train on the Mullan grade.

"I'm the fellow who's going to shoot you now," Orchard said, stepping back so the big man wouldn't fall on him when he went down.

"Aw, Gawd no!" Kildare gasped. "I come to warn you. I swear! They're tearin' things apart lookin' for you."

"Why would anyone be looking for us, Kildare?" Orchard said. "What do they think we've done?"

"Not him, just you," Kildare said, licking dry lips.

Orchard said, "Let's take him inside before we all freeze to death."

Questions were churning in his head. How had Kildare made the connection between him and Adams? And how had he found them? What else did he know? Were they suspects in the Independence Depot explosion? Was a posse on the way there?

Once in the cabin, Orchard searched Kildare. He was unarmed except for what seemed to be his weapon of choice, a large clasp knife. In his trouser pockets, Orchard found eight dollars and some small change, but it was in a vest pocket that he made his most interesting, if disquieting find. Folded in a neat square, its corners torn where it had been tacked, was a reward poster printed by the Pinkerton Detective Agency. It bore Orchard's picture, cropped from his wedding photo, and offered a five-thousand dollar reward for the arrest of Harry Orchard on suspicion of murdering Virgil McCormick and Mel Beck.

"What are you doing with this?"

Orchard was getting angry. The Pinkertons had his real identity and picture. They'd probably put his mug on every telephone pole in Colorado.

"I believe this horse turd was making sure I was here so he could turn me in for the reward," he told Adams.

"'tain't so. I swear to Gawd," Kildare said.

"How'd you know I'd be with Adams?"

"I seen you comin' out of a whorehouse in Victor together and then I seen you again, drunk, at the Colorado Belle. Figgered you was friends."

"How'd you find me?" Adams screamed.

Kildare was beginning to sweat.

"You told me you had a prospect on Grizzly Flat."

"Harry, let's walk this son-of-a-bitch into the trees and put some holes in him," Adams said, breathing hard. "You can't trust nobody no more."

"No. This big mick is going to break trail for me tonight. I've got some business in Goldfield."

They tied Kildare's hands and feet with his boot laces and dragged him outside and leaned him against a tree. Back in the cabin, Orchard gave Adams another fifty dollars.

"Best we both get out of here," he told Adams. "No telling who the bastard's talked to."

"Bet he'd tell us if we held his hand on the stove," Adams said.

"Doesn't make any difference now," Orchard said. "I'm going to see my wife one more time and then I'm gone for good."

"I have a little business in Altman," Adams said. "Soon's I take care of Neville, I'm headed down to Trinidad. See if I can get on as a trainman. I'm sick of workin' underground."

"That's coal country, anyway," Orchard said. "Coal mining's like being dead with a shovel in your hand."

That afternoon Orchard and Adams shook hands and Adams headed down the mountain toward Altman. Orchard untied the shivering Kildare's feet and followed him through deep snow on the trail which led to Goldfield. He felt bad about leaving his bag and his good clothes behind, but took only his new derby and his shotgun when they hit the trail. With the money Haywood had promised him for Frank Bromley he could buy twenty new wardrobes.

They didn't stop walking until Kildare, wheezing like an overloaded pack mule, collapsed in the snow and was unable to get up.

"Go ahead and shoot me," he gasped. "I cain't go no futher w'thout I rest."

Orchard helped him up and dragged him into a clump of trees. He didn't want to venture onto the street in Goldfield until it was dark anyway and the town wasn't that much further. He was down to two cigars so he gave one to Kildare and they smoked quietly while dusk descended upon them.

"You hear anything about the Independence explosion, Kildare?" Orchard asked at length.

Kildare gave him a startled look.

"You done that?"

"I asked what you'd heard about it," Orchard said.

"Paper said thirteen kilt," Kildare said. "More hurt. Some with arms and legs blowed off."

"Like your finger," Orchard said. "Let's go."

# CHAPTER THIRTY-FIVE

Siringo, though case hardened by his profession, was appalled by the havoc wreaked against the union in the days following the Independence Depot disaster. Having dropped his Charlie Dawes masquerade, he joined General Ben Sheridan, the National Guard commander and a detachment of soldiers on an inspection tour of Victor, where anti-union violence had been severe. They were accompanied by a bird-like little man named Hamlin who represented the Mine Owners Association.

It was late afternoon, with the muddy street shaded by the buildings' long shadows. They paused in front of the Victor union hall, a stout, two-story brick building whose facade was marred by broken windows. The street in front of the hall glittered with broken glass, where splintered furniture seemed to float on a sea of papers strewn about. A smashed typewriter lay next to a man's coat with blood on it.

Members of a hastily assembled Citizens' Alliance, consisting of business and professional men, who had invaded the union hall, were enraged by the discovery of a scab list posted on the wall: a collage of photographs and descriptions of non-union men known to be working in the district. Several of those pictured had died at Independence.

Surveying the carnage, General Sheridan, moustache bristling, exclaimed, "Serves the anarchists right. We're going to do up this murderous Western Federation once and for all!"

Further down Fourth Avenue, they examined the shambles made of a union cooperative store by an out-of-control mob. Sacks of flour, coffee, sugar and potatoes filled the street, split open and doused with coal oil. Tinned goods, sides of bacon and packaged items had been carried off by looters. Several of the union volunteers manning the store had been beaten so badly that they required hospitalization.

While they watched, a young woman with a drawn face, trailed by three little girls, marched defiantly past them to pick through spilled potatoes.

"You there," Hamlin called. "Get off the street and go home."

The woman gave him a long look, spit at him, and left with half a dozen small potatoes in her apron.

"Those that can't eat can't cause trouble," Hamlin told Siringo happily, stamping the life out of a lone potato for emphasis.

"I reckon that woman and her kids are ones to watch," Siringo said. "They looked like troublemakers."

Derisive shouts rising from groups of idle men loitering on either side of the street drowned out Hamlin's sharp reply. A contingent of soldiers appeared, escorting perhaps thirty sullen men toward the train depot. The growing crowd watching the forced exodus contained a number of tear-stained women with sobbing children in tow.

"That's the first batch," Sheridan told Hamlin. "We've got thirty-five more waiting in the jail and about forty locked up in Altman and Goldfield."

"Where are they headed?"

Siringo couldn't stifle a feeling of compassion for these grim-faced men who were being torn from their families, some for no reason other than their admission of union membership.

"These are going across the Kansas state line," Sheridan replied, watching the procession pass. "Tomorrow's bunch we're sending to New Mexico."

Campaign hat tilted low over his eyes, Sheridan adopted the pose of a tough professional, while in civilian life, he was a mild mannered druggist in Colorado Springs.

"You don't seem overly enthusiastic about all this, Mr. Siringo."

Siringo lit a cigar, eyeing Sheridan through the smoke.

"Deporting men against their will breeds the kind of hatred that leads to murder," Siringo said. "Besides, most of those fellows'll be back here in a week. This is their home."

Sheridan shook his head angrily.

"Not anymore it isn't. If I had my way, we'd send their families packing with them."

Siringo gave him a sardonic smile.

"I'm surprised you haven't, General. You aren't worried by the men's Constitutional rights. What makes the women any different?"

"Hang the Constitution!" Sheridan exploded. "This is a rebellion and rebels have no rights!"

Siringo, not wishing to engage the General in a public debate, turned to walk away.

"I would suggest, Detective Siringo, that you concentrate on the apprehension of the murderers and dynamiters and let me worry about the conduct of martial law."

Siringo tipped his hat.

"It's your army, General."

As he walked away, Siringo was thinking about the murders of Lyle Gregory and Walter Kenley. If there were ever men who deserved killing it was those two. Unless they were simply killed on general principles, there was one person whom he believed might still be hiding in the district, and who had a motive: Harry Orchard.

Later in the afternoon, to escape the depressing atmosphere of Victor, Siringo rode the trolley to Altman. He wanted to question Wyatt again about Adams and Orchard. Wyatt had been locked in the Altman jail since the day after the destruction of the Independence Depot. He steadfastly denied any knowledge of Harry Orchard's presence in the district, even when shown the reward poster with Orchard's picture. Maybe with the threat of deportation hanging over him, Wyatt might become more talkative.

If anything, the scene which unfolded in Altman was more oppressive than that which he'd just left in Victor. In addition to the surly crowds on the street, the local Citizens' Alliance, under the leadership of Stanley Nesbitt from Goldfield, was in the process of relieving all of the elected officials of both communities who were deemed to have union sympathies. Arriving at the city jail, Siringo discovered that the city marshal, his assistant, the jailers and the deputies were all new faces and uniformly unfriendly.

The marshal, nervous and ill at ease with his newfound authority, refused to accept Siringo's credentials without a pass signed by General Sheridan.

"That's it, Siringo," the marshal said, shaggy eyebrows rising with each sentence. "You may be good as gold but I don't know you and I can't afford to take no chances. I got some desperate men locked up in here."

"I'll leave my revolver with you before I go inside, if that's what you're worried about."

"You'll leave your revolver with me in any case," the marshal said. "Nobody but the soldiers and the law carries weapons of any kind in Altman."

He ran his finger around the inside of a collar which seemed too tight.

Siringo moved toward the door.

"You wouldn't want a lot of shooting right here, the first hour you're in office, would you, Marshal?" Siringo said easily. "That's what you'll get if you try to confiscate my weapon."

The marshal stared at him, open-mouthed, as did a middle-aged deputy, armed with what appeared to be a cap-and-ball Colt of another era.

Siringo was fuming as he walked toward the depot. That officious bastard was going to get himself killed before he learned how to pin on his badge

At the last minute, he decided to go to Goldfield. He didn't really expect to get much more information from Bella. He was thoroughly convinced that she'd been completely unaware that the man she married was Harry Orchard. On his second visit to her home, after Alford Kildare had reported selling the dynamite to Adams, which Siringo believed was used at Independence, her revulsion seemed overpowering. So much so that he was certain that she'd tell him if Orchard had tried to contact her.

Crime and criminals aside, Siringo found her attractive. Thus, even a frivolous interrogation would embody its own reward. It was near supper time, so he would stop somewhere before he got on the trolley, to pick up something to take to her. Sweets of some sort, he decided.

# CHAPTER THIRTY-SIX

Reaching Bella's house would be more difficult than he'd anticipated, Orchard concluded as soon as he and Kildare came off the mountain and waded through three-foot drifts behind some of the other houses. Darkness had fallen and the street lights had been turned on, revealing soldiers patrolling the street.

He and Kildare worked their way along the street, staying behind houses and buildings, their footsteps muffled by the snow. As they passed behind Nesbitt's store, an employee came out of the darkened building carrying a coal oil lamp. He set the lamp on the ground and entered an outhouse located a distance from the store.

"Stay here and keep your mouth shut or you're a dead man," Orchard warned Kildare.

Moving as rapidly as he could through the snow, and keeping an eye on Kildare over his shoulder, Orchard picked up the lamp. He rapped on the outhouse door with his automatic.

"Stay in there or you'll be shot," he told the occupant. Orchard tossed the lamp through the back door of Nesbitt's store and watched the flames spread across the floor. They brought back memories of the night he killed Fatty Kincaid. It seemed like a hundred years ago.

Orchard pushed Kildare ahead of him until they were several houses away, hidden in the shadows. When excited voices reached a crescendo and the soldiers patrolling in front of Bella's house ran toward the fire, Orchard pushed Kildare onto Bella's front porch and tried her door. It was locked. More people were in the street, running toward Nesbitt's, looking neither right nor left. Orchard kicked the door open and pushed Kildare inside, closing the door behind them.

Bella was at her sewing machine when they tumbled into the room. She raised a pair of scissors to defend herself.

"Oh, my God!" she said when she recognized him.

She looked from Orchard to Kildare and back again, obviously confused and frightened. Kildare just stood there, mouth open, breathing heavily.

"Bella, it's all right."

"How did you get past the soldiers?"

"There's a fire in the neighborhood," he said.

"A fire?"

"Never mind that," Orchard said. "I'm leaving the district tonight, Bella. I want you to come with me."

As the words came he suddenly realized how impossible that would be. He and Bella on foot in heavy snow with nothing but the clothes on their backs. And there was Kildare. Orchard had already decided he'd shoot the Irishman when he no longer needed him and that would make their departure a little messy.

Bella threw her scissors at him and screamed, "You must be crazy! I wouldn't..."

Kildare's shouted warning cut her off. Orchard glanced at the window in time to see a man's face. He pulled Bella to the floor as a shot shattered the glass and a bullet ricocheted off the sewing machine.

Orchard fired two shots through the wall next to the window. Outside, someone grunted in pain.

Nesbitt's store was completely involved when Siringo got off the trolley. He had taken only a few steps when he heard three shots, all coming from the direction of Bella's house.

Siringo tossed down the bag of candied fruit he'd bought for Bella and drew his revolver, heading down the street as fast as the deep snow would permit. He could see soldiers running toward him from the other end of the street. As he neared the house, a man staggered into the street and fell down. Siringo ran to him. It was Dumps Benton, gut-shot and bleeding.

"He's inside," Benton gasped. "I got one shot."

"Did you hit him?"

"No," Benton whimpered, "but he got me, twice. I don't think I'm gonna make it."

Soldiers surrounded them, a corporal in charge.

"What's the shooting?"

Siringo pointed toward the house.

"There's a wanted man in there. Have your men fan out. I'm going in there after him if he doesn't come out."

The soldiers took up positions. One paused long enough to stuff a dirty handkerchief into Benton's wound.

"Son-of-a-bitch peeped through her window every night," the soldier said, before loping away. "Serves him right."

Siringo cupped his hands around his mouth to yell, "Harry Orchard! Throw down your weapons and come out. The house is surrounded."

Actually the house was far from surrounded. The soldiers had taken up positions behind a berm of snow so if Orchard came out shooting, he, Siringo, standing fully exposed, would probably be the only one to get shot. Over the thump of his rapidly beating heart, he told himself it might be worth it, to finally bring this dance to an end.

Suddenly the house went dark. The front door opened to reveal a man in a derby hat who seemed to be looking frantically up and down the street. Five shots, fired in rapid succession, sent snow flying along the edge of the road.

Siringo, big revolver held in both hands, fired twice. Along the road, the crack of the soldier's rifles ripped the night. The impact of the bullets drove the man's body back through the open door.

Bella's screams were all Siringo could hear as he ran toward the house. Inside, Bella was on the floor, still screaming. Siringo scratched a match. In its flare he found that Alford Kildare had fallen on top of her, pinning her against her overturned sewing machine. He had been shot three times in the chest and was quite dead. Orchard was gone.

In the morning, the drifted snow outside the broken window was marked by the last impression Harry Orchard would leave in the Cripple Creek district.

# CHAPTER THIRTY-SEVEN

It was foggy and grim in San Francisco. On a clear day the bay was visible, the landlady had told him, but in the time that Orchard had been there, the bay had never appeared, so he had only her word for it.

He considered himself extremely fortunate to have found a room in a private home, in the same block of Washington Street as the Bromley townhouse. Mrs. DeParlier, his landlady, had recently lost her mother, who was the last occupant of the large, second-floor room. She'd placed a small sign in the window which Orchard had seen as he took stock of the neighborhood.

From his front window, Orchard was able to look down the street and get a clear view of the Bromley front porch. By this time he'd learned the identity of the servant girl and the cook, along with the well-regulated rhythm of the household.

Each morning at six, the milkman, with his horse-drawn cart, left a quart of milk in a glass bottle on the Bromley's front stoop. At seven, the servant girl, Clarice, appeared, to bring in the milk and the morning paper, which the newsboy left at six-thirty. Between eight and nine, Anna, the cook, or

Clarice, would go to Chaffee's Grocery at the end of the block, for the day's provisions. Promptly at nine, Frank Bromley would come through the front door. If it was raining, he'd enter a carriage brought around by a colored houseman. On fair days, he'd walk to his office, eight blocks away.

Between his observations, Orchard spent his time at Kilgallin's Saloon on Columbus or dining at Delmonico's on Pacific. He was in no hurry to attend to Frank Bromley. He felt he'd earned a well-deserved respite after the Cripple Creek ordeal and his narrow escape in a freighter's wagon, under a pile of stinking hides.

Haywood had wired five hundred dollars to him in care of the Bartenders Union, and Joe Wyatt, who had somehow escaped deportation, had arranged the transfer of his funds in the Victor First National Bank to the Bank of Italy in San Francisco. Thus, money was no problem and Bromley's schedule so consistent, that Orchard felt he could choose a time to do him in which wouldn't interfere with his personal activities.

He made a habit of being in Chaffee's Grocery when he knew Clarice would be there, to strike up casual conversations with the plump, bosomy servant girl. It turned out that Clarice was open to more than conversation and by the end of the first week she was in his bed and on top of him, her preferred position.

"I'll have more free time later this week," she whispered lovingly, on Monday evening of his second week in the city by the bay. "I might be able to see you some in the daytime. The Bromleys are going to Mexico."

"Are you sure?"

Orchard sat up in bed to look at her. She stared back at him with vacant eyes which reminded him of a kitten.

"Umhum. They told us tonight."

"How long will they be gone?"

"I dunno, sweets," she purred. "A month, maybe. Isn't that peachy?"

"Yeah," Orchard said. "Peachy. Get dressed, dearie. I've got things to do."

"Oh, not yet," Clarice said, trying to pull him down beside her.

"I said, now!" Orchard growled.

He swung around to put his feet against her and pushed her out of the bed. He rolled out on the other side to toss her clothes to her where she sprawled naked on the floor.

"You're really not a very nice man, are you?" Clarice said in an offended tone as she sorted out her garments.

"I've been told I have a good heart," Orchard said. "Hurry it up."

He hustled the pouting girl out of his room and down the stairs as soon as they were dressed. At the door, he tried to keep his options open by kissing her on the cheek. She pulled away from him and flounced down the street.

He returned to his room to drag his trunk out from under the bed to make sure he had everything he needed to send Frank Bromley on his last journey.

On Tuesday, Otto Hauser, the barkeep at Kilgallin's, gave him a letter addressed to T. S. Hogan. It was from Haywood advising that Jake Schultz had died in the hospital and that two days later, Johnny Neville had been found dead in his room, apparently from cyanide poisoning.

"The coroner thinks it's suicide," Haywood wrote, "even though there was another plate in the room. I wonder whose?"

Orchard drank his beer and thought about Steve Adams. He hoped he hadn't lingered in the district, for he was the only person alive who could link him to either the Vindicator or the Independence Depot—if you didn't count Haywood and Moyer.

On the way home, he picked up a large tin of biscuits at Chafee's and that night as he chewed on the biscuits, he fabricated the bomb with a fairly modest charge of six sticks of 2XX dynamite.

On Wednesday morning, he gave up his room, arranging for a drayage company to pick up his trunk. Carrying the bomb gingerly in his traveling bag, he took a room in a small hotel in a different neighborhood. That night he slept fitfully, worried about the timing for planting the bomb.

Too early and one of the servants might set it off, making all his efforts for naught. Too late and Bromley might catch him in the act, ruining any future opportunity he might have and exposing him to the possibility of arrest.

On Thursday morning at eight o'clock, Orchard, with the biscuit tin wrapped in a newspaper, waited behind a hedge across the street from the Bromley house. At eight-fifteen, Anna, the cook, bustled through the front door on her daily trip to Chafee's.

Orchard waited impatiently, checking his watch every ten minutes. She didn't return until eight-fifty-five. That gave him five minutes to plant the infernal machine on Bromley's doorstep. He hesitated for a moment, telling himself that it was too late. Then, in a rush, he crossed the deserted street, placed the bomb on the front porch and tied the trigger string to the front door handle.

He was a block away when he heard it go off. He was tempted to go back to assess the damage but went straight to his hotel room. The evening paper carried the story on the front page, with a picture of the house. The entire facade had been blown off. Bromley, though still alive when taken to the hospital, wasn't expected to survive. A fire marshal, investigating the explosion, hinted at a gas leak, an allegation vigorously denied by the gas company.

Orchard, pleased by all he had read, went to Kilgallin's to have a few drinks for the boys in the Coeur d'Alene, whose oppression had been avenged at last.

# CHAPTER THIRTY-EIGHT

Siringo's first real break in his search for Harry Orchard came when the cashier of the Victor National Bank reported the transfer of funds in T. S. Hogan's account to the Bank of Italy in San Francisco. The detective arrived in the city two days after Frank Bromley's house was partially destroyed by "leaking gas."

"My husband had no enemies, Detective," a shaken Mrs. Bromley told Siringo at the hospital. She was a handsome woman with abrasions on her face and one arm in a sling from a sprained shoulder.

"I can't believe that anyone could place a bomb on our front porch in broad daylight—in a civilized city like San Francisco. This isn't a mining camp, you know."

Siringo didn't press the issue. He could have told her that there were probably over a hundred people who considered themselves mortal enemies of Frank Bromley. He was unable to talk to Bromley himself, who was in a coma. It would have made no difference anyway. Neither of them could help him find the bomber.

The following day, Bromley's lawyers filed suit against the San Francisco Gas And Electric Company for one hundred thousand dollars. Late the same afternoon, doctors at the Good Shepherd hospital reported that Bromley had emerged from his coma and was expected to survive. He did suffer a major hearing loss and had only partial vision in one eye; conditions believed to be irreversible.

That night, Siringo got his second break in the form of a telegram from the Pinkerton home office in Denver. Postal inspectors who had been alerted to watch for postings by Western Federation officials, reported letters directed to a T. S. Hogan, in care of the San Francisco Bartenders Union.

The business agent of the union met with Siringo in his office on Polk Street. He shook his head when he saw Orchard's picture.

"He don't belong to this local, Mr. Siringo. And I know 'em all. I've never seen him around here, neither."

"I'd appreciate it if you'd put up this reward poster where the boys can see it. Somebody here might know him."

"I'm sorry, Detective," the agent said. "This ain't the post office."

"I'd see to it that you shared in the reward," Siringo told him.

"Well, then, gimme a couple them notices," the agent said. "We can help out the Pinkertons."

"You can reach me at the Sutter Hotel," Siringo told him as they shook hands. "I'll be here for a few more days. After that, I'll be in Denver. The address is on the poster."

The response to the reward poster came two days later while Siringo was dining at his hotel with a young woman he had charmed in the lobby. A bell boy paged him for a telephone call at the front desk.

The voice on the line had a trace of a German accent.

"Mr. Siringo? The Pinkerton man? My name is Otto Hauser. I work at Kilgallin's on Columbus. I have information for you."

Kilgallin's Saloon, despite being a San Francisco landmark, going back to the gold rush days, was no more grand than similar establishments in Idaho and Colorado. The brass foot rail and cuspidors were perhaps less battered, but there was sawdust on the floor, and the same smell of beer and stale cigar smoke lingered in the air.

Otto Hauser, a rotund man in a clean white apron, leaned on the polished bar top to speak in confidential tones. It was midmorning and the place was almost empty.

"This man, Orchard, you look for, tells me his name is Hogan," Hauser said. "He paid me five dollars to pick up his mail at the union hall."

Siringo drank some of the steam beer Hauser had set in front of him and wiped the foam off his moustache.

"When did you see him last?"

"A week ago. No more since."

"Do you know where he lives?"

"He said he had a room around Leavenworth and Washington. I never went there."

"Very interesting," Siringo said.

"When will I get the reward?" Hauser asked.

"We have to catch him first."

"What if he comes back here?"

"Call the police, Otto. Don't try to detain him yourself, unless you've got six friends who'd like to carry a heavy casket."

"He's that dangerous?"

"My friend, you have no idea."

His dining companion of last night was attending a school administrator's convention in the hotel. She had promised to meet him for lunch, and though the short-term future with her looked promising, Siringo headed for Leavenworth and Washington Streets instead.

There was one house in the neighborhood of stately old homes, with a room for rent. It was a once-elegant place in need of paint. From it, the Bromley residence was visible, down and across the street, with workmen on ladders pulling down the shattered facade.

"Why that's Mr. Hogan," Mrs. DeParlier exclaimed when Siringo showed her the reward poster. "He rented mother's old room for two weeks but was here only ten days."

She pursed her lips disapprovingly.

"Frankly, I was glad to see him go, the way he was carrying on with the Bromley's hired girl."

She made a clucking sound.

"Poor Mr. Bromley. I suppose you've heard what happened to him when the gas main blew up."

"Yes, I heard. Terrible. Do you know where Mr. Hogan went when he left here?"

"He didn't tell me," Mrs. DeParlier said. "I asked the drayman who picked up his trunk and he didn't know. I couldn't understand why he left when his rent was paid."

It was evident that Mrs. DeParlier was eager to talk to someone—about anything. She was explaining why she had to rent her late mother's room when Siringo interrupted her.

"Do you remember which company picked up his trunk?"

Mrs. DeParlier gave him a blank look.

"All I know is the wagon had a lightning bolt painted on the side. I didn't see a name. The driver was a colored man about four feet tall. I don't know how he could handle heavy things."

A lead which had seemed so promising had suddenly become dependent on a lightning bolt and a Negro midget.

Promise returned when Siringo located Lightning Transfer's small office and warehouse on Third Street. The dispatcher was thumbing through his orders when a black man entered the office. He wasn't a midget but he couldn't have been more than five feet tall. What he lacked in height he made up in width, with broad shoulders and the largest upper arms Siringo had ever seen.

"Whatcha got, Lemuel?"

"Jack's throwed a shoe," he told the dispatcher, "and Maudie's come up lame."

With that, he left the office.

"How'm I gonna pick up a piano and deliver it across town today?" the perplexed dispatcher asked Siringo.

"Maybe Lemuel could carry it on his back," Siringo responded dryly, anxious to get on the move.

"Might have to do that," the dispatcher said. "That little nigger's one strong son-of-a-bitch."

"I believe he's the one who picked up Mr. Hogan's trunk," Siringo said, wondering if that might help the dispatcher narrow his search.

"Here it is," the dispatcher announced finally. "Picked up a trunk on Washington and delivered it to the Southern Pacific express office."

The Southern Pacific freight agent, hurried by a gratuity of one dollar, said, "Yup. T. S. Hogan. We sent that item to Boise Idaho."

To Siringo, that could mean only one thing. Harry Orchard, having dealt with Frank Bromley, had gone to Idaho to assassinate Governor Steunenberg!

# CHAPTER THIRTY-NINE

The elderly sheep rancher from nearby Nampa won again, causing Orchard to give up his seat at the poker table for the second time that day.

"If the weather doesn't improve, you fellows are going to break me," he said laughingly, going into the bar for a beer.

There was an amused chuckle from the other players and one of them, a patent medicine drummer, called out, "We'll keep your seat warm, Hogan."

Orchard had been holed up in Caldwell's Saratoga Hotel for over a week, deterred from his mission by sub-freezing temperatures and an unusual amount of blowing snow. In that time, he'd become a well-liked regular in the hotel bar and at the poker table, where he won as often as he lost.

In the dining room, he carried on a mild flirtation with a red-haired waitress. Her name was Dora and she always rushed to serve him when he came in. He told himself it was his charm but, in his heart, knew it was his generous tipping which drew her to him. He told anyone who asked that he was a sheep buyer from Denver.

When he left San Francisco, his original plan had been the quick assassination of Governor Steunenberg on the streets of Boise. He had taken a room in an obscure boarding house, maintaining his distance from the other boarders. He had scouted the governor's mansion and the capitol grounds, catching an occasional glimpse of Steunenberg in his closed carriage but never seeing him afoot in a place where he would be an inviting target for the pump gun.

Finally, tired of exposing himself to the chilling wind and slushy streets, Orchard moved to Caldwell, where the governor owned a home. With the Christmas holidays approaching, and the governor known to spend time there, Orchard decided that Caldwell would provide him with the opportunity he sought. He also concluded that a bomb, hidden in the snow by the governor's front gate, would entail less risk than stalking Steunenberg with his shotgun.

Haywood had sent him another five hundred dollars so that Orchard, not pressed for funds, could bide his time for the right moment. Since he was in no hurry, he contemplated visiting some of his old cronies. Haywood had advised him that Joe Wyatt was now in Silver City, about sixty miles away, and that Steve Adams was working on a gold dredge in the Sumpter Valley of eastern Oregon.

He was, in fact, considering a trip to Silver City when he learned that Steunenberg and his family would be spending the next weekend in Caldwell, in anticipation of the Christmas holidays. This would be as good a time as any to finish the job; his last for the Western Federation of Miners, he had decided. It was with mounting excitement that he had trudged through the snow to have one more look at the Steunenberg gate before returning to his room to fabricate the bomb.

Orchard had liked San Francisco during his brief stay and decided that was where he'd like to settle, once he'd severed his ties with the union. He probably had enough money to buy an interest in a small saloon and card room, somewhere in the area known as The Barbary Coast, near Kilgallin's where his friend Otto Hauser worked.

The governor's office was dark and cavernous. Siringo had been admitted almost at once and found the governor to be open and cordial. He told him the reason for the visit and gave him a copy of the Orchard reward poster.

Steunenberg glanced at it dismissively and tossed it on top of other papers on his desk.

"No, Mr. Siringo, I don't fear the union," Steunenberg said. "They have no ax to grind with me. What happened in the Coeur d'Alene, they brought on themselves. We can't tolerate anarchy in the mining camps any more than we would on city streets."

"I doubt they feel that way, Governor," Siringo said. "You've heard what happened to Frank Bromley in San Francisco?"

The governor's smile faded and he shook his head sadly.

"Poor man. Blind and deaf, I'm told. A gas leak, the paper said."

"I'm afraid it was no gas leak, sir."

Siringo had taken an immediate liking to this big, affable man. It troubled him that Steunenberg seemed unwilling to entertain even the slightest notion that his life might be in danger.

"I guess that must be proven," Steunenberg said, rising to shake hands. "I do thank you and the fine Pinkerton Agency for your concern, but I fear you've made a long trip for nothing."

"I hope so, sir," Siringo said resignedly.

Steunenberg handed Siringo the reward poster. "I don't believe I'll be needing this," he said. "Now, you must excuse me, sir. Affairs of state, you know," he added wryly.

On Saturday afternoon, Governor Steunenberg and several local citizens enjoyed a late luncheon together in the Saratoga dining room. Orchard seated at his corner table, studied his prey over the top of his copy of the Idaho Statesman. A pleasant-looking fellow, he concluded, but looks notwithstanding, the bastard had called for federal troops and had broken the union's back in the Coeur d'Alene.

He remembered reading the governor's widely quoted words when he spoke of the union. "We have the monster by the throat and we'll choke the life out of it."

He had to pay for that.

Dora brought him more coffee, leaning close to him as she poured.

"That's the governor," she murmured. "Aren't you impressed?"

"Dora, you're the only thing that impresses me in Caldwell," he told her.

"He'll be here through the Christmas holidays," Dora said. "His house is just down the street."

"So I've heard," Orchard said. "Why don't you bring me a piece of mince pie so I can watch your hips when you walk?"

"Mr. Hogan, you're a caution!"

Dora's peal of laughter made the governor and his friends look up. For an instant, Orchard and Steunenberg made eye contact. Then the governor turned his attention back to the conversation around his table.

When he'd finished his pie, Orchard left a generous tip for Dora and seated himself in the lobby with his newspaper. He would observe the governor and his friends for a while and when it seemed that they would linger until dark, he'd place the bomb.

At five o'clock, while Steunenberg regaled his friends with some tale which made them laugh, Orchard passed through the lobby with what appeared to be a Christmas present, wrapped in colorful paper, replete with a large red bow.

"Hey, Hogan," the medicine salesman called from the poker table, "there's a hot seat open."

"Don't let it cool off," Orchard replied. "I'll be back as soon as I've delivered some Christmas cheer."

Snow had begun to fall heavily which, in a way, was a blessing. It would not only hide the bomb but it would cover his tracks leading away from the front gate.

Lights shined from all the windows of the Steunenberg home when Orchard arrived with his package. It took less than a minute to place the "present," cover it with snow and attach the trigger string to a picket on the gate. Satisfied that he'd done a good job, Orchard hurried back to the hotel.

Bending against the wind, he met no one until he was halfway there. Then, on the other side of the street, he recognized the heavily bundled-up man as the governor. Orchard increased his pace, hoping to reach the hotel before Steunenberg opened his gate. He was twenty yards from the hotel when the tremendous explosion of fifteen sticks of dynamite ripped through the darkness.

Reaching the Saratoga, he paused momentarily to mingle with the curious who had come out on the porch at the sound of the blast.

Orchard was shaking the snow off his coat when one of the poker players asked, "Did you see where it came from, Hogan?"

Orchard pointed in the direction of the Steunenberg house.

"I saw a flash," he said. "And then a hellacious noise. Don't know what it was."

"Maybe it was a meteor," a man suggested.

"I don't think so," Orchard said as he went inside.

He went directly to the bar and ordered a double whiskey. He noticed that his hand was rock steady when he lifted the brimming glass. Commendable, for a man who'd just killed the governor of the state.

The barkeep waited for Orchard to drain the glass before asking, "Are you any good at wrapping up a package, Mr. Hogan?"

"I guess I've wrapped up a few. Why?"

He could feel the increase in his heart beat. Had this man...?

The barkeep placed a small package on the bar in front of Orchard.

"Present for my sister in Portland," he explained. "I can't seem to get the damn thing tied up properly for mailing."

Orchard's nimble fingers did the folds, wrapped the strings and tied the knots, making a workmanlike job out of the barkeep's fumbling attempt.

The barkeep thanked him with another whiskey on the house, which Orchard drank before going up to his room.

He lay down on the bed, feeling suddenly as though all the strength had gone out of his body. Outside, on the street, he could hear excited cries as the news of Steunenberg's murder spread. Orchard closed his eyes. He'd killed the governor and now his union career was finally over. A feeling of great relief swept over him as he drifted off to sleep.

# CHAPTER FORTY

Siringo was having his supper at Boise's Capitol Hotel when the waiter brought the news of Governor Steunenberg's assassination. The detective laid his knife and fork aside, staring into his plate. For the past six days he'd been on the move. In Silver City he'd questioned Joe Wyatt to no avail. The former head of the Altman union said Orchard was probably still in Colorado, as far as he knew, and refused to answer further questions.

He'd ridden the train for a night and half a day to reach Baker City in Oregon for a meeting with Harvey Browne, who was working as a paid informant for the Pinkerton Agency in the nearby Sumpter Valley camps. Browne said he knew that Steve Adams was there but had detected no hint of Orchard's presence. The placid farming community of Caldwell was the last place Siringo would have looked for the most deadly man in the country.

"What was the governor doing in Caldwell?" he asked the waiter.

"He has a house there," the waiter said. "The family goes there for Christmas and such. They say the whole town's been sealed up."

After the waiter had gone, Siringo pushed his plate away, appetite gone. For the first time in his life, he felt that he'd failed. But he had tried to warn the governor, he told himself. The only way he could salve his conscience now was to find Orchard.

Siringo arrived at the Boise train station where his credentials permitted him to board a special train being made up for the trip to Caldwell. Aboard were Charles Steunenberg, the governor's brother, and Joe Hutchinson, a self-styled explosives expert.

"We'll be grateful for any help you can provide, Mr. Siringo," Charles Steunenberg told him when the train got underway.

Siringo sat next to a window, staring into the darkness. He refrained from taking part in any of the conversations going on around him. He hadn't mentioned Orchard's name, but sitting there in the swaying coach, he was absolutely certain that it was Orchard who'd planted the fatal device which had killed the governor. First Bromley, now Steunenberg. The legacy of the Coeur d'Alene.

By the time the train reached Caldwell, a hastily formed Citizens' Committee, under the direction of Canyon County Sheriff Mosley, had cordoned off the town. Siringo was disturbed to learn that a westbound train had stopped in Caldwell before the town was secured, but the stationmaster insisted that no one had boarded.

Inasmuch as there were only two hotels in town, the Saratoga and the Pacific, it was a relatively simple matter to find a T. S. Hogan registered at the former, in room nineteen. Siringo marveled at Harry Orchard's audacity in using the same alias he'd used in Wardner. Siringo's first impulse was to pound on Orchard's door and accuse him of the murder. However, recalling events in the past wherein Orchard had left no trail of suspicion, he elected patience as the alternative.

He went across the street to the Pacific and rented the last available room. He telephoned McParland in Denver to let him know where he was, before crawling into bed. With all the roads and the train station guarded, there was little chance for Orchard to escape and any attempt to do so would be tantamount to an admission of guilt. Bone weary, Siringo closed his eyes and was asleep in minutes.

As was his custom, Orchard came downstairs at a quarter past nine, purchased a copy of the Idaho Statesman in the lobby and went into the dining room for breakfast. He could feel the excitement which had pervaded the hotel. Every conversation seemed to revolve around the governor's murder.

According to the newspaper, Steunenberg had lived for an hour after the blast, dying in his own bed from the terrible wounds inflicted by the bomb.

From Dora, his friendly waitress, he learned that every exit from Caldwell was guarded by armed men.

"Can you imagine," she said, "that the person who did this is still here in Caldwell?"

"Maybe tonight we can pull your covers over our heads, sweetie," Orchard said, as he pinched her bottom.

Dora had trouble maintaining a somber demeanor as she skittered off. When she had moved away, he considered his choices, angry with himself for not leaving town while acrid smoke still lingered in the air. However, there was no reason for him to be a suspect, and since escape was impossible, there was no reason, he concluded, not to maintain his pose as an itinerant sheep buyer. When the excitement died down, he'd drift silently away.

After breakfast he accompanied several men from the hotel to the Steunenberg home to survey the damage. A blackened hole marked where the gate had been. It also appeared that the front windows in the house had imploded. A bloody path in the snow marked the route of those who carried the dying governor into the house.

"That's where they dragged him," one of the card players said.

"Joe Hutchinson found a piece of fish line tied to a picket last night," another of his companions said. "He thinks it might have been used to set off the bomb."

Orchard tried not to appear to be in a hurry to get back to the hotel but was unnerved by the thought that his room contained damaging pieces of evidence. The unused fish line was still on his dresser and he hadn't cleaned up all of the bits of plaster of Paris which he'd used to secure the acid bottle over the dynamite caps.

Back in his room, he put the fish line and the plaster chips in the chamber pot. For some reason, after he'd tidied up the room, he was reluctant to go downstairs to the bar as he would have normally. Instead, he lay on the bed for almost an hour, worrying about being caught. Luck, he decided finally, had always been his ally, and there was no reason to believe it wouldn't continue to be. He put on his derby at a confident angle and went downstairs for a drink.

He found several of his poker-playing friends at the bar, unusually somber.

"I'll buy, gentlemen," he said, "if you'll join me in a toast."

He raised his glass and found himself looking into the eyes of Charlie Siringo, reflected in the back bar mirror. Slouch hat, sardonic smile and all, not a foot from him.

"To the boys in the Coeur d'Alene."

Orchard downed his whiskey and turned to face Siringo.

They stared at each other, relaxed and sure of themselves.

"I never did thank you for returning my hat, Harry," Siringo said. "Let me buy you a drink."

He signaled the barkeep, who refilled Orchard's glass and poured one for the detective.

"You should take better care of it, Charlie," Orchard replied easily. "What brings you to Caldwell?"

"Murder," Siringo said. "And you?"

Orchard tossed down his whiskey.

"Just passing through," he said. "I might stay for the funeral, just to make sure the old boy's not playing possum."

They stood elbow to elbow for a long moment before Siringo broke the silence.

355

"The Western Federation always gets its revenge, doesn't it?"

"I don't know what you're talking about, Charlie."

Orchard looked around the room. Through the front window, several armed vigilantes were visible in the street. He might be fast enough or lucky enough to get Siringo, but he knew he'd never make it out of town alive. Suddenly, escape didn't seem that important. Maybe it was the whiskey or maybe it was his belief that his luck would somehow hold out.

"My turn," he said, flagging down the busy barkeep.

"I don't believe we have time for another," Siringo said. "Sheriff Mosley has some questions for you."

Sheriff Mosley, whom Orchard thought looked like a turkey, was standing near the door with one of his deputies.

"Can we go up to your room, Mr...Mr. Hogan?"

Orchard looked at Siringo. Luck had dumped him. He knew they had him.

"By all means."

Charles Steunenberg and Joe Hutchinson were waiting for them in room nineteen. On the bed, neatly laid out, was the contents of Orchard's trunk and traveling bag. Shirts, underwear, several changes of clothing, dynamite, giant caps, acid bottle, shotgun and shells.

"Can you explain these things?" Mosley asked.

"I don't know anything about them, Sheriff," Orchard replied with a shrug.

Joe Hutchinson dangled two pieces of fish line.

"This one was tied to what's left of the governor's gate," he told Orchard. "This one was under your bed."

"It's all over, Harry," Siringo muttered.

He reached inside Orchard's coat and removed his automatic pistol. He hefted the weapon curiously.

"You can keep the Colt if you want, Charlie," Orchard told him. "It's the latest thing and it's only been used once."

"It got the job done," Siringo said.

Dumps Benton had died on his way to the hospital in Cripple Creek.

He deferred to the sheriff, who gave him a nod of approval, before he tucked the Colt into his waistband.

Orchard was escorted to the Caldwell jail by the sheriff, Siringo and two deputies. At the cell door, he turned to look at them.

"You know, boys, I'm just forty years old and this is the first time I've ever been locked up."

He winked at Siringo.

"I reckon it's because I've never done anything to deserve it."

Formally charged the following day with the murder of Governor Steunenber, Orchard was returned to jail.

"Don't get too comfortable," Sheriff Mosley told him at the cell door. "We'll be taking you over to the state pen in Boise this evening for safekeeping."

The train ride to Boise and the transportation to the penitentiary afforded him the last opportunity for human contact for the next ten days. Once inside the grim penitentiary walls, he was placed in solitary confinement, without explanation.

He knew what they were up to. He'd read that solitary confinement was believed to be an effective method of extracting confessions. Supposedly, one's demons were loosed to prey on the conscience of the miscreant until he begged to tell all. Well, not Harry Orchard.

With nothing to do but think, Orchard relived his violent life a hundred times. When he was assailed by despair, feeling that the Western Federation had deserted him, he pulled his spirits up by the bootstraps. He recounted the women he'd had, the good poker hands he'd held and the interesting men he'd met in the mining camps of the west.

One night he dreamed of Amy Neville, with him being held back by rough hands, made to watch while she was assaulted and killed. He woke up with a violent start, sweat-soaked and tear-stained. When he finally went back to sleep, the men he'd killed marched through his dreams. This time he awakened, filled with anger. To hell with them! His job was death and he did it well.

Among his regrets, Bella was at the top of a meager list. He was sorry they couldn't have made a life together but he consoled himself with the thought that he'd brought some happiness into her otherwise bleak life.

He was startled on the tenth day of his confinement when the always silent guard who brought his meals and emptied his bucket, opened his cell door to announce, "I'm takin' you to see the warden, Orchard."

On the long walk through the cell block, he tried to comb his hair with his fingers so he'd be more presentable. However, he knew this was part of the treatment. The sleek, well-groomed wolves waiting to interrogate the bedraggled coyote.

As he was led into the warden's office, Orchard recognized the portly James McParland sitting next to Siringo. He'd seen pictures of him often enough and knew he was the head of Pinkerton's Denver office. He gave him a little bow.

"The head Pinkerton. I'm honored."

Orchard was directed to a chair and for a moment, no one spoke. McParland's alert eyes, peering at him through gold-rimmed glasses, were friendly. His voice, when he finally spoke, had a soothing quality.

"The state of Idaho wants to convict and hang you, my boy."

The old detective leaned back in his chair, hands clasped on his heavy watch chain. A huge Masonic ring glistened on one finger.

"I gathered that," Orchard said.

"It would be a shame to hang for the crimes of others," McParland continued.

"What others?"

"The men who pay you. The men who'll sigh with relief as you fall through the trap."

Siringo leaned forward in his chair.

"We've got you cold for killing the governor, Harry."

"In that case," Orchard said, "I hope the union sends a team of good lawyers."

"They haven't yet, have they?" McParland said.

He pulled a letter from his inside pocket and handed it to Orchard.

358

"This is Bill Haywood's response to an inquiry about you, made by my office," McParland explained. "None of the officials of the Western Federation of Miners has ever heard of you. They deny any knowledge of your activities."

"Your friend, Bill Haywood, calls you a mad dog," Siringo added.

"I can read, Charlie," Orchard said, trying to keep his growing annoyance out of his voice.

It was all there, over Haywood's flowing signature. They didn't know him. The Western Federation didn't condone violence in the prosecution of its responsibilities to the working man. There was no place in the organization for mad dogs who commit murder and mayhem.

Orchard handed the letter back to McParland. The bastards had tossed him to the wolves. Automatically, he felt his coat pocket for a cigar. Siringo came over to him with one and held the match while he lit up.

"Harry," he said softly, "You have no defense. Haywood's going to let them stretch your neck."

"Doesn't look like I can do much about that, Charlie."

Orchard stared at Siringo, remembering the night they'd met on the Northern Pacific train coming over the Bitterroots. He was enjoying the cigar Siringo had given him but would have paid a fortune at that moment for a drink.

"You're doomed, boy," McParland rumbled, "but you can still cheat the hangman."

"And how do I do that?"

"Confess, my boy," McParland purred. "Confess. Confession is not only good for the soul, but in your case, it promotes long life."

"Harry, the union wants you out of the way more than the people of Idaho do," Siringo said. "Big Bill Haywood'll dance a jig when you're gone."

Orchard studied his hands and puffed thoughtfully on his cigar. He knew he was hearing the truth. You couldn't kill the governor of a state without going to the gallows.

"Confess, my boy," McParland said again, his voice now almost a whisper. "Save yourself."

Haywood and Moyer always slipped away before the dirty work was done.

"The best lawyers in the world couldn't save you, Harry," Siringo said.

"Confess. Confess."

The Western Federation had to denounce him publicly, but he would have expected some token of encouragement from Haywood. Even an anonymous postcard would have lifted his spirits.

"Confess. Confess."

They took no risks. They let men like him do the killing and the dynamiting. He was going to hang, but they'd find someone else to spread the terror.

"Confess. Confess."

Orchard rose abruptly from his chair to go to the window. The guard lunged at him but the warden raised a restraining hand. In the bleak, snow-whipped exercise yard, men in gray prison uniforms huddled together, talking and smoking. One of them threw back his head and laughed.

Orchard took his seat again and looked at McParland and Siringo.

"Where do you want me to begin?"

"At the beginning, my boy. At the beginning."

McParland nodded to Siringo, who went to the door to bring in an owl-eyed young man who took a seat, pencil poised over his steno pad.

Orchard took a deep breath. There wasn't a sound in the room but the ticking of the clock on the wall behind the warden's desk.

"In Burke, Idaho, in 1889, I dynamited the tramway at the Imogene mine. That was my first job. Bill Haywood paid me forty dollars. In Telluride, Colorado, in 1892..."

# EPILOGUE

Harry Orchard's often rambling, always shocking confession took three days to transcribe. In all, he took full responsibility for acts of terror and revenge which had claimed the lives of nineteen men. His confession set off a chain of events leading to one of the most celebrated trials of the twentieth century.

Charles Moyer, William Haywood and Charles Pettibone, the top officials in the Western Federation of Miners, were arrested in Denver and turned over to Idaho lawmen. Denied habeas corpus, they were whisked aboard a special train, taken to Boise, Idaho, and locked up in the Idaho State Penitentiary with, but isolated from, Harry Orchard. They were charged with a series of crimes, including being complicit in the murder of Idaho's ex-Governor, Frank Steunenberg.

Steve Adams was arrested outside Baker, Oregon, after being identified by Pinkerton operative, Harvey Browne. When confronted with Orchard's confession, he too, confessed, becoming a corroborating witness against the union officials.

The trial of Moyer, Haywood and Pettibone stretched over a period of months, pitting the great legal minds of William Borah and Clarence Darrow against one another for the prosecution and the defense. In a startling finale, Haywood and Pettibone were acquitted and charges against Moyer were dropped. At subsequent trials, Adams was acquitted but Orchard was sentenced to death; that sentence later commuted to life in prison. He died there in 1954, at the age of eighty-eight. In his final years, he lived in a cottage outside the prison walls with his dog. He raised strawberries and vegetables for the prison kitchen.

After the trials, the bloody saga of the Western Federation of Miners seemed to be at an end. One final incident flaws the premise.

On September 30, 1907, Harvey Browne, who had become the sheriff of Baker County, Oregon, opened his front gate and was fatally mangled by a powerful bomb. The killer was never apprehended.

# Author's Note

Charles Siringo eventually left the Pinkerton Detective Agency to become a writer. A number of his books, chronicling his adventures, were published. He died in Hollywood, California, in 1924.

# About the Author

Descended from gold miners, Jack H. Bailey grew up in and around the locales frequented by Harry Orchard. It was while living in Coeur d'Alene, Idaho, that his fascination with Orchard began. Jack joined the navy at seventeen and served in WWII aboard the aircraft carrier *USS Lexington* until she was sunk in the Battle of the Coral Sea. He graduated from USC with a BA in English and spent sixteen years in aerospace during which time he wrote two critically praised novels, *The Number Two Man* and *The Icarus Complex*. Jack wrote prolifically until his death in 2010. Most notably, Jack was an annual participant in the prestigious Academy Nicholl Fellowships in Screenwriting, sponsored by the Academy of Motion Picture Arts and Sciences, and was one of only a handful of writers to have advanced in the competition seven times.